The clouds were dark and heavy and Catherine suspected it would snow before morning. She walked toward the woods, stopping where Cameron had held her and made her come alive as a woman. How she longed to feel his arms around her, lighting a fire within her to ward off the chill. The wind stirred the bushes and she shuddered as the cold wind whistled.

She started to turn, then froze. She sensed something, someone and held her breath in hope. A dark form detached itself from a nearby bush and walked toward her.

"Catriona."

She ran toward him without hesitation, her body bursting with joy. He swept her into his arms and into the cover of the bushes. Stopping, he drew her gently against his body, his arms tightening to mold her slender form to the hard, firmness of his. Her senses tingled with awareness, and she clutched at his jacket to make sure it wasn't a dream. . . .

HISTORICAL ROMANCE IN THE MAKING!

SAVAGE ECSTASY (824, $3.50)
by Janelle Taylor
It was like lightning striking, the first time the Indian brave Gray Eagle looked into the eyes of the beautiful young settler Alisha. And from the moment he saw her, he knew that he must possess her—and make her his slave!

DEFIANT ECSTASY (931, $3.50)
by Janelle Taylor
When Gray Eagle returned to Fort Pierre's gates with his hundred warriors behind him, Alisha's heart skipped a beat: would Gray Eagle destroy her—or make his destiny her own?

FORBIDDEN ECSTASY (1014, $3.50)
by Janelle Taylor
Gray Eagle had promised Alisha his heart forever—nothing could keep him from her. But when Alisha woke to find her red-skinned lover gone, she felt abandoned and alone. Lost between two worlds, desperate and fearful of betrayal, Alisha hungered for the return of her FORBIDDEN ECSTASY.

RAPTURE'S BOUNTY (1002, $3.50)
by Wanda Owen
It was a rapturous dream come true: two lovers sailing alone in the endless sea. But the peaks of passion sink to the depths of despair when Elise is kidnapped by a ruthless pirate who forces her to succumb—to his every need!

PORTRAIT OF DESIRE (1003, $3.50)
by Cassie Edwards
As Nicholas's brush stroked the lines of Jennifer's full, sensuous mouth and the curves of her soft, feminine shape, he came to feel that he was touching every part of her that he painted. Soon, lips sought lips, heart sought heart, and they came together in a wild storm of passion. . . .

Available wherever paperbacks are sold, or order direct from the Publisher. Send cover price plus 50¢ per copy for mailing and handling to Zebra Books, 475 Park Avenue South, New York, N.Y. 10016. DO NOT SEND CASH.

PASSION'S BLOSSOM
By Brenna McCartney

ZEBRA BOOKS
KENSINGTON PUBLISHING CORP.

*To my family and friends for their support,
my editor for the chance,
and a special thanks to my daughters
who were my inspiration.*

ZEBRA BOOKS

are published by

KENSINGTON PUBLISHING CORP.
475 Park Avenue South
New York, N.Y. 10016

Printed in the United States of America

Prologue

The heavy gray clouds of fall hugged the sky, the movements slow and labored as they rolled across the heavens. In the east, golden shafts of light streaked the misty darkness with the first glimpse of dawn. Neither the semidarkness nor the cold damp air bothered the tall slender girl gliding through the thick foliage. The barely noticeable path she traveled was familiar, and she hummed softly to herself in answer to the light chirping of the early morning birds. One hand lightly brushed the damp leaves to send them dancing against each other as beads of moisture dropped to the earth.

The path narrowed, and she turned sideways to squeeze between two trees. When she straightened around again, a small pond was visible. She sighed. It was already late fall. Soon the pond would freeze and the beautiful greenery surrounding it would turn a dull brown to match the coming winter.

She had first discovered the pond when she was fourteen. Its beauty and peacefulness contrasted her daily surroundings, and she fell in love with it. Each morning, from early spring to late fall, she escaped to her private haven to enjoy the beauty of nature. Unfortunately, the pond wasn't large or deep enough for her to swim in but she was able to bathe in comfort.

Pausing near the edge of the water, she picked one of the last wild flowers of the season. She twirled the stem between her fingers and brought it to her nose to absorb the fresh, sweet fragrance of nature. How she would miss the hours spent at the pond away from her nagging, spinster aunts!

She laced the flower through her hair, then studied her reflection in the water. This was the only place where she felt happy and content. Her aunts were not present to remind her of her shabby appearance, her subdued existence, or the debt she owed them. She could be herself—alive, happy and alone with her dreams and hopes of someday being free.

With a frown, she realized there was little chance of her fantasies coming true. Her aunts made sure of that. With the exception of the few hours she managed to sneak away before her aunts rose, she was constantly watched and badgered. She was repeatedly reminded of the debt she owed them, though Catherine did not believe it existed. She was positive her parents had left her funds when they had been killed six years earlier. but her aunts assured her the money had been depleted during the first three years—and now she was living on their charity.

They had taken the spunk and vitality of a twelve-year-old and beaten it down over the years until she was a subdued young woman who barely spoke or showed any enthusiasm for life. Her aunts thought they had broken her liveliness, but Catherine's spirit was free, though carefully hidden, so they would not try to suppress her further. She doubted her aunts knew what it was like to be happy.

Her eyes caught her reflection and she saw her

brows drawn together, the line of her smooth mouth grim. This was the expression she knew she assumed to pacify her aunts, and it haunted her whenever her thoughts strayed to them.

Reaching down, she picked up a handful of small pebbles and flicked them into the pond. Her image was temporarily blocked by the ripples. The motion of the water seemed to erase her sullen mood, and the lines of tension had disappeared when the water calmed.

Kicking off her shoes, she raised her dress to her knees and stepped into the cool water. Mud oozed between her toes and she giggled. She playfully splashed water at a frog on the nearby bank and with a croak of protest, it hopped away. Her laughter was light and bubbly and floated to the edges of the pond.

It disturbed a sleeping figure hidden from sight by the dense growth surrounding the water. He woke, his senses instantly attuned to his surroundings. It came again, the light melodic laughter unmistakably belonging to a woman. Puzzled, he eased himself to his knees and peeked through the bushes. His interest was immediately aroused at the sight of the alluring young woman standing knee deep in the water, her dress high enough to award him a glimpse of slender thighs. Her head was bowed, and she appeared to be studying something in the water before her. Her long, golden-brown hair shielded her face from his view, and he found himself eager to see what loveliness matched the slim form.

He noiselessly shifted his position on his bed of pine needles to afford a better view of the young woman. Her head jerked up suddenly as a rabbit scurried through the brush, and her lips parted in a smile, displaying straight, even, white teeth.

The stranger's breath lodged in his throat. Before him was the most beautiful young woman he'd ever seen. Her eyes were large and fringed with long dark lashes that enhanced their remarkable tawny color. Her nose was small and delicate. The skin covering her cheeks was smooth and creamy, with a slight flush from the cool morning air. Her upper lip was barely noticeable, but her bottom lip was curved and sensual. Her pink tongue slowly slid across her lips to moisten them, and the stranger felt his body tremble with rising desire.

Her rare beauty attracted him, but his senses responded to the aura of innocence that surrounded her. It had been too long since he had been with a woman and he longed to be the one to awaken this young one's innocence and feel her young, vibrant body writhing beneath his experienced hands. He usually did not make a point of becoming involved with young maidens but he sensed she was different, and his body could not deny its need.

Casting a glance at the sun edging the trees, he pulled out a pocket watch, checked the time, and swore softly. He had less than an hour to make an early appointment and he couldn't be late. His future depended on it!

Last night his luck had soured and his financial situation had made it necessary for him to select a bed of pine needles rather than a plush hotel. He was a skilled gambler, but the previous evening he had met another professional and lost everything. He generally made a point to set aside enough for another game but last night the stakes were high, and he had carelessly lost even that.

His eyes skimmed the girl again. Maybe last night's gambling had made him a winner after all. Besides learning the whereabouts of a man he had been searching for, this girl was certainly a prize worth winning.

The girl edged her way back to the bank, taking care to keep her dress dry. She paused at the edge of the water and in one fluid motion, lifted her dress over her head and dropped it on a bush. The stranger uttered a low groan of frustration as she stepped into the water. Pausing, she raised her arms to the sky and the sun's first rays struck her naked body, making her ivory skin bloom with a golden beauty that strengthened her goddess-like loveliness. Her breasts were full, firm and amply sized, and the cool morning air made them ripe for love-making. He suspected his hands could span the distance around her tiny waist. Her flat abdomen and round buttocks led to long, firmly shaped legs. She was magnificent!

Once again, the stranger considered forgetting his appointment, but he knew it was impossible. Even a short delay in his arrival could destroy carefully calculated plans. With a muffled groan, he turned and crept away. His body burned with a need for fulfillment, and he promised himself to learn who the innocent woman was. He wanted to awaken her body to the hidden secrets of her femininity and let her blossom from girl to woman, before he plunged to the depths of her being.

Catherine stayed in the water until she became so cold her lips turned blue. She glanced quickly at the brightening sky and hurried out of the water. She was later than usual and did not want her aunts to be angry at her. Effie would probably have their breakfast ready, and Catherine was expected to serve it. She threw her dress over her head and squeezed her hair until it stopped dripping. The cap she wore around the house would cover the dampness, and if she was lucky, her aunts would never know she'd been out.

She did not sing on her return to the house. Her happiness was a thing of the past, and she resumed her sullen, subdued personality. If only something would happen to change her life.

Chapter One

The two story gray frame house was not as large as many of the neighboring country homes nor as richly appointed, but it had a simple beauty that made it pleasing to the eye. The large, heavy front door was painted white to match the open shutters at the windows and succeeded in adding contrast to the house. The woods met a vast garden, covering three sides of the house.

In midsummer, the gardens were more beautiful than the house itself. They were a great source of pride to her aunts, and the envy of many neighbors. Narrow stone paths were lined by an abundance of varying flowers, arranged so the colors and fragrances blended to denote the beauty of nature. Bushes and trees towered over the flowers to add a touch of majesty, while providing coves for privacy and isolation.

A bright yellow summerhouse sat in the midst of the garden. It was enclosed but not heated, so its use was limited to warm weather. When the snows fell and Catherine could no longer retreat to the pond for her seclusion, she went to the little house.

Hesitating at the edge of the woods, she looked toward the house. The cold weather had turned most of the flowers to a dull brown. The trees had a final beauty about them as the early sun caught the yellow, red and orange leaves and made them stand out vividly.

She ran down the stone path to her room at the back of the house. The window was still open, and she hoisted herself to the sill and dropped inside. She always used the window when she went out on her own to avoid meeting anyone and undergoing a barrage of questions.

Her room was tidy for there was little to make it messy. Her narrow bed was covered by a worn, light-weight coverlet. It was not adequate for the cold nights ahead, but Catherine doubted she would get anything better from her aunts. Her dresser was actually a night table with three drawers in which she kept her few articles of underclothing. The top was bare because her aunts deprived her the luxury of a lamp or candle. At night when she'd completed her duties, she would return to her room and stumble around in the darkness.

On one occasion, she had borrowed a candle from Effie, but it was the first and last time. On a whim, Aunt Harriet had visited her room and flew into a tirade, screaming that Catherine was not permitted a light because she was expected to retire upon completion of her duties so she would be fresh for the next day.

Effie was a slave, but her position in the house was decidedly better than Catherine's. Effie was permitted contact with the outside world, but Catherine was forbidden to travel to town or meet her aunts' guests. She wondered how many of her aunts' social friends even knew of her existence.

Removing her damp dress, Catherine pulled some

clean underclothing from her drawer. She slid the coarse linen over her body and wished for something a little softer. At night, when she finally slipped into her nightgown, her skin was red with chafe marks. Smiling wickedly, she wondered what her aunts would think if she went without anything beneath her dress as she did when she went to the pool.

Pushing aside the curtain covering the small closet, she reached for one of two dresses, not stopping to decide which one to wear as they were both identical and the only ones she owned. The garments were a dull gray cotton, buttoning down the front with a fitted bodice and full skirt that ended just above her ankles. Two bands surrounded the bottom to keep the wind from making the skirt billow. She combed and pinned her hair up, then added a frilled striped hat and an apron that tied at the waist. She did not have a mirror to check her appearance but she knew if she wasn't presentable, one of her aunts would let her know.

The kitchen was just down the hall from her room and as soon as she opened her door, she could smell Effie's cooking. The corridor was carpeted, and she reached the kitchen without making any noise. Effie was bent over a pot on the stove. Smiling mischievously, Catherine tiptoed across the room and playfully poked Effie in the ribs. The spoon flew out of her hand as she swung around. Her face mirrored her surprise before she burst out laughing.

"Wha' iz yo' tryin' to do to po' Effie. Where'z yo' been? Yo' aunts been callin' fo' der breakfast and here yo' iz playin' 'round. When iz yo' goin' ta learn?"

"Oh, Effie," Catherine said, forcing a scowl. "Am I not to have any fun? You sound as bad as my aunts."

Effie's eyes widened in resentment, and her hands rested on her hips. "O' chile, how can yo' make such a comparison? Yo' knows I love yo' dearly, but one of des days, yo' pranks iz goin' ta catch up ta yo', and yo' aunts iz goin' ta know yo' been pretendin' ta be docile. I hates ta think wha' dey will do den."

"Yes ma'am." Catherine looked over Effie's shoulder into the pot. "Sure does look good. I'm starving."

Effie smacked Catherine's hand as she tried to take a taste. "Yo' aunts iz waitin', so yo' best serve dem first."

Catherine stepped aside while Effie served the oatmeal. The tray for her aunts already contained griddle cakes and sausages, and Catherine helped herself to a piece of meat.

"Catherine, wha' does yo' think yo' iz doin', eatin' yo' aunts' breakfast."

Catherine smiled and started to put the half-eaten meat back on the tray. "I really didn't think they would miss just a bite. You know they leave half the food you fix."

Effie shook her head. "I knows it chile, but I iz just followin' orders, and don't yo' dare put dat sausage back on dat plate."

"I never intended to," Catherine answered, plopping the remaining meat into her mouth.

"Yo' better calm down." She handed Catherine the tray. "Now git dis ta yo' aunts. I'll have somethin' fo' yo' when yo' iz done."

Catherine left with the tray and made her way through the house. Her aunts always had breakfast upstairs in a sitting room that joined their bedrooms.

Catherine's Aunt Harriet was older than her Aunt Charlotte by ten years, and Catherine found their closeness unbearable. Perhaps the bond had grown because they had never married.

Although Catherine was never allowed around when company was present, she was sure her aunts had a different face in public. They were not without friends, and they often went to town for parties and socializing. They were accepted by the upper society, and Catherine assumed it was because of their financial standing.

Her feet were silent on the plush carpet as she followed the curved oak banister to the top. None of the rooms opened to the landing, so Catherine followed the short hall to the entrance of the sitting room. Balancing the tray on one hand, she knocked and waited for permission to enter.

Both her aunts were seated at the small breakfast table in the center of the room. One look at the grim line of their lips, and Catherine knew she was in for a scolding. She just hoped they wouldn't notice her damp hair. She kept her eyes lowered while she set the food out before them, and wondered which one of them would be the first to speak.

"Catherine," her Aunt Harriet said sharply. "We have been waiting twenty minutes for our food. Why were you delayed?"

Catherine had her excuse ready, but she did not answer immediately. Her aunts expected her to be shy, and she lowered her head and softly said, "My dress was ripped, and I had to mend it."

"You have another one, don't you?" Aunt Charlotte snapped.

"Yes, but it was soiled. . . . I didn't have time to clean it."

"You will make sure it is taken care of today. We will not accept excuses for being late." Aunt Charlotte waved her hand. "Now open the drapes and set out our clothes."

"Yes ma'am," she answered meekly.

Catherine pulled the plush drapes across the windows and sunlight flooded the room. She hesitated to admire the scene before her. Her aunts' rooms faced the front of the house and commanded a beautiful view of the carefully kept lawn and drive. In the distance, she saw a carriage heading in the direction of town and wondered what it would be like to visit the city and see how much it had changed in the last six years.

"Catherine," her aunt said harshly. "Stop daydreaming and get on with your chores. I won't have you wasting time."

"Yes," she replied, moving to the adjoining bedroom. Aunt Charlotte's room was large and spacious. She opened the drapes and made the bed. Her hand lingered on the warm, thick quilt added the week before at her aunt's request, and Catherine's resentment grew, thinking of her own shivering body in her cold room.

She laid her aunt's clothes on the bed, grateful that neither of them had insisted on a bath. The water had to be hauled from downstairs, and she was still feeling a stiffness through her shoulders from the day before.

Rather than cutting through the sitting room, Catherine went down the hall to enter her Aunt Harriet's bedroom. Her room was a duplicate of her sister's, but done in green instead of yellow. By the time Catherine had completed her chores, she knew her aunts would be finished with their breakfast. Hoping to avoid another encounter with them, she stepped into the hall and waited until she was sure they were gone. She was putting the last of the dishes on the tray when Harriet stormed into the room. Her face was red with rage, and she looked all of her sixty years. Catherine braced herself for her attack.

Harriet flashed a green dress before Catherine's eyes. "I found this soiled dress in my wardrobe. I want to wear it at the end of the week, and I expect it to be clean." She shoved the dress into her niece's hand and stomped back to her room.

In a childish gesture, Catherine made a face at the closed door before slinging the dress over her arm and picking up the tray.

Effie was waiting for her in the kitchen and immediately noticed the scowl on Catherine's face. The dishes clattered on the tray when Catherine slammed it down on the table.

"I can tell yo' iz mad, but don't take it out on da po' china. Yo' aunts will have my hide if'n yo' break dem dishes."

Catherine forced a smile. "I'm sorry Effie, but sometimes Aunt Harriet and Aunt Charlotte are unbearable." She fingered the dress over her arm. "Aunt Harriet's dress didn't get clean in the laundry. I tried to get the stain out." She jutted her chin out in determination. "It is not my fault my aunt can't eat without making a mess. Besides, the stain is barely noticeable, and I didn't think she'd spot it."

Effie shook her head. "Yo knows yo' aunts look fo'

fault wit yo' work. Let me see wha' I can do."

"I better do it myself. If Aunt Harriet found out—"

Effie took the dress. "She won't. Besides, yo' knows yo' got mo' work ta do in a day dan me. Now sit down an' eat 'fore yo' breakfast gits cold."

Catherine sat at the large table and ate in silence. Effie cleared off the tray, then went to the pantry. Catherine didn't know how she could bear to live in the house if it wasn't for Effie. Effie was fifteen years her senior, and she often acted the mother figure in trying to comfort Catherine. Effie had been purchased at an auction seven years earlier but she was treated better than Catherine, a free woman.

After finishing her breakfast, Catherine went to the dining room, parlor and library to draw the curtains. Her aunts usually stayed in their rooms, but they expected her to clean each room daily. She also had to wash and wax the large hallway. Her aunts were particularly fussy about the parlor and entrance where guests were greeted. Cleaning the furniture in the vestibule took her more than an hour. The black walnut hatrack was intricately carved and dust collected in the tiny crevices. The mirrors running down either side had to be polished until her reflection could be seen without a smudge. She had the same problem with the grandfather clock and two chairs that matched the hatrack.

She usually had the hallway and parlor cleaned by midday when she was expected to serve a light lunch to her aunts. She arrived back in the kitchen shortly before noon to make sure she was on time. Catherine nibbled on some raw vegetables while Effie arranged the tray.

18

"I got yo' Aunt Harriet's dress cleaned, so yo' can stop worryin' 'bout her gettin' mad."

"Thank you, Effie," handed Catherine the tray. "Well, someone got ta, and it sure ain't goin' ta be dem aunts of yo'. Now git dis upstairs 'fore yo' iz late again."

Her aunts were waiting in their sitting room, and although the door was open, Catherine waited for permission to enter. When she received it, she placed the food on the table before them.

"Have you completed the parlor and hallway?" Aunt Charlotte asked.

"Yes. I also managed to get the spot out of your dress Aunt Harriet."

"Well, I would hope so," her aunt barked. "From now on, you are to inspect the laundry to make sure it is clean. Can you imagine either of us keeping an engagement with soiled garments? We would be the laughing stock of the town."

"You must be more careful, Catherine. You have been with us long enough to know we expect you to be efficient in your duties." Her aunt poured a generous amount of cream into her coffee. "We were kind enough to take you in after your parents died—despite the additional expense."

Catherine's anger flared, but she maintained her sullen expression. They had given her nothing. If anything, they owed her.

"I am grateful for everything you and Aunt Harriet have done for me," she answered humbly.

Catherine shuffled out, her shoulders slightly hunched, her head bowed. They made her future with them look hopelessly dismal.

"That girl needs to be reminded of her place," Charlotte said to Harriet after Catherine was gone. "We could have turned her out on the street when her parents died. We were more than generous."

"I certainly can't disagree with you there. She has brought us luck."

Effie usually joined Catherine for the noon meal. When they had finished eating, Catherine propped her elbow on the table and rested her chin in her hand. Her eyes took on a distant, thoughtful pose.

"Well, wha' is yo' thinkin' 'bout gal. I bet it'z somethin' ta git yo' in trouble."

"Ever wonder what it would be like to leave here?" Catherine asked dreamily.

"No chile, ain't no place fo' me ta go, and yo' shouldn't be thinkin' thoughts like dat. Why yo' ain't even been around anyone but me an yo' aunts fo' the past six years. Where do yo' think yo' could go?"

"Maybe I could get a job. Thanks to mama and papa I got some schooling. Perhaps I could take care of someone's children."

Effie shook her head doubtfully. "Ain't no woman gonna hire yo' ta watch over her chil'en when she can git a slave. Yo' looks iz trouble. Besides, wha' does yo' know 'bout the world outside dis house?"

Catherine's hand dropped, and she stuck out her chin defiantly. "Not much, but I am not afraid to learn."

Effie chuckled. "Yo' got spirit all right, but dat ain't all it takes." Her eyes swept Catherine's face. "Yo sure would be temptin' ta da men, but wha' does yo' know 'bout dem things. Yo' was ta young when yo' came here ta know much of anythin'."

"I know things," she protested. "Why, the summer before my parents died I was kissed by the neighbor boy. He was just a few months older than me, but all the same he kissed me." Catherine looked pleased with herself, but Effie only shook her head.

"Bein' kissed by a boy of twelve ain't nothin' like bein' kissed and loved by a man."

Considering what Effie said, Catherine's brows came together. She had not thought much of the kiss at the time, and she wondered what more there could be.

"Tell me what it is like to be loved by a man. I found a picture of a naked man in a book when I was thirteen, but Aunt Charlotte caught me looking at it and had it burned." She giggled, remembering her aunt's flustered face when she tried to ask her about the picture.

"Ain't somethin' fo' tellin'." She eyed Catherine a minute as though considering whether or not to speak further. She was old enough to know about love. "Surely yo' knows wha' a man and woman do."

Catherine smiled at Effie's discomfort. "Sure I know. They kiss and the woman has to submit her body to the man." She shrugged. "It doesn't seem like any big deal. Sounds like the man is the only one to enjoy himself."

"I don't knows wha' ta tell yo' chile. Yo' knows da general things, but ain't no one can tell yo' how yo' body will burn with desire dat nearly drives yo' wild when da right man touches yo'." Effie shook her head. "Yo iz gonna have ta watch it, girl. Yo' is beautiful, and sometimes wi' men, lust and desire ain't love. Just remember chile, ta wait till yo' marry, or yo' might find yo'self saddled with a babe."

Catherine ran her fingers through her golden-brown hair. "Am I really pretty?"

"Yo' sure iz chile. I jest hope it won't be a source of heartache."

"I can take care of myself." There was a determined edge to her soft voice.

"Chile, yo' stubbornness iz gonna git yo' in a fix someday. Yo' got a wild streak in yo' dat jest ain't ladylike." Effie shook her head. "I worry 'bout yo'. I sure don't want ta be around if'n yo' let dat temper of yo'z go on yo' aunts."

"I'm careful, and I don't want you worrying about me. Nothing is going to happen if I stay in this house until I'm an old maid."

Since Charlotte and Harriet lingered over their meal, Catherine wasn't expected to pick up their tray until two o'clock. When she left Effie, she checked the hall and parlor to make certain everything was in its place. Satisfied that her aunts would not find fault, she went to the library. Aunt Harriet enjoyed reading at night before she retired, and Catherine was expected to provide a supply of books. After selecting two novels, she went upstairs.

The door to their sitting room, usually open, had been pushed closed but not latched, and it was from the small opening that she heard their voices. Urged by curiosity, she paused at the mention of her name and put her ear to the opening.

"Harriet, I do not believe our good fortune. We made money on Catherine when her parents died, and now she is going to secure our position of wealth once again. I never thought she would bring such luck."

Catherine heard a snicker.

"We were just lucky six years ago that she was too young to know her real worth. She believes the money her father left her is gone. What do you suppose she would do if she knew it was her father's wealth that made us financially secure?"

Harriet laughed loudly. "Catherine will never find out and besides, she doesn't have the spunk to challenge us. I don't think I have ever seen such a subdued female. She doesn't look at us when she speaks. She acts like a frightened mouse."

Catherine's anger rose. A frightened mouse indeed! She fought the urge to burst into the room and let them see her as she really was, but a spurt of anger would not accomplish anything.

"Charlotte, what do you think she will say when we tell her about her future marriage?"

"She won't have a chance to say anything. Hasn't she always done what she was told? Besides, we can't risk having her disagree. She is worth a lot of money to us. We have gotten used to high living, and the money Duncan Alexander offered us will secure our future."

Catherine heard the rustle of paper and suspected her aunts were reading something.

"I still can't believe this letter. Imagine a man asking for a woman's hand in marriage without ever seeing her—and offering to supply us with a settlement instead of requesting a dowry."

"It is puzzling," Charlotte agreed. "How do you suppose he knew Catherine was here? We've tried to keep her presence quiet."

"I don't know, but it doesn't matter. Once the marriage agreement is signed, we will have a party and introduce her as our niece. We can say she has been away at school."

"I know her father made sure she had the best tutors, but that was years ago, and we never worried about continuing her education. Do you think she is intelligent enough to make people believe she has been at school?"

"I don't know," her aunt said thoughtfully. "If she was away at school, she would know proper etiquette. She doesn't know anything, and there isn't enough time to teach her. Besides, she is so shy, I doubt she could carry on a conversation. What does she know about the world outside this house?"

"We can say she just—" Catherine heard someone snap their fingers, then a giggle of satisfaction. "I've got the perfect solution. We can say she just arrived from England where she spent the last six years in a convent. People would expect her to be shy and somewhat subdued; after all, nuns teach obedience."

"Harriet," her sister exclaimed, and Catherine did not miss the note of pleasure in her voice. "You are brilliant. We will have to spend money on clothing for her. We can't expect her to go to her future husband in rags. He must be a man of substantial wealth considering the money he is offering."

"Just think. It will be the social event of the season. How about a party for the New Year and a wedding by the end of the month?"

"Wonderful idea." Charlotte paused, and Catherine heard the rustle of paper again. "His letter says he will call on us at three this afternoon. We will have to make sure Catherine is otherwise engaged. We don't want her to learn about her future just yet."

Harriet sniffed. "We also have that other problem to worry about. I wrote to Ben then tore up his letter. I wouldn't want Catherine to learn she had a choice."

Catherine could not bear to listen any more. Turning, she crept down the hall, her breathing rapid and irregular. She clutched the railing tightly as she ran down the steps. She needed time alone to think about what she had heard. The library was the closest so she raced inside, closed the door, and fell into a chair. She was still holding the books intended for her aunt's room and they dropped to the floor with a thud.

Her palms were sweaty, and she wiped her hands on her apron. She was stunned, her mind a whirl of what she had just heard. Her aunts intended to marry her to a stranger so they could maintain their wealth. Who was the man who had asked for her hand in marriage? Was he young, old? Why did he choose her?

The thought of being married to a stranger terrified her, and she was determined to get a look at him that afternoon. If her parents had not been killed, she would be part of a loving family and none of this nightmare would be happening. She felt uncertain about her future. If only she had a choice.

Choice. The word hung on her mind. Her aunt had mentioned a letter and an alternative, but what did it all mean? Was there another possibility for her future? If there was, how could she learn about it? There had to be a way, and she was determined to find it.

Rising, she took several deep breaths to compose herself. She could not let her aunts guess she had overhead their plans for her future. To her relief, they were not in the sitting room when she collected the tray. Her eyes darted over the floor and furniture for something that might give her a clue to their discussion, but there was nothing.

An hour later, she was summoned to the parlor. It was the prettiest room in the house and also the largest. Doors opened to the garden, and it was here her aunts' socializing centered. The large fireplace had a marble mantel with a portrait of her grandfather hanging above it. There was a sofa beneath the windows and in the center of the room, a low table with two plush chairs. There were several lamps on tables and two corners had shelves cluttered with books and curios.

Catherine found her aunts in the chairs before the fire. She approached them slowly, her hands clasped together in her apron, her head bent slightly so she didn't have to look into their eyes.

"Catherine, we are expecting a guest this afternoon at three. As usual, we expect you to stay out of sight."

"Yes, Aunt Charlotte. I will wait in my room."

"Not this time. The summerhouse needs to be closed. You should be safe enough there."

"An excellent idea. There is no point in wasting working hours. You may leave Catherine."

She nodded slowly. This time she didn't have to pretend to be subdued. She felt beaten. How much longer could she survive under the present conditions?

She was almost glad her aunt had suggested she close the summerhouse. It gave her time to be alone to try and decide what she was going to do. She took the covers from storage and followed the path through the garden. There were two small settees, tables and chairs. She carried the cushions to the house so they would not mildew, then covered the frames.

At last, she sat down on the hard bench. Just a few hours earlier she had hoped something would happen to change her life. Now, in view of changes, she was frightened. Marriage would be an escape from her dominating aunts, but would she only be fleeing into another prison?

She wanted to view her future hopefully. Perhaps the man she was to marry was young, handsome and generous. She guessed the caller would still be at the house and she wanted to know what he looked like. Leaving the summerhouse, she crept down the paths, taking care to remain hidden behind the tall bushes.

She didn't have long to wait. The door opened and a man of medium height stepped outside and walked toward a waiting carriage. He was richly dressed, indicating a strong financial position, but Catherine did not find his money or his appearance comforting. He was probably fifty or older—older than her own father would have been—and she hated the thought of marrying the man. She remembered what Effie had said about a man stirring her body with desire, but this man did nothing for her. Marriage would release her from her drab existence but propel her into a life with a man she did not love. She intended to try and keep an open mind about her future, but she could never discount the possibility of escape.

Chapter Two

Catherine waited for her aunts to inform her of her upcoming wedding but when nothing was said, she began to wonder if perhaps plans had changed. Nearly a month had passed since she had overheard them talking and she knew if the wedding was to take place, the engagement should be announced soon.

Catherine trusted Effie but decided to keep her future a secret. If things didn't work out and she had to flee, she didn't want to leave Effie behind as a source of information. The slave knew something was bothering Catherine, but when she asked what it was, Catherine explained she was depressed because of her aunts' nagging.

Effie accepted her explanation without question. Since the visit with the stranger, Catherine was pushed harder in her work. Her aunts demanded a thorough cleaning of the house and she worked from dawn till late in the evening, falling into bed each night exhausted. December was nearly on them, and Catherine expected the first snow any time. It was too cold to visit the pond, and she was too busy to visit the summerhouse.

Straightening the last of the rugs in the library, Catherine stepped into the hall and glanced at the grandfather clock. It was too early to take the tray upstairs and she didn't have enough time to get involved in another project until after lunch, so she decided to help Effie in the kitchen. As usual, Effie was bending over a small pan on the stove. She looked more nervous than usual, and Catherine's smile froze on her face.

"Is something wrong?"

"I ain't gonna git yo' aunts' lunch done on time. Yo' aunts got a message dis mornin' and when I took it up ta dem, dey kept me from my work."

Catherine relaxed. "I came to volunteer my help. What can I do?"

Effie hesitated and looked at the pots on the stove. She appreciated Catherine's offer but knew what happened whenever Catherine got near the stove. Everything she tried to prepare got ruined. It wasn't her fault, she just never had the opportunity to learn to cook.

"Yo' can set da dishes on da tray."

Catherine knew what Effie was thinking and started laughing. "Don't you trust me with the food?"

"Yo' knows I appreciate yo' offer, but nothin' seems ta go right when yo' git near my stove."

"Maybe I should have you give me cooking lessons," Catherine said in jest as she took dishes out of the cupboard.

"Ain't yo' got 'nough ta do wi'out tryin'ta take over my job too. Yo' aunts sure iz workin' yo' hard."

"I don't know when the house has looked cleaner."

"I wuz wonderin' why yo' aunts iz makin' yo' do all dis work?"

Catherine reached for two cups on the top shelf. As she turned around, she knocked her elbow against the counter and one cup shattered on the floor. Out of the corner of her eye, she saw Effie shake her head. Effie was right. Catherine was a disaster in the kitchen. After setting the other cup on the tray, she stooped to pick up the broken pieces of glass. Effie wouldn't scold her for breaking the cup, but if her aunts found out they would not spare a reprimand.

"Any idea what the messenger brought this morning?" Catherine asked casually.

Effie shrugged her shoulders. "I don't know, but yo' aunts sure wuz pleased with whatever it wuz. Dey wuz 'specially nice ta me dis mornin'." She set the food on the tray, and Catherine took it from her.

She could not help but wonder if the message had anything to do with her wedding, but when she left the meal and they didn't comment, she didn't know if she was relieved or disappointed.

Two weeks before the end of the year, her aunts called Catherine to their sitting room and asked her to sit down. They had never been so formal with her and she felt certain something was about to happen. Her aunts were smiling and for once seemed approachable. Catherine sat straight in her chair, her hands hidden in her skirt.

"My dear Catherine," Aunt Harriet said. "You don't know what a pleasure it has been for us to have you here."

Catherine tensed. They had never been approving, and she knew their praise was leading to something. She mentally braced herself for what was to come.

"We have always tried to consider your interests.

30

We have prepared you for running a house, although I understand from Effie that you need some improvement in the kitchen." Harriet waved her hand. "That is not really important to your future. We have tried to think of you and want to make sure you are provided for. A certain gentleman has shown an interest in you. He is a little older than you, but he will make a good husband."

Even with the knowledge of what her aunt was going to say, Catherine was stunned. "Husband," she echoed. "What do you mean?"

"It should be clear, Catherine," Aunt Charlotte answered. "We have arranged for you to marry Duncan Alexander."

The room became silent, and Catherine knew her aunts were waiting for her to say something. Her mouth suddenly felt dry.

"H—how can I marry someone I don't know?"

"Marriages are frequently arranged. This man is wealthy and eager to provide for you," Charlotte answered.

"Why does he want to marry me?" Catherine asked bluntly.

"Your parents were prominent in the community. You come from a good background."

"I can't believe this," she muttered under her breath.

"We have arranged a party for the end of the month, and we intend to announce your engagement at that time."

"We—ah—hope you will not disappoint us. We are thinking of you."

Catherine glanced at her aunts sharply and she

wondered if they could see the mistrust on her face. "Am I to meet his man before the party?"

"We hope so," Harriet answered. "We have also arranged for a dressmaker to come this afternoon and make a few garments for you. Since you have not been with people for the last six years, we are going to say you were studying at a convent in England. If you appear a little quiet and shy, people will understand."

"Might I get a visit to town so I know what it's like?"

Her aunts exchanged glances. "We will see what can be arranged. Until then, you will continue as before. Effie will need help. The party and clothes might set us back a bit, so we are unable to hire additional help until the day of the party."

They watched Catherine closely, but she made no comment. "That will be all then. We would like you to polish the silver this afternoon. The dressmaker will be here at four."

Catherine rose and silently left the room. In the hall, she stopped and took a deep breath. It had happened. Her future was destined to change.

Instead of working on the silver in the dining room, Catherine took it to the kitchen. Now that she knew what her future would be, she needed to confide in someone. Effie was making a bread pudding for the evening meal. Catherine set the silver on the table, closed the door, and sat down. Effie took one look at Catherine and shook her head.

"Iz yo' aunts givin' yo' trouble again?"

Catherine picked up a piece of silver and began working. "I just came from my aunts. It seems my life is about to undergo a change, and I'm frightened and confused."

"Iz yo' gonna tell me 'bout it?"

Catherine took a deep breath. "It seems I am to be married."

"Married," Effie gasped. "Wha' iz yo' talkin' 'bout? Yo' don't even know nobody."

"You are right, but my future husband was picked for me by my aunts, or at least he picked me and my aunts agreed." She sighed. "It seems my engagement is to be announced at a party in two weeks."

"Iz dat why yo' iz cleanin' da silver?"

Catherine nodded. "There is also a dressmaker coming here at four to fit me for new clothes."

"Well, it iz 'bout time yo' got some new clothes." Catherine gave a devilish grin. "Wha' iz yo' thinkin' now chile? I can see da gleam in yo' eye."

"I was just thinking how long it has been since I have had anything new. I think I will order the most expensive fabric. It will hurt my aunts where they will feel it the most—their pockets."

"Yo aunts iz gonna be mad."

Catherine dropped her soft cloth with disgust. "Yes, but I will only have to put up with them a few more weeks."

"Yo iz playin' wi' fire, if yo' asks me. Dey can make things miserable fo' yo'."

"But not much longer. I understand my future husband is quite wealthy. I won't have to do this kind of work again."

"So yo' iz gonna be a big boss lady an' tell yo' slaves wha' ta do," Effie said with disgust.

Catherine looked up quickly and knew what Effie was thinking. Rising, she put her arms around her friend. "You know I could never have slaves. I'm not owned like you, but I still know what it is like to be a slave." Catherine smiled. "Besides, maybe I can talk to my husband about buying you. Then I could set you free."

Tears clouded Effie's eyes. "Yo' iz dreamin'. Bein' free iz almost ta much ta believe." She wiped her eyes with the corner of her apron. "I ain't even gonna hope fo' somethin' like dat. Besides, yo' don't even know wha' dis man iz like. He may be worse den yo' aunts."

Effie turned back to the stove and Catherine sat down. "I know, but I have to believe the best will come from my engagement. I never thought about getting married. The man is older than I would have liked, nearly fifty, but maybe because of his age he won't make demands on me."

Effie finished the pudding and sat down to peel a bowl of potatoes. "If yo' iz talkin' 'bout wha' I think yo' iz, age don't make no difference, 'specially if he iz da one ta want yo'."

Catherine wrinkled her nose in distaste. "I guess I don't know much. I remember what you said about the right man lighting a fire within me, but I got a look at my future husband and I almost hate the thought of him touching me."

"I iz 'fraid ta many of da arranged marriages iz wi'out love and passion." Effie put her knife down and looked directly at Catherine. "Yo' ain't gonna have much choice when yo' husband comes ta yo'. It iz his right, and yo' better learn ta control dat spunk when he demands wha' iz his right."

Catherine shrugged. "Maybe things won't be so bad. I hope to meet him before the party."

Finishing the silver, she returned it to the dining

room, then stepped into the hallway and checked the time. The dressmaker was due to arrive within the hour. She started toward the parlor, but halted when she heard her aunt call from upstairs.

She found the sisters in Aunt Charlotte's room. Their eyes studied her from head to toe, and she heard a grunt of disapproval.

"Remove your dress, Catherine," Aunt Harriet ordered. "The dressmaker is due to arrive and we don't think your present attire is satisfactory for the image you must portray."

Catherine knew very well what her aunt was hinting at, and she couldn't resist the bait. "And what image is that? After all, I am merely a servant in this house."

Harriet's cheeks puffed and reddened, and Charlotte gasped. Catherine's sudden burst of temper had been a mistake, especially when she had tried so hard to let her aunts think she was timid. Now was no time to ruin her image.

Her hand flew to her mouth, her eyes widening in horror. "I'm sorry. I don't know what came over me. I am grateful to have my position in this house." She hated to humble herself, but she knew she had been successful when her aunts glanced at each other in satisfaction.

"We told you before you have just arrived from a convent. It won't do for the dressmaker to see you attired like a—like you are. We will have the fitting right here."

Catherine slipped out of her dress and stood before her aunts in her coarse, worn underclothing. The garments were barely presentable and she could imagine the dressmaker's eyebrows lift when she saw the cheap garments. Her aunts exchanged a concerned glance and Catherine had to bite back a smile. They had obviously not counted on her shabby underclothing.

Her triumph, however, was short lived when Effie showed the dressmaker into the room. Harriet went forward immediately and drew the dressmaker across the room to her niece. Catherine stiffened under the woman's quick, thorough appraisal of her body.

"Clarice," Harriet said quickly. "This is my niece Catherine. I am so glad you could come. I don't think I could bear to look at her deplorable state of dress any longer. The nuns in the convent made their students live in the same poverty they are accustomed to. Can you imagine wearing clothes like this?"

Clarice shook her head as her eyes once again ran down Catherine's figure. "They certainly are drab." Her fingers rubbed the fabric. "And most unsuitable to wear next to the body." Her eyes flickered to Harriet. "Do you want to dress her from the skin out?"

Harriet's lips compressed to a thin line and she nodded grimly. Clarice turned Catherine around and studied her slender form. "You will probably want about seven day dresses, several evening gowns, underclothing and accessories."

Catherine heard a small noise that sounded like a choke as Charlotte stepped forward. She knew her aunt was adding the cost of so much clothing.

"Right now, we were just thinking of one party dress and two day dresses. Catherine's future husband plans to outfit her completely after the marriage." Clarice's disappointment was evident. "Once the party is over, we will of course have you make Catherine's wedding gown."

Clarice seemed somewhat satisfied. "But of course she will need new underclothing."

Reluctantly her aunts agreed, and the dressmaker measured Catherine's figure, nodding approval for her excellent proportions. She would wear her creations to their best advantage and enhance the dressmaker's skills.

When the time came for picking fabric, Catherine gave Clarice her full attention. Her aunts were not consulted, and Catherine knew they were afraid to speak for fear of appearing reluctant to spend money on their niece.

Catherine took Clarice's advice on the best style to fit her tall, slender body and both of them agreed on the color. The dressmaker promised to have the garments ready by the first of the week. Harriet and Charlotte showed her to the door and Catherine dressed.

Catherine was satisfied with the dress fitting and was elated over the prospect of new clothes despite the reason for getting them. She did not know what her engagement to the stranger would bring, but she wanted to make the best of it and wait to see what would happen.

The week passed quickly. The fact that Catherine was to be married in a short time did not change her aunts' attitude toward her. Christmas was almost on them, and she spent most of the time getting ready for the holiday. A large tree had been brought to the parlor and decorated. Effie had been busy cooking and baking, and the smells were tantalizing.

The dressmaker came for a fitting and although the evening dress was not completed, Catherine felt special wearing it. The underclothing was finished, and she put it in her drawer next to her daily wear coarse linen. Her new clothes would never irritate her skin.

Christmas Day was no different than any other day. Catherine was not invited to join the festivities and because of unexpected guests, she was forced to stay in her room. After dusk, she decided to walk in the garden. After wrapping a thin shawl around her body, she climbed out her window into the brisk air. A light snow had fallen, and the bright moon made the grounds glisten. Feeling in a foolish, light-hearted mood, she blew into the night air and watched her warm breath hit the cold air.

Quickening her pace, she walked to the edge of the garden and stood before the woods. She rubbed her hands up and down her arms and stared into the darkness. She was eager to return to the pond. She was already tired of bathing out of a shallow bowl.

The brush in front of her rustled, and her eyes scanned the darkness. Probably an animal, she told herself, but a shiver raced up her spine. She took two steps backward and listened. She did not hear any further movement, but she did not turn her back on the woods until she was almost at the house. She lightly scolded herself for being so foolish, but she felt as though she had been watched.

When she was gone, the stranger let the bushes fall back into place and a smile of satisfaction curved his lips. Off and on for weeks now, he'd been watching and waiting for her to venture into the gardens. Late at night he'd caught glimpses of her through the windows as she drew the curtains in place, but this was the first time she'd come outside and stood a few feet away.

Since he'd first seen her at the pond, his interest had been aroused. He'd made discreet inquiries, but no one knew of a young woman living in the area. After returning to the pond and tracing her worn path, he found the house. It had not been difficult to learn the mansion belonged to two elderly women who were cared for by a slave. Certain the woman he searched for lived in the house, he waited until Effie went to the market and followed her to town. After placing her order, Effie mingled with other slaves, and he was lucky enough to overhear her mention how hard Catherine was being worked and treated.

Hearing her name stunned the stranger and at the same time brought relief. He could at last put a name to her face. Her position in the house, however, filled him with silent rage. The aunts were wealthy. How dare they take advantage of her dependence on them and treat her like a slave! It was unforgiveable.

There was nothing he could do for the present except watch her from a distance and be ready to protect her if necessary. Learning about the party had been easy. It was the talk of the town. He had not been able to learn the reason for the celebration, but he knew it would be his chance to meet Catherine, and he was determined not to let anything stand in his way.

He hated to admit it, but she had become an important facet of his life. He didn't know if it was love—he couldn't deny his desire to take her to his bed—but he wanted more than that. He wanted to take her away from her cruel aunts and protect her. A woman with her beauty needed a strong companion, and he wanted to be that man.

Turning, he crept into the darkness. Until the party he had things to do and plans to make — plans that would ensure his future with Catherine.

Aunt Harriet came to Catherine's room shortly after she had climbed back in the window. She carried a large box under her arm and Catherine sensed she was displeased.

"Duncan visited us this evening." She threw the box on the bed without entering the darkened room. "He sent this to you." She turned and left, firmly slamming the door as a protest to the gift.

Catherine opened the box the instant she was gone. Inside she found a heavy cloak in a burgundy print. The fabric was rich and thick beneath her fingers, and while she wasn't taken with the style of it, she realized it was a very generous gift and something she desperately needed. Her last thought before she slept that night was of the generosity of her future husband.

Her completed gowns arrived three days later, and Catherine admired their beauty before hanging them next to her shabby dresses. An hour later, she was informed by Aunt Harriet that Duncan would be dining with them, and she was expected to join them.

It was with some reservation that she dressed in the burgundy gown and nervously sat with her aunts in the parlor to await Duncan's arrival. Neither of her aunts had commented on her appearance except to say that her hands were too rough. She wanted to remind them it was because of the work she did, but she kept silent.

The minutes ticked by slowly. When the door finally opened, and Duncan stepped into the room, Catherine's heart was nervously lodged in her throat. He briefly acknowledged her aunts' presence and then walked toward Catherine.

She immediately registered his appearance, taking in the neat, clean cut of his clothes. He was by no means heavy, yet his face had a thickness that made his cheeks puffy. His eyebrows were bushy and shielded part of his eyes, but not enough for her to mistake the close intimate scrutiny of her body, and she instinctively pushed herself against the back of the chair. She had made up her mind to try and like the man, but she found it exceedingly difficult under his appraisal.

Stopping before her, he took one of her limp hands in his, his moist lips touching her flesh while his eyes searched her face. "My dear, I have been anxiously awaiting our meeting."

Unable to speak, Catherine managed a half smile. He seemed amused by her lack of response, and she quickly pulled her hand from his. Duncan took a seat on the settee, keeping his eyes on her the whole time. She moved restlessly beneath his gaze and looked hopefully at her aunts for an end to the unnerving silence that had fallen in the room, but she sensed they found her discomfort amusing.

Duncan finally tore his eyes away from Catherine and turned to the sisters. "It was good of you to invite me this evening." His eyes flickered back to Catherine.

"I am satisfied with my choice for a bride. How are the plans for the party coming along?"

Harriet beamed with pride. "Most of the acknowledgements have been returned and so far there are no refusals."

"It will be the grandest party of the New Year," Charlotte added.

Duncan smiled. "It is more than I had hoped for. Being new in this part of the country, I find it to my advantage to meet influential people, and I am sure you ladies know the right social class."

Her aunts glowed under his praise. There was a short discussion on the party, and the more Catherine heard about it, the more uncomfortable she became. There would not be any familiar faces. The lie about her being in a convent would excuse her from knowing the current events, but she would still be expected to converse with people, and it frightened her.

Effie announced dinner, and Catherine rose. Duncan was immediately at her side, slipping her arm through his. The dining room was large for the small dinner party. The best silver rested on the hardwood table, and she wondered what Duncan would say if he knew she had been responsible for the table's appearance. The sideboard with its ornamental back piece held an elegant silver service, and it glistened brilliantly.

Catherine was seated opposite Duncan with her aunts on either end. When Effie served the first course, she felt Duncan's eyes on her but refused to meet his gaze.

"Tell me Catherine, what do you think of this country?" Duncan prodded.

Her aunts had refused her a visit to the town, so consequently she didn't know anything about its appearance. "The—the ship docked at night, and I came straight to the house. I'm afraid I saw very little of the town," she answered shyly.

"I am afraid it is our fault that Catherine has not seen the town," Harriet explained. "We decided not to let her out in public until after the party. We want her presence to be a surprise."

Duncan met Catherine's eyes. "I am sure the guests will be surprised and delighted when they see Catherine. She is a real beauty."

To Catherine's amazement, she blushed. Duncan chuckled but made no comment. For the remainder of the meal, she sat quietly and hoped she could excuse herself soon after they left the table. When they rose to retire to the parlor, Duncan asked to see Catherine alone, and her aunts readily agreed.

Reluctantly, Catherine led her future husband to the library. She heard the doors close and seconds later she tensed when he pulled her down on the settee next to him. She fought the urge to run. She had to remember this man was to be her husband, and after the wedding he would demand more than just holding hands.

"This marriage is important and necessary to me. I hope you do not find it too distasteful."

"I—I really don't know what to think," she answered truthfully. "You could have chosen many young women. Why did you select me?"

"You are necessary for my plans, and I want you. You are far more lovely than I had hoped. You must have led a very sheltered life in the convent. I shall enjoy teaching you about life."

Catherine was certain there was more to his statement than what appeared on the surface. She gently pulled her hand from his. "Since that is the case, I hope you will be patient with me." She ventured a look at his face and found him watching her openly.

He smiled, but there was no warmth on his face. "I will be patient with you—until after the wedding." His eyes roamed over her body, lingering on her full breasts. The dress she was wearing was modest and high necked, but the gown for the party was quite revealing and displayed a generous amount of flesh. She laid her hand against her neck to break his gaze, then rose abruptly.

"Please excuse me. I am tired."

She swept out of the room before he had a chance to protest and hurried to her room. The night had been worse than she expected, and she needed time to think. Opening the window, she grabbed her cloak and slipped outside. She followed her usual path and walked near the woods. Tonight they did not look as dark as they had on her last visit. She pulled on some dried flowers, and they crumbled beneath her touch.

Catherine had mixed thoughts about Duncan. She genuinely wanted to like him, but there was something about him that frightened her. He was so much older and more knowledgeable about life, and the touch of his hand on hers did nothing but make her tense. There was none of the fire Effie had mentioned to make her want to fall into his arms, and she dreaded the touch of his lips.

She strolled along the path to the summerhouse. She had no option but to marry Duncan. He was rich and perhaps if her future with him became unbearable, she could steal money and start a new life. It was not an encouraging thought, but one she would have to consider.

Once again, she felt a strange uneasiness. She looked around the garden, then scanned the woods for a sign of what was disturbing her. If there was anything, it was hidden by shadows. Perhaps it was just her fears of Duncan that were making her nervous.

The party was still a few days away, and Catherine was kept busy with final preparations. Her beautiful evening gown had been placed in one of the empty bedrooms on the second floor. She would dress there but return to her old room to sleep.

Her aunts were spending the day in the parlor so she could clean their rooms. She had Charlotte's room completed in time to serve the noon meal, and after she had a quick bite with Effie, she went to the second room.

Harriet's chamber was never neat, and Catherine suspected it was to give her more work. Clothes were scattered around the room, and she carefully picked them up and returned them to the closet. After changing the bed, she gathered up the trash. Getting down on her hands and knees, she looked under the bed, dresser and tables for things she may have overlooked. She believed her aunt would jam something into a corner just to see if she'd find it. She discovered a piece of paper crumbled beneath the dresser. It was so far back, she suspected it had been there for a long time.

Instead of throwing it out, she sat on the bed and opened it. She immediately noticed it was only half intact, and her eyes widened when she saw the letter was addressed to her. She smoothed the paper out and read.

Dear Catherine, It has been some time since you heard from me, and I deeply regret the delay. When I received word of the death of your father, my brother, I wanted you with me immediately. It was not possible, so I decided you would be better off with my sisters. I feel I can now offer you a good life at my ranch near Santa Fe, and I hope you will join me. I have enclosed money for your trip. I have another reason for wanting you out here. It is extremely important, and I hope you will understand. . . .

Catherine frowned. The torn letter made it impossible to learn the reason behind her uncle's desperate plea. She knew the letter was from her Uncle Ben though it had probably been more than ten years since she had heard from him. He had gone west as an adventurer but had finally settled down and built himself a home.

She sighed. She had been offered an alternative to marrying Duncan, but it had been snatched away by her aunts as soon as it was offered. She knew the money from her uncle had gone to her aunts, so even if she wanted to go, she didn't have the funds. Her only possession of any worth was a misshapen gold piece presented to her by her father when she was ten. She had always considered it a lucky piece and doubted she could part with it.

Perhaps this letter was the choice her aunts had discussed. The thought of making the long, hard trip was frightening, yet she could not discard the possibility. Marriage to Duncan had been her only hope of fleeing her aunts, but now she had a choice.

Chapter Three

Catherine dressed for the party without assistance. Effie wanted to help her, but her aunts had made it impossible by assigning her extra work. Catherine stood before the mirror in her soft linen underclothes and admired the way they molded to her body. The dressmaker had included a corset among the clothes, but she had purposely left it off. She was slim enough to forego its confines.

She slipped into the dress and struggled with the back hooks. When she stood before the mirror for final inspection, she could scarcely believe the transition. The dress was a dark brown velvet that served to compliment her tawny eyes and matching hair. The neck of the dress was low, and the fullness of her breasts were pushed against a tawny gold collar that nearly matched the flecks of gold in her eyes. The skirt was full, and the many layers of petticoats made the three tiers flow in an easy line to the floor. Each tier contained a decorated band that matched the collar. The sleeves ended just below her elbow and were turned back to display the tawny gold trimming.

Her long golden-brown hair had been parted in the center and drawn back over her ears, so just the tip of her earlobes showed, and into a chignon at the back of her head. Although it was fashionable to wear a headdress, she decided to forego the custom.

She heard a light tap on the door, and Effie hurried in before Catherine had time to respond. Effie's face clearly showed her approval as she studied Catherine.

"I jest had ta come up ta see yo'. Yo' look so pretty. Turn so'z I can see da back." Catherine did as she bid. "Yo' sure iz gonna be da belle of da party."

Catherine smiled. "I'm so nervous. Has Duncan arrived?"

"He iz down in da parlor with yo' aunts. Dey is wantin' yo' ta come down 'fore da guests arrive."

Lifting her chin with determination, Catherine followed Effie. When she walked into the parlor, all conversation ceased. Duncan came toward her and led her back into the hall, away from her aunts. His eyes clearly showed his admiration.

"My dear, you do me great honor." Catherine smiled her appreciation, but she was still too nervous to speak. He drew a box from his pocket and placed it in her hands. "It would please me if you would wear these."

Her fingers shook as she raised the lid. She muttered a low gasp when she saw the beautiful necklace inside. It would compliment her dress and the gold chain would draw immediate attention to her eyes.

"It is just perfect for my gown," she said quietly. "I don't know what to say."

Duncan beamed with pleasure. The next thing Catherine knew, he had pulled her into his arms. She reminded herself he had every right to take certain liberties, but an unexplained tenseness crept through her limbs. His mouth crushed roughly against hers, and she tried to draw back from the iron-like hold.

49

She felt instant revulsion as his moist, clammy lips moved against hers. Just when she thought she would be sick, he released her. Her hand flew to her mouth, and she stepped back. A knock at the door announced the arrival of the first guests and rather than be seen, she turned and fled up the stairs. In her room, she tossed Duncan's gift on the bed. Marriage to him was going to be much worse than she thought. She felt nothing but revulsion for the man who was to be her husband. She dragged her hand across her mouth as if to wipe away the imprint of his lips. She had had to fight to keep from becoming physically ill. How could she endure his lovemaking?

She heard the musicians playing and knew if she didn't go down soon, her aunts would wonder what was keeping her. Reluctantly, she put the necklace on. Duncan would expect to see it, and she didn't want him to guess how she felt about him. She lightly fingered the gems and smiled. Perhaps she could pawn the stones for funds to go to her uncle. Duncan didn't realize it, but he had provided her with the means of being free.

With her confidence restored, she went downstairs. The guests in the hall watched her descent, and she saw many admiring glances in the crowd. Her aunts greeted her at the bottom of the steps, fully enjoying their guests' obvious approval of their niece. Duncan detached himself from a group of men and took her hand. Names and faced blurred, and Catherine's cheeks became tired from forcing a smile. She was quizzed about her life in the convent, and she tried to make sure her answers were always the same. Space had been cleared for dancing, and when Catherine didn't think she could stand the inquiries any longer, Duncan pulled her away for a dance. After that, she was claimed by an unending line of males, but she took little notice when one ended, and the next began. She had only danced as a child, and she felt clumsy and awkward.

She was escorted to the dining room for the buffet by Alfred Cavenage. Effie was serving, and Catherine caught her sympathetic look when she offered her the main course. Catherine forced a smile but knew she had not fooled her friend. The meal was delicious, but Catherine merely picked at her food. Alfred tried to keep up a conversation but failed miserably. Catherine had nothing to say and no opinions on things she didn't understand.

She hated trying to live a lie and felt drained to the point of exhaustion. After a time, she found an excuse to leave Alfred and slipped unnoticed through the crowd. To her relief, her aunts and Duncan were in another part of the house entertaining the guests. When it was time to announce the engagement, they would seek her out, but Catherine doubted it would be for several hours.

She strolled to the back of the house, and when no one was looking, fled to her room. She removed her necklace, grabbed her shawl and slid it over her shoulders. Using the window was impossible in the elegant dress, so she slipped out the back door. She stepped quickly away from the house, then paused to make certain no one followed. There was no moon and the night was unusually dark. It had not snowed for days, and the garden paths were clear as she walked away from the sounds of the party.

The eerie tingling started in her spine and raced quickly through her limbs. She scanned the woods, but as usual there was nothing visible to cause this fear. She had never been afraid of walking alone outside, but lately there was something different. Unable to turn her back on the dark woods, she walked backwards. She was halfway to the house when she came up against a solid object. Was whatever she feared in the woods now behind her? Clenching her fists, she swung around and stepped back.

"Who are you?" she asked the man standing before her.

"I didn't mean to frighten you. I saw you slip away, and the party was boring," a male voice answered huskily, and she suspected he had been in the spirits.

"Who are you?" she asked again, experiencing the first fear of being alone and so far from help.

"One of the guests at the party," he said, taking a step toward her. "The belle of the ball came outside, so I thought I would follow."

He was close to Catherine, but the darkness hid his face. She didn't recognize his voice, but she really hadn't paid attention to the young men. When he reached out and touched her cheek, she shrank back immediately.

"I think I'd better return to the house," she said, moving to step around him.

"Why? We can have more fun out here." He moved quickly catching her arm and pulling her toward him. She tried to twist out of his arms, but all she accomplished was the loss of her shawl. The man's hands slid up her arms to the bare skin on her shoulders. She pushed against his chest, but her struggles only made him laugh. Hot kisses were pressed along her neck and shoulders, each motion becoming more and more intimate. She tried to scream, but her tongue lodged in her throat, and all she could do was whimper. Tears stung her eyes and streamed down her cheeks.

His leg caught the back of her knees, and she was forced to the ground. Clenching her fists, she beat at his face. She hit him twice before his iron hard fingers closed on her wrists, rendering them useless. To further halt her struggles, he lay his body the length of hers, crushing her against the hard ground. Her breath became shallow and painful, her lungs struggling for air. His weight shifted, and his hands tore at her dress. One side dropped off her shoulder, his fingers falling roughly against her breast. She squirmed in a desperate effort to free herself from his unwanted attentions. Suddenly, his weight shifted off her, and she lay alone on the stone path.

Everything was disoriented as she struggled to clear her senses. She raised herself to a sitting position and stared in amazement at the two men struggling before her. A large man successfully warded off her attacker, and he limped into the darkness. Catherine stumbled into the cover of the bushes with the hope of finding a haven of security.

Distraught over the attack, she drew her knees against her chest and wrapped her arms around her legs. Her head dropped forward, her body overcome by a trembling fear she was not able to control. Tortured sobs of pain and terror ripped from her slender throat and shattered the quiet night. Was this what Effie meant by the desires of a man? The first time she had been among people, and she had been attacked.

She was supposedly safe at her aunts' house. What would the outside world be like? She felt alone and longed for someone to comfort her and to understand what she was feeling.

She felt a light, gentle pressure against the bare skin at her neck as her shawl was placed around her shoulders. With the shawl came the soothing security of an arm along her back, and she moved against the hard object. In her overwrought state, she found strength and love. Comfort was something she had not had since her parents' death, and slowly, her tears ceased, and her head dropped against a hard, firm surface. She felt a roughness against her cheek and heard a pounding like a drum beating in the distance. Sighing softly, her fingers reached out to touch the strength and security surrounding her. She touched warm flesh, and her fingers moved to discover the hand holding her firmly.

Fear was absent, and she thought only of the security and safety she felt. This man had saved her from a brutal attack, and his gentle understanding brought her relief. She ran her fingers along his arm and felt the strength of the muscles beneath the jacket. Unable to stop, she explored farther to find the hard smooth jaw.

" 'Tis nae for ye to fear, lass. 'Tis over now," a voice said softly, and Catherine found the deep masculine tones calming. "He canna touch ye again. Did he hurt ye, lass?"

Still unable to speak, Catherine shook her head. With her fingers against his cheek, she turned her face toward his. She longed for a moon to show her the face of her savior, but it remained hidden in the darkness. Moments before, she had experienced terror at the hands of a man, but she felt none of the same misgivings in the arms of the stranger.

His fingers brushed her cheek, catching the lingering tears. In the process, his thumb touched her lips, and a tingling spread through her body. She saw the dark shape of his head tip toward her, and in a fleeting second, she wondered what it would be like to be kissed by the faceless stranger. His long fingers slid to her jawline to hold her head firmly against his shoulder. His warm breath fanned her cheek, then she felt a soft pressure on her partially open lips, so light, that she wondered if she had imagined it.

Deep within her body she felt the uncertain beat of her heart. She strained to see the face above her, but the darkness was their blanket, creating a bond she was reluctant to break. The feel of his breath against her cheek stirred her senses. Her tongue slid out to moisten her lips in hopeful anticipation. When she didn't think she could bear it any longer, his mouth touched hers in a tentative, exploring kiss, then withdrew. All Duncan's kisses had been hard and forceful, and she did not have any experience with such tender, personal contact. The stranger's gentleness and nearness made her stomach twist, and her heart pound. Responding in a natural instinctive manner, her hand slid across his neck to touch the thick hair against his collar. His head moved, and her fingers opened into his hair. He rained a path of kisses from her tearstained cheeks to her mouth. This time his lips did not draw back, and she felt a deepening pressure. It came slowly, coaxing out her timidity, and she was not prepared for the passion that flamed and raged within her. Involuntarily, she edged closer to him, and his hold tightened.

Her body trembled with a new fever, and she touched his face in an eagerness to discover the man who could arouse such feelings within her.

"Dona be afraid. I wouldna hurt ye."

"I believe you. I am not frightened," she whispered. She did not fear this stranger, but she did fear her inexperience and the desire he had aroused.

He kissed her cheek and neck, and her shawl fell. His hands glided down her neck to the low front of her dress and exposed shoulder. She knew what he was going to do, yet her body no longer seemed to belong to her. He had taken possession of her, and she had willingly surrendered. His fingers inched under her dress to cup her breast. His caresses were gentle and persuasive, and she felt a growing need within her body—a hunger to become a woman. When his lips touched the top of her breast, she moaned softly.

Kissing her lightly on the nose, he drew her into the circle of his arms. She snuggled against him, and his lips brushed her hair. This was the moment the stranger had waited for. He had watched her from the edge of the woods, firm in the promise that he would hold and protect her. A tightening of his jaw was the only indication of his anger as he let his arms draw her closer. He had almost failed in his promise to her.

"Ye be so beautiful, my Catriona. I would kill any man that tried to hurt ye."

Catherine twisted to look up into his dark face. "But who are you? And your strange speech. Where are you from?"

"I be Cameron MacLennan from Scotland, tho' I

havena been to the country since I was a lad."

His lips touched hers, the kiss exploding to a burning pitch of desire. Her arms encircled his neck, pulling him closer. Her breasts were crushed against his chest, but she relished the hard, unrelenting form. She welcomed the intimacy of his kiss, and her senses swam until she felt herself floating on a cloud.

"Catriona, I ne'r thought I would fina woman so warm and passionate." She started to speak but was silenced by the persistent pressure of his lips. He broke from her abruptly and stared into the darkness. At length, he rose and pulled Catherine into his arms.

"I will see ye again." With that promise, he was swallowed up by the darkness.

"Wait," she called, but he was gone. Adjusting her shawl she moved in the same direction, but Cameron had vanished. She could hear the music clearly and realized the door to the parlor was slightly ajar. Had Cameron returned to the party?

He had appeared out of nowhere to rescue her. He had the hands of a gentleman, and the feel of his clothing indicated a well-cut suit. She had little doubt he was a guest at the party, and she remembered his words, *I will see ye again*.

Her body warmed, then suddenly a warning chill coursed down her spine. Tonight's party was to announce her engagement, and she had not told Cameron it was against her wishes. He would think she agreed to the marriage. With the announcement, her hopes of seeing him again would vanish.

She ran to her room and threw her shawl across the bed. She had to find Cameron and explain about her marriage. Her fear of not finding him was ever increasing. The darkness had hidden his face, and she only knew his features through the brief touch of her fingers. His hair was long enough to touch his collar, but was it light or dark? And what of the color of his eyes? The only thing she knew that could pin him down was the Scottish accent. Now, she wished she had paid more attention to the men who had danced with her. Cameron might have been one of them.

After putting on the necklace, she refastened her dress. Fortunately, the fabric had not been torn, and she was sure the two missing hooks would not be noticed. The dark color would hide any spots of dirt, but what was she going to do about her hair. Without a mirror her corrections were limited, and she knew it had to be a mess.

When she stepped into the hallway minutes later, her eyes scanned the faces of the men around her. She put a brilliant smile on her face, hoping Cameron would think it was for him and what had passed between them.

When Duncan approached her and tried to take her hand, she pulled away. He did not notice her response, and Catherine knew it was because he was too busy watching her breasts swell above the dress.

"I have been looking for you. Your aunts wants to announce our engagement."

"Al—already," she stammered. She had to postpone the announcement until she found Cameron and could explain. "Wouldn't it be better to wait?"

Duncan eyed her strangely. "Where have you been?"

Catherine moistened her lips, and her hand tried to smooth some of her hair into place. "I stepped outside for a few minutes."

"Your place is at my side," he said, taking her arm and pulling her across the room. The guests had congregated in the parlor and hall. Hungrily, Catherine's eyes roamed over the faces, but none of them matched her vision of Cameron. Her palms began to sweat, and the smile left her face. Aunt Harriet made the announcement of her forthcoming marriage, and Catherine knew it was the end of her happiness; her aunt had just proclaimed her doom.

Nevertheless, she continued to skim the faces of the men, watching for some flicker of disappointment on one man's face. Soon she and Duncan were surrounded by people offering their congratulations, and her search was abandoned.

An hour later, the guests began to leave. It was much later when Catherine managed to slip back to her room. Removing her dress, she put on her nightgown. Not finding Cameron left her feeling defeated. She wanted to ask someone if they knew him, but it would have aroused suspicion.

She drew the blankets to her chin. For a time this evening, she had felt like a real woman. Cameron had awakened her body to new sensations and tender emotions, while Duncan's touch only aroused revulsion.

Catherine closed her eyes and tried to picture Cameron's face. She had found the fire of desire Effie had told her about, and it had been with a faceless stranger. Now that she knew what it was like to respond to a man, she would never know anything but an unsatisfied longing from Duncan. She wanted Cameron, a faceless stranger.

Chapter Four

Catherine woke earlier than usual and snuggled down in her bed to keep warm. Her thoughts were pleasant, and she didn't want to rise and break the magical moment. She smiled, and a warm flush raced through her body. Last night, Cameron had awakened her senses as a woman and she was a new person, aware of her needs and desires. She was ready for Cameron to broaden her knowledge and teach her more about her smoldering passion. With a sigh, she remembered the announcement of her engagement. What had Cameron thought? Would he keep his promise to see her?

She had never thought it possible for a man to leave such an impression on her. Thoughts of Cameron completely filled her mind and left her aching to see him again. For years her aunts had dictated her life, and she had gone along with them because she lacked the experience to argue. Last night convinced her that she could never live in an arranged marriage with a man who stirred nothing but revulsion in her. The marriage was still weeks away. She would wait and hope that Cameron would come to her as promised. If not, the necklace from Duncan would provide the means for escape.

Tossing aside the blanket, she rose and dressed in

her usual attire. The hired help had gone, and she knew her aunts expected her to help Effie clean up from the party.

She hummed softly on the way to the kitchen. Effie had her aunts' breakfast ready, and Catherine took it upstairs immediately. Her aunts looked refreshed despite the few hours rest they had.

"Tell me, Catherine," Aunt Harriet said, "did you enjoy the party last evening?"

Catherine kept her head bent so her aunts would not see the unusual sparkle in her eyes. "It was very nice. Last night was the beginning of a whole new life for me and I would like to thank you both for all you have done."

Her aunts smiled at each other in satisfaction. Catherine was obviously happy about the events in her life, and it made things easier for them.

"Duncan is quite taken with you. We plan to have the wedding in about a month. Until then, we expect you to continue as you were. Clarice will come to fit you for your wedding dress."

Her aunts started eating and Catherine turned to leave. Her exit, however, was halted by Charlotte's commanding voice.

"Catherine, we think it would be a good idea if you let us keep the necklace Duncan gave you."

Catherine tensed. The necklace was her only means to freedom. Without it, she'd be trapped into marriage with Duncan.

"We also want you to keep all your new clothes in the room upstairs." Her aunt offered no reason for the decision, but Catherine knew it was to keep her in a state of poverty. Her aunts had succeeded in dampening Catherine's spirits, but she still clung to the hope that Cameron would come to her.

To keep her mind occupied, she went into her work full force. Time passed slowly and each day Catherine wondered if Cameron would contact her and how he would do it. She listened for the door knocker and took long walks in the garden at night.

Clarice came to work on her wedding dress and although it would be beautiful, Catherine found little pleasure in the fittings.

Duncan came to visit and Catherine showed him to the parlor. He frowned when he was forced to sit across from her. "Are you anxious for the wedding?" he asked, his eyes roaming hungrily over her face.

Catherine was unable to answer for fear of telling him how she dreaded becoming his wife. She felt his penetrating gaze, but refused to meet his eyes.

"Are you too timid to answer me?" he prodded, laughing. "You will overcome your shyness soon enough after the wedding." She knew his implications included the bedroom, and she twisted her hands nervously. "You act like you are afraid of me. What did the nuns tell you about men?"

"N—nothing." She still refused to look up. "You must give me time. After the wedding I might feel differently, but this is all so new and frightening."

"Ah, so you can speak after all. We don't have to wait until we marry to get to know each other better," he coaxed. "Come over here and sit with me." She saw him pat the cushion at his side. "Sit right here."

When Catherine refused to move, he lifted her hand and pulled her across to the empty seat. "Don't be shy." Without warning, he jerked her roughly against him and forced her head back against his shoulder. His mouth fell on hers with a desire that showed no gentleness. She stiffened and pushed against his chest, but his grip tightened, lessening her chance for escape. The pressure of his hand on her thigh nearly drove her into panic. Summoning all her strength, she scratched and beat against him until his hold lightened and she was able to jump up. Without waiting to see the startled and angry expression on his face, she fled the parlor.

She ran directly to her room, leaned against the closed door and listened for sounds in the corridor. After several minutes passed, she sighed with relief; he wasn't going to follow her. Her body ached from the roughness of his hands and she knew his lovemaking would be harsh, merciless and only satisfy his lust.

She stomped back and forth across her dark room. Two weeks had passed since the party and the wedding was getting closer. She no longer had the necklace and the financial means to leave, but she knew marriage was out of the question. Her hopes for Cameron coming to her had lessened with each passing day, and she was certain he had been discouraged by the announced engagement.

Distraught over the turn of events, she threw her thin shawl around her shoulders and slipped out the window. The clouds were dark and heavy and she suspected it would snow before morning. She walked toward the woods, stopping where Cameron had held her and made her come alive as a woman. How she longed to feel his arms around her, lighting a fire within her to ward off the chill. The wind stirred the bushes and she shuddered as the cold whistled through the shawl.

She started to turn, then froze. She sensed something, someone and held her breath in hope. A dark form detached itself from a nearby bush and walked toward her.

"Catriona."

She ran toward him without hesitation, her body bursting with joy. He swept her into his arms and into the cover of the bushes. Stopping, he drew her gently against his body, his arms tightening to mold her slender form to the hard, firmness of his. With her breasts crushed against his chest, and her hips pressed intimately against his thighs, her senses tingled with awareness, and she clutched at his jacket to make sure it wasn't a dream. Her tawny hair tumbled loosely over her shoulders and his warm fingers brushed the silky strands from her neck, teasing her skin with a light sensitive caress. Every part of her body felt alive and she eagerly welcomed his touch. His hands cupped her jaw and his thumb skimmed her cheek.

Catherine studied the dark head inches from hers. In a short time, he had become an important part of her life, and she wanted to hold and treasure the moments they shared. Shyly, her hands slid up his arms to rest on his shoulders. Her body was anxious to be with his, but she knew so little about making him want her.

It seemed natural to follow her instincts, and her hand glided across his shoulder. She rubbed her palm along the length of his hard jaw, it was smooth to the touch. Her fingertips brushed his lips and they quivered beneath the light caress. Finally, her hand slid into his thick, soft hair in eager exploration.

His hands tightened on her neck and her head was drawn forward. His lips lacked gentleness when they crushed against hers, but instead of pain, she felt a surging flood of satisfaction and release from days of wanting. Her body flamed with a desire that drove all reasonable thought from her mind. His body shifted, and he drew her down to the ground where she sat with her back against his legs, her side resting against his chest.

"Catriona, I longed to see ye. How I have missed ye these past days." His grip on her tightened possessively, and his lips made a path along her neck.

"I was afraid you wouldn't come. I wanted to explain to you about my announced engagement."

His grip slackened and sensing his withdrawal, she clutched at his arm. "Tell me, Catriona. I want to hear ye sae ye want to wed Duncan."

She snuggled back into the security of his arms, but she still sensed his reservations. Her earlier feelings of passion were halted by the fear of losing him.

"I don't want to marry him," she stated positively. "My aunts arranged the marriage, and I'm trapped."

"Couldna ye sae nae? What kinda life would it be for ye?"

Sighing, she clutched at his fingers. "There is nothing else for me to do. I have nothing of my own, and I live only by my aunts' goodness."

His fingers rubbed her shoulder. "Ye aunts goodness? Do they nae provide warm clothes for ye? Ye shawl canna keep ye warm."

"It is all I have," she offered. "I work for my keep, but my aunts are not very generous."

An angry sound erupted from his throat, but before

she could speak, his mouth silenced her with a deep kiss. "I must go Catriona, but I will see ye on the morrow." He drew her against him, his lips lightly brushing hers. "My Catriona," he muttered before his dark form vanished into the night.

Her sleep was restless, and she woke early without feeling rested. Remembering she would see Cameron that night, her body trembled. The feelings he aroused were new and exciting, and she welcomed his affections. She was eager for him to break through her innocence and teach her the way of love.

The warming glow on Catherine's face was unmistakable. Effie and her aunts attributed it to her coming marriage, and Catherine did nothing to make them believe otherwise because it gave her an excuse to be happy.

The day passed slowly but thoughts of being with Cameron made her heart race. Her aunts summoned her to the parlor after the evening meal. She had set a fire in the hearth earlier and the room was warm and cozy.

"Catherine," Aunt Harriet said, "Duncan is going to call soon and we would like you to change."

Catherine paled and she clutched at the chair before her. Duncan couldn't come tonight; she was meeting Cameron!

"Is something wrong?" Aunt Harriet questioned. Catherine saw a disapproving look pass between her aunts.

"No—I'm just surprised. He was here only yesterday."

66

"He is your intended, Catherine," her Aunt Charlotte pointed out. "Go and change. He will be here soon."

Defeated and discouraged, Catherine went to the upstairs room where her dresses were kept. Her animosity toward Duncan increased. Why had he chosen tonight to come? With him at the house, it would be impossible to keep her meeting with Cameron. Her anger slowly gave way to disappointment. She had to remember her future was with Duncan and not Cameron.

She chose a high-necked green dress in hopes of keeping Duncan's eyes from roaming to her bosom. She didn't want to do anything to attract his attention. When she returned to the parlor, her aunts were gone and Duncan was waiting. She took a deep breath as he ambled toward her.

"My dear Catherine," he said, touching her arm, "you look lovely this evening." He seated her on a small settee. His thigh brushed hers when he joined her, but the pleasure of such contact with Cameron was revulsion with Duncan.

"I was glad you were free this evening. My desire for you makes it impossible to stay away." His thick hand curled around hers and she felt a sinking pit in her stomach. "My desire to make you my wife has become an obsession. I will never let you go, Catherine. I will follow you everywhere."

His words were unsettling—too possessive. She tried to pull her fingers away but his grip tightened. "You're embarrassing me."

His fingers drew her chin up so she was forced to look into his eyes. "You are a beautiful, innocent young woman, and I shall enjoy you the night of the wedding and many nights after."

Catherine's face turned scarlet and she quickly dropped her gaze. Duncan chuckled. "Ah, I can see my frankness has made you uncomfortable. In time you will learn to satisfy and please me."

He drew her into his arms and tightened his grip. She struggled to draw air into her crushed lungs and ease the painful gasps. When his mouth moved toward hers, she turned her head so his lips landed against her cheek. Groaning low in his throat, he forced her head to his. His grip on her was bruising and the more she struggled, the tighter he held her. With one hand, he loosened the hooks at the back of her dress and she prepared herself for the feel of his hand on her bare flesh.

"Catherine," he said hungrily. "I cannot wait for the wedding. I want to make you mine."

She trembled in fear at his announcement, but she could not free herself. His hold on her was too demanding. If he sensed her fears and reservations, he ignored them and focused all his attention on his needs. Exhausted, her struggles ceased and she went limp in his arms.

Duncan uttered a quick chuckle of conquest before he claimed her mouth in a kiss that ground her lips against her teeth. He relaxed his arms to shift to a more intimate position and Catherine seized the opportunity to push him away. Caught off guard, Duncan fell to the floor with a thud. Catherine jumped to her feet and raced into the hall, nearly knocking over Effie who was bringing tea. Effie's eyes widened at the sight of her open neckline and flushed cheeks.

Catherine raced to her bedroom and slammed the door. Trembling, she sank to the bed. Duncan had known she hated his intimate probings, but it hadn't made any difference. He wanted her and he would have taken her, regardless of her feelings. It would have been a brutal and painful possession.

At length, she straightened her clothes and rose to stare out the window. Cameron was probably waiting, but she was afraid to leave for fear of someone coming to her room and finding her missing. Returning to her bed, she wrapped her shawl around her shoulders and stared into space, her mind blank. She was startled back to reality by a light pressure on her shoulder.

"Iz yo' all right chile. Wha' did dat man do ta yo'?"

"Oh Effie," she sobbed. "He didn't want to wait until we married to take me." Catherine shuddered. "It was horrible. His hands were everywhere, and I wasn't strong enough to stop him. He frightens me." She raised her tear-filled eyes to her freind. "What am I going to do?"

Frowning, Effie shook her head. "I don't know wha' ta tell yo'. Da man iz gonna be yo' husband."

"But how can I marry him? I hate it when he touches me."

Effie patted her friend's shoulder. "Ain't no way I can help yo'. I ain't got no money of my own and yo' aunts keep deres hidden. Besides, yo' don't have no other place ta go." Effie's statement reminded her of her uncle, but without money, it was an impossible alternative. "Try and rest. Duncan is gone, and yo' aunts have gone ta bed."

"Do my aunts know what happened?"

"No, Duncan left right afta yo' ran out on him."

Effie shook her head. "He wuz mad." She walked toward the door. "Wants ta borrow my candle dis evenin'. Yo' aunts ain't gonna be up."

"No. I don't want to take the chance."

Effie smiled. "Things iz gonna work out. I'll see ya in da mornin'."

When Effie closed the door, Catherine stumbled to the window, unhooked the latch and opened the lower portion. The cold air made her shiver and she clutched the thin shawl closer.

Her heart was pounding in hopeful anticipation. She wanted to feel Cameron's arms around her and hear his soft Scottish accent as he whispered her name. She ran down the path to their meeting place, her eyes scanning the darkness for the familiar dark shape. She was grabbed from behind, and she turned to the familiar feel of Cameron's arms. Her shyness left her when she felt the strength of the man she loved and desired. Her revelation was a wonderful awakening, and she flung her arms around his neck. His reaction was as instantaneous, and he drew her closer until her form molded against his.

"Catriona, I was afraid ye wouldna come," he whispered against her neck. The feel of his warm breath sent a tingling through her body.

"And I thought you would be gone," she answered.

His fingers tangled in her long hair, and he pulled her face toward his. Her mouth parted immediately beneath his, and the heat of their bodies mingled to a burning oneness. She pressed closer to the hard masculine form, hating even the slightest inch that kept their bodies from knowing the feel of the other's. She felt his hands at her neck and marveled at the skillful way they moved down her back, freeing her from the confines of her dress. He drew her against him and into the bushes. Together they sank to the ground. Catherine was pushed back until she felt a softness against her spine. He stretched out next to her and drew her body firmly against his.

She ran her hand through his hair, then across his cheeks, following the straight line of his brow, nose and clean-shaven jaw, trying to visualize the face of the stranger she had come to love. His fingertips brushed the sensitive area of her neck, then his lips followed their own path of sensual delight. Slipping his hand inside her gown, he gently cupped her breast. His caresses were unnerving and her body arched against the palm of his hand, creating havoc with her senses.

Her fingers touched his shirt, tenatively at first, then with more confidence as she sought the feel of his naked flesh. Finally, she pushed the shirt and coat and ran her hands up the hard muscled chest, feeling the soft curly hairs beneath her fingers.

Groaning, he rolled against her and crushed her beneath the weight of his body. His mouth teased her lips until she stilled his head, forcing the kiss to deepen.

Catherine was floating. Her body no longer belonged to her. The sensations Cameron aroused were new, but she wanted to know more, to experience the ultimate fire Effie spoke of. More than anything, she wanted Cam to teach her. His hand slid lower, and the words Effie once spoke came back to her. *Wait till yo' marry or yo' might find yo'self saddled with a babe.*

71

Locking her fingers with his, she drew his hand to her lips. "Cameron, I want to learn everything you can teach me, but I am to wed someone else and I fear having a child."

Cam kissed her lightly. "Catriona, I wouldna' want to saddle ye wi' a bairn when ye've nae husband, but surely ye didna want to marry Duncan?"

"I have no choice."

"Do ye have nae feelin' for me, Catriona?" he whispered in her ear.

Catherine's arms tightened around his neck, pulling her beloved closer. "I love you Cameron MacLennan."

"Then ye will wed me. I canna have my woman marryin' another."

Catherine felt something burst inside of her. "Oh Cam, do you really mean it?"

"Aye, and I wouldna like to give ye a bairn wi'out bein' married." He kissed her deeply, then rose and drew her to her feet. " 'Tis nae place for us to make love. Ye wouldna want to freeze." Bending over, he picked something up and placed it around her shoulders. "I thought ye should have somethin' warmer."

Her skin warmed beneath the heavy cloak. "Oh Cam, it was so thoughtful. I love you," she cried, throwing her arms around his neck. "How soon can we marry?"

He became thoughtful. "I have some business to take care of, but can ye meet me at the church in three nights."

"I'll be there," she promised, lightly touching his cheek. "I can't wait to see your face."

"I be anxious to see ye beauty again." She heard his

soft laugh. "I know wha' a lovely lass I be marryin', but ye may be disappointed when ye see me at the church."

"No. I have learned your face by the touch of my hands."

He drew her against him for a long kiss. "I will see ye in three nights."

Catherine watched him disappear, then walked slowly toward the house. She was happy; her life was full of promise.

Chapter Five

Catherine woke the morning of her wedding to Cameron feeling alive and excited. Marriage to Cam was the most important aspect of her life, and she was determined to get to the church that night for the ceremony. Her love for him gave her life purpose and she did not doubt the depth of her feelings for him. He had not told Catherine he loved her, but his gentleness and desire to marry convinced her that he did.

She had carefully planned her escape. When Duncan had called the night before, she had asked him to take her on a tour through the city. Elated that she wanted to be seen with him, Duncan agreed. If Catherine's aunts had any reservations about her leaving the house, they remained silent.

She spent an hour before Duncan's arrival getting ready. She dreaded time in his company, but it was the only way to learn the location of the church. It was too risky to ask her aunts or Effie.

In the buggy, Duncan covered their legs with a heavy lap blanket. "Are you comfortable, my dear?" he asked, taking one of her slender hands in his.

"Yes. Everything is fine."

Duncan seemed content to sit in silence, but when they reached the edge of town, Catherine turned to him. "Could you show me the church where we'll be married?"

"Anything you wish," he replied and called directions to the driver.

Catherine paid particular attention to the route to the church. Duncan pointed out various sights and she was captured and mesmerized by the changes in the town during the last six years. Even Duncan's presence could not dampen the happiness she felt on this special day.

They stopped for tea at a small inn in the center of town. Duncan did most of the talking, reciting stories about his work and youth. Catherine pretended to listen, but her thoughts were occupied with her love for Cameron. After an hour, she pretended to have a headache and asked to be taken home so she could retire for the evening. She couldn't afford to have Duncan stay for dinner. His disappointment was obvious as he covered her with the blanket.

On the drive back, Catherine concentrated on the road, memorizing the terrain and landmarks. Her thoughts were distracted by Duncan's hand on her leg, pressing intimately up her thigh. She ignored his touch until his motions became so persistent that she had to wrench his fingers away. Contact with him made her feel bruised and dirty. When the carriage stopped at the door, Catherine jumped out before Duncan could assist her.

"Thank you for a lovely afternoon," she called, before turning and running inside.

Her aunts had an endless list of things for her to do, but the hours passed slowly. Finally, the sisters settled into their sitting room for the evening. Catherine did not expect to be summoned again but she had to wait until they retired for the night.

Even the dark, dismal surroundings of her room couldn't dampen her joyful spirit. Tonight she would marry Cam, and he would take her away from the misery at her aunts. Her life was going to take on a new purpose and she was prepared to face the challenge.

Her fingers ran down her thigh, the coarse fabric of her dress irritating her skin. She wanted to wear something new and beautiful but her dresses were upstairs and she was afraid to risk discovery. Her father's gold piece hung around her neck in positive reinforcement of her future with Cameron. Removing her apron, she flung the cloak from Cam around her shoulders and slipped out the window, closing it behind her.

She cautiously followed the path to the front of the house and looked at her aunts' windows. The house was in darkness; she was free to leave. She estimated her walk to the church would take less than an hour if she maintained a brisk pace. She was on the outskirts of town when she sensed someone following her. Pausing, she glanced over her shoulder and scanned the blackness. She edged forward and stepped into a doorway. From her hiding place, she studied the dark corners, but didn't see any human form lurking in the shadows.

Catherine shook her head and chastised herself for worrying. She started forward, then froze. Duncan had told her he would pursue her if she ever tried to get away from him. Did he mean he was having her followed? The idea did not appeal to her, but she wasn't going to let her fears spoil her wedding with Cam. Cautiously, she stepped into the street and edged her way along the row of shops, taking care to remain hidden in the shadows.

The wind whipped her cloak around her body, and she paused to adjust it. In the distance she heard a shuffling motion and she whirled around. Several stores away, she saw a dark cloaked shape disappear into one of the doorways. It was such an abrupt movement on the part of the stranger, it increased her suspicions that she was being followed. Frightened, she pressed herself against the building and watched the doorway. She only had to wait a few minutes before the door opened again and a man staggered out, cursing loudly. The man fell, then climbed to his feet and wobbled off in the opposite direction. Catherine sighed with relief. She'd been watching the door of a tavern—a common place for people to come and go.

Nevertheless, she broke into a run and raced down the street. Fear wiped out all conscious thought and she was unaware of the noise made by her shoes as she shuffled down the dirt. She flew by couples out for a stroll, oblivious to the strange looks she received as she ran. The town was not large but the streets were an endless maze as she wove a path to the church.

She experienced a moment of panic when she feared she was lost, but when she left the cover of the buildings she saw the church. After glancing over her shoulder, she ran across the street and up the path. The heavy door squeaked a protest when she pushed it open.

The interior of the church was small and dimly lit by candles. Catherine glided up the center aisle toward a man leaning over a large book on a wooden pulpit. He glanced up and smiled.

"Catherine?" he questioned, and she nodded. "I've been expecting you. I'm Reverend Peters. Is something wrong?" he asked, noticing her disheveled state and breathlessness.

"I was afraid of being late."

The man chuckled. "Cameron has not arrived, so you didn't have to run."

She hesitated. "Actually, I thought I was being followed."

Rev. Peters became serious. "Are you certain?" He glanced toward the door. "You are safe here."

Catherine forced a laugh. "It was just my imagination."

The outside door opened and two women stepped inside. The reverend leaned forward and whispered, "The church is always open. Many come here at night to pray." He took her arm. "Cameron explained your situation, and I understand your need for secrecy." Another woman came inside. "Someone might recognize you. Come, I'll take you to a safe place."

Catherine followed him without question into the dark garden. She could barely see and she had to rely on Rev. Peters guidance. He paused deep within the garden where a circle of green bushes shielded everything from view.

"Wait here. I will go watch for Cameron." In the next second he was gone, and she was standing alone in the darkness. Her excitement was so intense, she was unable to get her breath or still the wild thumping of her heart. The darkness hid everything except shapes, and she wished for a moon to help light the area.

She did not have any warning when three figures

78

emerged from the darkness. She shrank back in fear but her terror was brief when she recognized Cam's Scottish accent. She welcomed the security of his arms as they folded around her and crushed her body against his.

"I be happy ye want to be my wife."

Catherine smiled. "I want it more than anything."

His lips brushed her cheek. "Catriona, the Rev. Peters saed ye seemed anxious when ye arrived."

"I was anxious to be your wife," she explained, wanting to forget her earlier tension.

Cameron was not prepared to let her forget. "Catriona, were ye followed?"

"I don't know. I thought someone was behind me but I think it was nerves," she said in a light voice so he wouldn't sense her uncertainty.

"Did ye know who it was?" he asked with a hint of anger.

Catherine shrugged. "Perhaps it was Duncan. He said something once about following me, but Cam, it is not important."

"I will find out who it was."

Catherine lightly touched his lips, silencing him. "Nothing happened. Don't let it spoil our night."

"I canna let it go. I must know." He released her abruptly and turned to the reverend. He kept his voice low, but Catherine detected the hint of anger. "We be ready to begin the ceremony."

Cam's arm slid around Catherine to draw her against his side. The third man, their witness, stepped forward and was introduced as Cameron's business counsel. Catherine focused her attention on Cam and the Rev. Peters' quietly spoken words. The Scottish voice was deep and sure as he accepted Catherine as his wife. Cam kissed the metal ring in his hand, then slid it on her finger. The holy man asked Catherine acceptance of Cam as her husband, and she answered without reservation. When they were pronounced man and wife, Cameron drew her into his arms. His lips gently found the softness of hers and they clung to each other in the biting cold, finding their warmth from each other. When Cameron stepped away and spoke to the other men, she ached with unsatisfied longing. The two men turned and moved away.

"Catriona, I must find out who followed ye." He sounded so determined that Catherine was shocked by his obsession. "Go back to ye aunts' home. Ye will be safe."

His words were like a cold sting of air. "Return to my aunts? But I do not want to return. I want to stay with you."

"Nae, we canna be together until I know if it was Duncan who followed ye."

"Duncan doesn't matter."

"I want to be sure he will nae haunt our future together." She felt the quick pressure of his lips. "I must go."

"Wait," she cried in desperation. Her hands unfastened the chain around her neck. "I love you Cameron. I want you to have the one thing in life I valued most until I met you. It was my father's lucky gold piece, and I give it to you because I have surely found my luck this night."

She dropped it into his palm, and his fingers curled around the unusual shape. "Oh Catriona," he muttered against her ear, and then he was gone.

Catherine stared into the darkness unable to believe the past hour. She had been married and deserted. She wondered about Cam's obsession to learn if Duncan had pursued her.

She returned to the church, but couldn't find the reverend or the man who had witnessed the ceremony. Stepping into the dark night, she wondered if Cam had been successful in his search. She was conscious of the slightest noise as she wove her way through the streets. Several times she paused to look behind her, but there was nothing out of the usual.

The thought of returning to her aunts' house depressed her, but she had no place else to go. She didn't know where Cameron lived, and with a start, she realized she knew very little about the man she had married. He had entered her life on a night when she'd needed strong, comforting support. He had given her hope and encouragement for what had appeared to be a bleak, hopeless future. For years, no one had treated her with such kindness and concern. She had responded to the strong, dominant influence and reached out with her love. Her awareness of him physically strengthened her feelings with a need that bound her to him in a bond she could not deny. But even as they had repeated their vows, Cameron had remained a faceless stranger, a husband she would not recognize if she passed him on the street.

In her dark room, she removed her clothes and donned her nightdress. She hid the cloak, slid into bed and curled up to keep warm. She had not been in bed more than a few seconds when the door swung open and Aunt Harriet stepped into her room. Catherine raised herself up on one arm and blinked, her hand rubbing across her eyes as though she had just awakened. Her aunt's eyes narrowed in close scrutiny to scan the tiny room. Catherine trembled in fear. Had her aunts learned about her visit to town? Or worse yet, did they know of her wedding? She slid her left hand beneath the pillow to hide the band of her marriage.

Without speaking, her aunt left the room and closed the door. Catherine sank against the mattress and sighed. Had her aunt's appearance anything to do with the evening's events? Or was she just making a spot visit?

The night had certainly not gone the way she'd planned, and her hand felt strangely weighted from the wedding band. She was now Catherine MacLennan, but she was to spend her wedding night alone.

Catherine knew it was still very early when she woke, her body floating on a sea toward undiscovered lands. A tingling raced along her spine, and a warmth spread throughout her body, making her tremble. "My Catriona," she heard whispered through the haze of her thoughts, and she reached out and clutched at the familiar nearness of her husband. Her hands closed around his shoulders and for the first time her fingers touched the bare muscles of his back. Her head turned to his and his mouth brushed her lips, cheeks and eyes. His hands entwined in her tawny hair and forced her head still while his lips nibbled playfully on hers.

His hands eased the nightgown from her body and her hands slid the length of his back to his buttocks.

Cameron drew her against him until his hard male form was pressed the length of her nude body. The feel of his nakedness sent a wave of shuddering awareness through her body. Never in her dreams or curious wondering about love-making had she imagined such wild sensations. His hands teased her breasts until they blossomed to peaks of sensual awareness. When she thought her body had reached its ultimate height, his hands slid on to teach her the passions of a woman.

Fear was absent from her thoughts. Cameron was too gentle, too persuasive and too thoughtful of her needs. Her head rolled to the side, his lips burning a line of kisses down her neck.

"Oh Cam, I love you," she whispered as his body shifted against hers. And then came the ultimate fulfillment as he broke her womanhood and inspired a new chain of emotions that left her mind and body weak and trembling. She was no longer responsible for her actions. Her body belonged to him; she was a slave to his hands and lips and she welcomed the new emotions that burst forth.

Cameron held her closely and lightly stroked her hair. Catherine's breathing slowed, her body lulled into a peaceful calm. She had had her wedding night; she had become his wife.

"Catriona, my beautiful wife. I couldna wait to make ye mine."

"Oh Cam," she said, snuggling against him. "Take me away from here. One of my aunts came to my room tonight. I think she suspects I was out."

His thumb moved slowly across her lips, and she trembled. "I canna take ye wi' me now, but I promise it willna be long. I must finish my business and ye will be safer here."

"Safer?" she quizzed, drawing back slightly.

"Did someone follow me tonight?"

"I didna find anyone."

"Is it your work? Are you in some kind of trouble?"

"I canna explain now lass, but trust me. I will see ye safely out of here." He gave her no opportunity to question him further. His lips expressed an urgency, and she relinquished all thoughts. She became more daring in her exploration of her husband's body, delighting in the sensations she aroused in him.

Their time together seemed so short when Cameron pulled away from her. "I must go. I canna let yer aunts find me here."

"Please don't leave me," she pleaded, clutching at his arm.

He slowly released her fingers. "I canna take ye wi' me, but I will come back as soon as I can. Leave your window unlocked." Hurt by his sudden parting, she stared into the darkness. He dressed quickly then kissed her lightly. "Ye take care, Catriona," he whispered.

She felt the cool winter wind when the window opened and he disappeared, leaving her to wonder if she had imagined all that had taken place. She knew of course she hadn't when she touched the gold ring on her finger. She loved Cameron MacLennan with all her heart and she felt his absence like a crushing blow. Clutching her pillow, she turned her face into the softness to hide the sobs that racked her body. He had never said he loved her.

Cameron moved briskly away from the house toward town, regretting the business that had taken him from Catherine's bed. He remembered the first time he had seen her at the pond, her long slender limbs and breathtaking beauty exposed freely to his gaze. He applauded himself for his correct judgment of her innocence, and for the first time, he felt satisfied. She was everything he expected in a young maiden. Her tentative shyness and clumsy exploring of his body had aroused him to an elevation that drove him wild with abandoned ecstasy. He wanted to go back and feel her body against his, but he had scheduled to sit in on a card game at dawn and any dallying would make him late. Catherine was his lucky streak and with that he felt sure he would win at the table.

Catherine woke shivering and missing the warmth Cameron had provided. Her eyes ached from the tears she had shed and she wondered how long it would be before he returned to her. There as so much she had to find out about Cam, so many questions to ask.

Rising, she quickly dressed. Her aunts wanted a warm sitting room when they sat down to breakfast and it meant rising early to start the fire. She stared at the ring on her finger and remembered the warmth of Cam's hand as he slid the ring over her knuckle. As much as she wanted to wear the ring, she had to remove and hide it. Her only chain was on the gold piece she'd given to Cam, so she secured it around her neck with a piece of twine. It fell between her breasts, close to her heart. She made her bed, making a note to clean the bloodstain from the sheets, another reminder of her commitment to Cameron.

Aunt Harriet did not make any reference to the unexpected check on Catherine during the night. Her aunts were demanding in their requests and the day slipped by in the usual routine. She was relieved to learn Duncan would not be calling that night and she retired to her room as soon as her duties were completed. After putting on her nightgown, she looked out over the garden. Would Cam come to her in the night? She made sure the lock was off the window and slipped between the sheets. She put the ring back on her finger and waited.

Her hope to have Cameron in her bed remained strong, but as the nights passed, she began to doubt him. Her temper and patience were short and she had to force herself to hold her tongue against her aunts' sharp taunts.

Duncan came to visit and she was forced to endure his company. She fought off his attentions and persistence until she felt bruised and battered. She hated to think what Duncan would do if he knew she was not the pure woman he suspected.

Alone and miserable, she crawled into bed one night and slept. The sliding of wood against wood woke her and she turned immediately to the window. The curtains fluttered open as a dark shape stepped inside. "Cam," she called, her body warming in anticipation. He walked toward the bed, undressing as he came, and her arms reached out to welcome him. He went eagerly into her grasp and drew her close. An angry exclamation erupted from his lips when he encountered her nightgown. Drawing back, he pulled it over her head, then covered her with his warmth. When his lips brushed hers and deepened into passion, Catherine groaned in pain.

"Wha' be wrong?" he asked, taken aback that he might have injured her. "Have I hurt ye?"

"No Cam," she whispered. "Duncan was here tonight and he tried—he tried—" She felt the tension in Cameron's body.

"Did he try to make love to ye?"

Catherine ran her hands down his back. "He always tries to get me to respond to him and I fight him off."

"I dona want another man makin' love to my wife," he said in controlled anger.

She ran her lips along his cheek. "He doesn't know how to make love. He is only trying to satisfy his lust."

Cameron buried his face in her hair. "I dona want to put ye through this."

"Then take me away."

He kissed her eyes. "Soon, soon," he promised.

When his lips touched hers it was with such gentleness that she felt no pain. His hands slowly aroused her body, teasing her until she squirmed beneath him and reached for the release her body demanded. In time with hers, his breath quickened and a rush of warm heat exploded from his body. Fulfilled, they collapsed in each other's arms.

"Cam, I have missed you. I was afraid you wouldn't come back."

"I will come back, but if ye e'er need help, go to the church. My legal counsel arranged for our marriage and asked the Rev. Peters to help ye if ye e'er needed it. He knows how to reach me."

His fingers traced a pattern across her breasts and

his lips lightly teased her neck. Questions fled her mind and she once again warmed to his touch. He held her close, and the cold winter air did not touch their heated bodies.

"Catriona, I must go, but I will try to come back soon. I be makin' plans to get ye awa' from here before the weddin' date set wi' Duncan."

"Why can't you take me now? I want to be with you."

"Do ye nae trust me?"

Even though Cam couldn't see her face, she lowered her eyes in embarrassment. There was so much she didn't understand, yet Cam seemed reluctant to calm her fears. Because of her love, her trust in him was complete, and when he came to her after that night, she put her fears and questions aside and responded to his presence.

The wedding to Duncan, which was to have taken place at the end of January, was postponed. Cameron didn't act surprised when she told him, and she wondered if he had heard about it in town. Her aunts were delighted to have her with them a little longer, and her work load increased. Effie was puzzled by Catherine's calm acceptance of her marriage to Duncan, and Catherine did not explain the true reasons for her carefree spirit.

Duncan was persistent in his ploy to possess her body and when she fought him off, she sensed his rage. She made excuses when he tried to get her alone and eventually his visits lessened. She knew he was only biding his time until after the wedding.

Her love-making with Cameron became intense. Each knew the responses and sensitiveness of the other, thus creating a mutually gratifying encounter. Cam welcomed her eagerness to please and in turn treated her with gentleness and respect in satisfying her needs. Catherine learned every inch of his body and memorized the lines of his face.

March began with a strong gusty wind and with it came good news for Catherine. She had missed her monthly time twice, and she was sure she was to have Cameron's child.

Chapter Six

Catherine felt lighthearted as she walked to the kitchen and her hand rested against her abdomen where Cam's child grew. She was anxious to tell him her discovery, but on his last visit, he had informed her his business would keep him away for a week. Tomorrow night was the end of that week and he would be back in her arms. Her smile was brilliant as she joined Effie.

The slave shook her head. "Chile', yo' sure iz happy dese days. I thought yo' hated da idea of marryin' Duncan?"

Catherine picked at a bowl of nuts on the table. "I guess I have decided to make the best of the situation," she replied with a sly smile.

"Iz yo' plannin' somethin', Catherine? Cause if'n yo' iz, yo' better stop. Yo' know da time iz gettin' close."

Catherine forced a frown to hide her jubilant feelings. "I'm marrying Duncan, but just because my life is going to be miserable doesn't mean I have to be sour all the time."

Effie regarded her closely, then set the bowls of gruel on the tray. "Yo' aunts iz gonna be wonderin' 'bout yo'. Dey iz an inner glow 'bout yo' dat just don't make sense."

"They'll think I'm happy about the wedding."

Catherine accepted the tray and went to her aunts' sitting room. Effie was right. She could not let her aunts see her happiness or they would immediately become suspicious. Thinking of the kind of life she would have with Duncan dampened her spirits, and she was frowning when she entered their room.

They were in their usual places, and she placed the tray between them. Charlotte grumbled about her breakfast, something Catherine rarely heard her do, and Harriet responded in much the same manner. Catherine was certain something was amiss as she opened the curtains.

"Catherine," Aunt Harriet said, and she turned. "Please come over here." She paused until her niece stood before her. "Duncan does not want to delay the wedding any longer. Your marriage will take place tomorrow afternoon."

Feeling faint from the announcement, Catherine scrambled for the nearest chair. "Tomorrow afternoon," she muttered. It was too soon. There would be no time to get Cameron's help. He wasn't due back in town until evening.

"Catherine," Aunt Charlotte said. "You look pale. Are you all right?"

Catherine didn't answer. "Do you have some reason to be disturbed by the wedding plans?" Aunt Harriet asked with skepticism.

"No—No," Catherine responded quickly. "It doesn't give me much time to get ready and I want to look my best." She hoped her aunts believed her. She had to stall for time. "Where will the wedding be held?"

"We don't know. Duncan is going to make the

91

arrangements."

Catherine struggled with her emotions. Their decision to proceed with the wedding would ruin everything. Why couldn't this have happened after Cameron's return? He would know what to do.

"You can retire immediately after dinner. You will want to be fully rested for tomorrow." Aunt Charlotte said.

"Th—thank you. I appreciate your kindness," she answered, too stunned to believe what was happening.

As soon as she was dismissed, Catherine retreated to her room. She was in a worse mess than she had ever thought possible. Cameron was not due back in town until after the wedding, so help from him was out of the question. The future rested heavily on her shoulders. She remembered Cam telling her to go to the church if she ever had trouble. His legal counsel had given the reverend information for getting in touch with her husband. Rev. Peters was the only link she had with Cameron and tonight she would have to make use of that fragile bond.

If Effie noticed her sullen mood, she said nothing. Catherine assumed she had been told about the upcoming marriage, and Effie's soft brown eyes reflected her pity. Catherine wondered what would happen to Effie when she was gone. Her aunts were too selfish to pay for additional help and Effie would assume all the household duties. Catherine wished the slave could flee with her, but she knew about the intense searches they conducted for runaway slaves and she could not afford to attract attention.

At her aunt's request, Catherine spent part of the morning making sure her wedding dress was pressed and ready for the next day. The gown was beautiful but Catherine hated to touch it, knowing the unhappiness she would have to endure if she wore it.

Just before returning to her room for the night, Catherine stopped at the parlor. She had searched every room but this one for the necklace from Duncan and it was her only means of obtaining cash. She checked the drawers, vases, and every conceivable hiding place but found nothing. Out of desperation, she went to the library and began a second search of the desk. In the back of the third drawer she found a small sack of coins. There wasn't much money, but it was better than nothing, and she was certain the necklace was unobtainable. It was doubtful her aunts would need the coins before she left but she was still uneasy when she returned to the back of the house.

In her room, Catherine counted the coins, relieved to find more than she first thought. The sum wasn't large but if she was careful it would last for days. After closing the sack of money, she gathered her belongings—the extra maid outfit, underwear, night-dress and shawl—and tied them in a sheet. She wanted to leave immediately but decided she had better wait until her aunts retired. Within the hour, she knew she had made the right decision. The door to her room opened quietly and she closed her eyes to feign sleep. Steps against the wooden floor warned her someone was approaching the bed and she forced herself to keep her breathing slow and steady. When the door closed, she opened her eyes to darkness. Had her aunts expected her to do something to avoid the marriage?

Certainly they would not return! She jumped out of

bed and dressed. With her belongings firmly clasped in her hand, she climbed out the window and closed it behind her. There was no turning back now. She was on her way to a new life with the man she loved.

Determined not to let anyone see her leave, she chose a path around the back of the house. She stayed three feet off the main road so she would not be spotted by travelers. Once in town, she took a direct route to the church. Pausing opposite the building, she scanned the area for anything suspicious. She had approached the church from the best angle and she had a view of every possible hiding place. Satisfied there was no one about, she slowly walked across the darkened street and up the narrow path. As before, the doors squeaked to announce her arrival. The empty silence brought a frown to her lips. Where was she going to find Rev. Peters?

"Reverend," she called, moving down the aisle. "Is anyone here?"

There were two doors off to the side. One she knew went to the gardens, so she approached the second. She tapped lightly and when no one bid entry, she unhooked the latch and stepped inside. The room contained a cot, desk and books.

An older man glanced up at her intrustion. A large pink scar marred his forehead and she noticed his brown eyes were dull with exhaustion or pain. Rising slowly, he smiled. "What can I do for you? It is unusual for me to get callers this late at night."

He sank back into his chair and gestured for her to take the one opposite. Catherine sat down and put the sack on her lap.

"I'm looking for Rev. Peters," she stated simply.

He gave her a warm smile. "I'm the Reverend."

Catherine's lower lip opened, then clamped shut. This was not the man she had seen the night of her marriage. "I mean the other Rev. Peters. I have urgent business with him."

Catherine saw his green eyes cloud with confusion. "There is no other Rev. Peters. I am the only vicar of this church."

His words threw Catherine toward the edge of panic. She could not be mistaken. "Is there another church in town?" she asked hopefully.

"No miss, this is the only one."

Her hands tightened around the small bundle. "But I was here several weeks ago and was married by Rev. Peters." She told him the date.

The man frowned. "I am sorry, but there has been a mistake. I remember the night you mentioned." His hand reached for the scar on his forehead. "On the night you say you were married, someone attacked me from behind and awarded me with a blow on the head. It nearly killed me. Up to now I could find no reason for the attack. Sunday's collection was in the drawer of my desk, but none of it was taken, so it appears robbery was not the reason for the assault." He shook his head in confusion. "It would seem someone did not want me to preside over your ceremony."

"What are you saying?" Catherine questioned anxiously.

"I'm sorry miss, but the only conclusion I can come to is that someone wanted to make you think you were getting married."

The blood drained from Catherine's face. Her wedding could not have been a farce. She loved

Cameron, and he had given her a ring to bind the vows. She extended her hand to display the band of gold.

"I have a ring."

Rev. Peters shook his head. "I'm sorry, but that does not make you married." He brightened. "Did you receive a marriage certificate? Perhaps if I saw it we could clear this up."

The dryness in her mouth made speaking difficult and she shook her head. "There was no wedding certificate." Stunned, she raised a trembling hand to her brow. "Why would Cameron go through the trouble of pretending to marry me?"

"That I cannot answer. What do you know about the man you supposedly married? Maybe we can find him." A blank expression clouded her tawny eyes. "What does he look like?"

Dumbfounded, Catherine could only stare at the vicar. How could she explain that she'd never actually seen her husband. She tried to speak, but the words would not come. Tears sprang to her eyes and ran down her cheeks. Why had Cam done this to her? Did he want to conquer her innocence so much that he would stage a false marriage just to get into her bed. She remembered how she had willingly accepted his attentions the night of the party. Her inexperience had made her prey to his affections, and he had used her.

Reverend Peters came to her side and offered her a handkerchief. She lightly dabbed her eyes.

"Miss, perhaps if you tell me his name, we could straighten this mess out."

"His name was Cameron MacLennan, and he told

me if I had a problem I should come here. His legal counsel was supposed to leave his name and address."

The reverend slowly shook his head. "I have none of the information you seek, and Cameron's name means nothing to me. Perhaps if you returned home things would look better in the morning."

Catherine looked up at him. "I have no home to return to. Tomorrow I am supposed to be married to a man I despise."

"Ah," the man said thoughtfully. "Would the man be Duncan Alexander?" Catherine nodded. "I have been asked to perform the ceremony."

Catherine panicked. "Please, don't tell him I'm here."

"No child. You have come to me for help, and I will not let you down. Have you a place to go for the night?"

"No, I thought I'd find Cameron."

"I can let you sleep on my cot. It is not comfortable, but it will be warmer than the street."

"I couldn't turn you out of your bed," she replied, touched by his kindness.

"I have another place I can sleep this night. Please let me help you."

Catherine thanked him for his kindness and waited while he gathered up his papers. When she was alone, she covered her face with her hands and burst into tears. The heaviness in her heart dragged her down and she felt deceived and used. How had she let herself be tricked by Cameron? She hated him for it, and she vowed never to trust another man.

Her love for Cameron crumbled before her eyes. Pulling his ring from her finger, she put it on a cord around her neck and let it fall heavily against her breast. This time the ring rested near her heart to remind her of the love she had given foolishly. She had paid the ultimate price for her trust — she now carried a bastard child. There would be no help for her in this town. Tomorrow she would make plans to leave.

Chapter Seven

Catherine's night was haunted by dreams of Cameron. His deceit made her bitter but she could not forget the response he had aroused in her body. He had tricked her, used her to satisfy his lust. Effie had warned her about men who would want her body. She was so naive about men, about life in general, that she'd been taken in by his smooth-talking manner.

Her love for him had soured and she wondered how long before she could drive him from her thoughts. Would she walk the streets looking at every male for some resemblance to the dark shape she remembered? Or would she listen for a voice she knew only as a soft Scottish whisper. His trickery had even included his voice. In the garden, her room, and even the church, their voices had been whispers. Perhaps Cameron had followed her the night of their wedding to frighten her and force the marriage to be held in the dark garden so she could not hear the true sound of his voice or learn the identity of his face. She had been such a fool.

Her hand rested against her abdomen. Now she carried the seed of his deceit. Her love for him was gone but her love for the child that grew inside her body was strong and thriving. The child was half hers, and she would love and protect the infant as best she could.

She knew that would not be possible in this town and she had to formulate a plan of escape. She decided it would be best to leave town before it got light, but the decision of where to go lay like a heavy burden. When her money ran out, she would have to find work. Effie had disillusioned her on the possibility of being a governess and if she took work as a maid, she would be dismissed when she began to get large with child.

Disheartened, her arm fell heavily across her forehead. There had to be something. Returning to her aunts was out of the question. Now that her marriage was not valid, she had no excuse for not marrying Duncan and she dreaded what he would do when he learned about the baby. Her only other relation was her uncle in the West. It was an option that frightened her. It was a solution, but could she make the trip alone? It would be a long and dangerous journey for a woman, but it would offer a fresh start for herself and her child.

If she decided to go, what difficulties would await her? In the short time she'd become acquainted with the outside world, she had made a mess of her life. What more could she expect? Even as she judged her uncertainties, she knew it was her only choice.

Swinging her legs over the side of the cot, she sat up. There were only a few hours of darkness left and she wanted to use it for cover to leave town. She'd find transportation to Santa Fe in another city where she couldn't be traced. Her finances would not support the whole trip, but perhaps she could find work along the way. She scribbled a quick thank you note to Rev. Peters, leaving out her destination in the event Duncan came looking for her. She didn't consider leaving a note for Cameron; she was sure he would never come back.

The streets were still dark when she crept out the door. Coaches left the town daily, and she hoped to find one leaving the city before daybreak. In the hope of concealing her identity, she used her shawl to cover her hair. It was an unusual shade and would be a quick means of identification. She kept to the back streets and walked rapidly toward the outskirts of town.

She paused to catch her breath and her eyes scanned the darkened streets. She saw a man in the distance disappear into the entrance of a shop, but she shrugged it off as a proprietor opening up for the day. She was certain she had not been followed. She was convinced it had been Cameron pursuing her the night of the wedding to scare her and force the ceremony to take place in the darkness.

On the outskirts of town, she spotted a small inn with a coach at the front. After locating the driver, she inquired about the fare to Philadelphia. The price he quoted was not high, but it still left a dent in her finances. She paid the fee and went directly to the coach. It was not particularly comfortable but it was built for speed, and she would be in Philadelphia by evening.

There were only three other passengers, all stopping at various points along the way. At the first sign of dawn, they left town, and Catherine leaned back against her seat in relief. She had not eaten breakfast, so when the coach made one of its stops, she purchased a hot meal. She hated to use the coins but she had to think of the baby.

The coach made excellent time and they entered Philadelphia ahead of schedule. The remaining daylight gave Catherine time to check on additional transportation and to find a place to stay. Unfortunately, the town was larger than she expected and very busy. After serious contemplation, she decided the best way to learn the options for going west was through a newspaper and she asked directions to the nearest office. She found what she wanted to know, but her heart sank when she read the paper. She did not know there had been a gold strike in California, nor that the fees for transportation would be so high. Ship transportation ran well over one hundred dollars, and she simply could not afford it. There were wagon trains leaving every spring for the West, and although she did not know exactly what a wagon train was, the fee was low. She considered it as a possibility for working her way to her uncle. The wagon trains left from St. Louis and Independence so her current problem was transportation to the point of departure.

The only low-cost option open to her was a steamboat. She had ridden on one with her father when she was a child and the thought of doing it again was exciting. They had traveled in a cabin but as she scanned the list of prices, deck passage was all she could afford if she wanted money left over when she arrived in St. Louis. After asking directions to the steamboat offices, she left to secure a place on the boat.

The steamship was scheduled to leave the next day,

and she was able to obtain deck passage for eight dollars. She needed a place to sleep for the night so she asked the ticket-taker if she could go directly to the ship. Understanding her anxiety, he wrote out a paper to be given to the captain.

With deck passage, she was responsible for her own meals, so she located the market area and purchased as much food as she could afford. It would have to be guarded carefully from unsavory people who chose the same cheap method of travel.

She was surprised to find several people already on the ship, claiming their place for the trip. She picked a spot in the center away from the rail where she would benefit from an overhang in the event of rain. The boat was clean and much more elaborate than the one she remembered as a child. The deck was hard and she had trouble finding a comfortable position. Finally, sleep claimed her and she was able to relax from the pressures of the day.

When she woke, the sun was already up and the deck was crowded with people. Every available space had been taken and she was glad she had come aboard the night before. A family had settled near her and the mother was giving instructions to two small children who were more interested in the happenings around them. Breaking off a hunk of bread, she leaned against the wall and watched the activity. There was a slight jerk followed by the sound of rushing water when the steamboat left the dock and started toward its destination.

By late morning, she found it necessary to find the washroom. She hesitated about leaving her things unguarded, but the mother near her introduced herself as Hetty and offered to watch her food. Hetty had already taken her two children to the facilities and warned Catherine she wouldn't like what she found.

Catherine wove her way through the clutter on the deck. The ship was new, but the people smelled dirty and some looked unhealthy. Hetty was right about the washroom. After waiting several minutes for her turn, she found it unclean and without any conveniences. The towels were already filthy from public use, and she refused to touch them.

She was glad to get back out on deck and went directly to the railing. Turning her back to the land, she studied the ship. The pilothouse was eight-sided with a gilded dome. The stacks were large and smoke poured from them. As she edged along the rail, the noise from the paddle wheel increased. An unhealthy smell filled the air and it wasn't long before she found the cause. Cows and horses were sectioned off on one area of the deck by piles of supplies. They could not be seen, but the odor was unmistakable. Moving away from the offending smell, she paused to look at the river. The scenery was beautiful and she found herself staring in awe. After a while, she became aware of someone standing close to her and she moved to make room at the rail.

Something drew her attention upward and her gaze was captured by brilliant green eyes. The man smiled and she was lured to his compelling good looks. He was tall and lean, his dress fancy and expensive. Short dark hair tapered slightly at the neck to just brush his collar. His cheeks were firmly chiseled, and his jawline hard and straight. His eyes were his most attractive feature and she found it difficult to look away.

He smiled, his eyes roaming across her face and down her cloak. His gaze was not insulting and Catherine found herself remembering someone else who might have looked at her in the same way. Tearing her eyes from his, she forced herself to look at the river. Would she see Cam in every man she met?

"Lass, pardon my forwardness, but I saw ye standin' alone, and I thought ye might like some company."

Catherine's hands tightened on the railing and her head slowly turned to the stranger at her side. The Scottish brogue had sent warning flashes through her mind and her knees buckled.

Suddenly, she was grabbed and supported against a hard chest. "Lass, what be wrong? Are ye sick?"

Catherine shook her head to clear her mind. This wasn't possible. She felt the ring against her breast as a reminder of the Scotchman she'd known, and she pulled away from the stranger. Her hands shook as she clutched at the railing.

"Thank you," she managed to say. "I just felt weak for a minute. I'm Catherine." she said, reluctant to use her last name.

He pretended to tip an imaginary hat. "I be Darrell Coleman." Catherine could not help but feel relief that he had not said Cameron MacLennan, and she let herself relax. "I did nae see ye in the dinin' room this mornin'."

An embarrassed tinge heightened the color of her cheeks. The expensive cloak from Cameron was delicately tailored and expensive and because of it, he assumed she could afford stateroom passage.

"I am not eating in the dining hall. I only purchased deck passage."

If he was startled by the news, his gracious smile concealed his surprise. "Then I insist ye be my guest for lunch. I canna think of anythin' I would enjoy more."

Catherine knew dining with Darrell was out of the question. His dress was immaculate, and her clothing beneath the cloak was shabby. She made a feeble excuse about needing to return to her place on the deck. Darrell was perceptive, yet Catherine did not feel embarrassed when he told her she would be the most beautiful woman there, regardless of what she or anyone else thought. Taking her arm, he escorted her back to her place on deck to make sure Hetty would not mind watching her things. Hetty, struggling to get her children to eat their lunch, was more than happy to watch her belongings.

The dining room was more lavish than Catherine expected, and she was once again conscious of her dress when Darrell took her cloak. He wasn't in the least embarrassed by her garments and proudly took her arm and showed her to a table in the corner. A large chandelier was suspended from the ceiling and the glass branches were breathtaking. Oil paintings decorated the walls and the ceilings and walls were painted with gaudy pictures. Catherine insisted that Darrell select a meal for her. It had been years since she'd eaten in a dining hall and she was unsure about ordering. Tea was brought to the table, and Catherine sipped hers slowly. Darrell leaned back in his chair and studied her.

"I be so glad ye could join me. Are ye takin' the boat all the way to St. Louis?"

"Yes, then I am going to my Uncle's ranch near

Santa Fe."

"Are ye travelin' alone?"

Catherine threw him an uncertain glance. "Yes. The trip was a quick decision on my part."

" 'Tis certainly my good fortune that ye are here. I shall enjoy yer company. I hope ye will dine wi' me again this evenin'."

"Oh, but I couldn't impose on you," she answered quickly. "You have been too generous with this meal."

"Nonsense, 'tis my good fortune," he repeated again.

The food was superb, and Catherine found herself enjoying both the meal and the company. Darrell walked her back to her place on the deck and told her he would call for her again at eight for dinner. As soon as he was gone, Hetty hurried over.

"That was sure a handsome man. Where did you find him?"

Catherine laughed. "Actually, he found me. I was standing at the railing and he insisted on buying my lunch. He said he'd be back for dinner."

"You are lucky to have someone to spend time with. They came and got my Hank to feed wood into the boiler." She sighed. "These two children of mine keep trying to run around the deck."

"I'd be glad to help."

Catherine could do little with her appearance other than to comb her hair. She watched Darrell saunter across the deck and she could not help but admire his cool manner and the way he carried himself. She had gotten over the initial surprise of finding him to be of

Scottish descent and believed it was merely coincidence.

The evening meal included live entertainment, thus offering little time for conversation. Catherine enjoyed herself in Darrell's company, but she remembered Cameron's deceit and was determined not to let it happen again. When he asked her for lunch the next day, she refused, citing her promise to help Hetty with the children.

The ship made daily stops at towns along the river for wood, and although not many left the ship, it seemed to slow the confusion on board. She avoided Darrell for two days because she did not want to become a burden to him, nor did she want to give him any false ideas. Toward dusk on the fourth day, their boat engaged another in a race up the river, and people gathered along the rail. When their ship pulled ahead, the deck rang with whistles and cheers. Catherine enjoyed the excitement and when she turned to leave the rail, she found Darrell watching her. He took her arm and helped her to a less crowded area.

"I have been lookin' for ye. Have ye been tryin' to avoid me?"

"N — no," she stammered. "I promised to help Hetty with her children."

"I have missed ye company. Will ye dine wi' me this evenin'?" His green eyes were soft but they still had the same compelling effect, and she found herself accepting.

The second ship began to gain on them and the crowd at the side roared their protest. There was a sudden jolt when the boat was caught in the river's current. Catherine was thrown forward into Darrell's arms. They tightened around her immediately, steadying her, and she clutched at him to gain her balance. She raised her head to thank him from preventing a serious fall, but nothing came from her mouth. Darrell's head was framed in the darkness and she was spiraled back in time to the garden where Cameron had held her and promised his love with the touch of his lips. The hard body against her was familiar, and she struggled to draw back into reality.

Darrell felt her resistance. "Catriona, ye need not be afraid."

The Scottish use of her name made her stiffen. It was the name Cam used for her.

"Why did you call me that?" she whispered.

" 'Tis just the Scotch form for ye name."

"Bu—but that was what Ca—."

Wrenching herself free, she raced down the deck and away from the memories. She heard Darrell call from behind, but the words were just a blur. The ship made a sudden lurch and Catherine reached for something to prevent a fall. She caught a wooden post and held on. Screams of terror erupted from the frightened passengers. The ship righted itself momentarily, then tilted at a sharp angle. Catherine lost her grip and fell forward, rolling with the uneven pitch of the ship. Terrified, she groped for something to stop her motion but everything around her was falling and bumping against her body. Her scream mingled with the confusion until the breath was knocked from her lungs by an unyielding object.

Stunned, she was totally oblivious to the chaos around her. Hands touched her bruised body in an impersonal search for broken bones and through the haze of shock, she recognized Darrell. She struggled to sit but was halted by a searing pain in her abdomen. She screamed as the pain ripped through her body. Darrell's arms tightened around her protectively, but it did not relieve the ache that brought tears to her eyes. Seconds later, her head rolled against his chest and blackness descended.

There was a misty cloud hovering about her mind, making everything move in slow motion. She remembered a torturous pain, but it was gone. Slowly, her eyes opened and focused on unfamiliar surroundings. A small lamp burned on a table near the bed but it barely lighted the room. A door opened and a shadowy shape walked toward the bed. This was something she remembered, and her arms reached out to the dark figure before her.

"Oh Cam, I knew you would come back to me."

The man sat at the edge of the bed and she clutched at him, drawing him close to her breast.

"Catriona, wha' are ye sayin'."

"Cam, I need you." She tried to sit up, but she was unbelievably weak. The dark figure moved and the lamp was turned up.

"Lass, try to remember wha' happened. Ye are on a steamboat. There wae an accident."

He watched her face twist with confusion as her mind tried to separate her thoughts. "What am I doing on a boat?"

"Ye saed ye wanted to go to Saint Louis."

"But how did I get here," she asked, indicating the

110

bed in the plush stateroom.

"I brought ye here."

Catherine looked at the expensive luxury surrounding her and thought of her meager funds. "I can't stay here."

Darrell sensed the reason for her anxiety. " 'Tis my room, Catriona. Ye be welcome to stay here."

"But I can't take your bed."

"Nae lass, I found a spare bed in another cabin. Dona worry."

Catherine was touched by the kindness of a man she'd met only a short time ago. He had been thoughtful and generous and had asked nothing in return.

"What happened?"

"Our steamboat engaged another in a race. The boats collided. We suffered minor damage, but the other boat caught fire and burned. Ye fell against somethin' and were injured."

She tried to sit up but fell against the bed. "I feel so weak. How seriously was I hurt?"

Darrell's gaze dropped to the floor and he took a deep breath. "Ye lost the child ye carried."

His words hit Catherine hard, and she raised her trembling hands to her face. She had lost her child; all ties with Cameron had been severed. She did not attempt to control the tears that trickled down her cheeks. From the first moment she had suspected she was carrying his baby, she had been elated. When the child had been conceived, her love for Cameron had been total. True, she had experienced moments of fear when she learned of his deceit, but she had still wanted the infant.

Catherine turned her face into the pillow. She had

suffered a terrible loss. A part of her had died with the baby, and she knew the painful scars would remain with her forever.

"Catriona, why did ye nae tell me?" Darrell asked when her crying slowed. "I would have helped ye. Where is ye husband? I found ye ring around ye neck."

"I have no husband," she said between sobs.

Darrell's expression sobered. "Who is Cam? Ye called for him."

Embarrassed, Catherine remembered how she had mistaken Darrell for Cam and begged him to come to her bed. Darrell was a gentleman not to have accepted the invitation.

"He was the father of my child," she admitted.

"Where is he?"

"I don't know—He tricked me—I believed he loved me." It was torture to admit what had happened. "He deserted me."

Darrell drew the blanket to her neck. "I think ye need to rest. Hetty has been helpin' wi' ye. She will be back later."

When Hetty came, Catherine learned the decks were crowded with people from the sunken ship. She enjoyed the older woman's company and they exchanged stories about their pasts. Hetty never asked Catherine about the man in her life, and she never mentioned the heartache she had experienced from Cam.

Darrell was determined to make Catherine relax, and he spent most of his free time at her bedside trying to cheer her. He amused her with stories about his gambling and he even tried to teach her how to play poker. She understood the difference between a flush, and royal flush and a straight, but she couldn't comprehend the betting. They chuckled over her attempt to keep a straight face when she held a winning hand. When her pile of chips quickly diminished, she knew Darrell was an expert at the gambling table, and he was not a man she would bet against.

After a week, she was strong enough to sit at the side of the bed. A few days later, Darrell helped her out on deck for a breath of fresh air. Throughout her illness, Darrell had been a constant source of support. He had offered his help and didn't demand payment.

When the ship's whistle blew to announce their arrival in Saint Louis, Catherine viewed the future hopefully. Her relationship with Cameron Mac-Lennan was in the past. She had carelessly given her innocence, but her love for him had been total and intense. If she wanted to make a life for herself, she had to try and forget the past. Her new life would begin in Saint Louis.

Chapter Eight

Saint Louis was not what Catherine expected and she felt overwhelmed as she stood on the steamship waiting to disembark. She was thin and weak from the loss of the baby, and she was grateful that Darrell had insisted on helping her find a place to live.

She was amazed by the number of people that flooded the streets waiting to start west to homestead or find gold. They were of every nationality and included the very rich and very poor. The confusion was frightening but Catherine found it exhilarating. She was one of the people preparing to stake her future on the unknown to start a new life.

She turned slightly at the light pressure on her elbow, and Darrell smiled down at her. "I managed to find us transportation, but 'tis nae much."

He escorted her to a crude carriage unlike those she'd seen in the East. When she pulled herself into the seat, the carriage dipped, and she realized it lacked the suspension that was the pride of the Eastern buggy makers. The seats were dusty but she had already decided dust was something she would have to live with.

She was grateful that Darrell had found transportation because it seemed the only way to get through the throng of people on the streets. On Darrell's orders, the carriage stopped before a two-story hotel.

"If ye will wait here, I will inquire about a room for ye."

Catherine appreciated his thoughtfulness, but he might forget about her small finances and take something she could not afford; or worse yet, pay for the room himself.

"If you don't mind, I think I'll accompany you. I would like to survey my possible surroundings."

The smile he gave hinted that he knew her real reasons, but he still held out a hand and helped her down. The hotel proprietor was in an angry mood as he argued with the people clustered around the desk. It seemed there was only one room remaining and six men willing to rent it. Several prices were mentioned, and Catherine knew at once she could not afford to stay.

She touched Darrell's arm. "I think we'd better go."

"Aye, 'tis nae the place for ye."

They stopped at three other hotels and Catherine insisted on following Darrell inside each one. The prices for a room were two or three times higher than she expected and while Darrell urged her to take a room and agreed to help with the cost, she refused the offer and the lodging.

Catherine was exhausted when they stopped before a two-story frame house. The rent sign in the window gave Catherine hope. A middle-aged woman answered the door with a welcoming smile and Darrell explained that Catherine needed a quiet place to rest.

"You sound like you'd be a perfect boarder," she said pleasantly and Catherine's hopes soared. But when the woman mentioned a price, her shoulders slumped, and she slid her arm through Darrell's.

"I'm sorry, but it's not what I had in mind."

"Wait," the older woman called as they turned away. "You could share a room, but you'll have to sleep on a mattress on the floor." The price she quoted was within Catherine's budget and she accepted.

Catherine thought she had made a bargain, but when Darrell saw the tiny room she would be sharing, he immediately voiced his disapproval. "Catriona," he said. "I canna let ye stay here. Let me find ye somethin' more suitable."

Her hand fell against his jacket. "You know I appreciate your help, but I cannot accept your charity. It will be at least two more weeks before I can seek employment and I must live within my means."

Capturing her fingers, he looked into her eyes. "Catriona, ye know it doesna have to be that way. I want to help ye."

Catherine still trembled when she heard Darrell speak her name. There were so many things about him that reminded her of Cam and she was grateful she had never felt the touch of his lips because it would either confirm or deny something that haunted the back of her mind—that he was Cameron Mac-Lennan. She wanted to like Darrell, but because of Cam, she wavered on the brink of uncertainty.

Pulling away from him, she turned so he wouldn't see the turmoil on her face. "No Darrell, I have to do it alone."

"But why? I want to help ye."

"I don't want to be indebted to you."

Darrell's hands closed on her shoulders to gently

turn her to face him. "Have I ever asked ye for anythin'."

"No, but I am used to relying on myself." Catherine bitterly remembered the one time when she had relied on someone and given her trust. It had taught her to be more cautious in the future.

"Catriona, ye are young, and I believe ye have led a sheltered past. Ye dona know much about this way of life." His green eyes softened. "Do ye nae trust me?"

Catherine wanted to trust him. There was no reason not to believe him, but she had been fooled once before. "I want to, but I can't—I'm sorry Darrell—I know I have hurt you."

"Is Cameron the reason ye canna trust me?"

"Yes," she answered and saw a tightening of his features.

Drawing her into his arms, he cradled her head against his chest. "Ye canna judge all men because of one. Ye must carry a great bitterness for this man, but ye canna let it ruin ye life." He ran his hand along her cheek and tipped her head up. "Do ye love him?"

"For a time, my whole life was centered around him. I loved him very much—but my love turned bitter."

"Ye must try to forget him."

When she was alone, Mary Cummings brought her a mattress and blanket. Catherine turned over all but a few pennies of her money. She still felt exhausted from the accident and spent most of her time in bed. Mrs. Cummings was an excellent cook and Catherine began to regain some of the weight she'd lost.

Several times a week Darrell came to visit and Catherine entertained him in a small parlor. Darrell had a room in one of the hotels and Catherine suspected he had been lucky at the gambling tables. Each time he visited, he tried to get Catherine to dine out with him, but she always refused. She thought it would be foolish for him to spend money on her dinner when she'd already paid for meals at the house.

Two weeks had passed since she had taken the room at the boarding house. She felt stronger and her figure had regained its curves. Darrell was persistent in asking her to go out with him, so she finally consented to go for a drive. On the day of the outing, she rose early and dressed in one of her maid outfits. All her clothes were starting to show wear, but she refused Darrell's offer of a new wardrobe.

The carriage he arrived in was more modern than the last one she'd ridden in and there was no driver. "We be goin' on a picnic," he announced, urging the horses into a trot.

It was a warm April day, so Catherine removed her cloak. She brightened at the prospect of leaving the confusion of the city and let the gentle breeze blow through her hair. Spring was starting to burst forth; the budding trees were a brilliant green against the cornflower blue sky. Tiny flowers had begun to peek above the ground and the sun's rays warmed them, bringing more life to the earth. As they left the town, the chatter of birds replaced the confusion of the city. Catherine raised her face to the sky and felt the sun warm her cheeks.

They found a comfortable place for their picnic beneath a large oak tree, and Darrell spread a blanket on the grass. Eager to explore, they held hands and forged a path through the woods. They found a shallow creek and Catherine sat on the bank while Darrell boldly skipped across the rocks to the other side.

"Would ye like to join me?" he shouted back to her.

Catherine hesitated. The water was not deep, but it still moved rapidly over the smooth stones. Smiling, she rose. She enjoyed a challenge and the worse that could happen would be wet clothes.

She reached the other side without suffering any more than a wet hem, and Darrell gave her a hug. "Ye made it." There was a teasing light in his green eyes. "I was hopin' ye might fall and need to be rescued."

She playfully pushed him back until water hit his boots. "You're the one who's going to need rescuing."

"Are ye goin' to get me wet?" he asked in mock horror.

Moving unexpectedly, Darrell swooped Catherine into his arms and carried her to the center of the creek where he held her over the water. "You wouldn't dare!" she said, tugging at his sleeve. "Put me down."

"Right here?" he asked with a humorous twist to his mouth.

Catherine's tawny eyes were twinkling with laughter, but her expression was stern. "I'll never forgive you if you drop me."

He considered her words. "It might be worth it."

She pretended horror at his comment but was laughing as he carried her across the creek and put her down. His hands remained on her shoulders and Catherine sensed a seriousness about him. Tension crept into her limbs as she looked into his face. She was unable to move as his lips lightly brushed hers. It was a brief, gentle kiss, and one she would have enjoyed if Darrell had not reminded her so much of Cameron.

They found their path back to the blanket and enjoyed the meal Darrell had provided. It was nearly dark when he drove her back to town. Catherine invited him in and he accepted. In the parlor, they sat on the small settee.

"How are ye managin'? Is there anythin' ye need?"

Catherine shook her head. As much as she needed money, she couldn't ask for his help. He had already done enough.

"Catriona, I've been lucky at the gambling tables. I am able to help ye."

She threw her head back and her golden-brown hair settled on her shoulders. "Darrell, we've been through this before. I will not accept your help. I wish you would not keep trying to force your good intentions on me."

"Is it me Catriona? Do ye nae like me? I have tried to be kind."

She hated hurting him, but her past pain was too fresh. "You've been wonderful."

"Is it because I be a man and ye be afraid of bein' hurt." His hand captured hers and her body churned in remembered torment. She didn't want him touching her; she was afraid she would respond and leave herself open and vulnerable. Darrell was so much like Cam—or he was Cam, she had never wanted to search for the truth. She hovered on the edge of panic and tried to tear her hand free but his grip tightened and he pulled her toward his body.

"Darrell, please don't do this," she pleaded, turning her head to avoid the touch of his fingers against her cheek.

"Why Catriona?"

"Why do you insist on calling me that?" she cried in anguish.

"I told ye before. 'Tis a Scotch name." Tears sprang in Catherine's eyes. "Why canna ye forget the man that hurt ye? 'Tis over."

"Why?" she cried in agony. "Because you remind me of him. I left my home to get away from his memory, but then I met you and you began to haunt me." She took a deep breath. "I have even wondered if you are Cameron."

Her eyes were too tear-filled to register the hurt look on Darrell's face. "Ye compare me wi' that scum. He hurt ye' Catriona. I have done nae to harm ye—I have been ye friend." His green eyes softened. "Let me show you how gentle I can be."

Dropping his head, he tenderly placed his mouth to hers. His lips moved in a warm, persuasive way, keeping with his promise to be gentle. His actions, however, filled Catherine with terror. Cam had been a soft, coaxing lover, and the memory burned through her mind.

Tearing herself from his embrace, she ran to the doorway and turned. "Get out. I never want to see you again." She was gone before he had a chance to comment. In her room, she threw herself down on her bed and wept. Cameron and Darrell—were they one and the same? Or were they two separate identities she had confused in her mind? Men were all alike, and she hated them.

Catherine never expected to see Darrell again but she was still nervous whenever the door knocker sounded. She experienced twinges of guilt for treating him so cruelly, but all she could think of was

Cameron. The landlady had been out the night of the argument and was unaware that Darrell would not be returning. When Catherine's rent came due, she graciously let her stay without payment, and Catherine knew she expected to get the money from Darrell.

Four days passed, and Catherine finally believed she was strong enough to find a job. She decided to take a day and scout the town before beginning her search for work. The streets were unbelievably crowded and people bumped and pushed her. Rain had recently turned the roads to mud and her dress was badly soiled.

She joined a group of people reading a posted sign and excitement tingled through her limbs. There was a wagon train leaving for Santa Fe in two weeks. Anyone interested in going along was to meet in Independence by the date given. It was the chance Catherine needed, but a frown caught the edge of her mouth. She needed money to get to Independence, and the only way she could do that was to find a job. Turning, she scanned the stores. Would one of the owners hire her? Tomorrow she would begin her search and hopefully by evening, she would join the ranks of the employed.

Chapter Nine

Catherine rose early to begin her search for a job. She took special care with her appearance and felt certain her poor but neat state of dress would not hinder her chances of finding one. Many people were experiencing the same state of poverty.

She had just put on her cloak when Mary Cummings came to see her. "Catherine, you are past due on your rent. If you cannot pay me today, I will have to ask you to leave. You probably think it is cruel of me to push you out but things in this town are expensive, and I must have money to buy supplies." She paused and eyed Catherine curiously. "If you are short of funds, perhaps you could borrow money from your gentleman friend."

Catherine knew Mary wondered about Darrell's absence but even if she wanted to ask for his help, she didn't know where he was staying. Times were hard, and she couldn't ask Mary to let her stay when she couldn't pay.

"I will pack my things and when I get a job, I will send you the money I owe you." She pulled the remaining pennies out of her purse and gave them to the older woman. "You have been very generous. I appreciate your kindness," she said, and began packing.

"I hope you understand," Mary Cummings said and quietly left.

While she folded her few items of clothing, she reflected on her association with Darrell. She was still bitter and anxious about the heated exchange she'd had with him. He had shown her nothing but kindness and until the last meeting, he had not made anything more out of their relationship than friendship. She suspected his kiss had been to ease her fear of him, but instead it had thrown her into a panic and she had bitterly lashed out.

After minutes of contemplating, she left him a note and apologized for her actions. She didn't have an address, but she did write her plans to be on the wagon train leaving for Santa Fe in two weeks.

The streets were crowded and she wondered if the constant flow of people ever ceased. Stopping before a small store, she smoothed her hair down with her hand and straightened her cloak. She had never had to seek employment before and there was a fluttering in her stomach. The proprietor was in his forties, and she noticed the approving gaze he gave her when she entered.

"Can I help you?"

"I am looking for a job. Do you have anything available?"

The man smiled slowly. "I might have. What are your qualifications?" He sensed her hesitation. "Have you ever worked in a store and handled money?"

Catherine frowned. She knew how to work with figures, but she lacked experience in dealing with merchandise. "No sir. The only position I've held was as a maid. Do you need someone to clean your store?"

"No, but we might be able to come to another understanding." His gaze wandered over her face, then down her cloaked figure. "Would you be interested?"

Catherine was shocked by his proposition. If she accepted a job from him, she'd only work from his bed. "No thank you."

She took a step backward but he caught her wrist. "What's your hurry? I've offered you a job."

"I'm not interested." Catherine clutched her few belongings and wished someone would come into the shop.

"Jerome," a high pitched voice called, and Catherine saw a large woman step out of a back room. Her eyes narrowed dangerously at the scene before her, and the proprietor quickly dropped Catherine's hands and stepped back.

"The young lady is looking for work." he explained nervously.

"We are not hiring," the woman said briskly, and Catherine left.

She received the same reception in three other shops. Without experience, no one would take a chance. She also suspected her youth and beauty were a deterrent. Finally, when she'd almost given up hope, she was hired to help in the kitchen of a dining hall. She was responsible to the cook for helping prepare the food. Catherine was eager and her intentions were good, but she poured too much salt in the soup and burned the muffins. It happened at their peak period and the owner was enraged. Grabbing her arm, he dragged her through the dining room, shouting that he should make her pay the damages. The people eating, mostly men, hooted with laughter. Catherine's cheeks flamed in embarrassment and she could not get outside quick enough.

Her stomach was empty, but without funds, she couldn't eat. She began walking to the opposite side of town. She was unfamiliar with most of the business establishments but she still went inside to ask for a job. Everyone turned her down and by late afternoon, she was totally disillusioned. If she didn't find something soon, she would be sleeping in the street.

Pausing, she leaned against a building to gather her thoughts. She scanned the businesses across the street. One of them had to need help. She tried to feel optimistic as she crossed the road. She received two rejections before she saw a tiny sign tacked to the wall of a new building advertising for a woman to serve tables. When she had eaten in the boat's dining hall with Darrell she'd observed the waitresses and knew it was a job she could handle. She would not be required to prepare the food, only serve it.

The outside of the building had a certain character she could not determine. There were no windows in the front and only two, two-way swinging doors. They were too high for her to peek over and she knew she'd look foolish if she bent to look under, so she pushed the door open and entered.

It took a few seconds for her eyes to adjust to the dim interior. The room was longer than it was wide and it was filled with tables and chairs. Opposite the door a long polished wooden counter spanned three-fourths the length of the room. A curving staircase with a similarly polished banister led to a series of doors on the second floor. The room was not crowded, but the patrons were predominantly male. Every pair of eyes in the room were focused on her, and her tongue nervously darted out to lick her lips. Tightening her grip on her bag, she squared her shoulders and crossed the room.

Pausing before the long counter, she watched the man behind it pour a drink for a man at the opposite end. When he came toward her, she noticed his hard, rugged appearance. His appraisal of her matched that of most men, but she did not flinch when his eyes roamed over her features. Catherine needed this job, and she thought serving beverage and food to the patrons would be easier than most.

"What can I do fer you, miss?" he asked gruffly.

Catherine placed a trembling hand on the counter. "I saw your job advertisement and I want to apply for the position." She heard his grunt of skepticism and once again he took in her appearance. "Has the job been filled?" she persisted.

"No, but this ain't the kind of job fer you."

She didn't like the smile he gave her, but his words only increased her determination. "I need this job. I will work hard." Catherine felt like she was begging, but it was getting late, and she had to find work. "Give me a chance to prove myself."

One of the men behind her shouted, "Give her a chance. We need someone to liven the place up."

The bartender snorted. "You got the job on a trial basis." He jerked his thumb toward the men at the tables. "If they like you tonight, I'll keep you on. You get the fourth room at the top of the stairs. Go on up. I'll send one of the girls to you."

"Thank you—thank you," she said as she started

up the steps. Catherine couldn't believe her ears. Not only had she gotten a job but it included a place to sleep. She felt the men watching her and decided not to let it bother her. Her job would require serving single men, and she had to get used to their crude comments and leering looks. She would stay just long enough to earn the money to get a place on the wagon train.

Her small but clean room was almost hidden from the steps. The bed was oversized and took up most of the space. Next to it was a dresser and night table. Her closet was a piece of rope strung across one corner of the room. Closing the door behind her, she tossed the bundle on the bed. Fortunately, the room had a window, and it gave her a view of the street.

Darkness had descended when she finally heard a light tap on the door. She opened it to admit a girl not much older than herself but quite different in appearance. After assessing Catherine's dress, she leaned over the chamber pot and spit out a mouthful of tobacco.

"I'm Candy." She put more tobacco in her mouth. "Sam said I'd have to make some changes in your clothes. Turn so I can see the back." Catherine did as she was told. "That dress is one of the ugliest I've ever seen. As you look now, most men wouldn't give you a second glance."

Catherine knew Candy wasn't right. All day long she'd been receiving crude glances from the male population, but it didn't bear mentioning. She didn't want men to look at her in the manner Candy suggested.

"Well, take off your clothes, and we'll see what we

can do for you." She threw something toward the bed but it was just a blur of red as it landed on the mattress.

"Do you mean they provide me with clothes?"

The look Candy passed Catherine was one of disbelief. "All the gals are given clothes to wear." She threw her hands on her hips. "Say, are you sure you want to get into this kind of work?"

Since it was her only opportunity to earn money, she lifted her chin. "Quite sure," Catherine responded and began disrobing. She was careful to remove her ring and hide it in her clothes. She didn't want Candy to see it and ask questions. Shyly, she threw aside the last of her clothes and stood for inspection.

"You've got a real nice figure," Candy praised, studying her nakedness. "You should earn a lot in tips."

"I was wondering about the wages. I was so excited when Sam hired me, I forgot to ask."

"Your salary ain't gonna be much, but you'll get extra from the men if you cooperate."

Catherine was determined to do all she could to be pleasant to the customers, but she couldn't understand why the shape of her body could make any difference.

"Try this on." Candy picked up the blob of red from the bed and handed it to Catherine. "It should fit. The girl before you left it behind."

Catherine shook out the dress and looked at it in stunned disbelief. There was nothing to it, and the flashy red color made the dress all the more hideous.

"This is what I'm supposed to wear?"

Candy laughed. "What did you expect? My dress is

even worse than that. Hurry up and get into it. I have to get ready and the place is getting crowded. I hate to lose business."

Catherine slid her legs into the skimpy costume and pulled it up over her breasts. It felt tight, and when Candy began to hook up the back, it molded to Catherine's body like skin and made her look like she was naked. The neck was cut low, and the tightness made her breasts want to burst from their confines. It was short and slit up the side halfway up her thigh. Long red ribbons of fabric covered the dress from the neck and descended to her knees. When she moved, they provided revealing glimpses of her curves.

"I can't wear this," Catherine protested.

"If you want to work here, you'll wear it." She shrugged. "If not, you can go back out on the street." She jerked her thumb toward the window. "After one night out there, you'll be back here; you might as well stay."

Catherine didn't have any place else to go. She had to remain for at least one night. "I'm staying," she told Candy.

Candy handed her a pair of red slippers. "You can wear these. Be downstairs in twenty minutes. Sam will tell you what to do."

It was more than thirty minutes before Catherine gathered the courage to open her door. Piano music and a general murmur of voices floated up the steps. Nervousness flooded over her when she peered around the corner. The room was full, but it did not cater to the family type clientele she thought she would be serving. Instead, the room was full of men smoking and drinking at the tables.

Taking a deep breath, she started down the steps. Several men called to her and Catherine quickened her pace to avoid unwanted attention. She went straight to the bar and waited for Sam to give her instructions. When he broke free from the customers and approached her, Catherine saw the flicker of lust in his eyes.

"You should improve business. The men are going to like you."

Catherine did not like the suggestive tone in his voice, but there was nothing she could do about it tonight. For the next twenty minutes, she carried drinks to tables. Men's hands brushed her legs and buttocks, and a few touched the tawny hair streaming down her back. One man even dared to touch the inside of her thigh.

Sam signaled her and Catherine joined him at the bar. He handed her a tray of drinks. "I want you to take these to the poker game."

"Which one?" she asked, knowing there were at least three games in progress.

"The *big* game behind the curtain," he said, pointing to the corner of the room. Balancing the tray on her arm, she cut a path across the room. She slipped behind the curtained area and set her tray on a small table off to the side. There were six men around the table and she began replacing their empty drinks with full ones. She saw hands reach for the pile of money in the center and she knew the game was over.

She was setting down the fourth drink when someone uttered a startled gasp. The sound drew everyone's attention to her, and she fumbled awkwardly. Looking up, her eyes locked on the man across from her.

"Catriona, wha' be ye doin' here?" Catherine's lower lip dropped as she stared into the disbelieving eyes of Darrell Coleman. Her initial shock soon gave way to embarrassment as his eyes slowly raked her figure. His brow arched at the generous display of flesh. She was certainly not the prim and proper lady he had left at the boarding house.

"Lass, will ye answer me?"

All attention focused on Catherine. "I—I work here."

"That's right," a third voice responded. "What else would she be doing here?" The man who spoke was on Catherine's right. His light brown hat was pulled low over his forehead so his face was hidden.

Catherine sensed Darrell's tension and his fingertips pressed against the table until his knuckles showed white. "Mind ye own business, Logan. 'Tis between the lass and me."

"Oh, I don't know," the voice said calmly. "Seems to me that a woman who would work in a place like this is anybody's property. She's here to service the patrons." Catherine watched the stranger calmly stack the money before him. He had been the winner of the hand and she suspected Darrell resenting losing to him.

"Well, this woman isna goin' to be anyone's property," Darrell said flatly. "Catriona, I want to talk to ye. Ye shouldna be here. Why did ye nae stay at the house?"

Darrell made it sound like it was his house too, and Catherine blushed. She appreciated his concern but she couldn't accept any more help; her debt to him was already too large. She didn't like working at her present job but thus far she'd been successful at fending off the roving hands and she had to get the money for the trip to Independence.

"I work here. This is my job." She looked at him hopefully. "Please don't interfere." There was a plea evident in her voice. Their exchange should be conducted in private and not before a group of strangers. Darrell's possessiveness made it sound like they were having a lover's quarrel.

"I want to talk," he insisted.

The set of his jaw told her he would be the winner. "I have a room upstairs. We can settle it there."

One of the men at the table hooted and the stranger called Logan jammed the money in his pocket. His gestures indicated anger but his voice retained a coolness she found unnerving. "Leave the lady alone." Putting his finger on the edge of his hat, he pushed it back and then turned to look at Catherine. He had the coldest, most piercing blue eyes she'd ever seen, and a tremor ran down her spine. The man looked merciless. "She's going to be otherwise engaged." Twisting slightly, his hand made contact with her leg. In plain view, his rough fingers traced an intimate line up her thigh. She tried to inch away but her exit was blocked by the chair next to her. Her tawny eyes made a silent plea to the stranger but he seemed amused by her trembling body.

"Take ye hands off the lass, Logan," Darrell ordered. "I tol' ye she be mine."

"Is that true?" the stranger challenged Catherine. "Do you belong to this man?"

The tenseness in her body increased. His hand had not ceased its caressing motion, and she could not collect her thoughts. "I don't belong to anyone."

"Hmm," the stranger muttered. "Is he your lover?"

Her eyes widened, and the implication of his words left her cheeks pale. How could the men discuss her so freely and submit her to such intense embarrassment? The other men at the table pushed their chairs away from the table, leaving the area around Darrell and Logan empty.

"How dare you!" Catherine ranted in protest. "I demand you take your hands off me right now."

The movement of his fingers became more suggestive and he parted the slit of her dress to caress her flesh. Catherine trembled uncertainly. What did this man think she was?

"You didn't answer my question," he stated flatly. "Is he your lover?" One of the men snickered, and Darrell shot him a cold glance. "Your lack of response confirms my suspicions," he drawled. Catherine tried to pull away, but the stranger's grip tightened possessively around her waist. Darrell's green eyes darkened with fury as he watched the caressing hand. "What's the matter?" the stranger asked in response to Darrell's reaction.

The tension in the air was thick; something had to give. In one final attempt, she wrenched herself from the stranger and cowered against the wall. Logan rested his relaxed hands on the table while Darrell's tight, nervous fingers drummed against the smoothly finished top.

"Logan, ye kind be the scum of the earth. Ye've nae regard for that which be good and beautiful. Ye want

134

to ruin everythin'. Just because ye got lucky at cards tonight doesna mean ye be goin' to win the lass."

Catherine saw Logan smile, but his eyes remained the cold, calculating blue. "Shall we play poker for her. I have no doubt that I'll win."

"Nae, I willna humiliate the lass by playin' cards for her. I canna let ye hurt her."

"We'll settle it another way then," Logan said, and she saw Darrell's head drop slightly forward in agreement. She didn't understand what was going on but the men never took their eyes off each other.

In a split second, Darrell's hand moved toward his jacket. It was a quick, smooth motion, but the stranger was faster. His hand dove under the table to the weapon at his thigh and it exploded before Darrell's gun cleared his coat. With a dazed expression on his face and a spot of red on his shirt, Darrell slumped over the table.

Catherine's breath was zapped from her body. Two of the men rose to help Darrell, and Logan calmly holstered his gun. Pushing back his chair, he rose. He was a tall man and as he turned toward Catherine, his height was overpowering. She shrank against the wall to avoid the look in his eyes.

"As you see I have won the prize." In one fluid motion, he lifted her and swung her over his shoulder. His arm rested heavily across the back of her legs to prohibit her kicking. He stepped from behind the curtains to the main room and was greeted by silence. All attention was focused on the curtained room where a man had just been shot and possibly killed.

A lady shouted, "Top of the stairs to your left — Room four," and the men broke out in a round of cheers. By the time they had reached the stairs, the noise had returned to normal and they were forgotten. Catherine saw the booted feet take the steps with ease and as hard as she struggled, she could not budge the arm around her body. The hallway passed before her eyes and she heard the opening then closing of a door. His grip lightened and she was thrown across the bed.

Catherine immediately swung her legs over the opposite side and moved as far from him as possible. He was standing with his back to the door, blocking her exit. His attention was focused on the generous display of flesh rising and falling with each breath. To make matters worse, her breath quickened in panic, and her breasts surged against the skimpy dress.

Catherine didn't know when she had ever seen eyes that were so cruel and blue in their intensity. There was hate written in their depths and she sensed that the hate was there for all women.

His hair was dark and long enough to brush his collar. His face was bearded to the extent that it looked like he hadn't shaved in several days which added to his ruthless appearance. A fresh scar near his left ear marred his otherwise unmarked features. Long tanned fingers reached for the belt at his waist, and his gun and holster slid off his hip, followed by a knife in a leather casing. He carelessly tossed them on the night table. Dusty, worn clothes told of long work or hard travel, and he also wore a red knotted kerchief around his neck. He moved slightly and Catherine noted the long supple motion of his limbs.

Cautiously, she crept toward the corner. She had to get past him and into the hall. Seeing her change of position he gave her a mocking smile. "What are you called?" he asked as if he really didn't care.

"I am—I am Catherine," she stammered, moving a little closer to the door. Although his eyes were not on her, she was certain that he knew every move she made.

Taking a deep breath, she lunged for the door, but Logan was ready for her and she came up against his hard chest. His hand laced itself through her hair and he let the strands fall through his fingers.

"Tawny eyes and hair," he muttered thoughtfully. "Catherine, you remind me of a wild cougar in captivity. Frightened—yet beautiful—and you are frightened."

"Let me go," she begged, refusing to look into his eyes. They frightened her yet something about them captivated her. "You don't understand. You can't just drag me into my room and hold me prisoner. I have a job to do."

"Ah, Cat, is that what you're worried about?" Twisting slightly, he slid his hand into his pocket and withdrew a gold piece. "There is your fee," he said, carelessly tossing it on the table.

Catherine didn't know why he was throwing money on the table. She wouldn't accept Darrell's help and she certainly wouldn't take money from a stranger. Sam was probably wondering what had happened. If she didn't get back to work, she'd be thrown out on the street.

"I've got to get back downstairs," she said, renewing her struggles for freedom.

"What's the matter, didn't I offer you enough?" he sneered.

Catherine was completely puzzled. "Enough for what?"

She saw a flicker of confusion in his eyes, but it was quickly masked by the icy blue gaze. "I don't have time to play games." His hand slid down the curve of her hip and she tried to wrench herself free.

"You're acting like a frightened maiden."

Logan's words stung. She had never been a frightened maiden and had willingly surrendered her maidenhead without a qualm to a man she had learned to hate.

"I don't know much about men," she lied, hoping he would take pity on her, but it only seemed to interest him more.

"If you were innocent in the ways of a man, then you wouldn't be working in a place like this and wearing a dress that leaves you practically naked."

One of his hands touched the small of her back, propelling her length against his. His body was hard and firm and she tried to pull back from the feel of it against hers. Waves of nausea surrounded her when his hand pinned her head in preparation for the touch of his mouth. When it came, it was like the man — cruel, hard and without emotion. Catherine fought him by throwing up a barrier of indifference and refusing to let him reach her emotions. Her tightly clenched teeth prohibited the entrance of his searching tongue. His hands glided up and down her back, pressing her closer until she felt the urgent need of his body spring forth. Soon he would be beyond control and she would be forced to submit to his desires. Her fists pounded at his back and her hands tugged at his arms.

Catherine's head was pushed to the side as Logan buried his face against her neck. His bearded stubble scratched her skin and her eyes widened when his tongue touched the tip of her ear. Her gaze locked on the gun and knife on the table. With a weapon in her hand, freedom would be within reach. Continuing her assault with one fist, she reached toward the table with her free hand. She didn't know anything about guns, so she went for the knife.

Logan slid his leg between hers and Catherine gasped at the intimacy of the position. A tremor of fear raced through her body as she pulled the knife from its sheath. His hands scorched the naked flesh exposed at her shoulder. Supporting her full weight, he pushed her back toward the mattress. Catherine knew the time had come to defend herself and she drew her arm back.

Logan caught the defensive motion, but his hold on her had been such that he was not able to move quickly enough to avoid the attack, and the knife buried itself in his side. Catherine fell against the mattress, then sprang to her feet.

Stepping back, Logan's arms dropped to his sides. Stunned, he stared at the knife protruding at an angle from his body. His expression was one of pain and disbelief. Looking up at her, he shielded his earlier emotions with a cold hatred that made her recoil. The animosity in his blue eyes made the hairs on the back of her neck tingle. Still looking at Catherine, his hand closed firmly around the hilt of the knife and in a quick motion, he pulled it out. There was no pain registered on his face, only an increased loathing for the woman who had tried to take his life. Blood spurted from the wound and Catherine covered her mouth to force back the heaviness in her throat.

The hard depth of his blue eyes remained unchanged as the color drained from his face and he collapsed across the bed. Catherine stood immobile, waiting for her body to cease its trembling. Logan's eyes were closed, but she doubted she would ever forget the hate she had seen in their depths. Taking a step toward the bed, she clutched at the bedpost. There was so much blood on his shirt and pants, and his face had a death-like stillness. Her hand stifled the groan of realization that crept from her lips. The broad, muscular chest was still, and his nostrils no longer showed the movement of life. She had killed him; she was a murderer.

She held her breath, hoping for some movement, yet dreading the stare of the blue eyes—eyes she would never see again except in her dreams. She had murdered him in cold-blood. She struggled with the feeling of panic, knowing she had to keep her head clear. Escape was her first consideration. Tossing her cloak around her shoulders, she grabbed her small sack of possessions and started for the door. She hesitated at the table long enough to pick up the gold piece Logan had thrown down for her favors. The money was dirty, but she would need it. She remembered the cash he had won at the poker game, but she couldn't bring herself to touch his dead body. By rights, the money should be used to bury him. She looked again at the face masked in death, knowing it would haunt her for the rest of her life.

Luckily the corridor was empty, and she ran to the back stairs. The noise from the bar area was louder and she could hear the giggles and moans from behind the closed doors. The warm air helped ease some of her tension, but it wasn't until she was two streets away that she relaxed.

It was too warm for the cloak and she received several questioning stares from people on the street, but she didn't dare remove it. The gaudy color and the skimpy design of her dress would arouse comment and remain in peoples' memories. She didn't want to be remembered and linked to Logan's death.

Her life had changed and she bitterly reflected on the events leading to her flight. Logan had insulted her and tried to rape her, and she'd responded in the only way possible; she had fought back. When she'd plunged the knife into his side, her only thought was of injuring him to obtain her freedom. She never believed it would make her a murderer. Life had been difficult before she met Logan, but he had twisted everything around and now she had to run for her life.

Her ignorance had been responsible and she felt foolishly naive. If she had been more knowledgeable in the ways of the world, she wouldn't have become trapped in an impossible situation. She would have known the kind of women who took jobs in saloons.

Weak from the experience and because she hadn't eaten for hours, she looked for a place to eat. Although the food took all her money, it was filling, and she was smiling when she ate her dessert.

Depression once again settled over her when she stepped outside. She wished she had not been so generous and left Logan's pockets full of money for his burial. She needed funds to get out of town.

She walked without direction or destination. She had seen Darrell shot and possibly killed, and she had murdered the stranger. Any thoughts of asking about

141

Darrell's condition immediately vanished. There had been too many witnesses to her association with Logan and she'd be walking into a trap. Darrell had been kind, but she had been wary of his generosity. Cameron had taught her not to trust people and she had not been able to return Darrell's friendship in the same way. In the back of her mind, she had always wondered if he was Cameron, but now it was something she'd never know.

Slowly, she adjusted her cloak. It was warm and she was exhausted. Without money, there was little hope of finding a room. In the distance, she discovered one of the covered wagons used to travel west. Staying in the shadows, she approached it. The streets were almost empty and there was no activity around the wagon. It was the perfect place to hide and she held her breath when she stopped at the back. The canvas was secured by knots, and it took several seconds before she had freed the fabric. After checking the streets to make sure no one watched her, she threw her bag inside and climbed in after it. She retied the flap in two places, then groped around in the darkness. It was full of merchandise and it took some time before she located a small space that would hopefully hide her. Her improvised bed was not the most comfortable, but she felt safe and was able to relax for the first time in hours. It was hot in the wagon and she removed her cloak and laid it with her small sack. After returning her ring to its resting place between her breasts, she sighed and drifted into a deep sleep. Things had to get better tomorrow.

Chapter Ten

Catherine woke slowly from the deep sleep that had claimed her the night before. Her body ached from staying in the cramped quarters and the uneven jolting of the wagon had added a few bruises. The flap at the back was secured, but light filtered through the canvas. Shifting her position, she looked toward the front. A man on a high seat whistled and called out to the team before him, and her fears and uncertainties returned. What kind of a situation had she gotten herself into? What would the man on the seat say when he found her hiding in the back? Would he know she was wanted for murdering Logan?

After careful consideration, she decided the best thing to do was disappear before the man discovered her. Her fingers tore nervously at the tight bindings holding the canvas down. She couldn't remember tying so many knots or making them so taut. Occasionally, she glanced over her shoulder to make sure she worked unnoticed.

The last knot was the tightest, and one of her nails snapped painfully close to her finger. She stopped to wipe the fleck of blood that appeared on the surface. The wagon hit a rut and tilted to one side. With a startled "Oh," she fell against a pile of boxes, then groaned when her shoulder slammed the hard surface.

She heard a "Whoa there," from the driver, and the wagon slowed. As the man turned, Catherine braced herself for their encounter, but the warming smile on his face made her fears vanish. He was a broad shouldered man with dark brown hair and pale blue eyes. The lines of age around his eyes and cheeks put his age near fifty.

"Did you hurt yourself?" he asked, climbing into the back. The wind caught the loosened flap and snapped it away from the wagon. It announced Catherine's intention to escape but the man seemed unconcerned. "You looked like you needed sleep, so I didn't bother to wake you."

"You knew I was here?" she asked in amazement.

"I found you this morning when I checked on the supplies." He gave her a generous smile.

"Aren't you angry to find me in your wagon?" she inquired cautiously. She had expected a totally different kind of welcome.

His tanned hand ran down the length of his jaw. "Not really." He shrugged. "Besides, I figured you had a reason to be here. It's my guess you're hiding. Am I right?"

Catherine was amazed by his uncanny perception. "I—I—," she said, unable to put her reason for being here into words.

"You don't have to explain. Many saloon girls decide they want to escape the demands put on them."

Remembering her revealing dress, her hand flew to cover her exposed bosom. The man did not throw her leering glances so she didn't feel threatened, but she was embarrassed.

"I needed a place to sleep last night. I was hoping

this wagon would be joining the wagon train in Independence."

"That's where we're heading."

Catherine beamed. "That's wonderful. I plan to be on the train. I'm on my way to Santa Fe." She lowered her eyes. "I don't have any money, but I hope to find someone who will let me work for them."

He sighed and Catherine looked up to find him shaking his head. "If it's work you're looking for, you may be in for hard times," he said grimly. "Many of the people have barely enough food to feed their own families. This will be the last train leaving this year and we will be lucky to make it over the mountains before it snows."

Catherine frowned. "I will just have to take my chances. I must get to my uncle's ranch." It was imperative that she find a place on the wagon train. If she remained in her present location, she'd be branded as a murderer. "Do you need help? I'd be willing to work hard." She felt a tinge of hope.

"Well, I don't know," he answered uncertainly. "I'm only driving this wagon. It belongs to the lead scout."

"I'll just have to ask him," she said with determination.

"I'm afraid that won't be possible for several days." His blue eyes twinkled. "We're meeting in Independence. You can ride along if you like."

"Thank you," Catherine said quickly. "I won't be a burden and I insist on helping."

"That's something you can talk to the scout about. Until then, you're a guest. Now, would you like to join me on the seat up front. It's a little cooler."

"I'd like to," she replied, "but first I want to get out of this dress. I loathe it." Her eyes darted over the stacks of merchandise for her tiny sack, but she didn't see it. "I had a bundle of clothes with me last night, but I don't see it." She moved a few boxes to intensify her search. "I know I had it with me last night when I crawled inside. Did you see it?"

He shook his head. "Sorry, but maybe it will turn up."

"I guess I'll have to wear the cloak," she said, frowning. "If I'm seen like this someone will get the wrong idea about me." She raised her eyes to the older man. "I'm not a saloon girl. I needed a job and this was all I could find." It was important to her that he understand.

His eyes softened. "I never thought you were." Smiling her gratitude, she reached for the cloak. The man caught the fabric in his fingers. "There ain't no one around here but me so you don't have to cover yourself up." Grinning, he winked at her. "You're a beautiful young woman, but I like 'em a little older."

Laughing, Catherine let him put her cloak over a sack of flour. She joined him on the wagon seat and he picked up the reins for the six animal team. The wagon jolted and she clutched at the seat until she became used to the uneven motion. They exchanged names and the man introduced himself as Lucas—no last name—just Lucas. He had an easy, friendly nature, and Catherine found him easy to talk to. The morning passed quickly and Catherine was relieved when they stopped in a secluded area for something to eat. Her back and buttocks were stiff and sore and she was glad to surrender the hard seat for the soft grass.

Lucas refused to allow her to help with the meal and he insisted she sit beneath a tree and rest. He worked with simple dexterity and before long he had a meal cooking over the fire. The food was simple but filling, and Catherine ate until she was stuffed. The heaviness in her stomach made her sleepy, but her hopes of taking a nap were shattered when Lucas climbed back on the wagon seat. When she joined him, the ring around her neck swung free of its confines. Lucas eyed it curiously but made no comment.

They reached Independence just before dusk and made camp outside of town. Catherine was amazed at the number of wagons gathered for the trip west. Lucas was right about the varied financial positions of the people waiting to leave. Some would make the trip in comfort; but most were like her, poor and unequipped. It made her realize how lucky she was to be with a man who was knowledgeable and self-sufficient. Not only were there wagons like the one she traveled in, but every other type, including a small two-wheeled vehicle. She could not imagine traveling very far in something so primitive, but perhaps they were desperate to begin a new life.

Again Lucas refused to let her help with the meal, so she sat near the edge of the wagon wrapped in her cloak. She found the disappearance of her clothing a real puzzle and was positive the sack had been with her. Lucas agreed to let her sleep inside the wagon and he rearranged things to make her more comfortable.

Catherine was stiff the next morning and felt the heat through the thick canvas. She loathed to wear the cloak but couldn't risk ruining her reputation by letting someone see how she was dressed. Their wagon was some distance from the others, yet she knew if she went without it, someone would notice.

Lucas had breakfast ready when she climbed down from the wagon. "Did you sleep well?" he asked when she joined him at the fire.

"I'm rested, but my muscles will have to get used to the bed."

Lucas laughed. "Perhaps you would find the ground more to your liking." Catherine wrinkled her nose, and he chuckled heartily. "I fixed you some water if you would like to wash. You won't get much privacy, but that is something you'll have to get used to if you plan on making the trip."

"I'm going to make the trip," she said with determination. She nibbled on the meat Lucas handed her. "When will the scout be here?"

"Sometime tomorrow."

"Do you think he'll let me ride with you?" Catherine's hope of going west rested with the man who would lead the wagons.

Lucas shrugged his wide shoulders. "Can't say, but I think it will depend on his mood when he rides in. He had some trouble back in Saint Louis and he's been as grouchy as a bear."

Lucas didn't sound encouraging, but she refused to get discouraged. She was determined to get to Santa Fe with or without the scout's help. She couldn't forget the man she had killed and until she was on the trail, she'd never be able to relax.

She washed in the water Lucas had thoughtfully provided, then found herself with nothing to do. Lucas refused her help and she didn't want to socialize with the other women until she had decent clothes.

Lucas rode into Independence late in the afternoon, and Catherine was alone and bored.

Late the next day, Lucas shouted the scout was coming in, and Catherine ran to the wagon to use the comb he had lent her. After adjusting her cloak to make herself presentable, she pushed open the corner of the flap. Her future depended upon the next few minutes.

The men greeted each other with genuine fondness. Catherine could only see the back of the scout, but Lucas was laughing at something the scout said and her heart quickened in the hope that he was in an amiable mood. Taking a deep breath, she pushed aside the flap.

"Here is Catherine now," Lucas said to the other man.

She started to step down as the scout turned in response to Lucas's remark. Catherine throat tightened, and the blood rushed to her head. Her foot failed to clear the wooden gate and she fell forward. The scout reached out to break her fall and she came up against his hard, masculine body. Catherine jumped back as though she'd been burned, her jaw clamping shut as she met the blue eyes that had haunted her dreams for several nights. Logan was not dead; he was the scout for the wagon train.

Her horror at seeing him was clearly reflected in her eyes, and his lips twisted into a bitter snarl. She involuntarily shrank back from the icy coldness in his blue eyes, a sign of his hated for her. Lucas disappeared as if on cue, leaving Catherine alone to face Logan.

"Well Cat, we meet again," he drawled, his eyes running down her cloaked figure. He reached for the

149

clasp and before she could stop him, the cloak had fallen to the ground and she stood before him as she had several nights before. He stared openly at the rise and fall of her breasts and she tried unsuccessfully to cover her nakedness.

"Why are you trying to hide yourself?" he asked in a biting tone. "As you know, I have already seen most of what you have to offer."

Grabbing her wrists, he yanked them to her sides. Catherine grew hot with embarrassment as his eyes slid slowly over her figure, mentally stripping away her clothes to see the hidden places of her body.

"Let me go," she screeched at him.

With a deep, throaty laugh, he pulled her roughly against his long frame. The coarse material of his clothing scratched the exposed parts of her flesh. She glared at him to display her contempt and hate, but he only saw an unquestionable fear in the depths of her tawny eyes. Her feeble struggles only succeeded in putting a mocking smile on his lips, and Catherine fumed that he would ridicule her. Her free hand snaked out and caught the side of his face. The blow was forceful, and her palm stung from the impact. The cold animosity in his eyes deepened and she cringed.

"Why do you feel outraged that I desire you? You are dressed like a trollop. Why should you care what man enjoys your body?"

"Because I hate you and every other man. I'm not a whore. I needed food and a place to sleep. I didn't know the kind of job I was taking."

He uttered a hoot of laughter. "Am I supposed to believe that? Once you put on that revealing dress,

150

you knew what would be expected."

She remembered her humiliation when she had first appeared in public. The male comments and actions made her want to hide her head in shame, but she couldn't risk being turned out on the street. She could never expect Logan to understand her fears or how desperate she had been.

"I didn't know. I've never—"

"Are you going to try and convince me you are an untouched woman?" he interrupted.

Her eyes flashed angrily at the reminder of the way she had been tricked into losing her maidenhead. "I am not the kind of woman you think I am. Let me go."

"I think not," he replied coolly. "I paid for your services, and I plan to collect."

"No," she cried in horror.

"Then I will take back the gold piece you stole." She saw the cynical twist of his lips. "You never rendered services."

Catherine closed her eyes. Here was the way of getting out of her debt to Logan, and she didn't have the necessary coin. "I—I don't have the money."

His hands slid down her spine. "Since you can't pay, I will collect what I paid for."

"No," she whispered. "You can't."

He chuckled deep in his throat. "You think not? I understand you want to go to Santa Fe. You have been enjoying my hospitality for several days now, and since you cannot pay I will have to employ your services." His fingers curved up her spine to the nape of her neck. "There is a shortage of women in your profession traveling with us, so I'll find good use for

151

your services. You can pay your way to Santa Fe by sharing my bed."

"I hate you," she whispered angrily.

"That is obvious," he said dryly. "Did you think you had killed me at the saloon?" His voice hardened. "Did you believe you were a murderer?" He saw the answer in her eyes. "Is that why you left me to bleed to death? I could have you thrown in jail."

Catherine paled. She had never considered the possibility of his retaliation. "You wouldn't," she accused.

One of his dark brows arched. "No? Try me!"

"Are you forgetting the man you shot?" she asked smugly.

"It was self defense. He went for his gun first." His jaw tightened. "You aren't going to get anything on me. You're the one who attacked me without provocation."

"You brought it on yourself. If you had left me alone, you wouldn't have been injured," she threw back at him.

"I've no intention of leaving you alone, but the next time I'll be more careful."

"If you touch me, I'll kill you."

Her threat amused him. His fingers entwined in her hair and he pulled her head toward his. She panicked as his lips opened to take hers and she pushed against his chest. His mouth was punishing, degrading, lowering her to the whore he thought her to be. Catherine remained rigid, feeling the vengeful lips and hating their touch. He released her abruptly and she fell back. His eyes clearly displayed his contempt.

"It won't be now," he said, smiling slowly. "But in my own time and place. I will let you think about when it will be."

"You are nothing but an animal," she screamed at his back.

Her eyes were blinded by tears as she crawled into the wagon and threw herself down on her bed. She hated him, and the punishment he intended would be far worse than he could imagine. When he tried to take her, she would fight him, and it would be rape. The horror of getting with child made her tense. It had happened once and the anguish of losing the infant still made her ache. Cameron's baby had been conceived because of her love, but a child by Logan would be conceived out of a mutual hate. Haunted by her fears, she was grateful when sleep finally claimed her.

She woke abruptly as something was flung in her face. She sat up, dragging it away from her eyes. Logan was framed in the entrance, watching her with amused interest.

"I don't mind your present attire but I don't want the other men on the train to get any ideas. You are for my pleasure alone."

Logan thought she was a whore, but at least he didn't intend to share her. She viewed the clothes with disgust. "These are men's clothes," she protested.

"Boy's clothes to be precise."

"I can't wear these."

"You either wear these or you stay dressed as you are. Dresses are not practical for the trail."

"I had my own clothes, but I can't find them."

"You mean the two gray dresses?" Catherine nodded. "I threw them out."

Her eyes widened. "But how?" It explained the mysterious disappearance of the clothes, but how did he get them?"

"I removed them while you were sleeping."

Catherine flushed at the thought of him watching her sleep. "But how did you find me?"

"When I finally regained consciousness, I needed someone to bandage my wound. I came to the wagon looking for Lucas, but instead I found you." His expression sobered. "If I hadn't lost so much blood and been so weak, I would have taken you then."

Catherine flinched. "But why did you take my clothes?"

"I wanted you completely at my mercy, and I wanted you in this wagon when I met the train in Independence."

"So you could get your revenge?" she asked bitterly.

"That's right."

"I'll get Lucas to help protect me," she threatened and Logan's eyes narrowed.

"Lucas won't get involved in our disagreements. I told him you were in the wagon and to let you stay."

Catherine had come to like the older man and was embarrassed to learn he knew about her earlier association with Logan. "Do—does he know I tried to kill you?"

"No. I haven't told him you were responsible—yet. Besides, he will probably figure it out for himself. Lucas and I ride together and get along because we mind our own business." He turned. "The meal is ready. Change your clothes and we'll wait for you."

Catherine was not happy at the prospect of wearing men's clothes. She'd never worn pants and the fit defined her curves in a provocative way. Despite what

Logan said, she didn't see why they were more practical for the trail. None of the other women were wearing them.

Jumping off the wagon, she strolled to the campfire. Logan's eyes flickered over her attire, but his expression did not reveal his thoughts. Lucas gave her a warm smile. "I hope you are hungry."

"It smells delicious."

He handed her a plate. "Logan tells me you will be going to Santa Fe with us." Catherine threw a quick glance at Logan but she couldn't tell by his blank expression if he had defined her duties. "It will be a pleasant change having a pretty woman along."

Catherine smiled at him. At least Lucas was sincere in his fondness for her, and she suspected they would share hours of warm discussion and companionship.

It was almost dusk when they finished eating and rather than sit idle under Logan's penetrating stare, she helped Lucas with the dishes. "How soon will we be leaving?" she asked the older man.

"Are you anxious to start?"

She sighed. "I am anxious to reach my uncle." With Logan alive there was no reason to fear her present location, but she wanted to reach Santa Fe and begin her new life.

"Logan wants to leave within two days. If we wait any longer there might be problems with the snow. Some of the people are going all the way to California to hunt for gold."

"Did you ever try your luck?" she inquired.

"I spent a few months there with Logan in '49, but I didn't like the atmosphere. Greed had begun to run everyone's life. I went back last year to take care of some business and things had settled down. I might like to try my luck again."

"Have you known Logan long?" she inquired after making sure Logan couldn't hear her.

Lucas handed her a dish to dry. "I've known him for years." Catherine could hear the fondness in his voice when he spoke of Logan, and she wondered what he would think if she told him why Logan wanted her along.

She was hanging up her towel when she felt Logan's hand against the small of her back. "I need your assitance." Catherine stiffened. Had he come to make her fulfill her commitment? "I'll be out later for our card game," he said, glancing at Lucas. "The men are expecting us."

Logan pushed against her back, forcing her to move toward the back of the wagon. Catherine wanted to ask Lucas to help her but she was so embarrassed by her past relationship with Logan that she bit her tongue. Once inside, he dropped the flap. The lamp hanging from one of the wooden supports was already lit and it bathed them in an amber glow. When Logan began to unbutton his shirt, Catherine backed away.

Logan watched her, his eyes taking in every tremor or line of fear in her body. A smirk of satisfaction twisted his lips in response to the terror that etched itself in her tawny eyes. Loosening his shirt from his pants, he eased it off his shoulders. The light made his skin bronze, and she found herself studying the solid lines of his shoulders and chest. He was sleek and fit, well proportioned without being over muscular. Dark curly hair covered his chest and gave him an unquestionable aura of masculinity—almost animal-like. Unwillingly, her eyes fell to the white patch on his side, covering the knife wound. He made a motion to move toward her and her eyes locked with his. There was a glint of satisfaction on his face and she colored at being caught staring at his half naked torso.

"Are you satisfied?" he queried.

Her flush deepened. "I don't know what you mean?"

"Don't you?" he asked sardonically. "Perhaps you are ready to share my bed."

"Never," she vowed, her voice filled with hate.

"My bandage needs to be changed. Since you inflicted the injury, I think you should tend it."

He handed her a bandage and water, then sat on one of the sacks. Catherine couldn't move. She didn't want any contact with his body.

"I'm waiting," he shouted impatiently. Catherine jumped nervously, then kneeled at his side. His skin burned beneath her fingers as she slowly eased the bandage off. The sight of the wound nearly made her sick and she had to turn away to catch her breath.

"What's the matter? Does it make you sick?" He sounded irritated.

"I've never seen anything like it?" There was still a thick feeling in her throat.

"*You* caused it. *You* tore the gaping slash in my side."

Catherine trembled. "Stop it."

"Do you regret sticking the knife in my side?"

Remembering his brutal attack, she regained her strength. Raising her chin, she looked straight into his eyes. "No, I don't."

His breath slowed and there was a tensing in his features. Catherine dabbed the wound with water and with her determination renewed, she worked without hesitation. Her eyes roamed across the flat stomach and she was stunned by the unexpected sensations it aroused in her. Her body betrayed her and she experienced the initial stirring of desire. Taking a deep breath, she fought to get control of her emotions. She consciously hated Logan, but her subconscious responded to the masculine virility surrounding him.

Quickly finishing the bandage, she stepped back. He sensed her inner turmoil and smiled in response. He was playing a game with her, and he held all the cards. Logan put his shirt on and left without speaking.

Alone, Catherine covered her face with her hands. How could her body betray her? She groped for the ring near her breast. It burned in her fingers as a reminder of how she had willingly given herself to satisfy the desires she and Cam had aroused in each other. Their parting had been painful and she promised never to let a man use her body the way he had.

She knew it would only be a matter of time before Logan forced himself on her. Despite her desire to reach her uncle, she knew it was impossible to make the trip with Logan. She couldn't live with the kind of pressure his presence dictated. Perhaps she could get a position with one of the wealthier travelers. Several more wagons had arrived that day and plans were being made for their departure. She would wait until she was sure Logan and Lucas had gone to play cards, then she would sneak out.

Much later, she threw aside the flap and glanced

out. Certain no one was around, she jumped off the wagon. The campfire was still blazing, but Logan and Lucas were gone. Their wagon was isolated from the others, so she walked into the darkness toward the distant campfires.

She had gone less than ten feet when she was seized in an iron-like grip. She fought and kicked, but her struggles were useless and she was dragged back toward her wagon. When they reached the light of the campfire, Catherine realized she was in Logan's grasp. His eyes were hard and the line of his jaw was taut beneath the partial growth of beard. He dumped her in the back of the wagon and climbed in after her.

"Where did you think you were going?" he demanded.

"Anyplace away from you," she threw at him in contempt.

"Just how far did you think you would get?" He laughed. "You don't know anything about being on a wagon train." He pointed his finger at her. "You better not try walking off like that again or you might find yourself in a lot of trouble." Dropping his hand, he rocked back on his heels. "Did you hope to get away without completing your payment?"

There was no reason to answer him; her response was obvious. "You owe me, Cat," he said and roughly grabbed her wrists. He tore a heavy piece of cord off the side of the wagon and lashed it to her wrists.

Never would she willingly become his prisoner. Her hands were immobile, but she kicked out with her feet. Her heel caught him in the side, and she heard his gasp of pain. Shifting his position, he pinned her against a sack and completed his work.

"You can't leave me like this," she cried in panic. "I'll scream."

His fingers tightened around her throat, cutting off her air. "If you do, I'll gag you. You're not leaving until you've made a full payment. Everytime you try to escape, I'll tie you."

His grip relaxed and she gasped for breath. Her bonds were not tight but they were uncomfortable and limited her movement. Logan left the wagon and she rolled to her side. How could she stand months of travel with a man she hated? She considered offering herself to him to fulfill her debt and ease the tension, but the thought of their bodies straining together in passion was a sensation she found disturbing as well as frightening.

Chapter Eleven

Catherine found the adjustment to male clothing difficult. They fit too tightly, revealing curves and roundings she could otherwise disguise. Logan had brought her two more outfits and boots which she sneered at but accepted since it was all she would get. She also got a hat like the men wore and though she would have preferred a feminine bonnet, it would have looked ridiculous with pants.

Logan was not around the wagon much and she knew he was getting ready to move the wagon train toward Santa Fe. He held a meeting and Lucas insisted she attend. She thought Logan was harsh with the people as he laid down rules for the trail and decided his demands were stupid and rough for people not used to living out of a wagon. They needed understanding support, but he was a hard, uncaring man. Most of the people were like herself, leaving a life in the East and totally unfamiliar with what to expect when they finally started the almost eight-hundred mile trek.

As one of the lead wagons, they were at the front of the long train. Lucas would do the driving and Catherine could either sit with him or walk next to the wagon. Logan would ride ahead of the wagons to pick the best route and watch for danger. There were two other men along to help Logan, but he was in charge. All scouts were responsible to the trail master who made all final decisions.

On the morning they were scheduled to leave, Catherine was up early. The first wagon would leave at sunrise and anyone not ready would stay behind. Catherine and Lucas enjoyed a cup of coffee while they waited for Logan's final call. Her earlier apprehension over making the long trip vanished. She was like everyone else experiencing a thrill and excitement over a new beginning. Someway she would get out of the debt she owed Logan, and he would leave her alone.

Logan rode up and swung off his horse. He wore his hat low over his forehead, so she was unable to see the piercing blue eyes. With long strides, he strode to the fire, accepted a cup of coffee from Lucas, and drained it in two gulps.

"Ten minutes before we start. Looks like everyone is about ready."

"Let's hope so. We can't afford any delays this early in the trip. There will be enough problems later."

The line of Logan's mouth thinned. "I know. We are almost two weeks late in leaving. Let's hope the snows aren't early and there aren't any other problems."

Lucas shook his head. "You know there will be trouble."

Logan ran his hand along the back of his neck. "You saw their faces at the meeting. I doubt if they listened to half the things I told them. They always think they know everything," Logan said gruffly.

"Some of your rules are harsh and stupid," Catherine interrupted without thinking.

Logan's gaze instantly focused on her, his fingers pushing back his hat to give her a clean view of the contempt in his eyes. "What rules are you talking about?"

"The rule about leaving the wagons without permission," she snapped coldly. "There are times when people have to have a moment of privacy. And what about this nonsense of keeping together? And why are you trying to scare everyone with the threat of Indians?"

"You think I was just trying to scare them?"

Catherine tossed the rest of her coffee into the fire. "I think you like being the boss and making the rules. You enjoy dominating people and watching them squirm when they make a mistake."

"The mistakes you refer to could cost them their lives," he stated firmly.

Catherine rose and faced him, her eyes flashing her disgust. "You are nothing more than an arrogant, conceited bore," she flung at him.

His eyes narrowed to hard blue slivers, and he grabbed her arms tightly. The look in his eyes removed any thought of trying to free herself.

"I don't care what you think of me, but I expect you to obey the rules I set up without question."

He threw her away from him in contempt, turned and mounted his horse. Catherine sighed her exasperation and looked at Lucas. He had observed the flare of tempers without comment, and she was unable to read his thoughts.

"That man makes me so angry," she fumed, kicking at the dirt with her foot.

"I've noticed the friction between the two of you, but don't let him upset you."

"The man is detestable," she protested. "He's always so sure of himself."

"Logan is carrying a heavy responsibility. Give him a chance, Catherine."

"Never," she stated firmly. "I hate him."

Lucas frowned and Catherine realized she'd been talking to Logan's friend. She hadn't been fair in letting her past problems with Cameron prejudice her toward men. Surprisingly, she didn't feel any pressure from Lucas and wondered if it was because he was older and presented a totally different image.

"I'm sorry Lucas, but it's the way I feel."

Lucas grinned and a teasing twinkle crept into his dull blue eyes. "if the two of you keep fighting, it won't be a boring trip. I'm going to be sure to stay out of the firing line."

Smiling, Catherine climbed to the high seat, and Lucas put out the fire and stored the cups. He swung up next to her and threaded the thick reins between his fingers in preparation for their departure.

When the call to move out came, the wagon jolted to a start. Catherine put her anger aside and let herself feel the excitement of the journey. She was getting a wonderful opportunity and was determined not to let Logan spoil the trip.

Two hours after daybreak, her back ached from sitting, and she climbed down to walk alongside the wagon. All signs of civilization were gone except for the semi-worn path of other trains leaving earlier in the season. Catherine turned to look at the long line of wagons. The number of people making the trip was staggering.

When Logan had made his speech, there had been a hopeless desperation on the faces of many people making the long hard trek. Some had sacrificed almost everything they owned to make the trip, except for a few priceless possessions that weighted their wagons. She remembered the shock on the peoples' faces when Logan told them to sell the things and leave them behind. Catherine thought he was being heartless. The women valued their heirlooms and wanted to take part of their past with them. From her observations, his advice had not been heeded, and she delighted in their defiance of his authority.

Most of the wagons were pulled by oxen and mules, but some had carefully selected horses. The wagons stirred up some of the dust but the cattle being driven at the rear created most of the brownish-colored haze.

Logan had warned that some of the wagons would never make it, but now she watched them in the long line. The carts were inadequate and she feared the hardships they would suffer without the comforts of a wagon.

The prairie grass was long and soft and would make excellent feed for the cattle. Pausing, she picked a wild flower. It was different from the kind she'd picked at her aunts' house, but it reminded her of mornings at the pond. When her thoughts turned to Cameron, tears stung her eyes. Would she ever stop thinking of him? She hated his deceit and he'd made her wary and cautious of other men. Her fingers absently reached for the band beneath her shirt. She carried his ring—a symbol of dishonesty. In a love-filled sentimental moment, she had given him the unusually shaped gold piece and lost the last memory of her father to a useless man.

Her hand brushed across her cheek, wiping the tears. It was part of her past and nothing could change what had happened. Her only resolve was her determination not to let it happen again.

Catherine's stomach cramped in hunger an hour before they stopped for the noon meal. Within minutes, Lucas had a fire started, and soon the smell of fresh meat filled the air. On Lucas's instructions, Catherine sat in the shade of the wagon. He seemed to sense her thoughtful mood but did not pry into her private life.

Logan rode up and had a conversation with Lucas. He ate his meal standing, then turned and walked toward Catherine. She did not miss the spite on his face.

"It's time you started earning your keep. I want you to take over the cooking. Lucas has enough to do with the animals," he ordered, then turned and left.

Dumbfounded, Catherine stared at his retreating back. He wanted her to cook and she didn't know the first thing about it. Everything she'd attempted in Effie's kitchen had turned into a disaster and campfire cooking looked even more difficult. She wished she had paid more attention to Lucas when he worked on their meals, but since she hadn't, she could only hope for the best.

It was early when they stopped for the day. There were at least two more hours of daylight and Catherine was surprised that Logan had ordered the stop.

She had the impression that he would drive the wagons and people without mercy.

Catherine was nervous about fixing the meal. She went to the stock of supplies and selected the ingredients for biscuits. Lucas had started the fire and a heavy iron pot hung above the flame. She sliced up meat and potatoes and put them in the water to cook while she worked on the biscuits.

Making the dough presented a problem. Flour slopped out of the bowl and covered the front of her shirt. When it failed to mix into dough, she added liquid, then flour to compensate. Finally, when the pile of dough was firm enough, she pressed it out into rolls and placed them over the fire. The first batch got too close to the flame and the bottoms burned. Fortunately, she had enough dough to make more, and she had a huge bowl full of biscuits when she decided the meat and potatoes were done.

When Logan and Lucas joined her, she handed each of them coffee, a tine of stew and several biscuits. Logan sprawled leisurely in the thick grass and forked a hunk of meat. Catherine was proud of her first attempt at cooking over an open campfire and waited hopefully when Logan popped it into his mouth. Seconds later, he made a choking sound and gulped down several mouthfuls of coffee. His fork stabbed one of the potatoes, and after a tentative taste, he tossed the plate on the grass before Catherine.

"This food isn't fit to eat. The meat is raw and the potatoes are rock hard. I haven't tasted the rolls," his eyes flickered to the large bowl next to the fire, "but I can see you made enough to feed half the wagon train."

Catherine was hurt and humiliated that her food was a failure, and she was furious with Logan for making a fool of her before Lucas. "You should have asked me if I knew how to cook," she spit at him. "I was a housemaid before I came here, not a cook."

"Am I suppose to believe that?" he asked, his eyes raking her figure to remind her of the revealing dress she'd worn on their first meeting.

"I don't care if you believe me or not, but it happens to be the truth."

Doubt was written all over his face. "I know differently," he whispered so only she could hear.

"I hate you," she seethed between clenched teeth.

He flashed her a sardonic smile. "So you have told me." He turned to Lucas. "Let's hope she gets better. The way she is wasting supplies, we will be out by the first week."

Catherine's hands flew to her hips, but Logan was striding away and her defiant gesture was wasted. "I'll do what I can to help you. I should have thought to ask if you knew how to cook," Lucas said gently.

"It's not your fault, it's his," she replied, swinging her hand at Logan's retreating figure.

"He can be hard at times," Lucas agreed.

"I don't know how you could stand his companionship for so many years," she said, knowing the fondness the two men held for each other.

"You two are a spur in each other's side." He dumped the contents of his plate back into the kettle. "It just needs to cook a little longer."

"What made Logan so hard and uncaring?" Catherine asked Lucas.

He glanced up, his face grim. "I don't really know,

but there is a bitterness eating at him."

"He hates women . . . at least he hates me," she said.

"So it seems," Lucas muttered thoughtfully.

"Was he hateful toward women before Saint Louis?" she asked, thinking his antagonism might be due to her attemt to kill him.

"He's been like that for some time, but whatever happened in Saint Louis didn't help matters. I'm sorry I can't tell you anymore, but I don't understand it myself. Logan will work it out."

The next morning Logan demanded that Catherine change his bandage. The wound was healing nicely but it would definitely leave an ugly scar.

When she'd finished, he mounted his horse. "I'll be back for breakfast." His jaw tensed. "I better amend that. I'll be back for coffee. It seems it's the only thing you are capable of making with any degree of success."

His remark was another sharp dig into her inability to cope with her given responsibilities. "Don't come back at all," she shouted at his retreating back.

When Lucas had finished hitching up the team, he offered to help Catherine. Breakfast was a success and Logan had two helpings. Finished, he left his plate by the fire and rose.

"Good breakfast, Lucas," he said, throwing a glance of mockery at Catherine as he mounted his horse. "I know you couldn't have done it," he added, fixing his gaze on her face. Chuckling, he turned and rode away.

"Oh that man," she stormed and tossed her coffee cup at his back. She had never expected to hit him, but it had helped vent some of her anger. "What am I going to do? she asked Lucas.

"Stay out of his way and don't do anything to make him mad," he advised.

She threw her hands on her slender hips. "That's impossible. As far as he's concerned, I can't do anything right."

Lucas chuckled. "You're like a bur under his saddle." He eyed her thoughtfully. "Did you do something to make him angry?"

As far as she knew, Logan hadn't told Lucas about the knifing, but that didn't mean he hadn't figured it out. "We met in Saint Louis, but I guess you already knew that."

Lucas nodded. "After Logan found you sleeping in the wagon, he told me to leave you alone."

Catherine twisted her fingers nervously. "I won't go into the details, but Logan saw me in the saloon and got the wrong idea about me." Lucas was watching her with interest. "He—ah—he—."

"Never mind, Catherine. I think I can figure out the rest." He put out the fire. "Like I said before, stay out of his way."

Catherine spent most of the day walking and enjoying the clean fresh air. They seemed to be making excellent progress, but Lucas told her they were on the easy part of the trail. Logan was scouting ahead when they stopped for the noon meal, so Catherine didn't have to be a party to his sharp words. By nightfall, she was exhausted, but there was no time to rest.

They had stopped near a creek and Lucas took the animals to the water. Catherine was deciding what to fix for dinner when Logan rode up and stopped at her side. He remained on his horse and she suspected he enjoyed the commanding height. Raising her chin, she met his look without flinching.

He reached for something across the horse's neck and handed it down to Catherine. "We'll have this for dinner."

When her hand closed around the plump rabbit, she felt a prickling of revulsion. The blood caked on its back made her shudder; Logan would have been a ruthless pursuer.

"Have you ever cleaned a rabbit before?" he asked doubtfully.

She shook her head, and he muttered something under his breath. Dismounting, he took the rabbit from her. "You are about to learn." He lifted his knife from his belt and threw the rabbit down on the grass. He made a series of quick cuts to display the tender meat.

The bloody grass and pile of entrails stared up at her in gross intensity. Her stomach churned and a heaviness crept into her throat. She had never seen anything so sickening. Uttering a small moan, her hand flew to her mouth. Logan glanced up and noted her anxiety with total disgust. His mocking laughter followed her flight to privacy, and her humiliation was complete when she retched into the dirt. Her throat burned, her stomach ached from the gagging motions, and she felt miserable when she climbed into the wagon and fell into bed.

When she woke, the sun was streaming through the back of the wagon and she knew immediately she'd overslept. Logan would expect breakfast to be ready and if it wasn't, she'd receive another tongue-lashing.

Both men were at the campfire finishing breakfast.

"How are you feeling this morning?" Lucas inquired. "Logan told me you were sick last night."

Catherine flashed Logan an indignant look. She could just imagine the tale he had told. "I am better, thank you."

The third day on the trail proved to be the beginning of their trouble. Wagons began to break down and slow progress. Toward the late afternoon, the sky clouded and rain fell with blinding intensity. Campfires were impossible, so cold meals were prepared. Cathering sought the sanctuary of the wagon and listened to the rain hitting the canvas. She was concerned about Lucas getting wet but didn't care if Logan got soaked to the bone. Her curiosity was soon dispelled when the back of the wagon opened and Logan crawled inside. He wore a thick poncho over his shoulders and when he took it off, water scattered everywhere. Catherine watched him curiously from her bed.

"I want you to change my bandage. It got wet before I put my poncho on." He quickly unbuttoned his shirt and parted the fabric. Reluctantly, she rose and picked up a clean bandage. The cut no longer needed to be cleaned and she doubted it needed the fresh dressing, but Logan wanted to make her uncomfortable. Her hands shook when she touched the warm skin at his side.

"Still playing the frightened maiden?" he drawled. Catherine refused to take the bait and she calmly smoothed the new bandage into place. "I wonder," he muttered. His fingers lightly brushed her cheek, and she shrank back.

"Don't—Please don't," she pleaded, her breath quickening in fear.

His fingers slid along the back of her neck and entwined in her hair. His lips brushed hers, then deepened into a hurtful, degrading kiss, and she grew hot with bitterness as he forced her lips open.

Tearing her mouth free, she pushed him away. "I hate you—I don't want you touching me."

His eyes narrowed and his nostrils flared. Without a word, he turned and left. Catherine threw herself against the bed. Her constant battles with Logan were unsettling. Her hatred for him had increased, but the sensations she felt when she saw his half naked body were disquieting.

Her sleep was restless and her dreams turned to Cameron and their lost child. She had loved him and the baby. Suddenly, her dreams changed, and she saw Logan forcing himself on her time and time again until she finally conceived his bastard. She woke shaking, her clothes drenched in sweat. She could no longer bear the thought of Logan touching her. She had to get away.

The next day, Logan ordered the drivers to move the wagons four abreast. The rains had stopped but the ground was still wet and the animals had to work unusually hard to keep the wheels from becoming stuck in the mud. It was just before noon when the wagon lurched and Catherine was almost thrown from her seat. Lucas's hands tightened on the reins, and he called softly to the team. The animals weren't able to pull the wagon free so Lucas jumped down, took the animals' leads and tried to edge them forward. Several men got behind the wagon and pushed. The wagon

173

rocked and mud sucked at the wheels. Before long, Lucas was covered with slop from the waist down, and his face was red from exertion.

Under his gentle coaxing, the animals strained to free the trapped burden. The wagon wavered, halted, then suddenly broke free and the team surged forward. Lucas lost his footing and went down in their path. Catherine screamed, someone shouted, but the words were dismissed from her mind as she centered her attention on Lucas beneath the powerful hoofs. Slowly, she became aware of someone on the seat next to her and of the slack reins on the seat being pulled tight. The wagon slowed and stopped. Catherine turned her head and met the icy contempt in Logan's eyes. Anger was etched in every line of his face and she shrank back.

"Why didn't you pull on the reins? Lucas could have been killed."

It was then Catherine realized she had had the power to stop the movement of the team, but her ignorance had prevented her action. "I—I didn't know," she said shamefully, before he climbed out of the wagon. Looking up at her, he shot her a look that made her feel totally inferior, then turned and went through the crowd to Lucas. Trembling, Catherine jumped down from the wagon and followed him. At least she could help care for him if he was injured.

Her offer was never made. Logan had taken complete charge of caring for the cut on his friend's leg, and the look he gave her when she came forward, warned her to stay away. Scowling, she returned to the wagon. The incident had not stopped the progression of the other wagons and they continued across the prairie.

She heard someone call her name and she looked up to see Hetty running toward her. She had not seen her friend since the boat and had no idea she was on the wagon train.

"Hetty, it is good to see you," she said, giving her a hug.

"It was Hank's idea. He decided he wanted to go to California. I'm not sure it's what I want, but the children are excited about it." Catherine waved to the children. "Can you walk with me?"

The prospect of escaping Logan's company was inviting and she agreed. She enjoyed the companionship of the loving family so much, she stayed for the noon meal with them. After eating, the children played — Julie fascinated by the flowers and Andy enthralled by insects in the grass. When Catherine learned Hetty was expecting a child, she was genuine in her congratulations, but experienced the pain of remembering the one she'd lost. She considered asking if she could stay with them for the rest of the trip, but when Hetty began to talk about their low stock of food, the thought vanished from her mind.

"How do you like wearing pants?" Hetty asked.

"I guess I'm getting used to them, but I wish my dresses hadn't been stolen." She reflected briefly on her worn maid gowns. Even they would be a pleasant change. She pulled her beige cowboy hat from her head. "I've certainly learned the value of my hat. I don't leave the wagon without it; the sun is murder on my skin."

Hetty touched her friend's arm. "Come inside the wagon. I might have something for you."

Logan's wagon ws full of food and staples, but

Hetty's wagon held furniture she'd bought cheap in Independence. "Everything was such a good bargain, I couldn't say no," Hetty explained. "The prices in California are even higher than Saint Louis." After rummaging through a trunk, she pulled out a worn blue frock. "I wore this about five years ago."

"It is a beautiful gown," Catherine said, examining the thick folds of fabric in the skirt. It was old and out of style, but at least it was a dress.

"Try it on," Hetty urged, and Catherine quickly discarded her clothes and dropped the dress over her head. "It's a little tight through the bodice, but I think you can wear it."

"Do you mean it?" Catherine said excitedly.

Hetty laughed, pleased that her small gift could mean so much. "I want you to keep it."

Catherine hugged her friend. "Thank you." She whirled around in the wagon. "It's wonderful."

"Fold up your clothes and come outside. I have to see about dinner."

When Catherine had her dusty pants and shirt folded, she joined Hetty at the campfire. Hank was tending the horses and the children were playing.

"Can you stay for dinner?" Hetty asked, throwing potatoes into the boiling water.

Catherine hesitated. She didn't know if Logan expected her back and she didn't want to short her friend. "You need the food for the family."

"Please stay. Hank got a rabbit so you won't be cutting into the food we brought along."

Smiling, Catherine said, "I'd love to."

It was well after dark when Catherine heard a horse ride up near the fire. Without looking up, she knew who it was.

His blue eyes pierced through the darkness. "You're needed back at the wagon," Logan said coldly.

Rising, Catherine thanked Hetty and Hank and picked up her clothes. Her slender body was rigid when she walked into the darkness. She had barely gotten ten feet when she was swept off the ground and planted on the horse's neck near Logan's thighs.

"Let me down," she hissed, but his hold tightened.

"What do you think you were doing leaving the wagon? You have been warned about wandering around without telling someone."

"I went to see a friend, and I doubt I was missed."

"In case you've forgotten, Lucas injured himself today and can't get around. You are supposed to be the cook." She did not miss the sarcasm in his voice.

"I will do what I can to help Lucas, but I am not your slave."

"You still have a debt to pay," he reminded her.

"One that will never be paid," she reassured him.

The hand at her waist moved to rest on the swell of her breast. His fingers burned through her dress and it felt like he was touching her naked flesh. When his fingers became more insistent in their search, she made a wild lunge for safety and fell off the horse. Logan looked down at her, but his face was hidden by the brim of his hat.

"The time will come," he said in a voice that both promised and threatened.

Logan rode off and Catherine realized she was at the wagon. Lucas was sitting against a wagon wheel and she went to his side.

"I'm sorry about the accident. I feel partly responsible."

Lucas covered one of her hands with his. "It was not your fault. I should have told you what to do." He hesitated. "I heard Logan was pretty upset with you. I had a talk with him, but I don't know if it will do any good." From the way Logan had greeted her earlier, she knew it hadn't. "I'm going to teach you to handle the team."

"If you really think it would help," she said agreeably. "I don't know much about this life."

"You can learn what you need to know. Just be patient."

"Logan is the one who needs to be more tolerant and patient."

Chuckling, Lucas shook his head. "Where you're concerned, I don't think he knows the meaning of either word."

"Neither do I," she agreed.

The next day was warm and sunny and most of the mud had hardened, making travel easier. Despite Logan's disapproval, Lucas drove the team and Catherine began her lessons. Fortunately, the scout was not around and she could work without his critical appraisal. Lucas was a good teacher and her confidence increased as the reins became more familiar in her hands. He praised her often but warned her that the flat driving she was learning was the easiest.

They day passed quickly, but Catherine was still relieved when they stopped for the night. A wide river ran alongside the wagons and she secretly hoped for the opportunity to take a real bath. At her insistence, Lucas sat near the wagon to rest while she took care of the chores. She did what she could with the team, then one of the men from another wagon insisted on taking them for water. Logan was out scouting and she hoped he'd be gone all night. Nevertheless, her eyes frequently scanned the horizon for a sign of him.

Catherine's meal was a success, and she enjoyed the light conversation with Lucas. She found herself liking the older man more and more, but she couldn't understand his strong relationship with Logan. It was even more puzzling that Logan returned the bond of friendship. He struck her as a man who would stand alone and never need anyone.

Catherine cleared away the dishes, then told Lucas she was going for a short walk. He warned her against leaving the train and she assured him she would only be visiting a friend several wagons back. It wasn't the truth, but she didn't want to worry him, and she believed Logan's rule about leaving the wagon train was useless and stupid. In the back of the wagon, she changed into her dress and decided she would visit Hetty after she bathed.

There was not much activity outside the circle of wagons. Nonetheless, she left their protection and walked toward the river. The livestock were being watered near the wagons, so she decided to go upstream to avoid being caught bathing. She kept the river on her left, but the overgrowth made it impossible for her to walk along the bank.

Her progress slowed when the terrain sloped upward. After one-hundred feet, it leaveled off, and she paused to look over the edge. She was surprised at how high from the river she was. The water swirled beneath her in great foamy masses and rushed against the bank in a roar. Feeling content, she sank against the rocks and stared into the dark night. This was beautiful country, and it offered her a new start. She kicked some loose stones off the edge and watched them fall into the depths below. She started to rise, then froze, her senses alert to the noise behind her. Coming to her full height, she turned. Her hands tightened into fists at the sight of Logan lounging against a tree.

Uttering a low gasp, she stepped back. "What are you doing here?" she hissed.

Straightening, he sauntered toward her. "I might ask you the same thing. You were warned not to leave the train." His voice was low and threatening, and she sensed in him an impatience and anger that had previously been lacking; it frightened her.

"I wanted a bath."

Logan's lips twisted humorously. "You should have waited for me. I would have made sure nothing happened to you."

Catherine tensed. "I wanted privacy." He was the last person she would want along when she bathed. "Don't you know by now I loathe the sight of you."

The muscles in his cheek hardened. "Is that right?" he asked doubtfully. His eyes raked the length of her body until Catherine felt stripped naked to his gaze. His intentions were clear and Catherine remembered another time when she'd fallen prey to a man's desires.

She stepped back to escape the certainty of what was coming. Her boots slid over the loose dirt and stone as she made her retreat from Logan's advance. Logan lunged for her but reached for empty air. The ground gave way and Catherine was pitched

backward. Her scream was a piercing echo of fear as
she fell toward the murky depths of the rushing river.

She hit the water with force and sank into its depth.
Panicking, she took a breath and liquid washed
through her nose and mouth. Coughing, she surfaced,
her hands clawing frantically for something to catch,
but she was unable to oppose the strong force of the
water. Her dress was a burden and her legs became
wrapped in the thick folds. The weight drew her down
and water rushed over her head. Her lungs felt like
they would burst and then she broke the surface. Before her, the grassy bank offered safety, but the current kept her away, its turbulent depths seeking to
take her into its clutches forever. Twisted around by
the swelling undertow, her arms and legs batted the
gushing wetness until powerless, her limbs relaxed
helplessly against the beckoning forces. Darkness
rushed before her eyes and she dropped beneath the
water.

A painful jolt to her shoulder revived her defeated
senses. Something tightened around her upper arm
and she grabbed at it. Above the rush of water, she
head a voice, but her groggy mind could not decipher
the words. Suddenly, the water was no longer the
commanding force, and she was moved by something
stronger. Her body was lifted free of the powerful
force and she found herself surrounded by strength
and security. Coughing spasms seized her slender body
as she sought to relieve herself of the water that had
entered through her mouth and nose.

Finally, her mind cleared, and she realized she was
on the bank of the river—exhausted but safe. Prop-
ping herself up on one arm, she looked around. She

was stretched out on a soft grassy clearing surrounded by bushes and trees. Twisting around, she found Logan in a like position behind her.

"I suppose I should thank you for saving me," she offered.

Logan shrugged as though his heroic rescue had been nothing. "You are lucky I know how to swim. Don't you know how?"

"I never had a place to learn," she said, thinking of the shallow pond. "Perhaps I'll learn at my uncle's ranch. I've always liked the water," she said, glancing up.

Water glistened off his dark hair and she was aware of the way the wetness molded his clothes to his lean body. He too was aware of her physical presence, and his eyes followed the line of her body. Her wet dress hid nothing from his searching gaze. Reaching out, he brushed aside a lock of tawny hair resting against her breast. The contact of his fingers burned through the fabric and she drew a sharp breath of awareness. She was too weak to resist when he rolled against her and imprisoned her body. From beneath his weight, she watched his lips slowly part and move closer. His warm breath fanned her cheeks as his hand slid the length of her body. Suddenly, his lips devoured the softness of hers in passioned lust, and despite the hatred she felt for him, she found herself unable to move away.

Logan had saved her life and she welcomed the security of his embrace. It never registered in Catherine's relieved, tired mind that she had once before welcomed the safety of a man's embraces the night she was attacked in the garden at her aunts' home. Then, she had clung to Cameron and accepted kisses.

Of its own accord, her body weakened to his demands. His teasing lips left her trembling and initiated the beginning of her traitorous desire. She felt his fingers glide down the back of her dress, then warm air fanned her naked skin as it slid over her breasts and hips.

Catherine's mind felt the urge to fight, but the calming sense of being alive was even greater. Logan's fingers circled her breasts, coaxing her body into a frenzy of need that washed all thoughts of resisting away. Slowly, his lips followed, teasing her and making her body a betrayer to her professed hate. He shifted, and she accepted the full weight of his body. His clothes dug into her tender flesh and their wetness sent a chill through her body and brought her to an awareness of what was happening.

Why was she permitting him such liberties with her body? Her arms fell against his shoulders and her lips turned away from his. "Stop Logan," she demanded, terrified of his possession of her body. "I don't want you to do this to me."

He flicked his fingers over her aroused skin. "You want me. Every part of your body tells me it does." There was something in his voice she couldn't pinpoint, but she knew it wasn't passion.

"No—I'm not the kind of woman you think I am. I've never—"

Muzzling her protests with his mouth, he fumbled with his clothing. She beat at him with her fists and dug her nails into his face and neck, but he easily pinioned her arms against further attack. He shifted to position himself above her and her scream of anguish died in her throat as she chilled in response to his driving need. She felt none of the rising desire that was part of a satisfying relationship. All she felt was disgust that she'd let herself be taken and humiliation at her initial response.

Sated, Logan rolled off of her, and her naked body was bathed in the moonlight. He rose and stood above her like the conqueror. Catherine twisted her naked body away from him in shame, but he planted his feet on either side of her and forced her to look at him.

It was impossible not to notice the hardened disgust on his face. "You were trying to play the innocent maiden with me when all the time you were nothing but a cheap whore. You dressed the part in the saloon, but your techinque needs to be improved."

His words were cruel. "I told you I'm not what you think."

He sneered. "No, your protests to my earlier attentions belonged to an innocent maiden. I found out differently," he said, grabbing her jaw and forcing her to look at him. "I'm not the first man you've known. Were you trying to make a fool of me?"

Catherine shrank from the contempt on his face. His hand dropped to her breast and he lifted the ring in his fingers. She was surprised it was still around her neck after the exhausting fight with the water.

"A wedding ring," he mused. "Is this why you are no longer pure? Did you sell yourself into marriage? Where is your husband?" he asked bitterly. "You are married to one man and respond to another."

"I didn't respond to you," she denied.

"It certainly wasn't rape. Where is your husband?"

"There isn't one," she flung back at him.

The reminder of her love for Cameron brought tears to her eyes. Now that another man had sought her womanhood, she remembered the tenderness Cam had showed her and she knew the gentleness two people could share. Even if Cameron had not loved her, he had showed her a kind of love that was absent with Logan.

"Get dressed," Logan ordered. "Lucas will be wondering where you are."

He watched her get to her feet. If there was ever a time she needed a bath, it was now, but she refused to ask Logan's permission. Turning her back on him, she dressed. The gown clung to her suggestively and she hoped she could get to the wagon without being seen.

"Maybe you'll start taking my advice and wear pants. Dresses aren't made for the trail."

Grabbing her wrist firmly, he pulled her through the woods toward the camp. Darkness hid their return and she was able to sneak into the wagon without being seen. After removing her wet dress, she collapsed on her bed. She felt used, bruised and degraded, and remembered her earlier response with shame. She had been so shaken by the fall into the river, his comfort had seemed right. When she snapped back to the present and began to fight him, she'd been ashamed that she'd actually welcomed his caresses.

Subconsciously, she began to compare the two men who had made love to her. Logan had been harsh and demanding, while Cameron had the ability to arrest her trembling fears and coax her into a love-making that was both rewarding and fulfilling. She had easily responded to Cameron, and she remembered a similar response to Logan. It was with a sense of uneasiness that she drifted off into a deep sleep.

Chapter Twelve

The sun hit Catherine's face and a cool wind rushed across her body. In her sleep-dazed state, she reached for a blanket. Her hand was unable to locate the light covering, so she opened one tawny eye and scanned the wagon. She froze when her gaze fell on Logan sitting on the sacks opposite her. Waking fully, she sat up. Logan made a slow sweep of her body, and she realized she'd fallen asleep without dressing and her pink skin lay naked to his inspection.

"Is this what you're looking for?" he asked, gesturing to a blanket near her feet. She shot him a sharp glance and reached for the blanket but he was quicker and kicked it out of reach. "There is no reason to hide your body," he baited. "I've enjoyed it and I know the secrets it holds."

"Don't be crude! You know nothing of the mysteries of my body. Last night was nothing but rape."

Logan tipped his hat back and his blue eyes lingered on her breasts. "It didn't start out that way." He grinned. "You were very responsive."

"And then I remembered who you were," she said smugly, and had the satisfaction of hearing his sharp intake of breath. "You are detestable," she said, shifting to hide her body from his open appraisal. "I consider my debt to you paid in full. I want to get out of here and away from you. The sight of you makes me sick."

She heard a deep throaty laugh. "Your words make me tremble in my boots," he rallied. "I will say when I have finished with you." He leaned forward. "You asked for a place in my wagon in exchange for work. I've yet to see much help from you."

"I may be forced to work, but you'll never put your hands on me again."

He gave a quick shrug and grinned. "I doubt that will be the case, but if you feel more secure in believing you'll never share my bed, then it's up to you." He dropped to his knees so he was eye level with her. Reaching out, he cupped the softness of her breast. Catherine started to flinch but stayed her motion. She was determined not to let him defeat her again. His eyes were hard as they searched the depths of hers. There was mockery on his face and the ever present hatred in his eyes.

His fingers began to move and a warm sensation flooded her limbs. His hand curved around her waist and flattened across her thigh. She felt an unwanted tenseness that rose from the need to feel his body against hers, and she blushed hotly at the thought. Logan was her enemy, yet his touch had the ability to scatter the barrier she'd erected around herself and to send her defenses reeling.

His fingers probed and teased, and she knew he could sense the turmoil in her body. He smiled his satisfaction at having conquered her, and she clenched her teeth to keep from snapping at him. When his smile of victory reached his eyes, her hand curved out and found the side of his face. The red print of her fingers darkened against the high part of his cheek where his beard did not cover. She had displayed her contempt with the slap and now he would retaliate. His hand closed around her throat and her supply of air slowly diminished. Rage made his features twist and darken. Hate surrounded him, but she believed it was against all women and not only herself. He was incapable of tender feelings, and she was almost sad to realize he would never know a loving relationship. Logan carried with him a bitterness that was a scar in his mind—a constant reminder of his hatred for something in his past.

Cam had brought forth her feelings and although he had ended up using her, she had learned to love. She could never hate him for that.

When Logan saw the pity reflected in Catherine's eyes, his fingers tightened. He didn't want or need a woman's sympathy. Women brought him nothing but trouble. Getting mixed up with Catherine was going to be dangerous but he was determined to maintain his barrier of contempt and hatred. He would use and discard her, but he would never let her near his heart; it was too painful.

Releasing his grip, Logan left the wagon, and Catherine gasped for breath. Her hand covered her throat where seconds before he had tried to squeeze the breath from her body. Shaking off her thoughts, she rose and dressed in pants and shirt. Last night had convinced her of the practical use of men's clothing, but she would never tell Logan he'd been right.

The wagons left soon after daybreak and Catherine saw the beginnings of the harsh, cruel life people had to face when they traveled on a wagon train. Graves stood out in evidence as the horror of sickness and accident. Debris scattered the trail and prized possessions brought great distances were left to rot in the heat of the day. The wagons traveled four abreast, and at midday Logan warned the people of the threat of Indians.

Panic and fear became etched on the faces of the men, women and children, and Catherine hated Logan for being so blunt and probably exaggerating the conditions. The men were instructed to keep their firearms within reach, but not to shoot unless instructed to do so.

When they stopped for the night, Catherine went to Hetty's wagon. Several women wanted to pick raspberries and gooseberries, so Catherine and Hetty got a pail and joined them. Men positioned themselves around the brush to act as guards. Catherine stayed close to Hetty, not because she was afraid, but because her friend jumped at the crack of a branch.

"Catherine," Hetty said fearfully. "I want to turn back, but my husband says we have to go on. I'm terrified of the savages."

"I'm sure everything will be fine," she reassured her. "I think Logan was magnifying the seriousness of the situation."

Hetty stopped picking berries and looked at Catherine with sympathy. "I know you don't like Logan. I wish I could offer you a place in our wagon, but we don't have the room or food."

Catherine put her hand on Hetty's arm. "I understand and don't worry about me. I will be fine."

Three days later, wagons began to turn back. Catherine could not bear to see the hopelessness on the faces of the travelers as they gave up their dream of going west. Teams tired from pulling the strenuous loads and women cried when they were forced to leave furniture on the trail to rot. Children, exhausted from days of walking, curled up in the wagons and slept.

The possibility of an Indian attack put everyone on edge. Guards were doubled at night and Catherine saw exhaustion and anxiety on the mens' faces. Indians were sighted on a rise early one afternoon and they followed the wagons until they made camp. Tension was thick, and the women kept the children in the wagons. Catherine wanted to go see Hetty, but Lucas warned her to stay near the wagon with him.

Catherine had seen the Indians, but she couldn't believe they posed a threat. Logan rode out every morning and returned at night without getting injured. She was sitting near the campfire with Lucas when Logan rode up and dismounted. Squatting down, he poured himself a cup of coffee.

"I think we'll have some company tonight," he said, staring into the fire. "The Indians are moving closer to the wagons. I don't think they'll attack, but they'll steal everything they can."

Lucas nodded. "I thought so. Have you found their camp?"

"Went by it yesterday. It's a big tribe, but the men following us are just a scouting party."

"Most of the women and children are frightened to death, and the men are so jumpy they'll start shooting at the first Indian who shows his face in camp."

Logan's expression was grim. "I know. If one of

them shoots, it could start a war. Let's hope the men on this train have more sense."

"Would you suggest that we just let them steal from us?" Catherine asked sharply.

The possessions in the wagons were important, and Logan was foolish to think the people were just going to allow savages to take things. Logan looked up, his hard blue gaze focused on her features.

"I'm saying people might have to look the other way and not start shooting just because an Indian sees a trinket he likes."

The tough, merciless side of Logan was in evidence, and Catherine fumed. He had no thought for other people and he couldn't understand their sacrifices.

"You're asking too much of them, Logan," she warned in opposition to his unreasonable attitude.

A muscle tightened in his jaw. "I'm trying to save their lives." He grinned. "What are you worried about? You don't have anything to steal."

His reminder of her poverty and dependency on him was painful. She was prepared to argue with Logan, but Lucas gave her a warning wink, and instead she took a sip of coffee.

"I want you to learn how to shoot," Logan said. "We might need your help."

"I doubt that," Catherine said flippantly and put her cup down. "You seem more than capable of protecting us singlehanded."

Coughing deep in his throat, Lucas excused himself. He knew his warning to Catherine had not been heeded, and he wanted to be clear of the battle about to begin.

Logan grabbed Catherine's arms and hauled her to

her feet. "You don't believe anything I say, do you?" he asked, his face inches from hers. "You think this is all a joke."

"I think you like authority and you enjoy making people squirm. You have terrified everyone with all the talk about Indians and what they do with their captives, yet you leave here every morning and return at night . . , unhurt," she added.

"And I suppose you hope I won't come back?"

"That's right," she edged sharply.

Logan's fingers bit into her flesh. She knew he was angry, but his face was hidden by the darkness and the brim of his hat. "Whether you admit it or not, you respond to me."

"My body may turn traitor, but I still hate you."

Logan yanked her against his length and the buckle of his pants dug into her flesh. Making a fist, Catherine swung at him, but he easily warded off the attack and rendered her arms useless. His fingers glided up and down her backbone until her body tingled in response to his nearness. His lips forced her mouth to part, and she was subjected to the intimate motions of his mouth as he sought to capture her sweetness and make it his. Just before she felt the urge to respond, he tore his lips from hers and followed the curve of her neck. The touch of his lips made her quiver, yet she steeled her body against feeling anything for him. Tugging her shirt free, Logan spread his hands over the flesh on her back. When his roaming palm curved over her breast, her stomach churned in unexpected weakness.

Logan was wearing down her defenses, but she refused to surrender. Pushing against his chest, she looked straight into his eyes. "It will still be rape," she said confidently.

His anger was displayed by a quick puff of air from his lungs. Swinging her into his arms, he carried her to the wagon and threw her down on the makeshift bed.

Looming over her, he rested his arms on either side of her shoulders. "If it is rape you want, then so be it. Your body wants to respond and I want you. Why are you holding back? What are you afraid of?"

For Catherine, the answer was simple. She was afraid of trusting and being hurt again. She had loved Cameron, but he had used her and destroyed her faith in men. She had conceived a child and feared it would happen again. With Logan, there would be no commitment.

"Certainly not you," she retorted.

Drawing back, he grabbed her shirt and ripped it open. "Is this the reason for your hatred?" he asked, holding the gold band.

Catherine felt the pressure of the cord against the back of her neck. "I won't discuss my past. It has nothing to do with the hate I feel toward you." She paused and regarded him curiously. "What is the reason for your animosity toward women? Did you love someone?" There was a faint flicker in his eyes and Catherine smiled smugly. "I bet she left you for someone else. Too bad, but she probably realized what an overpowering bore you are and hated the sight of you. She and I have a lot in common."

Logan fell against her, his fingers tearing at her pants. They slid off her hips and when he pressed his body to hers, he'd already shed his own clothing. Her cruel words had driven him past the point of reason-

194

able thought. All his past pains was directed at her, and he gave her no time to prepare.

She arched when she was forced to accept him, and her nails dug into the flesh of his shoulders. He was like an animal, lusting for satisfaction, and she knew it was his anger and hate that forced his body to drive onward. When he'd finished the attack, he lay heavily against her until he regained some sense of control. Catherine didn't hold him nor fight him. She felt empty and alone. When Logan finally left the wagan, Catherine rolled to her side and let the tears stream down her cheeks. She'd taken her anger out on Logan with her tongue, and she'd touched the sensitive feelings hidden deep within the hard man. He had retaliated with an animal assault against her body. Both had reason to hate, and their mutual need to lash out would cause them nothing but pain.

The next morning, Logan began her instructions in the use of a handgun and rifle. Priming the rifle was awkward and tedious work, but she managed with a positive degree of effectiveness. The six-gun was easier and lighter in her hand. Several other women were receiving the same lessons from their husbands, and Catherine wondered for the first time if there might be something to fear.

Logan held another meeting and warned that the next five to six days would be hot and dry. He cautioned against wasting water and instructed the people not to overwork their animals. Catherine had learned the importance of the team in respect to survival. She had dutifully listened to Lucas's lectures on driving the mules, and at times she relieved him so he could rest. His leg was nearly healed, but it still gave him periods of stiffness.

She had sat on the back of a horse for the first time and experienced a sense of freedom and power. Once she learned to control the animal, he could mean time away from the wagon train. For several hours a day, she rode next to the wagon, getting the feel of the awkward motions of the animal beneath her.

Logan's warning about the water turned into a real threat. The scenery changed from the lush, forested area to a flat, dull, lifeless brown. The days were hot and dry and Catherine was forced to give up her daily washing to save water. Logan was strict in his rationing, and she knew she would incur his wrath if she disobeyed him.

The wagons moved slowly, stopping early each day to rest the animals. Lucas said they were making good time and the news brought a smile to Catherine's lips. It meant she would be with her uncle sooner and away from Logan.

It was midday and Catherine was sitting on the wagon seat with Lucas when Logan galloped up. The heavy breathing of the horse and the glistening neck told of a strenuous run. Tipping his hat back, Logan looked at Lucas.

"We have big trouble. About four miles ahead, I found the wagon train that left two weeks before us." His lips thinned. "It's cholera."

Catherine straightened in her seat, and Lucas's hands tightened on the reins. "How bad is it?" Lucas asked.

"Bad," Logan replied grimly. "It has reached epidemic proportions. Over one-hundred people are either sick or dead."

"Does anyone else know?"

Logan shook his head. "No, and I can't see any reason to tell them."

"No reason?" Catherine sharply interrupted.

Logan glanced at her as if he had just noticed her presence. "That's what I said," he reinforced flatly.

Catherine met the cold, challenging look in his eyes squarely. She may have led a sheltered life, but she knew the deadliness of cholera. "How can you be so cool about something so serious? The people have to be told." She started to climb off the wagon. "If you aren't going to tell them, I will."

Logan edged his horse forward until he was level with the side of the wagon. His arm shot out, encircling her waist and dragging her onto the saddle before him. She met the fury in his eyes with equal anger. The line of his jaw tensed, but the mocking curve of his mouth warned her that he was enjoying the barbed confrontation and was sure of the outcome.

"Do you want to be responsible for a riot and panic among the people?" he barked at her.

"But the people need to know."

"Why? What good will it do to tell them? Everyday they would wait for signs of the sickness. We have enough problems, and we don't need to add this fear." Catherine tried to pry his arm loose, but when she couldn't her eyes rose to Lucas for help. As usual, Lucas was staring at the horizon and blind to her need. "I'm warning you to keep your mouth shut," Logan whispered in her ear. "We will go farther south and miss the train. No one needs to know."

"But the people on the other train might need

help—supplies. You can't just leave them," she spat in defense. She knew Logan was a hard man, but it was cruel to desert people when they needed help.

"But that is just what I intend to do," he replied tersely and felt her renew her struggle to be free.

"Let me go, you scum," she screamed. "You are the coldest person I've ever met. I hate you."

"So I've been told," he remarked indifferently and let her fall from the horse so she landed in the dirt. He towered over her, cutting her to shreds with the contempt in his eyes. "Remember my warning."

Without another word, he turned his horse and rode down the line of wagons. Rising, Catherine slapped at her thighs to remove the dust and to vent her anger. She glanced up and found Lucas watching her with sympathetic eyes. Catherine's cheeks reddened; it was bad enough to lose a battle with Logan, but worse when someone witnessed it.

"I hate him," Catherine muttered under her breath as she climbed up next to Lucas. "He doesn't have any feelings," she replied, plopping down on the wooden seat and wincing when her tender backside hit the seat.

"Don't judge him too harshly," Lucas advised. "He was right about the wagon train. There is nothing we could do to help. Besides, they have guards posted to keep us away. Everyone who travels west knows the risks.

Lucas snapped the reins and the wagon moved forward. Logan and Lucas shared a close bond of friendship, and Catherine knew she could expect little sympathy from the older man. As Logan requested, the wagons moved slightly south, but Catherine doubted anyone would question the slight deviation from the usual westward trail.

The weather was warm and Catherine grew restless as the afternoon progressed. For a while, she walked alongside the wagon, listlessly kicking at the ground with her toe. She dreaded her next encounter with Logan and was certain it would come when the wagons stopped for the night. For the first time since leaving her aunts, she questioned her decision to go to her uncle and allowing herself to get into her present predicament. She liked Lucas, but Logan was impossible, and she loathed and hated him for using her.

When she realized the wagons were stopping for the night, she scanned the prairie for a sign of Logan. She wanted to be ready for their next confrontation and not have him arrive without warning. Satisfied that he was not in sight, she started the fire while Lucas watered the team. Logan had still not returned when the meal was over so to avoid him, she went to the wagon.

Laying in the darkness, she stared at the canvas and listened in fear for Logan's return. He was like an animal, lacking in the gentle love-making she had once learned from Cam. Sitting up, she stared into the inky blackness and drew a trembling hand to her lips. What was she thinking? Both of the men she had known were animals, the only difference being that Cameron had used gentle, persuasive measures, invoking a response from her body to obtain what he wanted. Logan saw no reason for pretense; he just took what he wanted. Stretching out, she closed her eyes. Her past had been a bitter lesson. She wanted to remember her hatred, but her body was eager to forget.

Chapter Thirteen

They broke camp early the next morning and Catherine barely had time for coffee before putting out the fire and climbing up next to Lucas. She scanned the surrounding wagons for a sign of Logan, but there was none.

"He's already gone," Lucas answered in response to her roaming eyes, and she relaxed in the seat.

"Good," she said, finding no reason to hide her animosity from Lucas. "How far do you think we will get today?"

"Five miles ahead, we'll be coming to a river. We're going to try and get everyone across tonight. Logan has gone ahead to look for a crossing."

Logan, always Logan, Catherine thought. The great leader, the man who is always right. She smiled. For once, she would like to see him put down, and she wanted to be the one to do it.

"What are you smiling at, Catherine?" Lucas asked, interrupting her thoughts.

"Nothing," she answered, giving him a sideways glance. "Just thinking," she said, and the sly smile parted her lips, leaving Lucas to ponder her actions.

The gnawing ache in Catherine's stomach was not to be satisfied at the usual noon hour. The wagons had arrived at the river and the first group was ready to cross and set up camp. To temporarily ease the pain in her stomach, she pulled out a piece of salted beef, then joined the crowd at the river.

It was wider and faster than any they had crossed up to now, and she could not even guess at its depth. The first wagon to cross was near the edge of the water, the team eyeing the wetness before them anxiously. From horseback, Logan shouted orders to the men around the wagon. Catherine decided he liked to look down at people from his horse, thus strengthening his position of command, and she longed to yank him into the dirt in front of everyone. Her hatred for him once again boiled to the surface and when his eyes fell on her, he knew what she was thinking. Thinning his lips in mockery, his eyes challenged hers until his attention was drawn back to his work.

Temporarily forgetting her hatred, Catherine watched the first wagon begin the crossing. The driver flicked a whip over the head of the team and kept a firm hand on the reins. A few feet from shore, the water had covered the lower half of the wagon. Catherine watched the team strain to fight the swirling mass of water surrounding the wagon and threatening to wash it away. She joined the other concerned observers at the bank and watched nervously when the wagon swayed. Someone shouted, "Keep it movin', quicksand ahead."

Quicksand! Catherine had not considered the threats the river held beneath the flowing torrents visible to the eye, and she did not realize she had been holding her breath until the team pulled the wagon up on the opposite shore. A roar of cheers sprang from the lips of the people crowding the shore. The second team prepared to cross, but Catherine turned away from the river; the tension was too much.

There were at least six wagons ahead of hers, so she decided to visit her friend. Hetty's wagon would not cross for several hours, and she was fixing something to eat. The children were excited over the river crossing, but Hetty was nervous and upset.

"Hank keeps telling me everything will be all right, but I'm plain scared. Something might happen," she cried, touching her rounding abdomen.

Catherine put a comforting hand on her shoulder. "Try not to worry. I was just down at the river and the first wagon made it across without any trouble."

"I suppose I am being foolish, but it's the children I'm worrying about. Neither of them can swim."

Catherine knew Hetty, like many of the travelers, relied on Logan and trusted his judgement. "Logan wouldn't let us cross if he didn't think it was safe."

At the mention of his name, Hetty immediately perked up. "Would you stay and have a bite to eat with us? I have plenty."

"I guess I have time," Catherine replied, delighted to fill her stomach. She joined the children on a patch of grass near the wagon and listened to them talk about what they'd seen. When they'd finished eating, Catherine helped Hetty clean the dishes and put out the fire.

"Hetty, my wagon is near the front, so I better get back. I'll meet you on the other side." She gave her friend a reassuring smile. "Everything will be fine, you'll see."

Hetty shook her head. "Thanks for coming. You always make me feel better."

Catherine said goodbye to Hank and the children and left to join Lucas. Several new wagons had moved into the line to cross and she scanned them in search of hers. To her dismay, she spotted it several feet off shore. Frowning, she rested her hands on her hips and hoped Lucas would not be angry at her for not getting back on time. Hetty's wagon was more than halfway back, but it was the only way she'd get across. Turning to start down the line of wagons, Catherine found her way blocked by a horse and knew before she looked up it would be Logan.

"Missed your ride?" he asked with the arch of his dark brow. His mouth curled into a smirk. "Were you planning to swim across? If I recall, you're not much good in the water."

Remembering the time he had to drag her out of the river, Catherine's face burned. "I don't swim at all and you know it," she countered. "I will cross with Hetty."

She stepped sideways to go around his horse but found her way barred. "Let me pass," she said angrily.

"I think not," he answered coolly.

She glanced over her shoulder at the wagon pulling up on the opposite bank. "Lucas is not going to come back for me, so I'll go with Hetty. What difference does it make?"

"A lot," he answered levelly. "Lucas knows how to cross the river. I'm not sure about most of the others."

"Are you worried about my safety?" she asked, purposely baiting him.

His lips curled. "I would hate to lose my bed partner," he drawled. "Women are hard to find out here in the middle of no place."

Catherine clenched her teeth together. "You are disgusting," she said, flipping her tawny hair over her shoulder. "I'd rather take my chances with someone else."

"Well, I'm not willing to take the risk." Before she could flee, she found herself in the saddle before him. She fought him until she realized people near the bank were watching them with curious interest. In the beginning, she'd received questioning glances from the women because she was traveling alone with two men. Those wondering stares returned when Logan's arm tightened possessively beneath her breasts.

"I guess I'll have to see you safely across the river."

The horse stepped into the water, moving lightly and relying on Logan's firm hand. Water touched Catherine's booted feet, then seeped up her pant leg. They were only a few feet from shore when the current hit them in a churning mass of foam. The horse reared in protest to Logan's command to continue, its flaying hoofs just touching the water. Catherine clenched her hands together and closed her eyes in silent prayer. Logan's tanned fingers tightened on the reins and his soothing, low voice brought the animal under control.

The thought of being swept down the river terrified her. Even the solid bulk of Logan's chest and the strength of his arm around her did little to assuage her fears. They were halfway across when the water edged over the top of the saddle. The force of the current became stronger, pushing her from the saddle.

"Do you want to swim the rest of the way?" Logan teased.

She was about to utter a sharp retort when the horse stumbled. Shrieking, Catherine threw her arms around his neck, buried her face against him and pressed her trembling body to his. Water soaked through her shirt and Catherine waited for the water to wash across her face.

A voice in the distance finally reached through the swirling mass of fear and confusion in her mind. "I said, do you want to join me in the back of the wagon?"

Catherine's eyes flew open and focused on the men surrounding the horse. Lucas was one of them and the expression on his face was one of wondrous joy. She wrinkled her nose in confusion. What was Lucas so happy about? Sighing, her cheek brushed the solid object her arms held for comfort. Suddenly, it all became clear and her tawny eyes widened. Her arms flew to her sides and she slid off the horse.

"You," she screeched at Logan.

He bent low over the saddle so only she could hear his husky voice. "I asked if you wanted to join me in the wagon?"

Catherine's eyes narrowed so the golden flecks glared her hatred as she met the cool look in Logan's eyes. "That day will never come," she spat venomously.

He laughed. "It will come. You can believe it," he added confidently.

"Never, never," she vowed. Tossing her head in dismissal, she turned and proudly walked to the wagon, ignoring the stares of the bystanders.

She climbed into the back and sank against her bed. She still trembled from the confrontation with

Logan. Why did he always try to provoke her? She hated herself for needing him when they crossed the river and at the same time, she burned with the humiliation of finding her arms around his neck, drawing the strength of his body to the weakness of hers.

Shouts from outside the wagon brought her to her feet. Hours had past and Catherine realized she had fallen asleep. Pushing aside the back flap she looked outside. Most of the wagons were across and the bank of the river was crowded with people. From her elevated position, she could see the reason for their concern, and her stomach tightened. Two of the Conestogas were stopped in the middle of the river. Something was holding the wagons from moving forward despite the animals' struggles. A third wagon shifted to the left to avoid the blocked area and when the current hit the wooden side, it teetered.

Startled gasps rose from the crowd when the driver failed to steady the prairie schooner and it rolled into the water. Two heads bobbed to the surface and battled to stay afloat as the rushing torrents of liquid invited them to its depths. A man on horseback rode into the water and Catherine recognized Logan. His horse moved steadily, but his progress was slowed by the quickening current. One of the heads disappeared beneath the water and Catherine's nails dug into her palms. She watched the gray water swirl where the head went down and failed to reappear. Logan had almost reached the other person, a woman who had managed to grasp hold of a tree trunk jutting out of the water. When her hold was secure, she waved to the spot where her husband had gone down, and

Logan switched directions.

The missing man resurfaced farther downstream. Logan jerked the rope off his saddle and swung it high over his head. It flew through the air, landing partially atop the fighting figure. Grasping the rope, the man slipped it around his arms. On Logan's signal, a rider entered the river to pick up the woman, and he started toward the man. His horse faltered twice and each time Catherine held her breath. She did not doubt Logan's capability, but the man was being held by the rope and pushed by the current and there was still a strong chance he could drown. When Logan was inches from him, he carefully maneuvered his stallion and eased the man out of the water. With great effort and skill, he pulled the man atop the horse so that they both now sat astride the heroic beast. Shouts erupted from the bank to applaud Logan on his rescue. The other rider brought the woman safely to the bank and she was covered by a blanket.

The shouts of praise turned to shrieks of horror. One of the wagons stuck in the center of the river had tipped sideways and was being carried downstream. Logan and his rider had their backs to the downhill sweep of the river and were oblivious to the wagon bearing down on them. Curving her fingers around the canvas, Catherine joined the crowd in screaming a warning. After a few seconds, when Logan didn't respond to the cries, Catherine knew the rushing water had silenced the alarm.

The wagon hit a hind leg of the horse causing it to bolt and go down under the water. The jolt knocked both riders off and they disappeared into the muddy depths of the raging water. Lucas jumped on a horse and galloped into the river. A head surfaced, but Catherine couldn't tell who it was. The man began swimming against the current without much success, but at least managing to stay afloat. Catherine scanned the water for the second man but saw nothing. Logan's horse ambled out of the water, uninjured but exhausted.

Lucas reached the man and lifted him out of the water. Catherine strained to see who it was, but he was hidden by Lucas's back. Jumping from the wagon, Catherine ran to join the others on the bank, refusing to admit that her unexplained tension was due to the unknown identity of the rescued man. She hated Logan, but everyone on the train, except herself, felt confident that he was their only chance of surviving the long, dangerous journey.

Catherine made a path to the front of the crowd so that she was on the bank when Lucas came out of the water. Men pushed forward to relieve Lucas of the man slumped over the saddle, thus blocking her vision. Lucas's pale blue eyes found Catherine in the crowd and she knew by the look of pain in their depths that the man was not his trusted friend. Logan had disappeared beneath the frothing mass of water and not resurfaced. Stunned, Catherine watched Lucas ride away from the crowd and stare out across the river. His bond to Logan had been strong, and the sense of pain and loss was a heavy burden of grief. She wanted to offer words of comfort, but from her, they would be false. Lucas knew her negative feelings about Logan. The man she hated was dead, swallowed up by the very water he sought to protect her from when he carried her across the river. Logan, the man who knew everything about survival, the man everyone depended on, had finally fallen to a place of equality with all men—death.

Catherine had mixed feelings about his drowning. Logan had made her existence miserable, but she grieved the loss of a life. Slowly, the crowd began to return to their wagons. Many were saddened by the loss of their scout and women dabbed their eyes with handkerchiefs. The man Lucas had rescued was one of the married men on the train, and his wife clung to him in grateful relief. Catherine turned away from the happy scene and walked along the river. The second wagon, freed from the middle of the river, came up on shore and Catherine realized it was Hetty's wagon. When she climbed down, Catherine hugged her.

"It was horrible," Hetty cried in a choked voice. "We could have been killed."

"You and your family are safe," she said softly, knowing the time for hysteria had passed. "You can be thankful for that."

Hetty wiped her wet cheeks with the back of her hand. "We saw the other two wagons. Was anyone hurt?"

Catherine couldn't explain the thickness in her throat. "Logan—Logan went down with his horse and never came up."

"No," Hetty wailed in horror. "It is our fault. We got tangled with the other wagon and Hank couldn't free us." Her shoulders trembled. "Because of us, a man of great value to the train is dead."

"Hetty," Catherine scolded. "I won't let you think like that. Logan warned everyone of the dangers in making this trip. He knew the risks. . . . Let me help you take care of the children," she said, glancing up at the two eager faces on the seats. "I don't think they look too shaken by the experience."

Hetty uttered a short laugh. "They thought it was exciting."

In the distance, Catherine heard Lucas asking for volunteers to go down river to search for Logan's body. Catherine's heart cried out to Lucas and she wished she could ease his pain. She met his eyes in silent understanding and felt hers fill with tears.

After spending two hours with Hetty and the children, she excused herself and walked to the river's edge. All the wagons had made it across before darkness had fallen, and the glow of campfires lighted her path. Looking over the water, she wondered how many victims it had claimed. With her hands in her pockets, she strolled along the bank, listening to the chirping of crickets and the rustling of night life in search of food and water.

Logan's warnings about moving too far from the wagons sprang to her thoughts and she halted in her tracks and turned back toward the fires. He was no longer present to remind her of her foolishness, but his words of caution still hung in her mind. The men searching for his body had not returned and she silently hoped it would be beyond recovery. The river would have taken its toll and she wanted Lucas to be spared seeing the twisted, broken body of a man who was once a strong, commanding figure. She had to admit to herself that she wouldn't want to see it either. She had known the hard masculine strength of his limbs, and that was how she wanted to remember him.

She had eaten at Hetty's so she climbed into the wagon. A bath would have been wonderfully refreshing but she knew she dared not risk the currents even at the bank. After pouring a small portion of water into a bowl, she removed her clothing. The water helped her relax and without putting on a nightgown, she fell into bed and drew a light cover over her nakedness.

Catherine's sleep was troubled. In her dreams, she saw the rushing river claim wagon after wagon. She heard the cries of trapped men and women screaming for release. Logan rode into the water after them, pulling men, women and children to safety. When everyone was on shore, Catherine saw the wagon hit his horse and crush his body into a lifeless heap of mangled bones. Lucas hauled the twisted body onto shore and cried over the man who had once been his friend. Catherine stepped closer and found Logan's blue eyes staring at her, his lips curved in a grotesque smile that tormented her even in his death. She covered her face with her hands to blot out the memory but her fingers were forced away and she stared once again at Logan's mocking face. There was no escape from the horror and she screamed.

Her body jerked upright as she woke, and the sheet fell to her waist. Covering her eyes, she wept from the terror of the dream. Would she ever be free of Logan? Oblivious to the slight noise of the wagon flap being raised or of the stealthy movement within the wagon, she jumped when hands closed around her upper arms and forced her hands away from her eyes. A large, bulky form hovered over her, and she struggled to clear her confusion and grasp hold of what was happening.

The hands on her arms slowly began to massage her shoulders in a soothing motion and the tension vanished from her body. Closing her eyes, she swayed as the coaxing fingers played lightly along her spine. A tingling coursed through her body and fully aroused her senses from the sluggishness of sleep. She welcomed the touch as it moved from her back to span her waist. Fingers slid up her side to cup her breast, rubbing and teasing her to a frenzy of desire. She reached for the form, releasing any thoughts of stopping the straying fingers as her body betrayed her need. The naked flesh beneath her hands was familiar and for a brief time she was spiraled back in time to the bedroom at her aunts' home where Cameron had taught her the passions of her body. The sheet slid from her legs and she welcomed the exploring fingers as they glided up her thigh. She reached to the dark head for the identity of the man who had reached into the depths of her nightmare to bring her body to life. Her fingers threaded through the thick, unruly hair to turn the head toward hers. Her mouth ached to know the feel of his lips, as his experienced hands maintained the burning fire licking through her limbs.

She raised her head, and a thin line of light broke through the back of the canvas to bathe their bodies in a soft glow. He lifted his head and her heavy breathing broke into a startled gasp.

"You," she said, drawing back in shock to stare at the face that had haunted her dreams. His mouth twisted in mockery and the blue eyes held an air of confidence. "You are supposed to be dead!" she whispered.

Logan laughed, his fingers trailing lightly up her

side to caress her cheek. "Is that what you hoped?" Her fingers tried to push away his persistent probing. "I can't believe you want me to stop. A moment ago, you welcomed my caresses."

"That was before I knew it was you."

"Does that mean you would welcome the fondling of another man? Perhaps your job in the saloon in Saint Louis was real. We both know I wasn't the first."

Catherine's hand closed into a fist, and she slammed it against the side of his head. "How dare you! Don't you ever speak to me about my past. It is none of your business."

Unconcerned by her attack, Logan pushed her back against the bed and held her firmly with the length of his body. "I seem to have hit upon a tender area. Is it possible you dreamed it was someone in your past making love to you? I would like to know who it was. It is much more enjoyable to make love to you when you cooperate."

His mouth spread a line of kisses along her neck and his tongue darted against her flesh in a teasing motion, causing her body to deceive her and respond. She twisted to free herself, but he only shifted his weight to cover her completely.

"Love," she spat. "You know nothing about making love. You are only satisfying your animal desire, forcing me because your body is stronger than mine." Her lips twisted in a sneer. "Well, I hate you, and the feel of you against me makes my skin crawl with revulsion." She took a deep breath. "Don't confuse it with love. I doubt if you have ever loved anyone and I can assure you that no woman could ever love you."

He stiffened, and she knew she'd gone too far in

213

mentioning his past. Whatever memory Logan had of another woman was firmly locked in his thoughts and he did not like to be reminded of it. For some reason, it gave him an uncontrollable urge to hurt.

From past experience, she knew struggling would be useless. She had reminded him of his bitter past and she would bear the brunt of his emotion. Under his expert guidance, she was physically ready to accept him, but she hated his assault as he rode the waves of his hatred, until finally, his animosity washed ashore, leaving him sated. He lay heavily against her and she felt the rapid pounding of his heart against her breast. Finally, he rolled to the side and she inched away from the heat of his body, but knew there was no permanent escape.

Chapter Fourteen

When the first signs of dawn brushed the sky, Catherine felt Logan stir. She'd spent a sleepless night, too disturbed by his nearness to relax. To avoid a confrontation, she closed her eyes and slowed her breathing to resemble the state of deep sleep. Logan rose and dressed and when Catherine was sure he was gone, opened her eyes. Rising, she poured water into a pitcher and scrubbed every inch of her body Logan had touched. After dressing she waited until he had ridden out of camp before joining Lucas.

"We won't be leaving for a few hours," he said, handing her a cup of coffee. "Logan decided that the people need a rest."

"Logan," she muttered with contempt.

Lucas arched his brow in question. "He heard you scream last night. . . . You must have been dreaming." He carefully watched her expression. "Were you surprised to find him alive?"

She shifted uneasily. Lucas knew Logan had joined her in the wagon and probably assumed he had stayed the night. "What happened?" she asked, without answering his question.

"We rode downstream about two miles. We found him half unconscious and tangled in a tree hanging over the river. If the tree hadn't stopped him, he'd probably be dead."

Catherine knew how much Logan meant to Lucas and she didn't want to dampen his happiness. Their friendship had been built over many years, and they were close, trusted companions.

"I'm glad you found him."

Lucas looked at her in surprise. He was aware of the friction between them. "I'm glad you feel that way," he said with a smile. "Yep, I'm real glad."

The terrain changed once they left the river. The grass became shorter and they saw the first signs of buffalo. Lucas gave Catherine a burlap bag and told her to collect the buffalo dung for the fire.

It was one of the worst jobs she'd ever been asked to do, but she joined the other women and children in the grass. Her bag was half full when the sensation of being watched made her straighten. Logan sat astride his horse, one leg casually thrown over the saddle horn as he watched her work. The smirk on his face confirmed the amusement in his piercing blue eyes. The task itself was humiliating, but seeing Logan laugh at her was more than she could bear. Gripping the sack tightly in her hand, she spun around and let the sack fly at his head.

Logan had underestimated her anger and was taken by surprise. The bag caught him full in the face, nearly upsetting him from the horse. The stallion pranced nervously until Logan brought him under control with a firm hand and coaxing words.

As soon as she had let go of the burlap, Catherine turned and ran across the prairie away from the wagons instead of toward where she might find some protection from Logan's wrath. The terrain was flat and her booted feet slapped against the grass. Her ears strained for the sound of pounding hoofs to announce Logan's arrival. Throwing a quick glance over her shoulder, their eyes locked in open war.

Kicking his horse swiftly in the sides, he came bearing down on Catherine. She tried to increase her speed but she was already tiring, and Logan was on her within seconds. Jumping off his horse, he tackled her and they fell to the soft blanket of prairie grass.

"Let me up, you scum," she said, trying unsuccessfully to get up.

He flipped her over and she stared into the ice blue eyes. "You have a lot of spirit. Does it only show when you get mad at me?"

"I hate you. I'm tired of being bullied. If I was stronger than you, you would never get your way."

Logan's eyes wandered over her face. "Your spirit needs to be tamed—not broken, and I just might be the one to do it."

"My spirit is free. You will never tame me no matter how many times you force me against my will. Men are all the same, and I hate everyone of you."

His lips twisted in a cruel smile. "My, my," he replied thoughtfully. "Someone, sometime, must have hurt you badly."

"That is none of your concern," she said heatedly. Tears sprang to her eyes as she remembered Cameron and his cruelty. He had struck one score in their battle, but he would not be the winner. "You talk about me," she sobbed. "I would love to meet the woman who hurt you and made you the cynical man you are today."

The tightening of his jaw told her he was holding his temper in check. "It will never happen."

She waited for his assault, but it never came. He rose to his feet and seconds later she heard the soft pounding of the horse's hoofs as he rode away. Exhausted from their verbal battle, she lay on the soft grass. Each confrontation with Logan left her more shaken and she wished she had some of the powerful reserve he held. He could provoke her to tears and make her weaken before him, but he still remained strong. Only her reference to a woman in his past stirred his emotions.

When Catherine finally returned to the wagon, Lucas eyed her disheveled appearance curiously, but he refrained from commenting. To avoid another encounter with Logan, Catherine spent the remainder of the day in the back of the wagon. When they stopped for the night she knew she needed time away from the wagon train. She had at least an hour before she'd be expected to start the meal, so she decided to go for a ride. The prairie was flat and she'd be able to keep the wagons in sight and see trouble before it reached her.

Making sure no one was watching her, Catherine saddled a horse and rode away from the train. Logan was scouting their path for the next day and Catherine made sure she rode in the opposite direction. She cantered the mare until the wagons were just a small dot on the horizon. The land was not as flat as she had first anticipated and gradual slopes led to soft grassy hills. Catherine, feeling free and relaxed, urged the horse into a run. Sweat soon glistened on the mare's hide and its labored breathing warned her the animal was tiring.

Slowing the horse to a walk, she wiped the sweat

from her own neck. The wagon train had vanished from sight, but she wasn't lost. The horse pulled in one direction and she let the mare have its head. When they broke the crest of a small hill Catherine saw the reason for the animal's eagerness. A small pond lay between two hills, its water cool and inviting to a thirsty animal.

Dismounting, she took the canteen off the saddle and let the horse wander ahead to drink. She sat down on the grassy hill and took a generous drink from the canteen. The coolness was refreshing on her parched throat. The horse drank thirstily and she decided to tell Logan about the pond so they could replenish their dwindling water supply.

Stretching, she leaned back on her elbows. She would let the horse have a few more minutes of rest before starting back. As it was, she'd been gone longer than she expected. Lucas would be worried, and Logan would be furious.

She was staring at the cloud formations when she heard a startled snort from the horse. Glancing up, she saw the mare back away from the water. The animal made an unsteady jerk with its legs before snorting wildly and rearing into the air. Catherine scrambled to her feet, alert to danger from the surrounding area, but there was nothing visible to cause the disturbed reaction in her horse.

Uncertain and talking in low tones, she walked toward the mare. The horse's shrill scream froze her motion, and she stared as it twisted in agony. Her confidence with horses did not include contending with an animal that acted crazy, and she glumly considered her predicament. She needed the mare to get back, but its obvious discomfort made its use impossible.

A sharp crack splintered the silence around her, and she watched as the horse fell to the dust and lay still. It took Catherine several seconds to realize the animal had been shot. Spinning around, she scanned the hilltop, her gaze finally settling on a rider. Her confidence vanished when she recognized Logan. He slowly rode toward her and she knew he was angry by the rigid way he held his body.

"Just what do you think you are doing?" he demanded, stopping inches from her.

Catherine was determined not to let him bully her. "I am out for a ride."

Logan pushed his hat back on his head and a dark lock of hair fell against his forehead. "You've been warned against leaving the train without telling someone." He indicated the horse. "Now look at what you've done."

"What I have done?" she shrieked. "You shot the animal."

His blue eyes narrowed. "Don't you know anything? Your knowledge—or lack of it—has been nothing but a hindrance since we left Independence. You've ruined good food and now you've caused the death of a horse."

Catherine's hands flew to her hips. "Let me tell you again. You—shot—him," she said, emphasizing each word carefully.

"Haven't you ever heard of bad water. That pond is full of alkaline. Why do you think I avoided this route with the wagons? The animals needed the water."

Catherine's mouth dropped open. The water was poisoned. "I didn't know," she mumbled feebly.

His laugh mirrored his disgust. "You caused the death of a very important animal and all you can say is, 'I didn't know.' "

"That's right," she spoke in her defense. "I never pretended to know anything about this kind of life."

"Well, she finally admits she doesn't know everything. What you did was just plain stupid. Had you paid attention to the signs, you would have noticed the absence of animal tracks—a sure indication that the water is bad." His eyes flickered to the canteen. "At least you didn't have any. I would hate to shoot you."

Catherine shot him a look of disgust, then rallied to her own defense. "The horse drank it. Why didn't he know it was bad?"

Logan looked at the dead horse. "You rode him too hard. He needed water." His eyes shot back to her. "It was just plain stupid, Cat."

"All right, all right," she screamed. "You've told me repeatedly about my mistakes. I am glad you're so righteous that you don't make mistakes. The people on the train would be thrilled to know they have an infallible guide."

"At least I don't make mistakes like that one," he said, indicating the dead horse with a flick of his thumb. "Out here, a horse is one of the most important things you have, and it can mean the difference between life or death."

He dismounted and Catherine stepped back in fear of another attack. His mouth twisted in amusement and his eyes flickered over her dusty figure.

"Sorry, but I haven't the time."

Catherine's fingers curled into fists. How dare he think she would be interested in a romp beneath the blankets! She watched his lithe movement toward the dead horse with the apparent intent of gathering the saddle. Catherine had had enough of him and his arrogance. Grabbing the reins of his horse, she jumped on the stallion's back. He had killed her horse, so he could walk back to the wagon train. She wasn't about to share the only horse. Logan glanced up as she started to climb the small hill, and she shouted over her shoulder, "The walk will do you good."

Seconds later, a shrill whistle split the air. The horse reared, catching her unexpectedly and dumping her in the grass. Turning, the stallion trotted back to his master. Logan's rumble of laughter made her burn with humiliation; she was sick of being bested by him.

"Horse stealing is a hanging offense," he shouted. "Sure would hate to stretch that pretty neck of yours." Catherine glared back at him. It was just like Logan to teach his horse to return on his whistle. Beaten, she fell back on the grass. Logan had a solution for everything.

Her pleasant afternoon ride had been spoiled by Logan, and now she was anxious to get back to the wagon train. By now, Lucas would be worrying about her and they still had at least an hour of travel time. Sitting up, she watched Logan strap the dead mare's gear behind his saddle and then mount. Frowning, Catherine realized how intimately close they would have to sit because of the space the extra saddle took.

The horse slowly labored up the hill and Logan kept his eyes on her face. "We better get started," he said, shifting slightly in the saddle. Catherine expected him to extend his hand to help her on the horse, but he rode right past, leaving her to stare after him with her mouth hanging open in an unlady-like gape. He intended to make her walk. She wanted to scream at him to wait, but her pride held her in check. She would never beg Logan for anything.

Squaring her shoulders, she started after him. Logan was so confident she would follow, he never turned around to see if she was behind him. She would have liked to stretch out in the grass and ignore him, but she didn't want to be left in the uninhabited territory after dark. After an hour, her legs felt heavy and her left foot ached from a blister. Each step became more painful and although she wanted to sit down and rest, the deepening shadows cautioned her against losing sight of Logan. With every movement of her feet, her hatred for Logan grew. He was a cruel, arrogant, unfeeling man, and she couldn't wait for the day when they would arrive in Santa Fe and she would be free of him.

She stumbled on a clump of dirt and went sprawling in the grass. Exhaustion claimed her and her body refused to respond. Looking up, she saw his tall figure disappear into the darkness. She opened her mouth to call out but clamped it shut immediately. She would not ask for his help. He already thought her to be incapable of doing anything right, and she loathed him for constantly reminding her of her shortcomings. It wasn't her fault she didn't understand this way of life. The past few years she'd been taking care of a house and waiting on her aunts.

Stretching out, she rested her head against her arms and stared at the multitude of stars twinkling in the heavens. They were so far away but their beauty on the warm night was soothing, and she drifted into a deep sleep.

She woke slowly, stretching her limbs to ease the stiffness. She took a deep breath, expecting to smell the clean prairie air, but instead, the odor of meat assaulted her senses. Remembering where she was, she sat up and her abruptness knocked away a blanket that had been placed over her. Logan was behind her, squatting next to the fire. He looked up and a mocking twist curved his lips and haunted his eyes.

"Since you couldn't make it last night, I waited for you."

A small spark of fire ignited in Catherine and burst into a blaze. "I can assure you it wasn't necessary."

"Oh no?" he quizzed, lifting one of his brows in doubt. "And just how did you plan to find the wagon train all alone."

Rising, Catherine dusted off her pants and shirt, then reached for the blanket. She was determined to best him at his own game. "I was going to follow your horse's tracks. I am sure it would not have taken me more than an hour."

He shifted a portion of the meat into a tin and handed it to Catherine. There was no point in haggling over the offering. She had missed dinner the previous night and she was hungry.

"Not more than an hour, huh," he said, returning to their conversation. His shoulders trembled with laughter. "I doubt it."

"Any why not?" she asked tartly, her hands tightening around the plate.

"It hasn't rained for weeks, and the ground is like rock. There would be no tracks—at least none you could follow."

"I don't believe you. You told me I should have looked for tracks at the pond."

He threw her an impatient look. "Water softens the edge of the bank and you would have seen the tracks." Shrugging, he said, "If you don't believe me, just try to find my tracks from last night. I went another hundred yards out on the prairie before I realized you'd decided to take a nap."

"How dare you!" she seethed. "I had spent most of the day collecting buffalo dung and I had every right to be tired. If you had any manners, you would have offered me a ride on your horse."

Keeping his eyes on her, he ate several strips of bacon and poured himself a cup of coffee. "I've never admitted to being a gentleman. If you thought I was, it's an oversight on your part. I have no time for gentlemanly manners where you're concerned."

"Is it me—or any woman?" The cup stopped on the way to his lips. "You have taken me by force or when I was asleep so I didn't know what was happening." She saw the narrowing of his eyes but she smiled smugly. "Maybe you're no good with a woman. Maybe you play rough because you can't please them."

The coffee spilled from his cup as he tossed it aside. Catherine, aware of his intent to attack, threw her plate at him. He caught it easily and tossed it aside. She scrambled to her feet but Logan tackled her knees and she fell to the grass. Quickly, he eased his weight over her to end her feeble struggles. His fingers twisted through her tawny hair, forcing her head still and making her look at the open antagonism in his eyes. With his free hand, he loosened the buttons of her shirt and slipped his hand inside. As with other times, Catherine waited for his assault, but his hand only curled around her ribs. Some of the hardness left his eyes as they roamed over her face. Her defenses slipped when his eyes dropped to her lips. An unbidden breathlessness surged through her body and created a weakness in her limbs.

Her gaze followed the curve of his lips, dwelling on the sensuous lower lip that could bring unbidden pleasure. Inside her shirt, his hand cupped her breast, and her heart pounded in response. She sunk her teeth into her lip. Her subconscious sent out warning signals of what was to come, but her body ignored them. His demanding fingers and cool blue eyes burned where they touched and slowly, her need began to awaken.

Raising her eyes, she studied the head that hovered over her, and for the first time realized how attractive Logan was. Weather-beaten bronze skin stretched over his cheekbones and disappeared beneath the bearded growth lining his jaw. Dark hair fell thick and loosely over his forehead, and she had a ridiculous drive to run her fingers through the silky strands. The scar near his ear had darkened and did nothing to detract from his looks.

The cold, hard hatred usually present in his eyes was gone, and the startling blue color had a hypnotic effect. She watched breathlessly as his lips dropped to brush her cheek and travel along a path to her neck where his mouth and tongue nibbled against the throbbing pulse. His hand flattened across her breast, and while she welcomed the touch, it left her unsatisfied.

Slowly, Catherine's hands crept up his arms. The hard muscled shoulders flexed beneath her palms and she sensed the hidden strength of the man who was making her body weaken in comparison. Shyly, she loosened the buttons on his shirt and slipped her hands inside. Warm flesh invited her exploration, and her fingers tugged and caressed the soft curling hair. The bandage from the knife wound was gone, and her fingers lingered on the still puckered flesh.

Logan's lips traveled down her chest to the sensitive area of her breast, teasing and driving her into a frenzy of total desire. Her hands threaded through his hair to draw him closer in wild abandonment, and her body arched against his. Her pants slid from her hips and for a few seconds, his lower body left hers. When he covered her again, his naked flesh pressed against hers.

He was no longer the arrogant, hated Logan, but a lover to satisfy the raging fire burning through her limbs and threatening to consume her if she didn't achieve release. His lips teased the sweetness of hers until hers parted in eagerness and they became one. The fire flaming between them burned with uncontrollable intenseness until the rushing tide swept across them, cooling the searing passion in welcome release.

She was trembling when Logan left her, and she rolled to her side and curled into a ball. She felt spent, satisfied and humiliated. Because of her snide comment about his ability with women, he had forced her into responding to prove his manliness, and she hated herself for weakening. Never again could she accuse him of not knowing a woman's desires, and she knew there would be a smile of satisfaction etched on his features.

When they were ready to leave, Logan put Catherine on the horse in front of him and left the gear until he could return for it. After the intimate confrontation they had shared, Catherine felt shaken by the feel of his arm across her middle. Several men and women looked their way when they rode into camp, and all Catherine could do was lower her head in abject disgrace. She went straight to the wagon and remained inside until they stopped at noon. When she finally came out, Lucas looked at her in silent understanding but offered no words of support.

Much to Catherine's relief, she saw little of Logan over the next few days. He was busy with the scouting and when he came to the fire she was in her wagon. During one of their midday breaks, he rode into camp and called a meeting. He maintained his usual position of authority atop his horse where he could look down on the ignorant peasants.

"I have found some Indian signs." Several women grabbed onto their husband's arms. "Don't get alarmed," he warned. "If you follow the instructions I gave you about leaving the wagon train, everything will be fine." Catherine saw the twist of his mouth, and his eyes sought her out in the crowd. "I expect *all* of you to abide by my rules." Catherine's hands clenched into fists. How dare he single her out! His eyes swept the crowd. "We will double the guard at night and I want all the livestock inside the circle."

There was a general discussion on the set-up for the train that night, but Catherine turned and walked away. She had more than enough of Logan's condescending attitude.

That afternoon they passed a large rock, and Logan

halted the train so the men, women and children could add their identities to the already existing slew of names chiseled on its surface. Catherine read many of the names and dates and felt a little more in touch with the people who had passed before her.

When they stoped for the night, the wagons were drawn into a tight circle with the front of one locking into the back of the other. As Logan instructed, the livestock was grouped in the center and sectioned off. The guards were doubled and Catherine felt the uneasiness that existed among the men and women. The circle of wagons was large, and it took Catherine nearly ten minutes to find Hetty's wagon. Hetty had just fed the children and was cleaning up the dishes.

"I was so grateful Logan was not killed in the river," the older woman told Catherine. "It is frightening to be in this savage land. Logan knows how to take care of us; without him him, we'd probably be dead."

"You're worrying again," Catherine reminded her friend. "It's not good for the baby."

"You're so strong. I wish I was more like you," Hetty praised and Catherine blushed. Her strength rose from the need to survive. For years, there had been no one to depend on but herself. "Aren't you just a little frightened?" Hetty queried.

Logan's speech had frightened most of the people but she wasn't convinced there was an Indian problem and she wasn't afraid. "No," she said honestly, but her negative reply did nothing to ease the worried frown on Hetty's face. "You've told me many times how you trust Logan's judgment. Why can't you believe him when he says everything will be all right if everyone does as instructed?"

Hetty smiled. "You're right, of course. You are lucky to have a man with experience in this part of the country. I wouldn't trade my Hank, but you've got a man who knows how to survive. There are several girls of marrying age on the train, and they'd like to know him better."

As far as Catherine was concerned, any woman could have Logan. She detested everything he did, but she didn't let on to Hetty about her true feelings. A while later, she said goodbye and returned to her wagon.

Lucas was sitting by the fire loading the spare rifles and pistols they carried in the wagon. Catherine sat down next to him and he glanced at her.

"Been wonderin' where you were. I hope you know better than to leave the train."

"Yes," she said, pushing her lip out in a pout. "I've been warned enough times."

Lucas's pale eyes regarded her doubtfully. "Then I hope you will take heed of the warning. So far things have been simple."

Catherine watched as he loaded a rifle and checked it. "Are there really Indians around here?"

Lucas glanced up sharply. "Of course there are. Didn't you believe Logan this afternoon?"

Catherine poked at the dirt with a stick. "I think he likes to exaggerate things to make himself look important."

Lucas shook his head. "I don't know what is between the two of you that accounts for the open hostility, but I have been with Logan for years. He knows this country. If you want to keep yourself and those around you alive, you better listen to what he says." He handed her a handgun. "Keep this in the wagon with you." Catherine took the weapon. "One other thing. Make sure you know who you are shooting at before you pull that trigger." He sobered. "I would hate to have someone shot by accident."

Catherine looked at him, her expression blank. Suddenly his implication registered in her mind and she laughed. "Yea, it would be a shame if I mistook our guide for a savage—even though he acts like one."

Shaking his head in wonderment, Lucas watched her walk away. He wasn't sure he wanted to be around when Logan and Catherine finally met in a real battle. He liked both of them and wished there wasn't so much antagonism. No matter how tense things got between them, he would not meddle. They would have to make their own mistakes just like they would have to find their own happiness—if it was ever meant to be.

Standing in the shadows, Logan watched Catherine climb into the wagon. On his instructions, Lucas had given her a gun. Grinning, he stroked his jaw. Tonight would not be a good night to visit her, or she might find the excuse she needed to get rid of him permanently.

For the past hour, he had watched her visit Hetty. He knew she didn't believe danger existed. Leave it to her to try a foolhardy stunt! For himself, he didn't care, but he knew Lucas had grown fond of her and that did matter.

Catherine woke abruptly from her sleep and sat up. Her hand automatically closed around the handle of the gun while she waited for her eyes to become accustomed to the darkness. Logan had told them to

231

sleep in their clothes and be ready to move in an instant and from the noise outside the wagon, something was going on. Scrambling to her feet, she pushed the canvas flap aside. Other than a few men running in the circle, it was quiet.

Driven by curiosity, she jumped down from the wagon and started a search for Lucas. A cry of agony from somewhere in the darkness sent shivers up and down her spine. Two men ran past her, and in blind panic, she ran along with them. A small crowd had gathered around one of the wagons and Catherine saw movement of men outside the circle. When someone shouted to stand ready for possible attack, the men ran back inside the circle.

Logan and Lucas were among the men returning, and they were supporting a limp body between them. They laid the man near the fire and Catherine's hand flew to her mouth to combat the nausea rising in her throat. Trembling, she turned and staggered to the nearest wagon for support. One of the women ran toward the figure by the fire and a man moved with her, offering support. When the lady got close enough to see the man, she screamed a tortured sound that sent an icy chill through Catherine's body. The woman slumped in a faint, and Catherine turned and vomited into the dirt. She was sympathetic toward the woman who had just seen her husband with the top of his head missing; it was a gruesome sight.

Catherine stumbled back to the wagon and climbed inside. She did not return to her bed but huddled in the corner, clutching the gun in mortal fear. Throughout the night, she listened to every noise, but there were no more screams. Logan had been right about the Indians, but it had cost a man's life to make her believe him.

At the first stirring of the camp, Catherine climbed out of the wagon. Logan and Lucas were not around so she set the fire herself and started breakfast. She was nervous and jumpy and kept the pistol at her side the whole time. Some of her tension eased when Lucas joined her and he immediately noticed her reddened eyes from lack of sleep.

"A man was killed last night," he told her grimly.

Catherine had been reaching for the coffee pot but she began to shake so badly, she let her hands fall to her lap. Lucas was quick to notice her uneasiness and put his hand on her shoulder.

"What is it, Catherine?"

"I know a man was killed." Her voice cracked. "I saw him." She began to cry and Lucas pulled her into the comfort of his arms. "It was horrible," she sobbed.

"Don't think about it," he said softly.

Catherine turned her head and through her tear-filled eyes saw Logan standing a few feet away, his eyes a hostile blue. She immediately pulled away from Lucas and wiped her hand across her eyes. She didn't want Logan to see her cry; it was a weakness he would never understand.

Lucas offered him a cup of coffee. "Hope I didn't interrupt anything," Logan said smoothly. His eyes rested on Lucas for an explanation.

"Catherine saw what happened to Fred."

Logan took a sip of his coffee and watched Catherine over the top of his cup. "So she's upset," he drawled. "It could be her if she doesn't start following instructions. I warned the men on guard not to leave

233

camp even if they heard something in the surrounding brush. Fred decided to be a hero. Now he's dead."

"You are a cold, uncaring excuse for a man," she spouted. "It's a shame it wasn't your hair that got separated."

Logan chuckled. "You better worry about your own head of hair. It is an unusual color and it would be a mark of great bravery if an Indian wore it on his belt."

Catherine's hand flew to one of the tawny curls on her shoulder. Logan was trying to scare her and he'd succeeded. Turning, Catherine fled to the wagon.

There was a small memorial service for the dead man. Catherine found it hard to look at his grieving widow and children who would have to make the remaining trip alone. By Logan's order, he was buried in their path so each wagon would cross over his grave and eliminate the chance of discovery by Indians or animals.

Catherine refused to walk alongside the wagon and sat on the seat next to Lucas, clutching the gun in her hand. Lucas tried to draw her into conversation but gave up when he realized she was not interested in talking.

Their wagon was the first in a long line, and Catherine was conscious of Logan riding off to one side. The uneven terrain offered numerous places for Indians to hide, and it made their route even more dangerous.

"Relax, Catherine," Lucas said. "You've been tense since this morning."

"I keep expecting the savages to attack and massacre everyone." Logan spurred his horse forward and Catherine anxiously jumped to the edge of her seat. "What's wrong?"

Before Lucas could respond, Logan turned and rode back, his hand raised to signal a stop. Logan looked first at Catherine then Lucas, and she was certain there had been nonverbal communication between the men. Their actions heightened her anxiety.

"What's the matter?" Her question was answered seconds later when ten Indians appeared on a small hill and rode toward the wagons. Stiffening, Catherine moved closer to Lucas and fumbled nervously with the pistol.

"Put it down on the seat next to you, Cat. I wouldn't want it to go off accidentally."

"I will not," she retorted. "I want to be able to protect myself."

Logan eased his mount closer to the wagon and plucked the gun out of her fingers. "I won't have you shooting someone and starting trouble." Their eyes met in challenge. "If you kill one of the Indians, even by accident, they will bring war upon the train."

Logan's gaze swung back to the approaching Indians and Lucas squeezed Cat's hand to give her courage. A tightness crept up her throat and her eyes remained riveted on the savages. Their hair was long and many had feathers stuck in a band around their head. Some were dressed in a small loincloth, while others wore buckskin leggings. Their bare chests were covered with painted streaks and many of the horses had similar markings. They stopped a few feet short of Logan, and Catherine saw several lengths of hair hanging from one of their belts. Involuntarily, she shuddered and Lucas whispered, "Easy girl."

Catherine shifted her eyes to Logan. He made a sweeping gesture with his hands in response to a motion the leader made. The Indian spoke in low, flat tones, in a language completely foreign to Catherine. To her surprise, Logan answered him in his own tongue. Logan never took his eyes off the men before him and she noticed he sat his horse with a sense of command; something she suspected the Indians recognized. They stopped speaking and Logan turned to Lucas.

"Get the boxes out of the back. I think two should be enough."

Nodding, Lucas climbed into the wagon. Catherine watched him disappear, wishing he did not have to leave her side. She knew his rifle rested on the floor, primed and ready, but her confidence in firing it suddenly vanished. Glancing at the Indians, she found the leader staring at her. Fighting her initial urge to cower in fear, she straightened in defiance. He said something to Logan and he turned to look at Catherine. She could read nothing in his expression and tried not to let her nervousness show.

Logan said a few words to the Indian and he started laughing and gesturing to his companions. All eyes turned on Catherine and they began joking among themselves. Her anger flared. They were discussing her, and she put the fault with Logan. He spoke again, and their laughter increased.

Urging his pony closer to the wagon, the leader waved one of his offensive scalps in her direction. When he reached up to touch the tendrils of hair on her shoulder, she bit her lip to keep from crying out. He said something to her and Logan's chest rumbled with laughter. Furious, Catherine slapped the Indian's hand away and glared at Logan. There was another exchange of words and everyone roared with amusement.

Much to Catherine's relief, Lucas appeared at the side of the wagon with two open boxes. Inside, Catherine saw mirrors, beads, trinkets, watches and things that were an everyday occurrence to white folk but probably treasures to the savages. Two Indians jumped off their horses and grabbed the boxes. A few more words were exchanged, then they turned and rode off.

Lucas glanced at Logan. "Looks like they were satisfied. I don't think we'll see them again."

"I agree, but we'll take precautions just in case," Logan said. "I'll ride down the train and let the people know everything is all right."

"Just a minute, Logan," Catherine said in a tone that demanded attention.

"I'll close up the back," Lucas said, certain a battle was coming and eager to get out of the line of verbal fire.

"How could you give them presents when they were probably responsible for killing one of the men on the train?"

"There is no probably about it," Logan said flatly. "Whose scalp do you think the Indian waved at you?"

A bubble of nausea rose in her throat. Logan was cold and heartless about another man's life and gave his murderers gifts. Sickened, she leaned over the side and retched. When she sat back on the seat, she was humiliated to find Logan watching her.

"Haven't you got anything better to do?" she seethed.

He grinned. "Sure, but I was wondering if you were

done questioning me? You might be interested to learn the gifts we have them will probably save many lives. They may seem like trinkets and junk to you, but they are gold to an Indian."

"I suppose the wagon is full of your little presents."

"We have several more boxes."

"The next time I'm confronted by an Indian, perhaps he'll find the trinkets more amusing than me."

"Don't underestimate yourself," Logan warned. "I could have saved all my gifts and traded you."

"What!" she spat in astonishment. "How dare you!"

"I dare nothing. Had it been a choice between a war or surrendering you, I probably would have sacrificed you—for the good of all."

"And what would *you* have done without me to satisfy your lust?"

He ran his hand along his bearded jaw. "Ah, I took that into consideration and told them you were not too bright. When they heard about the trouble you've caused, they believed me. I guess you could tell they thought it was funny."

"How could you tell lies about me?"

Logan casually rested his arm over the horn on his saddle. "I am beginning to wonder if they are lies. You have an uncanny knack for doing the wrong things."

Catherine wiggled in her seat. "You think you're so perfect, but you have overstepped your bounds of authority. The people on the train might be interested to learn what you gave a white man's murderer."

Logan's eyes narrowed ominously. "I'm surprised by now you haven't learned to trust my judgment. I won't have you causing trouble. I did what was best for the train. If I hear any of this being discussed, I might be tempted to trade you to the Indians." The corner of his lips curved into a smile. "The leader liked your tawny hair. I told him the sickness in your brain made your hair turn the color of a cat."

"Oh you!" she screeched and disappeared into the back of the wagon. Throwing herself on the bed, she beat against it with her fists. Logan's laugh as he galloped away added fuel to her raging temper. He had tried to make her appear feebleminded, and his words *the color of a cat,* hung in her memory. Since their first meeting, Logan had shortened her name to Cat and made a similar comparison between her and a cougar. She'd never seen the wild animal, but Logan obviously thought there was some likeness between them, and she didn't know if it was good or bad.

Chapter Fifteen

Catherine tried to forget the incident with the Indians but it remained in her thoughts as a bad dream. She managed to keep her distance from Logan, and he did not attempt to join her at night in the wagon. Relief flooded her when her female time had come and gone, thus assuring Logan's seed had not found a home in her body. The possibility of conceiving a child frightened her. With a deep sense of grief, she thought of the baby she had lost. Despite the treacherous, deceitful character of Cameron, Catherine would have taught their child to be trustworthy and honorable.

They came to the Arkansas River after a long hard day of traveling. Catherine was elated to find a calm river and considered the prospects of a bath. She went to Hetty's wagon to ask her to join her and was surprised to learn that a semi-secluded area had been set up for the women to bathe.

The water was icy, but Catherine welcomed the refreshing coolness and washed her hair and body until she tingled. She sat on the bank with some of the other women and talked while the warm sun dried her tawny mane.

When she returned to the wagon, Lucas was cleaning a rabbit Logan had provided. She poured herself a cup of coffee and stretched out in the grass.

"Did you enjoy your bath?" Lucas inquired.

"It was wonderful."

"Once we leave here, our water supply will be scarce. We could all get pretty thirsty."

"Is there any real danger?"

Lucas threw some chunks of rabbit meat into a pot over the fire. "There are always dangers. We will have to be careful with the water." He looked up and smiled. "It is the unforeseen things that catch you unprepared. We will be leaving early in the morning, but perhaps you might like to take another bath before we leave."

Catherine grinned. "Sounds like a good idea. Thanks for telling me."

The friendly atmosphere immediately changed as Logan rode up to the campfire. He was dusty from the trail and Catherine could not help wondering if he planned to take advantage of the river. He helped himself to a cup of coffee, then swung around and caught Catherine watching him. She shifted uncomfortably and pretended an interest in the dirt at her feet. Chuckling, Logan drained his coffee cup.

"I'll be down at the river. I might as well enjoy the water while we have it," he said, his gaze switching to Cat. "Would you like to join me for a bath? You could wash my back."

"Wash your own back," she snarled.

Laughing, he sauntered away. Catherine glanced at Lucas, but he was involved in his work and as usual pretending ignorance of what passed between her and Logan.

Catherine overslept the next morning and didn't

have time for a bath. The water barrels were checked and she joined the other travelers at the river for a long drink. It was already a warm day and she knew how quickly the sun could make the throat burn for liquid.

It got hotter as the day progressed, and Catherine was relieved to be at the front of the long line of wagons where the dust was minimal. Logan insisted on rationing water as though there wouldn't be any for miles, and the animals were given a measured portion at night. A small ration of water was given to Catherine and it quenched the undeniable dryness that had plagued her most of the day. Much of her thirst came from the knowledge that water was no longer available in unlimited quantities. Logan had called another meeting before they left that morning and warned each man to be responsible for their water. If they were careless and misused their allotted supply, they could not expect to get more from another wagon.

The night was warm and when Catherine woke the next morning, her body was bathed in a light sheen of perspiration. She needed a bath and decided a small amount of water would not be missed. Lucas had put a barrel in the wagon, and she helped herself to a tiny bowl. Stripping her clothes away, she let the liquid cool her body. Just as she was returning the cloth to the water, the back flap of the wagon opened. Her hands flew up to cover her naked breasts and she stepped behind some boxes to shield her lower half. Logan climbed in, glared at the water in the basin, then at her.

"What do you think you're doing with the water?"

"Washing myself," she snapped back.

His eyes ran the length of her partially covered figure. "As much as I enjoy seeing your naked body, you had no right to bathe."

"I only took a small amount of water," she said, grabbing her shirt and putting it on.

"You took enough to keep a dying man alive."

"Aren't you being a little dramatic? We will have water at the Cimarron."

"How can you be sure?" he asked, his hands on his lean hips.

"Huh!" she scoffed. "Don't you ever tire of your role as boss."

His eyes flickered his disgust. "If everyone on this train caused as much trouble as you, we would never get to Santa Fe."

"Get out," she said tightly, fighting to control her anger.

Logan took a step toward her. "Let's remember whose wagon this is."

"If that is the way you feel, I'll be glad to find someplace else to stay."

The line of his lips twisted humorously and a glint of mischief touched his blue eyes. "I think not. I'm not finished with you yet."

Cat tossed her tawny hair off her shoulder. "I can't wait to reach Santa Fe and see the last of you," she said spitefully.

Shrugging, Logan pointed to the water in the bowl. "When you have finished dressing, give the water to my horse. At least you had the foresight not to use soap in it, and it can still be salvaged for animal use."

"The only reason I didn't use soap was because I ran out of it at the river."

Logan left without further comment and Catherine ran her hand through her thick hair. Whenever she had a confrontation with Logan, she always seemed to come out on the worse side.

Two more days passed without reaching the Cimarron. Water was still plentiful, but only because Logan made sure it was not wasted. To ease the strain on the animals, they stopped traveling when the heat was at its peak and left by the cool of the early morning. Tempers were strained and one night Logan organized a dance to break the tension. Catherine was surprised he would think of something so simple and effective, and she noticed an immediate change in attitudes.

The next day they saw the Cimarron. Logan had ridden ahead and returned with the good news that there was enough water to satisfy their needs. The smooth line of wagons broke and the drivers urged their teams to reach the water first. It took several hours to get everything back to normal.

Catherine was returning from the river when she saw Logan, Lucas and two secondary scouts involved in a heated discussion. The men seemed agitated by something Logan had said, and Catherine's curiosity was immediately aroused. She couldn't hear what was being said but was determined to find out, especially if it meant Logan being wrong.

At the evening meal, Lucas told her there would be a camp meeting, and Catherine wondered if it had anything to do with the argument. She decided it did when Logan came to the fire, his features etched with anger.

"I don't know why they can't take my word for it,"

Catherine heard him tell Lucas. They walked out of earshot, and Catherine didn't hear anymore. She silently hoped that whatever happened at the meeting would not be decided in Logan's favor. For once, she wanted to see him bested.

The two men Catherine had seen talking to Logan sat on their horses before the crowd of curious travelers. She scanned the crowd for Logan and found him on his stallion off to one side. There was no tenseness in his body, but she was certain of the angry glint in his ice blue eyes. Joel, one of the scouts, raised his hand to quiet the crowd, and his gaze briefly touched on Logan before addressing the crowd.

"You've been called here because Willy and I," he said, indicatine the second man Logan had spoken to, "feel you have a right to know about the choices open to you when we leave this river. As you know, Logan is the chief scout, but Willy and I disagree with him on the journey from here to Santa Fe." He moved uncomfortably on his horse. "Willy and I favor goin' upstream. It would be safer for the stock, plenty of wood and lots of water. Logan wants to go downstream because it is fifty miles shorter." He pushed his hat back on his head. "If you go with Logan, there is no guarantee of water and the trail is not marked. If somethin' happens to Logan, you'd be lost." He scanned the anxious travelers. "I suggest we take a vote."

"Before the poll is taken, the people have a right to a few more facts," Logan said, edging his horse forward and into the light of the campfires. "Fifty miles could save days, maybe weeks of travel. We left Independence late in the season. Some of you want to reach California, so you must cross the mountains before the snows. A wagon train left Independence a few years back and got stuck in the mountains. The people who lived went through a nightmare before they were saved. The choice is yours."

Finished, Logan eased his horse back into the shadows. He had made his point, and now it depended on the people. Catherine didn't know which route was better but knew she didn't want Logan to win.

"All those in favor of followin' Willy and I stand off to the left," Joel said.

There was a hum of voices as men and women voiced their fears and considered the alternatives. Slowly, the crowd began to separate. Catherine's gaze locked with Logan's and she stepped to the left. She wanted him to know her choice was not with him. When the crowd had divided, several families had gathered on Logan's side, but the bulk remained with Joel and Willy. One of the men from Logan's side stepped forward and Catherine recognized Hetty's Hank.

"I'm thinkin' that Logan has led us right since we started on this trip. I believe all of you should put your trust in him." He turned to Logan. "We want you to lead us down your trail. We're not willin' to risk gettin' trapped in the snow. I know what those people went through that got stuck in the pass, and I don't want it for my family."

Another man stepped forward and said, "We're goin' that way with or without you."

Catherine heard the murmurs of agreement from several other men. When the crowd finally returned to their wagons, it had been decided the train would separate. The wagon master was against the split, but he couldn't sway the crowd, so he went with the two scouts and the majority. Catherine was satisfied in her decision to join Willy and Joel. For once she was sure Logan was wrong.

The wagons would all stay by the river through the morning before dividing, and Catherine was determined to use the time to find someone to travel with. She was delighted at the prospect of finally getting away from Logan and his forceful attitude.

She climbed into the wagon without seeing Lucas. He had frowned when she made her choice not to travel with them. Although she would be sorry to leave Lucas, there was no other choice; Lucas would never leave Logan.

While she undressed, she considered the friendship and trust that flourished between the two men. They used only one name, and she wondered if it was to hide their true identities from the law. The twenty or more years that separated them didn't seem important. A few times she had caught Lucas in a thoughtful mood and seen sadness reflected in his pale blue eyes. If Logan knew what troubled the older man, he kept it to himself, and Catherine never asked. Lucas stayed out of her business and she felt obligated to do the same for him.

She had almost fallen asleep when something hit her elbow. Opening her eyes, she focused on the dark form above her and knew instantly it was Logan. Tonight, she'd refuse to respond.

Logan tossed the last of his clothing aside and began to ease his body down on the narrow bed.

Taking a deep breath, Catherine swung at him with her fists. The attack caught him unaware and she managed several blows to his chest before he caught her wrists and dragged them above her head. She twisted her body and kicked out with her feet, but he eased himself over her, stilling her motion.

"I can't wait to get away from you," she panted, exhuasted from the fight.

A gruff laugh rumbled from his throat and she knew she was just amusing him. "Why don't you cooperate one last time?"

"Never," she professed. "You can't make me want you."

"We both know that's not true." The positive tone of his voice infuriated her.

"Don't delude yourself. It won't happen tonight."

"You are right," Logan assured her. "I haven't the time."

Catherine tensed and her mind became a blank frenzy of hate as he slowly aroused her body and satisfied his lust. When he rose and dressed, she curled into a ball and let the tears spill. Tomorrow when the wagons split, she'd be free of him. Tonight had been the last time.

"I'm glad I'll never have to share my bed with you again."

He chuckled. "Don't be too sure. You leave with me."

"I will not," she said defiantly, but she spoke only to the darkness; Logan was gone.

Catherine was determined not to be on the wagon train with Logan, but her carefully laid plans for finding space in another wagon were abruptly interrupted when he demanded that she mount her horse and ride with him.

"I'm not going with you," she said, throwing her hands on her slim hips. "I think you're going to get the people killed."

Logan's dark brows came together and his blue eyes flashed his annoyance. "You're coming with me!"

"You don't own me Logan. You have no right to try and dictate my life."

Seizing her upper arm, he jerked her against him. "If you go with Joel, you'll probably get yourself killed. They aren't going to make it through the mountains before it snows."

"It's still my choice and I don't want to stay with you." She didn't finish when his grip tightened painfully. "I'm tired of being used. You treat me like a plaything without any regard for my feelings."

His lips curled into a sneer. "You respond to me, Cat. You just won't admit it."

There was no point in denying what he said. She had enjoyed his lovemaking on at least one occasion. "It doesn't change anything. I'm still leaving with the other wagons."

"I'm going to save your life. You are going with me if I have to tie you on my horse."

"You wouldn't dare." She tried to pull her arm free.

"You know I will." There was a tightness along his jaw. "There isn't another family who could take you on. Supplies are low. No one would take the risk."

Still holding her arm, he took her to her horse and mounted. "Don't try anything. You'll only humiliate yourself."

Logan led the small party of twenty-four wagons

along the creek bed. Logan kept Catherine at his side, despite her attempts to drop behind and disappear. It was his final promise to tie her in the wagon that forced her to abandon her escape attempts.

They made camp early that night so the women could do extra baking and water barrels could be filled. Once they left the river, water could get desperately scarce. The small children were sent out to collect buffalo dung for use when wood got scarce. Catherine had already collected a substantial amount so Lucas said it wasn't necessary to get more. He did insist, however, that Catherine do some baking while he filled the barrels.

Logan had disappeared, so Catherine went about her work with a carefree attitude. She was late in starting her fire, so most of the loose sticks near the wagons had already been collected. Instead of spending time searching the woods for twigs, she decided to use the buffalo dung. The fire was hot by the time she had the batter ready. She marveled at her expertise in building the fire and the makeshift oven. She had even achieved some culinary talents that would certainly have surprised Effie.

She put two loaves of batter bread in her campfire oven, then sat back to work on potatoes for the meal. She suspected Logan would bring some kind of wild-life for their dinner and she was hungry for stew. The spuds were soft and wrinkled from the heat and long white eyes stood out to mark their age. Effie had always discarded old potatoes, but when she suggested it to Lucas, he told her food was precious and they were still good enough to eat.

Logan rode into camp and her knife was set aside.

Rising, she brushed her hands down her pants and waited for the nice plump rabbit he had dangling from the saddle. Stew was definitely on the agenda for tonight, and with the fresh bread, it would make a special meal.

Catherine expected him to dismount and have some coffee, but when he didn't, she stole an upward glance. Logan was looking at the fire and Catherine smiled. For once, she would show him she could do something right. The corners of his eyes took on definite lines of amusement as he swung off his horse.

"Baking bread?" he questioned.

Pulling the batter bread from the fire, Cat smiled. They were perfect. "Would you like some? It is always best hot."

"No thanks, but don't let me keep you from trying it." He crossed his arms over his chest and watched her. "I wonder if it is as good as you think it is?"

Logan was baiting her, and Catherine could not resist the opportunity to prove him wrong. The bread would be delicious, and she would prove it by having a piece. She cut off a generous slice. "Are you sure you won't change your mind?" she asked, holding out a slice.

"No, but let me know how it tastes." The corner of his mouth curved in a smirk.

Catherine's anger had started to bubble when she bit into the bread. Logan's mocking grin deepened as she began to chew. In the next minute, Catherine's eyes widened, and she spit the bread in the dirt.

She heard the deepening rumble of Logan's laughter. "Didn't anyone tell you never to cook breads over buffalo dung? It assumes the flavor of the dung."

He rocked back on his heels. "Why do you think we stopped here for the women to bake? There is a plentiful supply of sticks and twigs—if someone is not too lazy to collect them." Grinning, he said. "I bet that piece of bread was a real mouth full."

"You could have told me," she said spitefully. "You knew what it would taste like," she said, wiping her hand across her mouth. The taste had been terrible.

Barely concealing his laughter, Logan turned away. "You wouldn't have believed me . . . You never do." Picking up the hot loaf of bread, Catherine threw it at his retreating back. It hit his shoulder and fell to the dirt. Stopping, he turned and looked at her. "Why not keep it to remind yourself of how little you really know about this life?"

Catherine's hunger for stew vanished and she butchered rather than cleaned the rabbit. When Lucas came for the meal, he could not help but notice her agitated state. But as usual, he said nothing.

They started crossing the broad, shallow water early the next morning. Their only problem was the thick sand along the bottom, but Logan kept the wagons moving and everyone crossed without incident. They only made five miles that day, but it was distance that had taken a toll on everyone. The threat of an Indian attack was still a possibility and the small train had to stay close together. Uncertain of where their next supply of water would come from, Logan ordered rationing.

His prophesy became true as the hot, dry days passed and they did not find water. The people became disheartened and disillusioned as their thirst increased. One afternoon, Catherine heard Logan telling Lucas they were only about ten miles from Rabbit Ear Creek where he hoped to find water. Her spirits lifted, and she rode next to Lucas to watch for the river. It was nearly dusk when they saw it in the distance and Logan rode ahead to check for water.

Several of the drivers sensed his hope and they pushed their animals beyond their limits to reach the water they'd been so long without. Catherine was as eager as everyone else, but Lucas said it would do no good to tire out the animals. If the creek was empty, it would only make their thirst greater. Half the wagons were at the river when Lucas guided the team in. Catherine saw the disappointment mirrored on their faces before she saw the dry, sandy bed of the river. Huge cracks in the earth gave evidence to the lack of water for weeks, perhaps months. Women and children sobbed to vent their disappointment and Catherine turned to Lucas to find his expression grim.

"What are we going to do? The animals are half dead with thirst now." As Catherine spoke, one of the hard-driven animals faltered and fell to the dirt.

"It is not good. We might find a little water if we dig in the sand." He shook his head. "I just hope everyone has followed Logan's instructions for rationing. The animals will be watered first. You won't see any more coffee or stew until we find water."

Catherine ran her tongue over her dry lips. "I need a drink. My throat has never felt so dry."

Lucas looked at her briefly before turning back to study the disillusioned travelers. "We always have the mule ear."

"What is that?" she inquired, eager for something to quench her thirst.

"We cut off a mule's ear and suck out the blood to ease our thirst."

Catherine shuddered her horror. She never believed she would get thirsty enough to suck blood out of a mule's ear, but she'd learned to accept many unusual things as a part of survival.

A short time later, she joined the men, women and children at the dry creek bed to dig for water. She chose a spot away from everyone else so she could work without hearing the moans and cries of thirsty children. Using a flat stone, she pulled the first pile of sand toward her. Dust flew through the air, and her mouth and throat soon felt like dirt. She longed for a drink, but knew she wouldn't receive her ration until after the sun went down. Someone in the distance shouted that they had found a little water and a round of cheers burst forth.

Exhausted, Catherine sat against a rocky portion of the bank to rest. The sun beat down on her and she adjusted her hat to shield her eyes. She longed to be sitting beneath the shade of a huge oak, but the trees she had known had long since been replaced by leafless, dry brush.

A shadow passed over her and she glanced up at Logan. His blue eyes flickered over her slender frame in a way that made her redden and squirm to avoid the betrayal of her body. Chuckling, he dismounted and squatted next to her.

"I thought I should warn you about walking around and sitting in places like this." Catherine looked up at him, already resenting his tone of authority. "Poisonous snakes and scorpions often make their homes under rocks."

Jumping up, she scanned the ground around her. "What kind of snakes?" she asked nervously.

"There are many kinds. Stay away from all of them. The rattlesnake is the easiest to recognize because of the rattle. You'll usually find them out in the cool of the night. The sun will kill them so they sleep in shaded areas." She glanced at the rocks, expecting to see one slither into view. "The coral snake is deadly. You can recognize them by the black, red and yellow rings. The red and yellow are always next to each other. It resembles the king snake which is harmless, but the colors are not in the same order. You do not want to get close enough to determine the order of the rings," he emphasized.

"I have never liked snakes but I had no reason to ever fear them. Are you just trying to scare me?" she asked hopefully.

His eyes hardened to icy slivers. "I'm just trying to keep you alive. You wander around by yourself and I would hate to see your body twisting with the agony of a deadly bite." She had recognized the slight emphasis on the word body, and she had to bite back a sharp retort.

"What is the other animal you mentioned—scorpion?"

"It has a small straw colored body about two inches long, long pincers and a stinger on the tail. One scorpion is deadly, the others will just make you sick. I suggest shaking out your boots if they ever lay on the ground."

Catherine nodded, hating the thought of having one crawl out of her boots. "Anything else I should know about?"

"Are you squeamish about spiders? There are black widows and tarantulas. The lizards to worry about are twelve-inches long and are appropriately called gila monsters. They are poisonous. Centipedes are not deadly and the ticks and mites—"

"Stop," Catherine screamed, throwing her hands over her ears. "I've heard enough. You have succeeded in frightening me."

She expected to find an amused grin on his face, but his expression was hard. "I'm not playing a game. Ignorance is the best way of getting hurt."

Catherine rubbed her hands down her arm and her body tingled as though she'd been touched by each serpent or insect he had described. All interest in looking for water vanished, and she raced back to the wagon. At camp, her fear did not abate, and when she sat next to Lucas, she was constantly twisting to watch the dirt.

"Is something wrong?" Lucas asked, noting her uneasiness.

Catherine was glad the scout was not around. "Logan told me about the deadly reptiles and insects and it has made me kind of jumpy."

"If you're careful, you don't have to worry about them. They will only attack if they get frightened or pinned in a corner. They don't look for trouble."

"Thanks Lucas, that makes me feel a little better."

The next morning Catherine learned water had been found, but not enough to replenish their dwindling quantities and there was no promise for finding more soon. When they left the river bed, it was cluttered with heirlooms and treasures as families sought to lighten the load of their wagons. Catherine had seen the tears in Hetty's eyes when Hank put one of her prized possessions off to the side.

As the days past, the sun beat down mercilessly and the water problem got worse. Catherine's silent hope for rain disappeared when Lucas told her it rarely rained this time of year. Animals fell everyday from thirst, and she heard the sharp cracks of guns as they were put out of their misery. Catherine's lips cracked, and the ration of water lessened with each day.

When several wagons carelessly used their supply and ran out, Logan gathered all the water and put it in his wagon, so he could ration it out. There was fear, uncertainty and anger on the men and women's faces, and the threat of trouble hovered over them. Catherine didn't know how much longer people would blindly follow Logan, but even she had to admit he was keeping them alive.

One morning, Catherine heard a succession of shots and knew more animals were being killed because they could not go on. It was only when she left her wagon that she learned a man, driven by thirst and fear, had killed his wife and child before turning the gun on himself. The burial service was short, the atmosphere tense and strained. If they didn't find water soon, there would be more deaths and suicides.

Catherine visited Hetty when they stopped that night and learned some of the men intended to relieve Logan as scout unless they found water soon. Upon her return to her wagon, she told Lucas, and he promised to let Logan know.

Logan called everyone together and told them he had hopes of finding water within the next few days, but they would have to be patient until then. Several men angrily voiced their opinions but in the end, everyone retreated back to their wagons without trouble.

When Catherine went to bed, she heard Logan and Lucas outside the wagon. Easing back the canvas flap, she strained to hear what was being said. The words were mere whispers, but Catherine knew by the subdued tones something was wrong.

"I didn't tell them the worst of it, Lucas," Logan murmured.

"You mean you don't expect to find water in two days? The Canadian isn't usually dry this time of year."

"No, it's not. I believe we'll find water, but the animals are tired and tempers are hot. If the people find out how little water remains, I'm afraid they will panic."

"How bad is it?"

"There is only enough water to feed the animals in the morning."

The words fell on Catherine's ears like a lead weight. They were almost out of water. She raised her fingers to her dry lips. Would she have to go without water until they met the river? Frightened, she crept back to her bed and for the first time trembled with real fear.

Her opportunity to sleep never came. Logan's shouts echoed throughout the camp and she dressed and scrambled outside. Lucas was putting the leather harnessess on the mules.

"What's going on?" she asked.

Lucas threw the reins over the seat. "We're leaving."

Looking around, she saw the other men readying their animals. "But we only stopped four hours ago. The animals are exhausted."

"Logan wants to move while its cool. Climb up on the seat. We're ready to go."

They traveled all night and when the sun rose and the heat of the day renewed their thirst, Logan stopped the train. The animals were given water, and Catherine knew by the way Logan and Lucas guarded the barrels, the last of it had been used. Logan told the people they would get their share after the sun went down, but Catherine knew he would have to tell them there was no water.

That evening, the people met the news about the water with anger and panic. Logan, however, did not give them time to react, and he ordered Lucas to start the wagon train across the dark, dry land. When morning came, Logan did not stop. Without water, it was essential to continue as long as they could. Food tasted dry and boring and eating was overlooked. It was late in the day when Catherine thought she noticed the team perk and move at a livelier pace. Glancing at Lucas, she found him grinning.

"They smell water," Lucas said flatly and pointed to a rider in the distance. "Here comes Logan."

Catherine scanned the horizon until she saw Logan galloping toward them. He waved his arm and Catherine knew he had led them to the much needed water.

It was a large river with a small waterfall where the river changed elevations. Catherine jumped down from the wagon and ran to the bank. Remembering what Logan had told her about snakes and insects, she studied the surrounding territory before kneeling at the edge. She splashed water on her lips and face before taking a long drink to relieve her thirst. When the thick, cottony taste had abated, she sat back and watched the children splash and play.

Logan ordered a day of rest, and he and Lucas discussed the best method of crossing the river. Catherine could see their dilemma. Most of the terrain near the water was covered with rocks, making it impossible for a wagon to pass. Where the rocks were absent, cliffs made the drop to the water an impossible feat. Quicksand made the flat areas upstream impassable.

The next morning Catherine learned they were going to cross near the waterfall where the rapids were the worst. Logan gave specific instructions, and the wagons crossed one at a time. It took half a day, but everyone reached the other side without incident. The spirits of the people had improved when they turned slightly south. The terrain changed abruptly and they ascended to the high tableland and passed a shoe-shaped mountain. From then on, mountains stretched across the land on the right, then left and held the promise of nearing Santa Fe.

Catherine's eagerness to end the journey grew each day. Logan had not come to her bed for days, but she didn't know how long it would last. Her opinion of Logan hadn't changed, but she had to admit he had led them to water.

Six days after leaving the river, they came to the place where all the trails west met, Rio Gallinas, and Catherine saw the first signs of the Mexican adobe huts and civilization. They were forty-five miles from

Santa Fe, but the trail was rough and progress slow.

The night before they rode into Santa Fe Lucas asked Catherine to join him for coffee. Something had been troubling him most of the day, and she hoped she could help in some way.

"What are your plans once we reach Santa Fe?"

"I'm going to my uncle's ranch," she answered and took a swallow of coffee.

"Is it in town?"

"It is one or two days north. I'm going to have to find out for sure."

"How are you going to get there?"

Catherine stared into the coffee cup. She had not given it any thought. Until she had money, she couldn't buy supplies or hire someone to take her. "I'll get a job and send word to my uncle."

Lucas stared at the dirt before him and Catherine sensed a shy awkwardness about the gentle man. Reaching out, she touched his arm. "What's troubling you, Lucas? I'd like to help."

"I wouldn't feel right leaving you in a strange town. I'd like to take you to your uncle's ranch."

Catherine smiled warmly. He had a fatherly image and she felt close to him. His offer was more than she could hope for, but she didn't want to appear too eager. "I appreciate your offer, but it is asking a lot."

"Nonsense," he scoffed. "Besides, it will keep me from worrying about you."

Catherine clapped her hands together. "I'd love to spend more time with you. Are you sure you don't mind? You're supposed to go to California."

"I can catch up to the train later," he said with an indifferent shrug.

Leaning over, Catherine threw her arms around his neck and gave him a hug. "Thank you, Lucas." When she pulled away, she found the haunting blue eyes on her; she couldn't get away from Logan too soon.

Santa Fe was larger than Catherine expected. The architecture was similar to what she had seen on the way into town. The flat roofed adobe houses lined the dirty, unpaved streets. In the better areas of town, the houses were painted white and heavily shuttered. The men wore laced trousers with bright colored sashes. Their boots were made from fancy embossed leather, and if the man was wealthy, silver spurs jingled. It was the women's dress that surprised Catherine the most. Short skirts displayed their ankles and lower leg, and their thin blouses, made from bold prints and gaudy colors, were cut low in the neck.

The wagon train passed through the town to the outskirts where they made camp. When the evening meal was finished, Catherine went to Hetty's wagon. She would be continuing to California and Catherine would miss her. Hetty wanted to thank God for bringing her family through the perils of the trail and asked Catherine to join her at the famous church of San Miguel built in 1636. Catherine had much to be thankful for and agreed to join her.

On their return, they had to pass through the market place where despite the late hour, men and women had their booths of food to sell.

They stopped near a group of men betting on two fighting cocks, but after a few seconds, the gruesome sport forced them to continue on their way. When they stopped to watch a fandango dance, Catherine lost herself to the music. Closing her eyes, she felt the

262

music run through her body. When she opened her eyes, her gaze was drawn to the man standing on the opposite side of the circle. The intensity of Logan's blue eyes pierced through the darkness and Catherine felt an uneven pitch in her stomach. How dare he follow her and invade on her privacy! Catherine touched Hetty's arm and they proceeded back to the wagons. The women cried and embraced when they bid each other farewell, each wishing the other a life of happiness.

Catherine hummed the tune from the Spanish guitar on the way back to the wagon. Tomorrow Lucas would be taking her to her Uncle Ben's ranch, and Logan would continue out of her life.

The wagon train was just a spot in the distance the next morning when Catherine joined Lucas. He obviously wanted an early start to her uncle's. Logan rode up and she was determined not to let him rile her on their last meeting.

"I wish you a safe trip to California," she said haughtily. "I consider all debts to you paid in full."

A sly smile touched his lips. "Are you trying to get rid of me? I thought you enjoyed my company."

"Never." She pointed to the retreating wagons. "Don't you think you better catch up with the wagon train before they get too far ahead?

"It doesn't matter," he stated with an uncaring attitude. "I am not going with them."

His words rang a warning bell in Catherine's mind and she glanced at him sharply. "But aren't you the guide to California?"

"I was only hired to Santa Fe. Someone else is taking them."

"What are you going to do?" she asked suddenly, afraid of his answer.

"I'm going to take you to your uncle."

"Lucas is taking me, not you."

"Didn't Lucas tell you? We always travel together?"

Logan turned his horse and rode toward town. Would she ever be rid of him?

Chapter Sixteen

At Lucas's insistance, they spent an hour in town outfitting Catherine with a new hat, boots, pants, shirts, two skirts and matching blouses. She didn't know how she'd repay him, but Lucas said he wanted to buy the things for her and wouldn't take money even if she had it. Lucas was one of the kindest, most understanding people she knew, and she loved him for it.

Catherine was sitting next to Lucas when they left Santa Fe for her uncle's ranch. When the town was behind them, Logan rode alongside the wagon and talked to Lucas. Catherine's disapproval of the scout's presence was apparent, but there was little she could do to protest. Once she got to her uncle's house, she would be rid of him forever.

The road out of Santa Fe was little more than a path. The dry, barren land with its short crop of grass made it difficult to believe her uncle owned a prosperous cattle ranch. She found the tall yucca plants a flower of beauty. Narrow flexible leaves grew from a central core and radiated out at angles. In the center was a long stem with white flowers clustered at the very top. Lucas told her they were hearty and could withstand the droughts that plagued the land.

They stopped for an hour at noon to eat and rest

the animals. Because of Logan's presence, Catherine spent the time in the wagon to avoid his close scrutiny. She stayed inside throughout the afternoon, but the heat and lack of air forced her outside when they stopped for the night. Sitting on the ground with his back against the wheel, Logan watched her. Catherine tried to ignore him, but his self-assurance was like a thorn in her boot.

"When do you think we'll get to the ranch, Lucas?" she asked, ignoring Logan's presence completely.

"If we get an early start it will probably be late tomorrow afternoon. Logan got the directions from the storekeeper, so I don't expect we'll have any trouble locating it."

"Are you eager to see your uncle, or do you just want to get rid of me?" Logan challenged.

"You should know the answer to that," Catherine hurled back. "I never asked you to come along."

His partial smile deepened. "Ah, but I knew deep down you couldn't bear to part from me."

Catherine's jaw dropped. She couldn't believe his conceit. "You egotistical bore! I'd leave right now if it meant I could be rid of you by morning."

"But then we wouldn't have the night," he said in a lazy drawl.

The underlying meaning of his statement tinged her cheeks with color. Uneasy, she glanced at Lucas, but as usual he was pretending not to notice their barbed confrontation. The older man's kind gesture of taking her to the ranch was overridden by Logan's cruelty. Rising, she muttered a good night to Lucas, shot a warning glare at Logan and went to the wagon. She considered closing and securing the canvas flap, but it wouldn't keep Logan out and she needed all the air she could get.

After removing her clothing, she stretched out on her bed. She heard Logan and Lucas discussing California, but she wasn't interested in eavesdropping. Her mind floated to the meeting with her uncle. What would he say when he saw her? Would he welcome her into his home? She tried to picture his ranch, but she'd never seen one and didn't know what to expect. Engrossed in her thoughts, she wasn't aware that the voices outside had stopped, but at the creak of a floor board in the wagon, she stiffened. She closed her eyes to feign sleep but knew it wouldn't do any good. Logan had never let her exhaustion bother him before.

The rustle of clothing warned that Logan's naked body would soon be on the narrow bed next to hers. She tried to steel herself against his touch but she remembered the fire he could ignite within her when he coaxed her into responding with a gentleness that was uncommon to him. Opening her eyes, she watched the dark form move in the semidarkness. He stripped off his shirt and she saw a thin film of moisture glistening off his skin from the night's heat. His upper body had a dominance and strength that even she had to admit added to his virility. The muscles in his arms stood out boldly as they followed a line to his shoulders and met the brawny chest. He twisted slightly, and she saw the wide hard back, indicating the strength he possessed. Shifting, he turned back, and her eyes dropped to the hard flat stomach and remembered running her hand over the firm muscles. He was sleek and well proportioned, his body a

267

physical specimen of manliness and strength. Bending over, he slid off his pants, and her gaze was drawn to the sturdy thighs that tensed with each movement.

Slowly, he eased himself down next to her, and the touch of his skin shattered her reserve. She let her body tense in a last effort to fight off his advances, but his fingertips glided down her arm and she lost her self-restraint. His hand pressed against her back and she was guided against his length. Lightly running the length of her back, his hands closed over her buttocks to gently ease her into a state of submission. His lips touched her neck and her head fell back as his mouth moved along her shoulder. No longer denying her need or desire, she reached for him.

His lips lightly brushed hers and when she opened her mouth to accept his deepening kiss, his lips transferred their attention to her cheek, leaving her with an unassuaged desire. Gently, he cupped the side of her face, his thumb stroking the soft skin and acting as a guide for his following lips. His fingers curved over her neck and across her shoulder.

Her mind floated, her body climbing to heights that seemed impossible to reach. His palm curved against her breast and the contact sent a shot of fire through her body. Lightly stroking the peak with his thumb, his mouth finally sought her lips. She welcomed their hardness, the urgency against hers.

Urged by her passion, her fingers lost themselves in the long, thick texture of his hair. Pulling him closer, she accepted the intimate probing of his mouth. The building pressure surging through her veins carried her higher and higher toward the burning inferno of her desire. She waited for the cooling tides to ease the blazing fire within her, but he only added kindling as his fingers stroked and his tongue teased.

"Logan," she whispered.

Every inch of her body tingled in expected release. The waves of their passion curled toward the shore as he shifted and they became one. Together they rose to whirling heights until their surroundings became their sanctuary. Through the swimming senses of her mind, Catherine heard Logan mutter her name. Gathering her close, he carried her to the final crest, and they washed over the sand of contentment.

When Logan rolled to the side and rested his length against hers, she let her hands fall to the sheet. What had happened minutes before was over, and she was ashamed of her wanton desires. After a short time, his breathing slowed until it became the rhymthic motion of sleep.

Catherine put her hand behind her head and stared into the darkness. Her mind was in a muddled state of anxiety and sleep would not come easily. How could she hate a man, yet respond to his touch? She wondered what Logan's lovemaking would be like with a woman he loved. Catherine had responded to two different men — Cam who she learned to hate, and Logan who she hated from the beginning. Could her hate for either man turn to love?

Perhaps her uncle would be the kind of man who would understand her fears and doubts. Lucas would, but he was too close to Logan.

She was only semiconscious when she rolled to her side and touched the hard body next to her. When arms tightened around her, she woke instantly and looked directly into Logan's eyes.

He smiled crookedly. "Did you sleep well?"

"No, not really," she managed to say. What she had felt toward him last night when they made love was gone. Now he was Logan her enemy, and she wasn't going to give him the opportunity to make her body betray her again. She had to tear her eyes away from the hypnotising affect of his blue eyes. Sitting up, she grabbed her shirt from the pile of clothes next to the bed and slid it on.

Logan propped himself up on one arm. "Does that mean you don't want a romp beneath the blanket?"

Catherine shot him a look of contempt. "It certainly does. I don't want a repeat of last night."

She watched his grin deepen to display his even white teeth. "I find it hard to believe, but I won't argue. We want to get an early start." He rose and started dressing. Refusing to look at him, she busied herself with straightening the wagon.

"I suppose I should thank you for seeing me to my uncle's ranch," she offered reluctantly.

Logan pushed his shirt into his pants. I'm only along because Lucas volunteered to take you, and we usually travel together." Logan strapped his gunbelt to his lean hips and secured the tie against his thigh. "Despite all the trouble you get into, Lucas likes you and wanted to make sure you reached the ranch safely. I suppose he sees himself as a father figure for you." He shrugged. "I guess sometimes for me too, though he would never admit it. He saved my life once and ever since he's been watching out for me." Grinning, he said, "I do the same for him, and he's kind of nice to have around."

Catherine looked up at Logan, surprised to find a

soft side to the hard, unrelenting man. "Have you got a father?"

The change in Logan was immediate. His eyes glared with hatred, and his bearded jaw tightened. If Logan had a father, he hated him, and Catherine was warned off from saying anything more. He started to leave the wagon but stopped and turned around. His eyes slowly roamed Catherine's body, lingering on the shapely legs displayed beneath her shirt.

"You won't have to share your bed with me again. After we take you to your uncle, Lucas and I are going to California. I guess we'll try to find a vein of gold."

When he was gone, Catherine finished dressing. She was glad to learn he would soon be gone and hoped he had not left his seed growing in her belly. A tear slid down her cheek as it always did when she thought of her baby—and Cam.

Catherine was dozing on the wagon seat when Lucas nudged her in the ribs. "The *hacienda* is just ahead. Logan went to announce your arrival."

"You mean my uncle's home?" she asked eagerly, standing to get a better view. "What did you call the ranch?"

"A *hacienda*. It's a Spanish word. This used to be Spanish territory and many of the words are used with English." Catherine wrinkled her nose in confusion and Lucas laughed. "You'll get used to it."

In the distance, Catherine recognized Logan's tall form next to a man several inches shorter. "I hope that's my uncle," she said, raising her hand to shield her eyes. It had been years since she'd seen him, and she couldn't tell from this distance.

"Does he know you're coming?"

"No. There was no time to notify him." She briefly reflected back on the day she learned her uncle wanted to see her, and her aunts' subsequent deceit. So much had changed since then.

The *hacienda* resembled the adobe structures she'd seen in town. The house was large, with flat roofs stretching across the top. Two cottonwood trees shaded portions of one side and a large patio ran across the front and disappeared around the corner.

The men were closer now and her gaze focused on the man talking to Logan. There was no mistaking him for her uncle. The light hair streaked by the sun was reminiscent of the memory she had of her father. There was a smile on her lips as the wagon stopped and he came forward to help her from the seat.

"Catherine, I don't believe you are really here."

Impulsively, she threw her arms around his neck. "You don't know how good it is to see you," she said, grateful for the warm welcome. Looking past her uncle, she saw Logan watching the exchange with interest. His blue eyes were noncommittal, but one corner of his mouth curved in mockery. Wanting to escape his cynicism, she broke free from her uncle. "Would you mind if we went inside?"

Her uncle's expression changed to one of concern. "Forgive me Catherine for neglecting my responsibilities as host, but I'm so glad to see you." He took her arm and ushered her toward the house. "I'll have somthing cool prepared for you to drink." His gaze switched to Lucas and Logan. "Perhaps the gentlemen would like to join us."

Catherine stiffened, but there was little she could do about the invitation. "I could use something wet,"

Lucas said, jumping from the seat.

Catherine was both surprised and pleased at the interior of the house. The ceilings were covered with beams that made the small rooms appear large and spacious. Colorful rugs scattered the floor and contrasted the heavy furniture arranged carefully around the room. The inside was pleasantly cool, and she welcomed the relief from the scorching heat. Her uncle introduced Juanita, his cook and housekeeper, when she brought the refreshing drink, and the maid welcomed Catherine to the house.

Catherine sank into one of the chairs while Lucas and her uncle sat on the couch. Logan preferred to tower above them by leaning against a wooden mantel, his long legs crossed casually. Everything about the man irritated her, but she could not deny the attraction between them.

"Why didn't you let me know you were coming, Catherine?" Ben asked. "I wrote your aunts months ago, but when I got a letter from them stating your intentions to remain with them, I gave up hope of seeing you. What prompted you to change your mind?"

She felt Logan's piercing blue gaze directed on her, and she swallowed thickly. "It's a long story uncle, and I promise to tell you all about it, but for now, I'm just glad to be here."

"You have definitely brought sunshine into my life," her uncle said, grinning. "Was it a difficult trip?"

This time she stole a glance at Logan and saw the familiar mocking curl of his mouth. He knew how hard the trip had been on her, and it was his way of daring her to tell her uncle the truth.

"Let's just say it was an experience," she said, switching her attention back to her uncle.

"I understand you traveled with Logan and Lucas." She nodded. "I owe both of you a debt of gratitude for helping my niece. She was young when she lost her parents and I'm not certain how my sisters prepared her for the world." The glance he cast Catherine was full of questions, and perhaps in time she would supply the answers.

"Catherine was a real pleasure to have along," Lucas added, smiling at her fondly. "Wasn't she Logan?"

Logan straightened. "She certainly was a *pleasure* to have along," he drawled.

Catherine's cheeks flamed and she quickly took a sip of her drink. There was little doubt in her mind what Logan had meant. She had been a pleasure in his bed. "It's been a long day, Uncle Ben. I think I'd like to rest," she said, coming to her feet.

"Of course, my dear, Juanita can show you to your room. I'm going to ask the men to stay for dinner, so I hope you'll join us later."

Catherine's room was spacious with two large windows overlooking the back of the house, and a door that led to a wide patio. When she was alone, she threw herself on the thick mattress and stared at the ceiling. As usual, Logan had been impossible, and she couldn't wait until he was gone. Her uncle had welcomed her warmly and she was certain she would find a real home with him. It was certainly a relief to be beneath his roof and in his protection. Catherine had come home.

Chapter Seventeen

The last of the sun was sliding behind the mountains when Catherine woke and stretched. Uncertain of the time, she rose, poured water into a bowl, rinsed her face, then went to the door. It wouldn't be polite to be late for dinner her first night. The dining room was empty but the table was set, so she hadn't missed the meal. Stepping into the main room, she stopped short at the sight of Logan stretched out on the couch.

With a start, she realized she was looking at a very different man. The rough growth of beard was gone and her eyes followed the long hard jaw before dropping to the tanned throat exposed by his half-unbuttoned shirt. His stomach was flat and his pants hugged his thighs tightly to hint at the power of the man. A low sound erupted in her throat and she stepped back at her unexpected response to a man she hated. Never could she afford to let her defenses slip where men were concerned. Cameron had taught her a painful lesson about trust, and she would never forget it.

"Did you say something?" Logan asked, his booted feet dropping to the floor as he rose.

Without the beard, he was an even more striking man, and his blue eyes deepened in their intensity. "No. I was just looking for my uncle."

Logan grinned. "That's funny. I thought I heard you sigh." He ran his fingers through his dark hair. "Didn't you like what you saw? Or *did* you like it?"

Catherine stiffened. "I don't know what you're talking about. I came in here to find my uncle."

"Well, when you saw he wasn't here, why didn't you just leave?" His question threw her off balance. Had she stood and stared at him longer than she remembered?

"I just walked in," she offered as an excuse.

Logan took a step toward her. "Now we both know that isn't true. I know you were watching me." He reached for her arms, his fingertips sliding in a caressing motion that sent shivering rays of pleasure through her body.

"Your arrogance is unbelievable," she retorted, jerking her arms away. "Why would I want to stare at you?"

"Perhaps because you find me attractive." His blue eyes twinkled, and she couldn't tell if it was a gleam of mischief or mockery.

"Oh," Catherine sputtered, her tawny eyes widening to mark her surprise. "Attractive," she repeated. "I loathe you, and there is nothing about you I find attractive—nothing at all."

"Are you sure?" he baited, his fingers jerking her against his hard length. "I think you're wrong."

"Let me go," she cried, pushing against his chest. "I'll scream for my uncle."

"Go ahead. He went out on the range with Lucas to check on some cattle, so you'll just be wasting your time."

His fingers laced through her long hair, spreading it

over her shoulders. "My beautiful, wild, Cat." She became mesmerized by the intent look in the blue of his eyes. "You want this as much as I do."

His mouth parted seconds before he touched her lips, and he ignited a smoldering ember. One hand pressed against her lower back to fit her tightly against his hips. Catherine's initial urge to fight was drowned by the sensual cravings of her body. Logan knew every trick, and he played with her mouth until she returned his kisses with equal ferocity. Raising her arms to his shoulders, her fingers spread through his hair, drawing his head closer and fusing their lips in an undeniable union.

Her breasts strained against the linen of her shirt, begging to be freed from their confines and to feel the weight of his palm. When her lips were swollen and bruised, his mouth dropped to her neck to tease the sensitive skin. Unbuttoning his shirt, she pushed aside the fabric and lightly teased the mat of hair curling his chest. Groaning deep in his throat, Logan pulled her shirt free and spread his hand over her back.

A door slamming in the distance tore them apart, and Catherine looked at Logan in bewilderment before turning and running to the sanctuary of her bedroom. Confused and frightened by her response, Catherine dropped into a chair and buried her face in her hands. Why did her body betray her and respond to Logan's lovemaking? She despised the man and could never trust him, yet everything fled her mind when he touched her and she became wanton in his arms.

As always after a physical encounter with Logan, her thoughts strayed to Cameron. He had been such a gentle lover, their passions exploding in similar ways until her body begged for the ultimate sensation. How could two men who were so different create such desire in her body? Where was Cameron now and why had he deceived her?

Her uncle knocked on her door ten minutes later and asked her to join them for the meal. Smiling so he would not guess her inner tension, she tucked her arm through his and let him seat her at the table across from Logan. Lucas was at her right, and she asked him about his afternoon ride.

"This is beautiful country," he responded. "Your uncle has quite a ranch."

"I am anxious to see his land."

Juanita brought bowls of chili, bread, fruit and wine and placed them on the table. Catherine had never tasted such spiced food and had to reach for water after almost every spoonful.

"I'm sure you'll be happy here," her uncle assured her. "I plan to give you a thorough tour over the next few days, and I want you to think of this as your home."

Catherine flashed him a warm smile. "Thank you. I already do. . . . Do you employ many ranch hands?"

"It's a large ranch and I need help to run it. Right now, I'm low on help. I had some trouble last week and lost my foreman."

"Did you find someone to replace him?" Catherine asked, knowing the importance of having a second in command.

"As a matter of fact, I have. Logan has agreed to accept the position." Catherine choked on the chili in her mouth, her eyes watering, and her breathing heavy with a cough as she struggled to clear her air passage. Her uncle was at her side immediately. "Catherine, are you all right?"

Shaking her head, her breath slowly returned to normal, and she waved her uncle back to his seat. "I'm fine, but I'm going to have to get used to eating the spicy foods."

Out of the corner of her eye, she caught the doubtful gleam in Logan's eye. He didn't believe she had choked on the food and he attributed it to his intention to remain at the ranch.

"Isn't it wonderful news about Logan and Lucas?" her uncle asked. "Logan has experience for the job as foreman, and Lucas is skilled in working with cattle."

Turning to Lucas, Catherine smiled. "I'm glad you're staying. It will be like old times."

Lucas grinned. "I've gotten used to having you around, and I'm glad your uncle had a place for me. We'll still be able to chat like we did on the wagon train."

"What about me?" Logan asked casually, but deliberately pinning Catherine down for an answer. In front of her uncle she wasn't likely to voice her true feelings.

"I thought you were anxious to get to California and try to find a vein of gold." Her tawny eyes challenged him.

"Prospecting for gold is unpredictable," he said, shrugging his broad shoulders. "The job here is a sure thing." He grinned. "Right now the ranch has a lot more to offer."

Catherine knew she was what the ranch had to offer, but she refused to let Logan bully her. Turning to her uncle she said, "I'm so glad I'm here and under your protection. There have been times over the last few months that I've been frightened."

"You don't have to worry. I'm not going to let anything happen to you."

Catherine smiled smugly at Logan, and he responded by narrowing his eyes and tightening his jaw. He wouldn't dare try anything with her in her uncle's home, and if he did she was determined to get him fired. Satisfied that she had won the battle, she sat back in her chair and enjoyed the rest of her meal.

After dinner, Logan and Lucas retired to the bunk house and Catherine joined her uncle on the patio. She kissed him lightly on the cheek before sitting in one of the chairs.

"I'm so happy to be here with you," she said enthusiastically. "Your home is beautiful."

"I'm glad you like it, and I hope you'll be happy here. I've wanted to have you with me for years, but I thought it would be better if I left you with my sisters. Did they provide a good home for you?"

Catherine hesitated. She didn't know if she should dampen his fond memories of his sisters' gentleness or tell him the truth about their treatment of her.

"I suppose they did the best they could, but I wasn't really happy with them."

"Then why did they say you wanted to stay with them?"

"It was their decision, Uncle Ben. I was never offered a choice. I only found out about your invitation by accident."

He shook his head. "I'm afraid I don't understand? Harriet's letter said you hated the thought of coming to the ranch. She said you were caught up in the social whirl."

Until Duncan came into her life, social gatherings had been nonexistent. "No," she denied. "I would have jumped at the chance to join you." She sighed. "I might as well tell you the truth. I was treated as little more than a slave in their home."

"What?" her uncle exploded. "Are you telling me you worked for them?"

She nodded. "Everyday from sunrise to sunset. I was in charge of the house. A slave did the cooking, but I took care of everything else." She laughed softly. "I am quite capable of running a home, and I suppose I have them to thank for that."

"Your father was a wealthy man. What happened to your funds?"

"I was told they ran out."

Her uncle shook his head. "The money had to be mismanaged — unless — " He regarded Catherine thoughtfully, and she knew he was wondering if his sisters had stolen the money.

"It's in the past. I'm here with you and nothing else matters."

"They had no right stealing from you and using you for their own gains," he said, frowning. "I had no idea! My sisters and I never got along, but I never suspected they would treat you cruelly. I believed you would be better off with them. At the time of your parents' death I was a bachelor without a home. I promised myself that one day you would join me. . . . Oh, Catherine!" he cried in anguish. "Can you ever forgive me for leaving you with them?"

Catherine went to her uncle's side and knelt by his

chair. "There is nothing to forgive. You had no way of knowing what my life was like, and I am so grateful that you have taken me in and offered me your home."

He ran his hand down her hair. "It is your home for as long as you like. I can only try to make up for what my sisters did to you."

"My life has been totally different since I left their home. I have learned and experienced many things, and my life is fuller because of it. Due to my sheltered past, I have made some mistakes, but they are in the past and I intend to start a new life with you."

"You're a very wise young woman," her uncle said, regarding her thoughtfully. "Did you leave someone special behind?"

Catherine stiffened momentarily but relaxed when she realized there was no way her uncle could know about Cameron. "What do you mean?"

"Did you have any special girl friends or male interests?"

"There was a slave in the house who did the cooking. I'll miss Effie, but other than her, there wasn't anyone worth mentioning."

"Well, I wouldn't be surprised if some of my ranch hands take a fancy to you. You are a lovely young woman."

Rising, Catherine returned to her chair. "Thank you, but I'm not interested in getting involved with anyone."

Her uncle frowned. "Did you have a bad experience with a man?"

"Aunt Harriet and Aunt Charlotte were trying to arrange a marriage for me. I went along with them for a while, but I knew I could never marry Duncan."

"Duncan?" he queried in interest.

"Yes, Duncan Alexander was his name. He was an older man, probably in his fifties." Remembering the way he touched and kissed her, she trembled. "He was a horrible man."

Her uncle's interest was aroused, and he edged forward on his seat. "Was he a friend of the family?"

"No. From what I understand, he wrote a letter to your sisters and asked for my hand in marriage." She wrinkled her nose. "I never did learn how he knew I was at the house. My aunts never let me appear when they entertained, and I never went to town."

Her uncle sadly shook his head. "I'm afraid I have done you a great wrong." He slapped his hand against his knee to lighten the mood. "I intend to make it up to you."

"I don't want you to feel guilty, Uncle Ben. Aunt Harriet and Aunt Charlotte had something to gain by my marriage. Duncan had agreed to give them money instead of requesting a dowry."

"That is puzzling," he said, stroking his jaw. "It usually works the other way around."

She nodded. "I thought the woman was expected to provide a settlement."

"She usually does. . . . Are you opposed to the idea of an arranged marriage?"

Catherine leaned back in her chair and let her hair swing off the back. "I suppose in some instances they are necessary, but I would like to marry the man of my choice."

Chuckling, her uncle nodded. "Being a confirmed bachelor, I believe I would object to someone trying to force me into a marriage I didn't want."

"Why are we talking so much about marriage?" she asked. "Are you wishing I had a husband or a man to love?"

"Forgive me if I sound like I'm pushing, but I want you to be happy. Someday this house and all the land is going to belong to you, and I want you to share it with a man who can fulfill your needs and make this a prosperous spread."

Tears sprinkled Catherine's eyes, and she and her uncle rose to hug each other. "I don't want your land or home. I just want you live here with you and be happy."

"I'll do my best to make your stay a memorable one." There was a slight noise off to the side, but Catherine couldn't see what it was. "Remember, when you meet the right man I want you to know you have more than yourself to offer him."

"Well, I can tell you, I don't know any man I would want to love and share a life with." Sighing, she hesitated. "I guess there never has been."

Her uncle gave her a brief hug and let his arms fall. "Was there something you wanted, Logan?" he asked, and Catherine noticed him standing in the shadows looking directly at her. He despised women and treated them with contempt, but the cold, unleashed hatred she saw reflected in his blue eyes made her step back. She couldn't imagine what she had done or said to anger him, but it really didn't matter. He hated women and she hated him.

"I think I'll go to my room. I'm still tired from the trip," Catherine said.

Her uncle put his hand on her shoulder. "My offer

still stands for tomorrow if you'd like a tour." Catherine nodded. "Good. We'll leave after breakfast."

After kissing her uncle on the cheek, she turned and went to her room. Her wardrobe had been neatly arranged in the dresser and closet, and she was searching for a nightgown when Juanita knocked on the door.

"Would you like a bath? I could heat some water," the maid offered.

"That would be marvelous, and I insist on helping you," she said, remembering the hard work involved in preparing a bath.

"Your uncle has a small room off the kitchen he uses for bathing, then the water doesn't have to be hauled through the house."

"Lead the way," Catherine said, picking up a towel and change of clothes.

They spent the next fifteen minutes heating water and pouring it into the tub. When she was alone, she stripped off her clothes and slid into the heated liquid. It was a wonderful feeling to rest against the high back and let the warmth soothe her tired muscles. When the water cooled, she washed and reached for the towel. Just as she was stepping out of the water, the door on the far side of the room opened, and Logan stepped inside. He stopped short, his eyes widening at the generous display of naked flesh. A smile settled over his lips when Catherine struggled to cover herself.

"Get out of here," she ordered, trying to keep the towel over her vulnerable parts. "You have no right to come barging in here and interrupting my privacy."

Pulling the door closed, he tossed his towel over a chair. "I came to take a bath. It is an extra bonus to find you here." His gaze flicked briefly to the tub. "I'm only sorry I didn't arrive a little sooner. I would have joined you."

"Oh," Catherine fumed. "How dare you!" Her cheeks flamed at the thought of Logan joining her in the tiny bathtub.

Chuckling, he said, "I can see you might have liked the idea."

"I would hate anything that had to do with you. I've told you over and over again, and I will keep telling you how much I despise you."

Leaning against the wall, he made a leisurely study of her body, searching for a place where the towel might separate. "You've told me, but your body sends out a different signal."

"Get out," she ordered. "I want to get dressed."

He crossed his arms over his chest. "Go ahead, I've seen it all anyway."

Infuriated by his cool, naked gaze, she turned, grabbed her clothes and ran. Once inside her room with the door locked against intruders, she sank to the mattress. She had looked forward to a start in her uncle's home, but she could never be free of the past with Logan constantly reminding her of the passion they shared.

The sun had just peeked above the land when Catherine woke. Today she was going to get a tour of her new home. Climbing out of bed, she dressed, washed and went to the kitchen. Juanita was already preparing the meal for the men in the bunkhouse. Catherine, remembering the mess she'd always made in Effie's kitchen, cautiously offered her help, and Juanita handed her a plate of biscuits.

"You can add these to the things on the table. The men eat in the bunkhouse, but I cook everything here." When she had completed the job, the maid handed her a large platter of meat and potatoes. "You can take this to the bunkhouse. They'll be waiting."

Although it was early, there was a sticky warmth to the air and Catherine knew it would be a hot day. The door to the bunkhouse opened when she stepped on the porch, and a stranger welcomed her inside.

"You must be Ben's niece." Catherine nodded. "It's nice to have a pretty face around here to brighten up the place." Catherine blushed and smiled warmly at the man. "My name is Tom, and this is George, Spur, Jim and Pete. I guess you know Lucas. The rest of men are out back, and you'll meet them later."

There were no leering glaces directed at her, and she relaxed under their curious glances. It was natural for them to wonder about her unexpected arrival, and if she was going to live here, she wanted to be on the best of terms with everyone.

"It's nice to meet all of you," she said, turning to leave. "I better get the flapjacks and biscuits or you'll be eating cold food."

"Would you like some help?" Lucas asked.

"I'd love it," Catherine said, and they walked toward the house.

"Do you like your uncle's place?"

"It's wonderful. It's different from my last home, but I'm determined to make my future here."

"I'm glad, Catherine," he said, running his fingers down his jaw. "I hope you're not too upset about my staying on."

"I couldn't be happier. I got used to having you around," she teased, reflecting on the time they spent together on the trail.

"You can tell me to mind my own business if you want, but I don't think you are happy about Logan being here."

Catherine sighed. "You know how it is between us. We are always arguing. We just can't get along."

Sadly, Lucas nodded his head. "You're both stubborn. Something is eating at Logan, but he won't talk about it, and I suspect there is something haunting you." He paused. "Am I right?"

She nodded. "I can't talk about it."

"Does it have anything to do with Logan?" he pried gently.

Catherine shook her head. "No. It has something to do with someone I met before Logan." There was a momentary softness in her eyes as she thought of Cam, then the hardening of anger when she remembered his deceit. Would she ever be able to think of him without experiencing the bitter memories? They had shared some tender moments, and his gentleness was something she would never forget. Despite his deceit, she didn't think that part of their relationship had been a lie. At least she wanted to believe she had sparked some tender feelings in him.

Lucas lightly touched her shoulder. "Have I stirred up a painful past?"

"You have refreshed some memories, but not all of them are painful." She forced a smile. "I think time will heal some of my bitterness."

There was a momentary sadness reflected in his eyes. "Time has a way of lessening pain, but you never forget."

Catherine studied him curiously. There was something of his past reflected in the statement, and she realized somewhere in his life he'd known hurt and understood her turmoil.

"I want you to remember I'm here if you need to talk."

"Thanks Lucas. I'm glad to know you're my friend."

They collected and delivered the rest of the food in silence, then Catherine returned to the house to have breakfast with her uncle. "Are you ready to see the ranch?" he asked when they'd finished.

Catherine smoothed her new pants over her hips. "I'm ready and eager."

"Two of the men are going to town for supplies. If there is anything you need, tell Juanita and she will add it to the list."

"I can't think of anything. Lucas bought me new clothes when we came through Santa Fe. If you could use my skills around the house, I'd like to earn the money to pay him back." She knew Lucas wouldn't accept it, but she wanted to offer and perhaps buy him something for his kindness.

"I don't expect you to work here," he said gruffly. "I'll settle things with Lucas, and in the future, if you need something just ask."

His generosity brought tears to her eyes. Her aunts had never considered her needs and she had lived many years without being able to give or receive happiness. Even the time with Cameron, when she thought she'd entered into a giving, loving relationship, she'd been used and misled. Now she was certain of her uncle's genuine concern for her future and her relief filled her with joy.

"What's the matter, Catherine? Why are you crying?"

She wiped her cheeks on her shirt sleeve. "You're spoiling me."

"It's about time somebody did," he said, chuckling,

Catherine put on her new beige cowboy hat and followed her uncle outside to three waiting horses. "You ride the gray mare. She is surefooted and gentle."

Stroking the animal's neck, Catherine spoke softly to her. "She's perfect, Uncle Ben."

"She's yours." He smiled at his niece's pleasure. "Take care of her and she'll be like a trusted friend."

Walking to the left side, she pulled herself into the saddle. Her uncle mounted a spotted stallion and reined him away from the third horse. Catherine's heart sank when she recognized Logan's mount. The door to the bunkhouse slammed and he crossed the dirt yard to his horse.

"Morning," he said to Catherine. "I trust you slept well."

Beneath the brim of her hat, Catherine's eyes narrowed. "Yes I did. In fact, it was the best undisturbed sleep I've had since I left my aunts."

A muscle tightened in Logan's cheek, but there was no other indication that her statement had had any affect on him.

Her uncle led them out of the yard and across the range. For the next hour, Catherine listened to the men discuss the land, her uncle's hopes, and the cattle. She was in awe of his holdings. While most of the grass was short, it was plentiful and supplied the cattle with a continuous grazing land. Berry bushes and apple trees scattered the land and offered an array of seasonable fruit. Catherine couldn't have asked for a more beautiful home.

Chapter Eighteen

At noon, they stopped at a chuck wagon for lunch. The men were working in a pen with some of the cattle and Catherine perched on the fence to watch. The sounds of the bawling cattle created a noisy confusion, but she enjoyed watching the small calves struggle to stay with their mothers. One little calf stopped right beneath her feet and looked up at her, its wide brown eyes haunted by curiosity before passing on with its mother.

"Enjoying yourself?" her uncle asked, stopping at her side.

"There is so much to learn. I've never seen anything like it."

"We will be starting the branding soon, then we have to drive the cattle to market. It is not going to be an easy trip, but we have to make it."

Catherine's gaze slid over the hundreds of cows before her. "Why don't you wait until next year?"

A haunted look appeared in her uncle's eyes. "I can't afford to wait. A ranch like this takes money to run and I have to get the cattle to market this year."

It was none of Catherine's business, but she was about to ask if he was experiencing financial difficulty when one of the men called him and he left. Leaning forward, she put her chin in her hand. She certainly hoped her uncle wasn't having money problems. The ranch obviously meant a lot to him and she didn't want to see him lose it.

"I don't like you sitting on the fence," a deep voice commanded, and Catherine twisted sideways.

Her eyes narrowed to meet Logan's gaze. "And why not? I'm not doing any harm and my uncle didn't object."

"You seem to forget your uncle has only known you a short time and hasn't learned the trouble you can get yourself into. I am fully aware of how dangerous you can be."

She swung back to the front and rested her chin on her hands. "I'll thank you to mind your own business. I'm not one of your hands. You can't boss me around."

She heard Logan's sharp intake of breath. "Regardless of what you think of me, it is not safe for you to be sitting there."

Before he could reach for her, Catherine decided to shift her position farther down the rail. Just as she swung her foot to the side, her heel caught the wood, pitching her forward. There was nothing but open space and cattle before her panic-stricken eyes. Continuous cries of terror ripped from her throat as she slammed the back of a cow and landed on the hard dirt. Either her scream or her abrupt movement into the pen frightened the cattle, and they shifted restlessly around her prone body. Terrified of seeing the numerous cattle legs and hoofs, she threw her hands over her face. Something struck her and she felt a stinging pain in her side. Whimpers of fear ripped from her throat and were blocked by the restless cries of the cattle. Escape was the only means of avoiding injury, but she was too terrified to move.

She heard a low soft voice seconds before strong arms closed around her body and lifted her from danger. Grabbing Logan's shirt, she buried her face against his chest.

"Oh Logan," she sobbed, as he carried her to safety and sat her on the ground. Still pertrified, she refused to release her grip on his shirt, and he gently pried her fingers loose. When he laid her back on the dirt, the tender spot at her side made her wince.

"Where does it hurt, Cat?" he asked quickly, his fingers already beginning a study of her limbs for injury.

"Something hit my left side."

He deftly freed her shirt from the band of her pants and ran his palm over the soft flesh. Despite his searching attention, there was a caressing quality to his touch and some of her fear vanished. She glanced at his eyes, but they were remote.

"Does it hurt to take a breath?" he quizzed, and she shook her head. "Good. I don't think you broke anything, but you will be sore for several days."

"Catherine," her uncle called, running across the yard with several other men. "Are you all right? Pete just told me what happened."

Wincing, she managed to push herself to a sitting position and readjust her blouse. "I'm a little stiff."

"I just left you a few minutes ago. How did you manage to fall into the pen?" he asked, kneeling at her side.

She shrugged. "It just happened. I caught my boot on the rail," she answered, refusing to let her uncle know it was because of a disagreement with Logan.

"She doesn't need an excuse to get into trouble," Logan told Ben, and Catherine clenched her jaw in anger. How dare he humiliate her in front of her uncle and hired hands! "Everything is okay now men, so you can return to your jobs."

The observers left Catherine alone with her uncle and Logan, and she unleashed her fury. "How dare you tell everyone it was my fault I fell into the pen! You are responsible."

Her uncle threw a sharp, curious glance at his foreman. "Is it your fault she fell into the pen?"

"No," he drawled. "But your niece would like to put the blame on me. We had several similar incidents on the trip from Independence." Logan grinned. "Now that they are in the past, some of them would make good tales. I'll have to tell you about Cat's antics."

Catherine silently fumed. He wouldn't dare tell her uncle about her inexperience with life. It had not been her fault she'd led a sheltered life.

"Uncle Ben, could you take me back to the house?"

"Of course," he said, helping her to her feet. "Do you think you can ride?"

"I'm a little stiff, but I'm fine."

"Logan, will you handle everything here until I get back. I want the men to start branding tomorrow at dawn."

The ride back to the ranch was pure agony. Catherine's muscles were so sore, she felt like she'd been trampled on in more than one place. A warm bath helped ease some of the discomfort, then she let Juanita help her into a gown and into bed.

Resting comfortably between the sheets, she tried to

relax. The experience with the cattle had been frightening and painful, but her worse memory was the humiliation she suffered because Logan saw her do something stupid. It was reminiscent of the times on the wagon train when she'd made a fool out of herself because of her inexperience. If today was an example of her life at the ranch, she'd be constantly ridiculed and hounded by Logan. The only way to prevent it from happening was to stay out of his way, and she didn't think it was possible.

Turning her head to the side, her cheek brushed the pillow. When she had fallen from the rail, she had screamed something. What had she said? Had she called to the man she despised or had she just screamed her terror? Her body warmed with the memory of his hands on her waist, probing for injury in her body. His touch had been impersonal, yet it had been a disturbing feeling.

Very little air entered the windows to cool her heated thoughts, so she rose, discarded her nightgown, crawled back into bed and drew a sheet over her nakedness. She couldn't let her thoughts become obsessed with Logan. Despite the tightening in her stomach whenever he came near, she refused to admit her desire. Rolling to her stomach, she slammed her fist into the mattress. She would not think of him any longer. He had no place in her life.

She stirred hours later to a stabbing pain in her side, then sighed as something massaged away the agony. Her tawny eyes slowly slid open, widening sharply as she met the piercing blue ones of Logan.

"What are you doing here?" she asked sharply, wondering how he'd gotten in. A quick glance at the open windows confirmed her suspicions.

"I came to see how you feel."

"I — I'm fine," she choked as his gaze fell to her lips.

She was on her back and the sheet was down around her waist. She started to reach for it, but Logan captured her hands and drew them to his lips. His tongue slid out to glide over each knuckle and up her arm. Waves of pleasure shot through her limbs in response to the sensitive caress. Suspended above her by his arms, Logan buried his face in her tawny hair. The heat of his body and the familiar scent of his skin spanned the inches between them to enfold Catherine in a cocoon of sensual awareness.

Her fingers freed themselves from his to reach for the buttons on his shirt. His playful teasing of her earlobs made her tremble, but at last she parted the shirt and eased it off his shoulders, Pausing briefly from his passioned caresses, he discarded the rest of it, and she raised her hands to run them over his chest.

His blue eyes drank in her beauty, starting at her face and moving slowly over every part of her body visible above the sheet. He reached for one breast, his fingers tracing the pink crest, taut with desire. Gradually, his palm opened to spread and cup the mound of flesh. Catherine's hands crept up his chest, her nails digging into his shoulders.

The indifferent glare usually present in his eyes was absent, and instead they were glazed with a passion that both stirred and frightened her. Their eyes met in a searching study of the other. At the same time, they moved to come together, their bodies arching until his muscled length met the contour of hers. Slowly and sensuously, his mouth closed over the softness of hers to tease and persuade a response. His mouth freed itself to badinage her neck and finally close on her breast. Arching to the playful attentions of his body, her fingers ran the length of his back to draw him closer and to feel the muscles flexed from their love-making. Her head rolled from side to side until he threaded his fingers through the tawny mane to stop the motion with a searing kiss. Deftly, he flicked aside the sheet at her waist, and his palm spread over her abdomen. The muscles in her stomach tightened as his fingers slid down her thigh to her parted legs. With his free hand, Logan loosened his pants and yanked them off.

His body covered hers, crushing her into the bed with the weight of their combined passion. When Logan excited her body to this pitch, there was no denying him the ultimate satisfaction. She would loathe him later, but now her body sought the same release.

Nuzzling her neck, his hands skimmed over every part of her body, thus maintaining the height of her desire and making sure she would not deny him his need. When she thought she could no longer bear the agony of waiting, his hands stopped and he pulled himself above her. His eyes, still clouded with the passion he felt, were now glazed with a hint of contempt—the look that was so often evident in his eyes when he looked at her

"My beautiful, wild Cat. I hate you for making me want you." With that declaration, he took control of her mouth and body and carried them away in a tide of passion that made them soar to supreme heights and descend together to the land of contentment.

Catherine was still feeling the satisfying aftermath of their lovemaking when Logan swung his legs off the bed and rose. He dressed, retrieved his hat and looked at her. His blue eyes had an unleashed hate that made her recoil. Logan had meant what he said just before taking possession of her body. He hated her and had finally verbalized his animosity.

She propped herself up on her arm and drew the sheet over her breasts. "If you hold me in such contempt, then why do you repeatedly come to my bed? I would perfer you to leave me alone." As she spoke the words, she knew they weren't entirely true. Only one other man had ever made her feel like Logan did, and he was gone and out of her life. Not even the few kisses she had shared with Darrell and Duncan had unleashed the same kind of need as Logan and Cameron did.

Cameron had been the first to awaken her feelings with tender love, but Logan had been the one to spark the fire—despite her animosity toward him. If she remained near Logan, there would be another repeat of their lovemaking, and eventually she might find herself unmarried and with child. Tears sprinkled her eyes as she reflected briefly on her lost child. It was a painful memory she didn't want to repeat. She had to make this man leave her alone.

She raised her tear-stained eyes to Logan and briefly saw confusion etched on his features before he carefully masked it with an emotionless expression that gave little hint of his thoughts.

"Well, are you going to stay out of my room and leave me alone? I don't have a place in my life for the kind of complications your lust could invoke."

"Do you mean a child?" he quizzed bluntly, but she remained silent. "Would my son or daughter be distasteful to you?"

Catherine never wanted to conceive a child without the commitment of marriage. "Yes, it would."

Logan's jaw clamped shut, and he glared his hate. "You are a cold-blooded female — just like all of them. If you want me to leave you alone, then stop sending me signals. You may not desire me, but your body does."

Catherine rose to her knees. "Now just a minute. I didn't send you any signal to come to my room. I was in here sleeping."

His mouth curved in mockery. "You wave the invitation around like a flag. I'd be a fool not to take advantage of the offer." Turning, he sauntered to the door.

"Don't go out that way," she cried in horror. "My uncle or Juanita might see you leave."

"What's the matter? Don't you want them to know you've been sleeping with the hired help? Don't you want them to know you paid your way across the country by bedding me?" He chuckled. "Oh, and I forgot the time you were working in a saloon." He touched his side where she'd stabbed him. "There is a lot I could tell your uncle."

Before she could respond, he had turned and left the room, slamming the door loudly behind him so it would be heard all over the house. Throwing herself back against the mattress, Catherine covered her face with her hands. She would never be able to face her uncle if he knew about her affair with Logan.

Rising quickly, she threw on some clothes and

stepped into the hall. She had to know who was in the house and knew Logan had been to her room. She nearly cried with relief when she discovered the house empty. For now, her secret was safe, and she still had time to convince Logan to leave her alone.

She didn't see her uncle until the next morning when she found him behind the small desk, studying some papers. "Good morning."

Glancing up, he smiled. "Catherine. How are you feeling?"

She gingerly patted her side. "I'm a little sore, but it's nothing for you to worry about."

He sat back in his chair. "You are lucky you weren't seriously injured."

"I know. I have a lot to learn about the ranch, and I hope you'll be patient with me."

"You'll learn. The men have started the branding. Would you like to watch?"

"It might be fun," she agreed. There wasn't anything for her to do at the house, but she could keep her uncle company and maybe learn enough to help in some way. "When do we leave?"

Frowning, her uncle tapped the papers on the desk. "I have to go over some business first."

"Can I help?" she offered eagerly. "I can read and I know figures."

There was a defeated expression on his aging face. "No, Catherine. This is something I have to take care of myself."

She studied him for a minute. "Is something wrong? I know you told me you had to get the cattle to market to keep the ranch operating, but is that all?" His uneasiness troubled her.

He grinned to brush away her thoughtful mood. "There is nothing for you to do or to worry about. Everything is fine." He made a waving motion with his hands. "Now go get yourself something to eat. We'll have lunch with the men."

From her days on the wagon train, Catherine had learned to always eat a hardy breakfast, and she accepted the oatmeal and bread Juanita gave her. Her uncle was ready when she'd finished, and she mounted Ribbon, the gray mare. The trip to the branding area was covered in less than an hour and Catherine was surprised to see twice as many cows as yesterday. Their cries were heard long before they became visible, and Catherine hated to imagine the pain they experienced when the hot brand touched their flesh.

When they rode into camp, she immediately scanned the area for Logan. After yesterday, she wanted to avoid a confrontation with him at all costs. Most of the men were at the pens, and she decided it was where Logan would be.

They tied their horses with the others and her uncle put his arm around his shoulder. "You can wander around camp, but please stay off the fence. I don't want another accident."

Catherine smiled. "I promise."

He walked toward the cattle pens and Catherine turned to the wagon serving coffee. Lucas was sitting by himself and after grabbing a cup, she joined him.

"I heard about your accident. Were you hurt?" Lucas asked when she had sat down.

"No—I scared myself and felt like a fool," she said

remembering Logan's public remarks about her clumsiness.

"You were lucky Logan was there to get you out."

Catherine took a sip of coffee. "If Logan hadn't been there, I wouldn't have fallen in the pen in the first place."

Lucas's pale blue eyes swept her expression. "Were the two of you fighting again?"

Catherine nodded. "I wish he would leave me alone. He is always trying to humiliate me, and I know he hates me."

Lucas arched one of his dark brows. "Did he tell you that?"

"He has told me and shown me how he feels. What is the matter with him?" she asked, staring at the ground thoughtfully. "I think he hates all women, not just me."

"We've talked about this before, and I don't know what to tell you. Logan has some bitterness locked up inside and he won't talk about it." Lucas shook his head. "I've tried to make him listen to reason, but it's no use."

Catherine shrugged. "I was glad to learn you were staying at the ranch, but Logan's presence is something else. I don't know if my uncle has picked up on our tension or not, but he soon will."

"Are you afraid of getting Logan fired?" Lucas asked, chuckling.

She sniffed. "If I did, it would be because he deserved to lose his job." She would probably get him fired immediately if she told her uncle about Logan's uninvited visit to her bedroom last night.

"Are you interested in seeing the branding? I have

some time before I have to go back to work."

Rising, Catherine brushed off her pants. "I'd like to see it and maybe if I'm with you, I can stay out of trouble."

Lucas was chuckling as they crossed the yard to the holding pens. The noise and confusion increased near the cattle. Wood smoke, burning flesh and dust clouded the air. The animals were contained in large pens and sent through wooden shoots to the branding area. Every branded animal was counted and tallied for future reference.

The cows, sent down the shoot one by one, were roped at the feet and head. The dust was unbelievable and most of the men had their noses and mouths covered with a knotted handkerchief. From a safe position at the fence, she watched one of the men rope and tie a small calf. A red hot iron was pulled from the fire and laid on the brown and white hide. The tiny animal squirmed to get free of its bonds as the stench of burning hair and flesh assailed her nostrils. Trembling, she covered her nose.

"Are you all right?" Lucas asked, touching her shoulder. "I reckon this is a sight I'm used to, but I can understand how it could bother a city girl."

She removed her hand from her face long enough to smile. "I'm not a city girl any longer. This is just one of the things I'm going to have to accept if I stay here."

Lucas lightly slapped her on the back. "That's what I like to hear—a gal with some spirit."

Laughing, Catherine turned her attention back to the branding, but her smile froze on her face when her eyes locked with piercing blue ones. Even with the bandana covering most of his face, there was no mistaking the man as Logan. She returned his gaze as a challenge and thought she saw his head nod forward in acknowledgement.

Recognition was the last thing Catherine had expected from Logan after their heated encounter the night before, and she wrinkled her nose in confusion. She was even more startled when he finished with the cow and sauntered toward her, pulling off his leather gloves and slapping them against his dusty chaps.

"You can take my place," he said to Lucas, and the older man climbed the fence and dropped to the other side. After adjusting his neck bandana over his nose, he walked into the dust.

"I'm surprised to see you here," Logan said, swinging over the rail.

"Why? I'm interested in my uncle's ranch. If I'm going to make this my home, I want to know how everything functions."

"So you are determined to remain."

"Of course. I wouldn't have come otherwise."

Removing his hat, he ran his fingers through his hair. Beads of sweat clung to the dark strands. "Let's see if we can find some shade." When he reached for her arm, Catherine avoided his searching fingers, and he whistled between his teeth. "What do you think I'm going to do? Make love to you in front of the men."

"Of course not," she retorted. "I just think it would be better if you kept your hands off me."

Logan's lips quirked in a smile. "Are you telling me you are not totally indifferent to my touch?"

"You know I'm not," she snapped. There was no point in denying her attraction, especially after her reaction the night before. If she did, she would only be trying to fool herself.

They stopped beneath a stand of trees bordering a small stream not far from the cattle pens. Catherine sat on an isolated rock, careful to keep her distance from Logan. He flopped down in the short grass and leaned against a tree.

"Do you think your trip was worthwhile?" he asked, tipping his hat forward to hide his eyes.

Catherine reflected on her life with her aunts and what would have happened had she stayed in their home. Marriage to Duncan had promised nothing but a lifetime of misery. For a short time, she'd found happiness with Cameron, but that too had been an impossible future. There was nothing left for her in the East.

"There was no place else for me to go."

"Ah yes, I'd forgotten you were running away from something or someone," he baited. "Which was it?"

"My past is none of your business," she reminded him sharply.

"My, my, but you're sensitive about something." He tipped his hat back to give her a hard, searching look. "I wonder what secrets you have hidden away."

Catherine threw one of her hands on her hips. "I'm sorry to disappoint you, but there are no secrets that would interest you." She eyed him cautiously, wondering if she dare accuse him of the same thing. "I was wondering if there is something in your past that haunts you."

Logan pushed himself up on one arm. "What are you talking about?"

Catherine shook her head and her tawny hair

306

settled like a cloud over her shoulders. "I think you're hiding something, and I believe it has to do with a woman." She noticed the tightening of his jaw and knew she had hit a tender spot. "Perhaps there was something about your mother that upset you."

Throwing back his head, he laughed. "Sorry to disappoint you, but your imagination is taking control of your mind. . . . You are on the wrong track, but I have to get back to work and can't take the time to listen to your ridiculous theory." As he strode away, he turned and shouted, "Stay away from the pens. I don't want a repeat of yesterday."

Catherine silently fumed as she watched his retreat. Logan always managed to get the last word in, and she hated the way he could make her look like a fool. The bubbling stream stirred her interest and she decided to explore. She remembered what Logan had told her about snakes and she was careful as she cut a path to the bank. Although it was not a large stream, it was a source of water, and she had learned how precious it was in this part of the country. It had to have a beginning and an end, and she decided to ask her uncle if there was a lake on his land. If there was, she intended to use it in place of the tub at the house.

Picking up a handful of stones, she tossed them one by one into the water. With the exception of the noise from the cattle, it was a peaceful place, and she was grateful for the time alone.

It was well into the afternoon before she approached the chuck wagon for something to eat. Food was always available and plentiful, and she was delighted to find it lacked the spicy taste she'd become accustomed to in Juanita's cooking.

Dusk had settled when Catherine learned her uncle was ready to leave. Most of the men were staying the night, sleeping on bedrolls they carried on the back of their saddles. She did not envy them sleeping on the hard ground and was glad when they left camp for the ranch. There was just enough time to wash and change before Juanita was calling them for dinner.

When they'd finished eating, she joined her uncle on the patio. It was a clear, cool night, and the stars were plentiful in the dark sky. "Thanks for letting me go with you, Uncle Ben," Catherine said.

"You are welcome anytime."

"Is there a lake nearby?" she asked, thinking of the stream she'd seen that afternoon.

"Yes, there is. I can show it to you tomorrow, if you like." Shifting in his seat, he crossed his booted feet. "We'll be leaving on the cattle drive in the next few weeks. I hope you will find enough around here to keep you busy."

"Is everyone going?" she asked, not sure of being left alone on the ranch with Juanita. She was becoming more familiar with the West, but she wasn't foolish enough to think she didn't need protection.

"A few of the men will be remaining behind," he assured her.

It was on the tip of her tongue to ask if one of them would be Logan, but she thought better of it. She didn't want to give her uncle any hint that there might be something between them.

"Is it necessary for you to go?" she asked, thinking how she would miss having him around.

Ben shook his head. "It is imperative that I go. This has got to be a successful sale, and I want to make

308

sure everything is covered as expected." He winked at her. "Don't worry, Logan will make sure nothing happens to you while I'm gone."

A lump rose in Catherine's throat and she forced herself to swallow the rising panic. Logan was the last person she wanted to stay behind. Without her uncle, she wouldn't have any protection against his advances, and he could openly move in and out of her bedroom.

"I think I'd like to go with you," Catherine said eagerly. She could not risk being left behind if Logan was staying.

Her uncle smiled. "You've just made a very difficult trip, but going on a wagon train is nothing compared to a cattle drive. . . . No, I think you'd be better off to stay behind."

"Why don't you leave Lucas with me? Isn't it important to have your foreman along?"

There was a questioning light in her uncle's eyes. "Logan is responsible for the ranch in my absence. One of us must be here. I have explained the situation to him, and he knows how I want things handled."

There was an unusual tone in her uncle's voice, and it put Catherine on edge. "Are you worried about something happening?"

He swatted at a fly on his leg. "Catherine, in this part of the country you can never be sure about anything."

"I suspect there is more on your mind than you're telling me." She hesitated. It was not usual for her to intrude into someone's private business, but she had to know. "You've made a few comments that tell me something is not right. I've seen you tense and anxious." She paused to take a breath before plunging on. "You have already explained the importance of selling the cattle, but will it be the end of everything you've worked for if you don't?"

Her uncle sighed, and he suddenly looked ten years older. "Catherine, you are new to this way of life and I don't want to frighten you."

"You are scaring me now by not telling me what is happening. You're my family, and I care about you."

"Maybe you're right," he said, nodding. "About two months ago, someone rustled more than one hundred head of cattle. We managed to get some of them back, but I still suffered a loss. One of the smaller watering holes was poisoned and I lost more cattle. Two weeks before you came, someone broke into the ranch house and stole most of my cash."

Catherine was distraught to learn of her uncle's plight. "Is someone out to destroy you? Do you have enemies?"

He shrugged. "Things like this happen all the time. There isn't any real law and order. You have to take things into your own hands. The trouble is not just focused on me. My neighbor is having trouble."

Catherine's eyes widened. "You have neighbors?"

"Yes, but it's not like walking next door to see them. It takes most of the morning to get the their ranch. I'll have one of the boys take you over some day. It would give you another female to talk to."

Catherine was delighted at the prospect. "It sounds wonderful."

"Logan already knows where the ranch is, so he can take you while I'm gone."

Standing, Catherine stretched. "If we are going to the lake in the morning, I think I'd better get some sleep." She leaned forward and kissed her uncle's cheek.

He caught her hand when she started to leave. "I want to ask you something, but if you think I'm interfering, you can tell me to mind my own business." The seriousness of his tone frightened Catherine.

"What is troubling you?" she asked, dropping to her knees at his side.

"Is there something between you and Logan?"

Catherine could read neither approval nor disapproval on her uncle's face, and she was almost relieved that he had asked. Hiding her animosity toward Logan was becoming impossible. "From the time we met, Logan and I have been at each other's throats. There is something between us that creates friction." Catherine wasn't about to admit to their shared passion. It was a secret she wasn't ready to tell.

"Is that why you'd rather not be left here with him?" She nodded. "I won't pretend to be happy about this. I've become quite fond of the man. He really knows about ranching and has pulled a lot of weight off my shoulders."

"It wouldn't be fair to Logan if you let my prejudices influence your feelings for the man. This is your ranch, and I want you to employ a man who will help ease your burden." She lightly patted his hand. "Don't worry about me. Logan and I have drawn our battle lines, and we understand each other."

"Still, I can't help being concerned."

Catherine shrugged. "Who knows, maybe things will change between us?" She doubted anything could erase their spite for each other, but she wanted to give her uncle hope. He had enough problems with the ranch, and she didn't want him to take on the added worry of her relationship with his foreman. "I'll see you in the morning."

Catherine was ready and waiting by her horse when her uncle came outside the next morning. After a quick greeting, they mounted and rode out of the yard. Riding was becoming an easy chore, and she was surprised at how well she had made the adjustment to prolonged time in the saddle. Her muscles had tightened, making her slim figure even more attractive.

They took their time, and Ben pointed out landmarks and scenic points of interest. Without roads, it became essential to memorize the land and learn the movement of the sun.

The lake was due west and situated on a small rise. It was larger than Catherine had expected, and the beautiful blue water sparkled in the sun. Brush, trees and flowers covered most of the bank around it, although there were rocky ledges and areas where cattle and animals approached to drink.

"I never expected anything like this," she said with a pleased smile. Her love of the water went back to the pond near her aunts' house where she'd enjoyed the isolation.

"It is the only large water supply in this area, and that makes it very valuable. When the small bodies of water dry up, this is all the cattle have." He raised his arm and pointed to the stream running off the lake. "That is the stream by the cow pen. I own the lake, but I share it with my neighbors."

"That's generous of you," she said, but she already knew he was a charitable man.

"It's necessary if we are both going to survive."

They rode to the water and let the animals drink. "Is the lake deep?" she asked.

"Not near the bank," he explained. "Do you swim?"

She shuddered. "No. On the way out here, I almost drowned. Logan had to pull me out of the river. It was frightening."

Her news was a complete surprise. "I had no idea. I'm beginning to believe your trip was harder on you than I thought."

Catherine stared at the water. "I didn't know much of anything when I left your sisters' home. The things I've learned since then have been through experience. Perhaps that is the best way, but I've made a fool out of myself too many times."

"Everyone makes mistakes. I know I've made my share," he said, easing the horse back from the water. "Are you coming to the cow pens, or would you rather go home?"

"Could I stay here?" she pleaded. The prospect of spending time by the water was inviting.

"I don't know," he said, stroking his jaw.

"Please. I know I can find my way home. I remember everything you told me about the landmarks, and I promise to be back at the house by noon."

"I suppose it will be all right, but I'll be sending Lucas back to the ranch in an hour to make sure you're there."

"I will be," she answered, grinning. "Thanks, Uncle Ben."

After a quick wave, her uncle rode toward the cow pens and Catherine slid off her horse. She securely tied him to some brush to avoid the humiliation of having the mare return without her. It would only give Logan something else to laugh at.

Sitting on a nearby log, she removed her boots and socks. With her pant legs rolled up to her knees, she stepped into the water. It was probably fed by an underground stream and it was icy cold. Her toes curled in the mud as she reached forward to run her fingers across the moistness. It reminded her of the pond at her aunts' home. She had been an innocent maiden, raising her arms to the sky in worship of her freedom. Now she was a mature, experienced woman skilled in the ways of making love. She had already had two lovers and experienced more than most women her age.

She stepped forward, stubbing her toe on the edge of a large rock. Further exploration with her foot revealed a rock of some size, and Catherine stepped on it. She turned to get a view from all directions, and her weight caused the rock to shift. Screaming a quick, "Oh," her arms flew up in the air and she fell sideways into the waist deep water. She was soaked from her head to her toes when she finally got her feet beneath her and stood. Brushing the hair from her face, she stumbled toward the shore. She had almost reached the edge of the water when she stopped and focused on a man on horseback. For a few seconds she tensed, then her shoulders sagged with relief. A chuckle burst from Logan's throat and Catherine glared at him.

"What are you laughing at?" she barked, trying to restore some order to her soaked clothes.

"You. That was a very nice demonstration," he mocked.

His statement confirmed her fear that he had appeared in time to witness her fall into the water. Why did he always show up at the wrong time?

"What do you want?" she snapped, finally reaching the bank. Her clothes were a mess and clung provocatively to her figure.

"Very nice," Logan drawled, his eyes doing a leisurely sweep of her body.

Catherine raised her hands to shield herself. "Get out of here. I'd like some privacy."

He ignored her request. "I saw your uncle and he told me you were here. I thought I better stop and see how you are doing. I was certain you'd find yourself some trouble."

"I'm not in trouble," she denied. "I just slipped off a rock."

The quick smile came to the hard line of his lips. "I know, and it was quite a show."

Catherine responded to his teasing with a smile of her own. "I imagine I did look kind of silly."

"You should learn how to swim," Logan said, swinging off his horse. He removed his hat and hooked it over the saddle.

"Who is going to teach me?"

"How about me?"

"Are you serious?" she asked cautiously.

"Of course. Your clothes need to dry anyway."

She took a step backwards. "Are you suggesting that I swim without my clothes on?"

Logan arched one of his brows. "Have I shocked you?" There was a mocking hint in his voice. "I suppose you've never had the chance to swim naked. It's a wonderful sensation."

Catherine didn't need to be reminded of the sensuous feel of the water on her flesh. She had experienced it many times, and enjoyed the soothing touch. Had Logan not appeared, she would have removed her clothes and bathed while they dried. Now it was impossible. Despite their past lovemaking, she could never undress before him.

He reached for the buttons on her shirt. "What's the matter? Are you shy?"

"Don't, Logan," she said, brushing his hand away. "I don't want to go swimming with you."

His fingers became more insistent and he managed to break three buttons free and cup her breast before she jerked away from him, her eyes tawny flecks of rage. "I said no. You are not going to get your way with me." She stepped back. "I told you before I don't want to be used to satisfy your animal lust."

"Why not if it satisfies something in both of us?"

Catherine whirled around and presented him her back. "I don't want that kind of relationship with a man." The past that so often haunted her and had left scars in her memory created a stream of tears down her cheeks. "Please, just leave me alone."

"What are you afraid of?"

Catherine swung around. "What are *you* afraid of?" she threw back at him and got the satisfaction of seeing him flinch. Their eyes locked in silent battle, then Logan's hands fell to the buckle on his pants.

"Since I'm here, I intend to take a swim. Feel free to stay and watch."

Brushing her wet cheeks, she reached for her socks and boots. With her back to him, she put them on and buttoned her blouse. When she rose and turned, her breath lodged in her throat. Logan stood before her in all his manliness. Their eyes met, then hers broke free to skim the length of his nakedness. Something tightened in her chest as the familiar wave of longing washed over her. Her hands knew every muscle and line of his masculine length, and her body knew the weight of his. None of her past knowledge could prepare her for the dizzy awareness she experienced. There was no flat on the well-formed stomach or thighs, and his upper chest showed the strength of a man who had spent his life at hard, demanding labor.

"Are you sure you won't join me?" he asked, breaking the spell.

Catherine licked her dry lips. "No—No, I can't." Turning, she ran to her horse, mounted and without a backward glance rode away from the lake and her haunting desires.

Chapter Nineteen

It was ten minutes before Catherine slowed the horse to a walk. She felt as though she'd ben chased by the urgent need of her body. By appearing naked before her, Logan had brought her awareness of him into sharp focus. Her hunger for him frightened her. If he didn't have that barrier of contempt surrounding him, would she see him differently? Could she forget Cameron and the deceitful tricks he had played on her and start a new relationship with another?

Twenty minutes later, Catherine knew she was lost. She had left the lake in such a hurry, she had neglected to watch the markers her uncle had pointed out. She checked the position of the sun but without knowing the time of day, it was little use in telling her how to proceed. Turning the mare, she rode across the short grassland. When she emerged alongside a hill her hopes quickened. Perhaps she would see something from the top. The horse made the climb easily and Catherine reined her mare to a stop at the top. Below, resting along the sweep of the land, was a house, corral and barns. It was a spread equal to the size of her uncle's ranch, and she decided it must be the neighbor he had mentioned. Whoever lived there she was certain would offer help and comfort from the blazing sun.

There weren't any ranch hands visible when she rode into the yard and dismounted. After securing her horse to the rail, she brushed the dust from her already dried clothes and approached the front door. Two sharp knocks brought no response, so she banged harder against the wooden panel. She was about to try the back of the house when the door opened and she came face to face with a woman at least thirty years older than herself.

The woman smiled warmly, the door opening wider to admit Catherine. "Good mornin', lass. Welcome to my home."

The greeting was genuine and Catherine returned the smile, but the hairs along the back of her neck tingled in apprehension. There was a warning bell signaling in her mind, brought about by the sound of the woman's voice.

"I'm Catherine Winslow. Ben is my uncle. . . . I was out riding and got lost."

"Ach," the woman said. "Ye are nae far awa'." She reached out her hand. "Come in, lass." Catherine stepped inside, the tingling apprehension growing stronger. "I be glad to meet ye. Ben mentioned ye when he came doon the last time."

Catherine's eyes narrowed. "Who are you?"

"I be Alana MacLennan."

The color vanished from Catherine's cheeks and she dropped in a silent lump to the floor. A cold cloth against her forehead was the first thing she was aware of when she regained consciousness.

"How be ye feelin', lass?" Alana asked, smiling.

"Better," she muttered, pushing herself to a sitting position. "I'm sorry. I feel foolish for fainting like that."

"Ach, t'was the heat. 'Tis hard to get used to it."

Catherine wasn't about to tell her it had been her last name and not the heat that made her faint. She was still stunned to meet someone with the same last name as Cameron. "I think I'm strong enough to get up off the floor."

Alana slipped her hand under Catherine's arm to assist and even after she stood, Alana insisted on helping her to a chair. "I will get ye somethin' to drink."

"Thank you," Catherine responded. While Alana was gone, Cat's eyes darted around the room. The house was beautifully furnished, the wooden furniture polished and coordinated with the rugs. Ruffled curtains in the windows and tiny nicknacks around the room indicated a woman's touch.

Returning, Alana handed her a drink, and she took several sips before setting it down on a nearby table. "It tastes wonderful, thank you."

"Be there anythin' else I can get ye?"

"No, this is fine."

"Good. After ye have rested, I will take ye home."

"Are you here by yourself?" Catherine asked the question uppermost in her thoughts.

"Most of the men are out workin'. I dona mind bein' alone."

Catherine curled her fingers around the arm of the chair. "Even with help this looks like a large ranch for a woman to run."

"Ach," she said, shaking her head. "I can see ye uncle didna' tell ye anythin' about us."

"He mentioned neighbors and promised to bring me over for a visit. Other than Juanita, I guess you are the only female company for miles."

Alana smiled. "Now I have ye. I have been here less than a year myself. The hired help doesna come to the house much and 'tis lonely. With my son gone, I feel isolated."

"Son?" Catherine asked, her mouth becoming suddenly dry.

"Aye, I have a son Cameron."

If Catherine hadn't been sitting, she was certain her legs would have buckled beneath her. "Cameron? You have a son Cameron MacLennan?"

Alana cocked her head to the side in confusion. "Aye, but he be gone now."

A clammy sweat broke out along the back of Catherine's neck. She didn't want to show too much interest in the son of a woman she'd just met, but Cameron MacLennan was not a common name. "Will he be home soon?"

The woman's blue-green eyes softened. "Cameron be gone for more than a year. He went to the East on business and so far he hasna returned. He posted a letter to me from Virginia more than a year ago, and he saed he wouldna be home for several months. I came here after he left, so I be anxious to see him."

There could be no mistake, the man Catherine had loved was Alana's son. Stunned, she sank against the back of the chair. Never had she imagined her uncle's neighbor would be the mother of the man she thought she'd married. Her love for Cameron had been intense, yet at times when she thought back to it, she wondered if anything so painful could be real.

"Be somethin' wrong? Ye look pale." There was concern in the older woman's voice and Catherine glanced up.

Alana's hair was a very dark brown and covered with flecks of gray. Her eyes, though not sharp in color, were a deep shade of blue-green. Did Cameron have any of her features? Did the face she had touched in the darkness resemble this woman?

"Catriona, are ye all right?"

The Gaelic use of her name washed over her in a flood of remembering, and she quickly rose. "I should be getting back to my uncle's ranch. I promised him I'd be back by noon and I'm already late. I don't want to create any problems by being gone."

Alana looked at her oddly. "Are ye sure 'tis nae troublin' ye?"

Catherine shook her head. All she wanted to do was get away so she could reflect on the disturbing discovery. "I'm just tired."

"I'll get my hat," Alana said and disappeared to another part of the house.

They were walking down the path to Catherine's horse when they spotted a rider in the distance. Recognizing Lucas, she smiled her relief. At least Logan hadn't come looking for her. Lucas slowed the horse as it came into the yard, his gaze gliding over the women. As he came closer, Catherine recognized an unusual tightness around his mouth and a haunted look in his eyes. It was not like him to be so troubled, but over the past months she'd given him reason to be anxious about her. Catherine bound forward as he swung from the saddle.

"I saw Logan and followed your tracks here." His voice sounded forced. "Did you get lost?"

"Am I going to get scolded?" she teased, trying to

erase the tension from his face.

Lucas's gaze slid past Catherine to Alana. "No—no, of course not. I know how unpredictable you can be." Catherine didn't mind Lucas's teasing. There was nothing derogatory behind it like there was with Logan. "Is—is this your neighbor?" he asked, nodding toward Alana as he removed his hat.

Catherine touched her hand to her forehead. "Forgive me. Alana, this is Lucas." She paused and looked at her friend. "You never did tell me your last name."

Lucas chuckled. "Last names aren't important out here." He hesitated. "You'd never remember it anyway."

Catherine shrugged. "Lucas, this is Alana Mac-Lennan. She lives here with her son who is away on business."

"It is a pleasure to meet you, ma'am." The haunted look had left Lucas's pale eyes and instead, Catherine saw a flicker of interest.

"Thank you," Alana said quietly, returning the same curious glance.

"Alana," Catherine said, and the older woman's gaze left Lucas's face. "Thank you for all you've done."

"Will ye come and visit me again soon?" Alana asked, and Catherine agreed. The older woman turned to Lucas. "Would ye like somethin' cool to drink before ye start back?"

"Thank you, I think I would. It has been a long, dusty morning." Lucas handed Catherine the reins of his horse. "Take good care of Pancho while I'm gone. I'll only be a minute." Surprising at not being invited

323

to join them, Catherine accepted the reins and watched them walk to the house.

It was nearly twenty minutes before Lucas stepped back outside with Alana. "Thanks Catherine, I was thirsty," he whispered in her ear and took the reins. "Branding is a dusty job."

Swinging into the saddle, Catherine renewed her promise to visit Alana as soon as possible. Lucas did not pursue conversation on the return to the ranch and Catherine was grateful for the silence. There was so much she didn't understand about her meeting with Cameron's mother. If she remained at her uncle's home, she would see him when he returned home. Would she fall into his arms, vowing the love she once felt? Or would she hate him for his deceit?

Another nagging suspicion planted itself in her mind. Had their meeting at her aunts' home been planned? She reflected on the night Cameron had appeared to save her from the attack. Never once had she questioned his sudden arrival. She had only welcomed the rescue and comfort offered. He had been very secretive about himself, even to the point of hiding his physical identity. What did it all mean? Could her uncle supply answers to her plaguing questions? What would he say if she told him about Cameron tricking her into a false marriage?

She was a bundle of nerves by the time she reached the ranch. Logan was casually leaning against the patio support when she swung off her horse. He immediately noted her heightened color.

"Did you have a nice ride?" he quizzed as she started to pass him. When she didn't answer, he grabbed her arm. "I asked if you had a nice ride."

Catherine snatched her arm from his grip. "Leave me alone."

His eyes narrowed, noting her agitated expression. "What's the matter?"

"None of your business," she spouted and ran inside.

Once in her room, Catherine couldn't relax and she paced the room. Memories of her past flew up to haunt her. When she left the East, she thought she was leaving her misery behind. Instead, it had followed her to create more havoc with her life. She would never be able to relax until she had answers to the questions plaguing her thoughts. The future frightened her. For the most part, the past had been a living nightmare, and now she was once again caught up in the feelings she had tried to lock away. She never expected Cam to reenter her life.

Her teeth dug into her lower lip. There had to be a solution. If she discussed her problems with her uncle would he be able to ease some of her uncertainty? Her uncle's open, casual, concerned nature made him someone she felt she could talk to, but she could never tell him everything. Parts of her life were just too personal and private to discuss.

She skipped dinner and when it was dark, she put on a jacket and slipped outside. She walked away from the main house to a secluded area where she would not be disturbed. Stopping by a tree, she stared at the sky. Did she dare go to her uncle for an explanation?

A quiet noise behind her made her wheel around. Logan stood a foot away from her, his thumbs caught in his belt loops.

"You startled me!"

"I saw you leave the house," he said, his hands

falling to his sides as he stepped forward. "Are you upset about something?"

She flicked her long hair away from her cheek. "No. Why do you think I am?"

She felt the piercing blue eyes on her face. "It's just a feeling I have. You were agitated when you got back from the ride. Were you still mad at me for asking you to come swimming?"

The incident at the lake was the farthest thing from her mind, and she laughed softly. "No. I'd forgotten all about it."

"Good. I'd still like to teach you some time."

Catherine shrugged. "Perhaps." There was a serious note in his voice that surprised her.

"Did you enjoy your ride this afternoon? Lucas told me you'd gotten lost."

Catherine bristled. Was he making fun of her? "It is your fault I lost my direction," she snapped. "You made me so mad, I forgot to watch the landmarks when I left the lake."

"Hey Cat, slow down. I'm not poking fun at you." He reached out and caught her chin. "Friends?" he asked to banish the battle lines.

Catherine had never thought of Logan as a friend and didn't know if she could. There was too much rivalry between them, but if she stayed at the ranch with him, there would have to be some sort of compromise between them.

"Friends," she muttered softly, and Logan let his hand fall.

"Would you like to walk?" he asked, taking her arm and slipping it through his.

Baffled by his casual demeanor, all she could do

was follow. They walked in a wide circle around the ranch, avoiding all evening activity. Catherine, aware of Logan's arm against her, was puzzled by his change of mood. Perhaps this was just a side of him she didn't know.

"Lucas told me he found you at the MacLennan ranch."

"I stumbled on it by accident, and Lucas tracked me there from the lake."

"The ranch is as large as your uncle's. I've been over there a few times to check on things and get acquainted with the men. Their cattle will be joining your uncle's herd for the trip to the market."

Catherine remembered Alana mentioning the men were busy, but she had not made the connection. "I didn't know."

"It's going to be a large herd, but we've got the men to handle it."

Catherine moistened her lips. "My uncle told me you wouldn't be going." It still troubled her to know he'd be remaining behind with her.

"No," Logan agreed. "He wants me to stay here and take care of things." Unconsciously, Catherine's nails dug into his jacket. "Does my staying trouble you?" He stopped walking and turned to look at her. "I can see it does." His hands slid up her arms. "My visits to your room won't be any more frequent with him gone. I'll be too busy. This is a large ranch and I have the added responsibility of taking care of the MacLennan ranch while Alana's son is gone. Your uncle is fulfilling that promise now."

"I didn't know," she muttered, her lips suddenly thick. She hadn't realized her uncle's friendship with the neighboring ranch was so involved.

"I'm surprised he didn't mention it. In this part of the country friendships are important." His hands slid along her shoulders. "He did mention the ranch to you, didn't he?"

She shrugged. "He said he had neighbors, but until today, I hadn't met anyone."

Logan chuckled. "Lucas has been asking a lot of questions about Alana. He's never shown so much interest in a woman. I'd say she definitely left an impression on him. Do you suppose it could be the soft Scottish accent?"

Catherine didn't want to continue talking about the MacLennans, but she didn't know how to end the conversation without making Logan wonder why it upset her.

"Alana seems to be a warm person." She was fond of Lucas and hoped he could find happiness with a woman. "Has Lucas ever been married?"

Logan shrugged. "He's never said, but I think there was someone special in his life when he was a young man."

"Perhaps Alana will provide a romantic interest."

"Who knows," he said, laughing. "Maybe her son will be your type. We received word tonight that he is in Independence and will be home in two months. You'll get to meet your new neighbor before your uncle gets back, and I will lose half my responsibility." His hands began a slow sensuous motion over her shoulders and down her back. "It will free up more of my evenings to visit you."

Catherine's body tightened like a coil. Cameron, the man she once believed held the future of her dreams, was coming home. "Relax," he muttered and continued his coaxing motion. "You're too tense."

Her tawny eyes widened. Logan was going to help out at the MacLennan ranch until Cameron came home. When he arrived, the two men would meet, and Catherine would be caught in the middle between two men. Cameron, with his gentle persuasive lovemaking, who first taught her the meaning of passion; and Logan, who promised everything with his hands, lips and body. What was she going to do?

A soft anguished cry broke from her lips. Cameron was coming home to torture her memory with their nights of passion and desire. She glanced up sharply at Logan but didn't really see his face. Instead she saw the mocking twist of his mouth and his piercing blue eyes, which were covered by the silhouette of Cameron's head. Her two lovers would meet and tear her apart with their wanting—two men so different, she couldn't believe she could be drawn to both.

Throwing her head back, she opened her mouth and screamed. The sound shattered the stillness, the tortured cry for help echoing across the land. But there was no answer to her call, there was only the haunting knowledge of what was to come. Her future weighted down on her until it surrounded her in darkness, and she fell forward into Logan's arms.

When she woke, she was in her bed and her uncle was at her side. "What happened?" she asked, forgetting her thoughts before she fainted.

"You'll have to ask Logan," he said, indicating the man at the side of the room.

Her gaze shifted to the man at her right. Logan's face was an emotionless mask, not giving any hint of what had happened. Slowly, Catherine's memory returned, and the dawning recognition in her eyes brought a smile to Logan's mouth.

"Catherine, what happened?" her uncle persisted. "You were screaming. What frightened you?"

Catherine wasn't ready to confide in her uncle. She still needed time to think. "Don't look so worried, Uncle Ben. I just saw a snake."

She stole a glance at Logan, silently hoping he would back up her story. "Cat has never been a lover of animals, serpents, or insects that scurry about in the dark," Logan supplied.

Her uncle shook his head. "I'm glad that was all. You really had me scared." He patted her arm. "You better stick close to the house after dark. My heart can't take much more activity like tonight," he said, rising. "Try and get some rest. I'll see you in the morning." He glanced at his foreman. "Coming, Logan?"

Logan straightened his tall form and followed her uncle to the door. When they were gone, Catherine breathed a sigh of relief and sat up. Why had she reacted to Logan's discussion about the MacLennans like she did? Cameron had been gentle and understanding, and she should have no reason to fear him.

Her head jerked to the side as the outside door to her room opened and Logan stepped inside. Pushing the door closed, he leaned ·.gainst the wall and crossed his arms over his chest. "Do you want to tell me what really happened out there?"

"No, I don't," she said, hating to be under the scrutiny of the piercing eyes. "Thanks for supporting my story about the snake."

Straightening, he strolled toward the bed. "I gathered there was something about the whole incident you didn't want your uncle to know." He regarded her thoughtfully. "Am I right?"

She nodded. "There are some things I need to work out in my own mind before I talk to him."

"Does it have anything to do with what we were discussing? You were tense."

Catherine looked up at him. "Can we just leave it alone, Logan? I can't talk about it."

He shrugged. "There are things that bother you, Cat. I've seen it in your eyes. Talk to your uncle about whatever is troubling you, but don't keep it inside. If you do, you might be sorry."

Turning, he sauntered to the door. "Logan," she called, as he pulled the door open. "Thanks for keeping my secret." Nodding, he vanished into the night.

Unconsciously, her fingers grasped the ring around her neck. She wore it as a symbol of Cam's deceit and her hatred for him. In a few weeks he would be home and the reminder would be a reality. Slipping the ring from her neck, she dropped it in the drawer of the night table. The memory of what he'd done to her was firmly embedded in her mind, and she no longer needed the reminder.

Stretching out on the bed, she thought of Logan. She hadn't expected him to be so considerate and to comply with her wishes. He was right about talking to her uncle. It was something she would have to do, but it could wait until morning. Right now, she needed a good night of rest.

Chapter Twenty

In the morning, when Catherine finally gathered the courage to talk to her uncle, she learned he had already left to check on the branding. Logan and Lucas were outside saddling their horses.

"Are you going to join us this morning?" Lucas asked. "We are riding over to the MacLennan ranch."

It was the last place she wanted to go, but she was curious about Cameron. He wasn't due back for weeks and she could use the time to learn about him without anyone knowing what her relationship with him had been.

Logan was watching her make the decision with undisguised interest. When she agreed, he walked past her to get her mare. Stopping briefly, he whispered in her ear, "Maybe we can start our swimming lessons today." He was gone before she could respond and returned minutes later with her horse.

On their ride to the ranch, Catherine paid strict attention to the land and made note of landmarks to tell her how to get home. Alana came outside when they rode into the yard, smiling warmly at the men and asking Catherine into her home.

She was making bread, so Catherine joined her in the kitchen. "It smells good in here," she said, sitting on a stool at the side of the table.

"Aye, I've been up for hours. The brandin' be almost finished, and the men will be returnin' tonight. I want to have somethin' special for them."

"Can I help?" Catherine offered, hating to sit idle while the older woman worked.

"I've got some pies to take out of the oven, so ye can work on the bread."

Jumping off her stool, she watched Alana dump the dough on the flour covered table. On the trip west, she'd made batter bread, but had never worked with dough before. She'd seen Effie make it, and it looked easy enough. Alana went to the stove and Catherine rubbed flour on her palms.

It was not as simple as it looked. Despite the flour, the dough kept getting stuck to the wood, and it lay like a blob instead of conforming to a nice round shape. She laid it over her thumb and tried to push with her palm, but the dough splattered out on the table in a flat lump. She tried again, lifting the back up over the front. Unfortunately, she pulled it too far, and the momentum carried it off the table and onto the floor.

"Oh no," she cried. "Look what I've done." Alana, in the process of pulling a pie out of the oven, turned and looked over her shoulder. "I'm so sorry," Catherine apologized.

Alana smiled. " 'Tis nae to worry about. We can make more."

Catherine had just bent over to retrieve the ruined dough when booted feet sounded on the kitchen floor. Glancing up, her heart sank at the sight of Logan.

"Been trying your skills in the kitchen?" he mocked.

Glaring at him, she lifted the dough and dropped it

back in the bowl. "It was an accident," she excused.

"I'm sure it was," he drawled humorously.

Alana turned from the oven. "Dona tease her, Logan."

"Yes ma'am," he said, removing his hat. "I knocked at the door but no one answered. I need to know what you want done with the calves that won't be going with the herd?"

Alana frowned. "I came after Cameron left, and I dona know. I'll trust ye judgment," she said and turned to Catherine. "Did ye hear the good news? My son be comin' home."

Catherine forced herself to remain calm. "I heard last night. You must be very happy."

"I canna wait 'till ye meet him. He be a fine lad."

"I'll be glad when he returns home to ease the work load," Logan said, reminding Catherine he was still in the room.

"Are ye bein' worked too hard?" Alana quizzed quickly.

Logan's eyes met Catherine's. "I'm not being worked too hard, but once your son is back, it will free up my evenings. And I have something I want to do."

Logan had warned Catherine his visits to her bed would increase once his responsibilities slacked off, and his statement reinforced his wishes. It also reminded her of the two men who desired her. Although she hadn't seen Cameron for months, she doubted she would ever forget the passion they shared. It had been good for both of them. Through marriage and love, she had invited Cameron to her bed. She had never extended the invitation to Logan, yet she felt sure he would not be brushed aside.

Eventually, the two men would meet, and the thought sent a wave of terror through her body.

"Lucas will be taking care of the repairs around the house. Ladies," he said, setting his hand back on his head. "if you need anything, call." Turning, he left.

"Ye uncle was lucky to find Logan when he did," Alana said, removing the ruined dough and preparing to make more. "He recently lost his foreman, and we've had trouble wi' rustlin'. I understand he was wi' ye on the wagon train."

"He was the scout. I rode with Lucas."

"Yesterday when I offered Lucas a drink, we had a few minutes to talk. He seems like a very interesting man," she said thoughtfully. "Do ye know him well?"

"All I know is that he and Logan have ridden together for years and have a deep friendship. He has been good to me, and I look upon him as a father figure."

Alana looked up quickly. "I understand ye lost ye father when ye were young. It must have been hard for ye."

"It's all in the past," Catherine said. "I came here to start a new life."

" 'Tis the perfect place to do it, and I have come here to do the same thing. I just wish things were more settled." She dumped some flour into a bowl and added water. "There has been trouble since Cameron left."

"Why did your son go East?" Catherine asked, hoping she did not appear too nosey, but determined to learn all she could about Cameron.

"He had business and from the letter I received, I think he met with success." Catherine wondered if she had anything to do with his reasons for the trip. If she was, she couldn't believe he'd been successful. "Cameron said he won back his losses from the stolen cattle."

"Won his losses?" she repeated in confusion.

"Aye, he won it gamblin'. Cameron likes to play, and he's good at it, but he prefers ranchin'."

Catherine nibbled her lip thoughtfully. Had Cameron left her on those cold nights to play cards? Had his business taken him to other towns and more gambling halls? Darrell had been a gambler with a Scottish accent. Was there a connection?

"Lass, what be troublin' ye?" Alana asked when she saw Catherine's brows drawn together.

She laughed lightly. "Running a ranch like this must be difficult," she said, to put her thoughts on other things.

Alana shook her head. " 'Tis nae harder than any other. 'Twill be fine as long as ye uncle continues to supply Cameron with water. If he didna, Cam would lose everythin'."

"I understand your herd is going to market with Ben's."

"Aye. Everythin' but the wee ones. We can get a good price if we take them to California." Thousands of people were trying to strike it rich in the gold fields and beef would bring a prime rate.

"I wanted to go along, but my uncle said it would be too hard and dangerous."

"Aye, 'tis nae place for a woman. Ye can come and stay with me. I would enjoy the company."

Catherine swallowed thickly. She couldn't be in this house when Cameron came home. What would he think? Would he want her for his wife? Did she want it herself? If he hadn't deceived her, she would want him with all her heart. Now, besides her bitter memories, Logan was a shadow in her life and it confused her.

Fortunately, Lucas arrived at the right time and she didn't have to respond. While Alana gave instructions on the work to be done, Catherine slipped outside and walked around the house. It was a beautiful home, warm and welcoming. The men were working on some horses in one of the corrals, and Catherine paused to watch. After an hour, she returned to the house.

She joined Alana for a cool drink and slice of pie, and it was mid-afternoon before Logan rode by and told her it was time to leave. Lucas was going to stay behind and finish his work, so just the two of them rode out of the yard.

"Feel like going swimming?" he asked, heading toward the lake.

"That depends," Catherine replied with hesitation. "Are you going to teach me to swim or are you out to satisfy your lust?"

Logan threw her a sideways glance. "Would you blame me if I tried both?"

Catherine laughed at his honesty. "I'll go on the condition that you keep your hands off me."

He paused to consider the request. "I'll try." It was the closest he would come to a commitment, and she was satisfied.

The water was freezing, but Catherine still stepped into the wetness. Logan cuffed his pants to his knees and joined her. "Swimming would be more fun," he argued.

"Yes, but I'm not in the mood to get my clothes wet."

His gaze was suggestive. "You don't have to. . . . take them off."

Backing up, she raised her hands in protest. "You promised." She stumbled over a rock, catching her balance just in time to prevent herself from getting soaked. Logan grabbed for her and she playfully avoided his grasp. Turning, she raced through the water with Logan on her heels. They were both soaked by the time he finally caught her. His expression was serious when he looked into her eyes. He was leaning forward to touch her lips when the horses whinnied and jerked against their reins. On sheer reaction, his thumb released the catch on his gun and his palm closed over the handle. He quickly scanned the area around the watering hole for danger. Seeing nothing out of the usual, he ran to the bank to quiet the disturbed animals.

"What's the matter?" Catherine asked, following him.

"There must be an animal around. It's probably coming in for a drink."

Catherine edged closer to Logan and his arm came around her shoulders protectively. A few seconds later, he pointed to a rocky incline one-hundred feet from them. Moving cautiously toward the water was a golden-brown cat. The animal paused, his head raised, and turned toward the horses and spectators.

"He's beautiful," Catherine muttered, awed by the beauty of the wild animal.

"Beautiful and dangerous," Logan agreed. "He's a lot like you, Cat."

"Me?" she quizzed, turning in the circle of his arms. His fingers tangled in her hair. "Your hair has the same coloring, and if you ever got close to one of those cats, you'd see flecks of gold in the eyes, just like yours. Beautiful but dangerous," he muttered again to himself.

"I'm not dangerous," she protested, puzzled by his statement.

His voice hardened and there was an angry glint in his eyes. "You're dangerous because you're a woman reaching out to capture and de—" Logan threw her from him and untied the horses.

Catherine was stunned by his statement. It was the closest he had ever come to admitting the reason for his hatred toward her. Logan had almost confided in her. What a wealth of understanding it would be if she could understand this man's bitterness. It might also provide the basis for a whole new outlook toward him.

Their return to the ranch was filled with tension. Logan never glanced her way, and she felt the barrier of hate surrounding both of them. He was a puzzling man and she doubted she'd ever understand him.

At dinner her uncle asked her about the Mac-Lennan ranch. "I hope you and Alana will see a lot of each other while I'm gone. It can get lonely for you."

"She asked me to stay with her," Catherine offered without committing herself to the plan.

"I'm glad you and Alana are getting along," he said, smiling. "You've certainly brightened this house since you came."

"I'm very happy to be here," she assured him, feeling a bond toward the uncle she had missed for years.

"I hope you and Logan have stopped quarreling. I

don't want the two of you fighting when I'm away."

"Don't worry. We won't." She reflected on the way Logan had treated her at the lake. For a time, there had been a playful companionship between them, but she always had to be ready to draw the lines of war.

"Logan has been a big help to me, and I know he has pulled the load off Alana's shoulders. When she first came here, I thought she was too soft to survive. I was wrong. She's a tough woman."

Catherine was once again reminded of Cameron's return. There were questions to ask her uncle and hopefully answers to ease her mind. "Uncle Ben—I need to talk to you."

He threw his napkin on the table and leaned back. "I'm here to listen whenever you're ready to talk."

"Now?" she asked, afraid her nerve would desert her.

"Fine. Do you want to go outside?"

After putting on a jacket to ward off the autumn chill, she followed her uncle outside. When they were seated, Ben leaned forward and took his niece's hands. "What's on your mind?"

The sound of thundering hoofs interrupted Catherine's response and they glanced up as Logan rode up and reined in his horse. With a quick glance, he took in the cozy atmosphere.

"There has been an accident on the range. Joel's horse went down and he's hurt bad."

Her uncle rose. "I'm sorry, Catherine. I have to go."

"I understand. I hope your man is all right," she said to his retreating back.

"I get the feeling I interrupted something cozy. Were you about to take my advice and confide in your uncle?" he asked from his horse.

She rose. "We'll never know now," she flung at him and retreated to the house.

She was already in bed when her uncle returned so she didn't see him until breakfast. When she joined him at the table, he apologized for the interruption. "I know you were troubled last night, and I'm sorry we couldn't talk."

"How is Joel?" she asked, remembering their meeting at the bunkhouse.

"He broke his leg and sprained his arm. He'll be laid up for weeks." He sighed. "He is one of my best hands."

"I'm sorry, Uncle Ben. I can't take his place but I'd like to help."

"Thank you Catherine, but we'll manage." He took several sips of his coffee. "If you'd still like to talk, I'd be willing to give you time this morning."

Catherine hesitated. There were still many questions on her mind and she knew she wouldn't relax until she had answers. It was time to face her doubts. "I'd like that."

"Good. I'd hoped you'd agree. Logan and Lucas have gone to the MacLennan ranch to make the final arrangements for the cattle drive. Do you think you could find your way back to the ranch from the lake? I thought we should do our talking where there is less chance of being disturbed."

Catherine couldn't think of a better place. "I'll get my hat."

Her anxiety didn't begin to build until they crested the small rise and saw the lake. Her uncle picked a small rock-filled area where they could sit above the water. It was the highest point at the lake and would give them a wonderful view of the surrounding land. Catherine made the short climb unassisted and flopped down on a rock.

"What is troubling you?" he asked, leaning against an odd shaped boulder.

Catherine drew her knees up and wrapped her arms around her legs. "Do you know why Cameron Mac-Lennan went east?" she asked bluntly.

Her uncle whistled softly. "You come right to the point, don't you gal."

Catherine raised her head. "Did his business have anything to do with me?" There was such a tightness in her throat, it made speech difficult.

Her uncle pushed his hat back and gave her a clear shot of his eyes. "He didn't go east because of you, but he knew where you were living," he said, watching the conflicting emotions on his niece's face. "Did you meet Cameron while he was there?"

Her gaze fell to the rock-filled dirt at her feet. "Yes."

"Do you want to tell me about it?" he coaxed.

"You already know your sisters arranged a marriage for me. The night of the engagement party, I took a walk through the garden." She covered her eyes with her hand. It was horrible even now to remember how useless her struggles had been against the stronger man. Even when Logan had assaulted her, the same cowering fear had not existed, and she contributed it to the loss of her innocence by Cam. "A guest attacked me and tried—" Her uncle's sharp breath caused her to glance up. "Nothing happened. A man came out of the shadows and fought him off. The man was

342

Cameron."

Her uncle had a pleased, satisfied expression on his face. "Did you see him often after that?"

"Your sisters would not have permitted it, but we met secretly in the garden." Her voice changed to one of wishful longing. She wanted to confide in her uncle, he had to know the whole truth. "I was desperate for comfort and understanding and Cameron provided it. I fell in love with him," she said, smiling at the memory of her deep feelings.

Her uncle dropped to her side. "I'm so pleased to hear that. Cameron is a wonderful man. You couldn't have made a better choice." He looked at his niece and noticed her smile did not touch her eyes. "What is it? Didn't Cameron return your feelings?"

Her lower lip trembled as she bitterly recalled his careful coaxing manner and the way he had deceived her. "I thought he did. I trusted him and I believed we would have a future together."

"What happened? Why did you run away?"

"Cameron knew I was being forced into a marriage I hated, and he asked me to wed him. I loved him so much and he gave my future new hope." She was unable to stop the scalding tears pouring down her cheeks. The pain was as intense as the day she had learned of his deceit.

"If you loved him, then why didn't you marry him?" he asked, concerned and confused about his niece.

"We arranged to meet late one night at the church. Because of Duncan and your sisters, we had to be married secretly. The church was crowded, so I was taken to the garden and we were married in the darkness."

Smiling, her uncle took her hand. "I didn't know you were Cameron's wife. Alana will be thrilled to have you in the family."

A sob broke from her throat and her shoulders shook with bitter sobs. "I loved him intensely. I waited for him every night." There was no stopping her now. She was going to tell him the whole truth in the hope of lifting some of the burden from her shoulders. "He was tender and gentle when he came to my room. I never once doubted his feelings." When she paused, he handed her handkerchief and she wiped her eyes.

"Tell me everything, Catherine."

"Cameron had to go away on business, and I stayed behind at your sister's home. No one knew about my marriage and plans for my wedding to Duncan continued. The date for the ceremony changed and was to occur before Cameron returned. I couldn't stay, so I went back to the church where we were married." She brushed her cheeks. "The wedding had been fake; the ceremony was never real. Cameron had deceived and left me. I was carrying his child. I needed help, so I came to you."

Her uncle drew her into his arms. "My dear Catherine. I didn't know you'd been through such torment. What happened to the baby?"

"The flatboat I obtained passage on was wrecked, and I lost the infant." Her sobs became broken gulps for air. Her bitter memories of Cameron had been shared with another, and now someone could help shoulder her anguish.

"What are you feelings for Cameron? Do you still love him?"

She brushed her long hair from her cheek. "Everything has become so complicated. I tried to put Cameron and the passion we shared out of my mind. I was burned by his deceit and convinced myself I hated him. I feel so much resentment and bitterness toward him, I don't know if the love I felt for him is dead or just smoldering beneath my hurt." She looked at her uncle for help. "After all the pain he's caused me, I should be sure of my hate."

He looked at his niece turning to him for answers. He didn't want to fail her. "Love is often challenged by misunderstandings. Through your love, you have to believe and trust."

"Are you saying I shouldn't feel hurt and bitter? I did trust him, but he fooled me."

"Are you going to give Cameron a chance to explain?"

"With him living so close, there won't be much way to avoid him." She clutched her uncle's sleeve. "I'm frightened."

"Once you talk to him, things might be explained."

Shaking her head, she pulled out of his arms. When Cameron returned, it would only introduce new, confusing problems. "It's not going to be that easy. There could be trouble," she said, thinking of Logan's explosive temper. She didn't know what he would do if challenged for rights for her bed. Logan didn't appear to be the jealous type, but he was unpredictable in regards to women.

"You see—ah—Logan and I have—"

Her uncle's eyebrows shot up in surprise. "Logan—but I thought the two of you hated each other?"

"We do. I don't know if it's me he hates or all women, but after we're together he hates himself for taking me."

"And what are your feelings? Do you really dislike the man?"

Cameron had been the gentle and persuasive lover, while Logan exhibited a wild animal-like passion that she responded to with equal eagerness. "I don't know. My experience with Cameron has left me bitter and wary toward men. My dislike—my fear—" She paused to consider her own admission. Did she hate him or fear him because he represented a threat to the defense she'd erected to keep from feeling? Logan had found her vulnerability and through it made her awareness of him an undeniable need. It was a frightening realization. "He has made me need him."

Rising, her uncle shook his shead. "Both Logan and Cameron are good men."

"But they are so different," she protested. "How can I be drawn to two men who are opposites?"

Her uncle's face took on an embarrassed flush. "There must be something about both of them that appeals to you. You need to talk to another woman. Why not go see Alana? She might be able to help you."

Catherine was appalled. Alana was Cameron's mother. She could never discuss her relationship with Cameron, then proceed to talk about Logan. It was unthinkable.

"I can't Uncle Ben, and I want your promise not to say anything."

"You have my confidence," he assured her, but he wasn't happy about her decision. "There are some things you don't understand about Cameron. Once I straighten them out you might comprehend his actions and perhaps you'll be able to make a choice between the men."

Turning away, her uncle dropped his hand into his pocket. "Cameron is a good man—one of the few I would trust with my life. We settled here about the same time," he said, turning to face her.

A sharp crack and the strangled sound of his voice made Catherine glance up. There was a funny, dazed expression on her uncle's face. His eyes were wide, his mouth open and trembling as he tried to speak. Jumping up, Catherine ran toward him. There was another sharp explosion and his body twisted.

"Uncle Ben," she screamed, raising her arms. Staggering, he reached for her support. He was a large man and his momentum pushed them back. She gripped his shoulders and a warm liquid spread over her palm.

"Catherine," he choked. "Get down."

There was another sharp retort and his body jerked forward, carrying both of them toward the edge of the rocks. Below them the water glimmered invitingly. Catherine used all her strength to push him back, but he was too strong, too heavy for her slight frame, and they went backwards off the cliff.

The distance to the water was not far, but Catherine lost her grip on her uncle. Water closed over her face, filling her open mouth with the icy liquid. She went down, the water covering her hair and twisting it around her head like a weighted mask. She hit the bottom, her legs pushing hard to force her head to the surface. Tearing the water and hair from her eyes, she tried to see where she was. She went down again, she estimated it was two feet before she hit bottom and could push herself back up. This time she hit her shoulder on something and reached out to clutch the massive boulder.

Exhausted and frightened, she clung for life. Overcoming her shock, she scanned the area for Ben. He was a short distance away, wedged between two rocks. Catherine twisted to her left to grab hold of an adjacent rock. The boulders reached into the water from the stony shore and offered a path. She was gasping for breath when she finally reached her uncle. His face was ashen and she couldn't tell if he was breathing.

"Uncle Ben, Uncle Ben," she screamed, but he remained unresponsive. Fitting her arm across his chest and over his side, she tried to pull him free. Her delicate positioning in the deep water and his position between the rocks prohibited her from getting a sturdy enough grip to move him. There were tears of panic when she pulled her arm across his chest. When her hand left his shirt, it was covered with a wet, sticky substance. She could only stare at the blood in horror before dashing her fingers through the water to make the red disappear. She had been in the West long enough to know the sharp sounds had been gunfire. Her uncle had been shot.

Catherine leaned against his chest to listen for his heart beat, but water slopped into her ear and made it impossible. She had to have help; she would never move him alone. She briefly laid her hand on his shoulder before reaching for the next rock to take her toward shore. It was a long difficult process, but at last she stumbled into waist deep water and staggered to the shore.

Exhausted, but urged by fear and love, she stumbled to her horse and pulled herself up on its back. She hesitated long enough to get her bearings. The MacLennan ranch was closer, and that's where she would find Logan and Lucas. She rode the mare hard, the wind whipping thorugh her wet clothes and throwing her hair out behind her. Tears dried on her cheeks and she leaned against the mare in determination. She crested a small rise and the ranch sprang into view. Screaming Logan's name, she galloped into the yard and slid off her horse. Logan ran out of the barn, his blue eyes filled with questions.

"What happened, Cat?" he asked, supporting her trembling figure. His gaze skimmed over the damp clothes and tangled hair.

"Uncle Ben," she sobbed. "Someone shot him — at the lake —"

She didn't realize her grip on his arm was so tight until he tried to pull away. "I have to go to him," he said, gently prying her fingers free. He called for his horse.

"Logan, I — I couldn't help hm. I tried, but there was nothing I could do."

Logan smoothed her hair from her cheek. "You've got to calm down and tell me what happened. Did you see anyone?"

"No. Oh please, we've got to hurry."

One of the men brought his horse and Logan reached for the reins. "I'll see you when I get back. Go to the house with Alana."

Catherine's tawny eyes widened and she seemed to get a grip on her emotions. "No, I'm coming with you."

Logan started to argue, then changed his mind. "Get her a horse," he called to one of the men. "Lucas, I'll want you with me."

They rode at a fast, tiring pace back to the lake. Catherine's tears dried and she experienced the horror of what they might find. Who had done this to her uncle and why?

"Where is he, Cat?" Logan asked when they rode to the lake's edge.

Stopping next to him, she pointed to a rock formation. "He's wedged between two boulders."

Logan and Lucas swung off their horses and ran into the water. Several minutes passed before Catherine saw them lift Ben's body and carry him toward shore. She was waiting when they gently laid him on the grass. She started to go down on her knees, but Logan stepped in front of her and caught her shoulders.

"He's dead, Cat."

She looked up, the tawny gold flecks looking at him first in hope then utter disbelief. In the depths of his blue eyes, there was a sympathy and understanding she'd never seen before. Catherine had lost a man she loved, and Logan understood her pain. Stepping forward, she rested her head against his chest and put her arms around his waist. His hands slid down her hair, then his arms curled around her shoulders protectively. He led her to a tiny stand of trees and they sat on the grass-covered earth.

"I need to know everything that happened," he said gently. "Can you talk about it?"

"We were talking—all of a sudden there was an explosion. I didn't realize at first what it was." Her lower lip quivered. "My uncle got a strange look on his face and there were more shots. I reached for him, but he was too heavy, and we both went into the water." She shuddered. "I thought I was going to drown, but the water wasn't deep, and I managed to get hold of a rock. . . .Ben was caught and I couldn't get him out."

Logan covered her hands with his. "Are you sure you didn't see anything?"

She shook her head. "Nothing," she said, raising her eyes to his. "Why would anyone want to kill my uncle?"

Logan shrugged. "When I hired on, your uncle said someone was rustling cattle and poisoning water holes. Maybe this is connected."

"Stealing cattle and murder are two different things."

"I promise to do what I can to learn who is responsible." Rising, Logan drew her to her feet. "Would you like to stay with Alana? Another woman might be a comfort to you."

Catherine shook her head. Until she saw Cameron, she would not be comfortable at his ranch or with his mother. "I want to go home." She looked past him to Lucas. "What about my uncle?"

"Lucas will take care of everything. I'll call the men and we'll have a service for him."

Logan led her to the horses and waited patiently while she mounted. The trip back to the ranch was accomplished in silence. Leaving Catherine at the house, Logan rode to gather the men and give them the bad news. A heavy depression settled over Catherine as she washed and changed. She had come west with high hopes for her future. She had found a home, a loving, caring uncle, and she felt his loss intensely.

Just before dusk, a small service was held beneath a large cottonwood tree. Logan took charge of the ceremony and several of the men made comments about their boss and friend. Catherine was too numb to cry, and she said her own silent prayer for the man who had welcomed her into his home. When the service was over, she went to her room, changed and climbed into bed.

Resting on her side, she wondered what she would do with her life now. What would happen to the ranch and where would she go? The last time she had been forced to leave familiar surroundings and start a new life, it had been disastrous. In the end it had worked out and brought her to her uncle, but now she had lost a man who had loved and tried to understand her. Moistness crept into her eyes and a sob escaped her throat. There was a reassuring touch on her shoulder, then a familiar length pressed against her back.

"Cry, Cat," Logan whispered in her ear.

Turning, she buried her face against his naked chest and cried for all the things in her life that would never be.

Chapter Twenty-one

Logan became Catherine's source of comfort over the next few nights. He would appear before she fell asleep and be gone the next morning when she woke. He never tried to make love to her, but she slept snuggled against his body, their limbs entwined. When she went out to breakfast one morning, she found Logan seated at the table.

"You are starting to relax more when you sleep," he commented and her cheeks reddened.

"I'm beginning to feel better."

Logan took a drink of his coffee. "Good. There are things we need to discuss."

Catherine accepted the oatmeal from Juanita but refused the offer of eggs. "You want to talk to me?"

He handed her a folded paper. "This is your uncle's will. He left everything to you."

She took the document and opened it. "I—I don't believe it," she said, after skimming the contents. "He told me it would someday be mine, but what am I going to do with a ranch?"

"Live on it for one thing," he said in a mocking tone. "Or have you got a better place to go?"

She shook her head. "You know I don't."

"Do I?" he asked with a lift of his dark brow. "You might have family in the East."

She wasn't going to get involved in a discussion about her aunts. As far as she was concerned, they didn't exist. "There isn't anyone."

"If you don't want to stay here, you could sell the ranch. Maybe the MacLennans would buy it. You now own the only water for miles."

"The lake will be shared."

"I'm sure they will be glad to hear it."

"Are you worried about your job?"

"Why? Are you going to fire me?"

Resting her fingers against her chin, she regarded him thoughtfully. "Perhaps." It was a definite consideration.

Logan leaned back in his chair. "You need me."

Catherine's mouth dropped open. "Of all the nerve," she sputtered.

"I'm only stating the truth. You've got a herd of cattle that need to get to market. On top of that, you need money to pay the men."

"Are you saying I should go ahead and take the cattle to California?"

"No," he said with a shake of his head. "I'm saying I should take the cattle."

"You!" she exclaimed. "And why should I trust you to do it? My uncle wasn't even going to let you go along."

"I was staying here to watch over you. Now that won't be necessary."

Catherine tossed her napkin on the table. "And why not?"

"Because you're going with me."

She was flabbergasted. "You can't be serious. My uncle said it was too hard for a woman. Look what happened on the wagon train." She had made so many mistakes.

"I'm trying to forget the stunts you pulled," he teased.

Catherine glared at him. "I'm not going anyplace with you." She shook her head. "It's simply out of the question."

"I haven't been able to learn anything about your uncle's killer. You can't stay here alone."

"Leave Lucas with me." There had to be a solution in her favor.

"Lucas is staying, but he's going to split his time between here and the MacLennan ranch. You'd be left alone too often." He rubbed his jaw. "I'll let you remain behind if you agree to stay with Alana until I return."

"When will that be?"

"A few months. I can't really say. We could hit snow in the mountains."

Cameron was due home in a short time. If she stayed, she would be at his ranch when he returned, and she wasn't ready for a confrontation. Thrusting her chin forward, she looked at Logan. "When do we leave?"

"At dawn in two days. I want you to stay with Alana tonight. I'm not going to be here and I don't want you alone."

"Juanita is here." She didn't want to spend a night in Cameron's home.

"Juanita goes to her husband at night. Your uncle gave them a house in the hills. Lucas will take you over this afternoon." He rose. "I've got to get to work." He pointed to the paper on the table. "Several men will be staying behind to look after things, but you better find a safe place for the will."

"By the way," she said before he left. "Where are you going to be tonight?"

Logan put his hands on his lean hips. "Are you jealous there might be another woman? Or are you anxious to have me in your bed?"

"Neither," she snapped. "I just wanted to be sure you'd be available if something came up."

"I'll be around," he said and left.

Picking up the documents, Catherine went to her uncle's desk. She only meant to find a place to hide the will, but she ended up spending the morning studying his records and learning about her holdings. If the cattle sale went through as planned, she'd be a very rich woman.

Catherine and Lucas rode to the MacLennan ranch shortly after lunch. Alana welcomed her to her house, and they spent the bulk of the afternoon discussing Catherine's trip. Lucas made several trips through the house and each time Catherine noticed the eye communication between the older couple. There seemed to be a spark of interest and given time it might burst into flame. She'd like nothing better than to return from the cattle drive and learn Lucas and Alana were contemplating a life together.

Lucas joined them for the evening meal, and when the dishes were done, they adjourned to the patio to talk. Lucas amused them with tales of his days on the wagon train, and Catherine contributed some of her antics. Forty minutes later, she decided to leave the older couple alone.

Alana led her to the middle bedroom. "You can

sleep in Cameron's room."

Catherine stepped through the doorway and closed the door. There was an odd breathlessness about her as she studied the spotless room. Crossing to the closet, she opened the door. Clothes, dusty from lack of use, hung in a neat row. Two pair of leather boots sat on the floor next to a fancy tooled saddle. Closing the door, she turned and walked to the bed. She changed and climbed between the sheets. This was where Cameron slept and where they would have come as man and wife. It seemed like years since they had stood in the garden outside the church and repeated their vows. She was another person—she had known another man and experienced more than she ever thought possible. People changed with time. Perhaps they would no longer share the bond they once had.

She rolled to her side, her body curving into an arch. This was the first night since her uncle's death that Logan wasn't in her bed. He would not come to her tonight, and it was just as well. How could she explain to him they would be sleeping in the bed of the man she thought she'd married?

Lucas was in the kitchen enjoying a cup of coffee when Catherine came out the next morning. "Would you like to join me?" he asked. "This woman makes the best coffee this side of the Mississippi."

"Dona believe him," Alana scolded. "Logan tells me ye be a good cook," she said to Lucas. "I might let ye fix me dinner some evenin'."

"It's a deal," Lucas agreed, glancing at Catherine. "I'll take you back to the ranch in about an hour."

"I'll be ready," she agreed.

They left on schedule and when they reached the

ranch Catherine spent the afternoon preparing her belongings for the trip. She checked on her mare, then paused to watch the men gather up the horses that would accompany them. There was an unusual excitement surrounding the men, and Catherine got caught in the anticipation of the trip ahead. After eating an early dinner, she went to bed. Logan didn't join her and she realized she missed not having him with her.

It was early when Logan entered Catherine's bedroom and shook her awake. Still in a sleep-filled daze, she propped herself up on her arm and ran her hand over her eyes.

"What do you want?" she asked, her voice thick from slumber.

"It is time to leave," he said flatly.

Catherine's gaze shifted to the darkness outside her window. "What time is it?"

"Two hours before sunrise."

Groaning, she said, "You aren't serious about leaving now, are you?" She flopped back down on the mattress. "Wake me when the sun comes up." She didn't know what kind of a joke he was playing, but she was exhausted.

"Move over," he said gruffly, and she pulled the blanket over her head. "I said move over," he repeated in warning tones.

She pushed the covers back and peeked at him. He was standing less than a foot away from the bed, and his fingers were loosening the buttons on his shirt.

"What are you doing?" she asked, her eyes widening.

"If you aren't going to get up, I'm going to join

you." He grinned. "It might be the last time I can enjoy your pleasures. That is, unless you'll let me bed you in camp."

Clutching the sheet against her neck, she said, "You'll do no such thing. It is enough that you barge into my bedroom and force me to submit to your lust, but I won't have you touching me on the trail."

Logan's brow shot up. "I don't have to *force* you. With a little persuasion, you're ready whenever I am."

"How dare you!" she said, sitting up. "I have *never* asked for your attentions and I certainly don't welcome them."

Leaning over, Logan rested his fists on the mattress. His eyes were inches from hers. "The day you appeared in the saloon dressed in that skimpy costume, you invited me and any other man to your bed."

"That's a lie."

Raising one hand, he lightly caressed her lips. "You had already been free with your favors. . . . Both of us know I wasn't the first." She sucked in her breath.

"I would like to meet the man who took your innocence. . . . Did the two of you enjoy the same passion and desire we share?"

Catherine's hand fell against his cheek in a stinging slap. "Don't you ever speak to me about him!"

Logan straightened, his hand going to rub his cheek. "Do I detect a smoldering flame for the man? Were you in love with him?"

"My past is none of your business."

"Why are you so touchy?" he asked. "You can't blame me for wondering about my competition."

Catherine brushed her hair off her shoulder.

"Would you like me to cross-examine you about the women in your life?"

Smiling, Logan crossed his arms. "What would you like to know? Days—dates—names."

"You're disgusting. I don't care anything about your past. What you did or who you slept with is none of my business as long as it isn't me." She rose to her knees. "And let's get one thing clear. When we are on the trail, you're to keep your hands off me. I will not have the men making snide remarks about my character behind my back. I am the owner of this ranch, half the herd, and your boss, so you'd better do what I say."

"What are you going to do if I refuse, fire me?"

"Maybe."

He shook his head. "You need me." His eyes pierced hers. "Whether you'll admit it to yourself or not, you need me. You proved it the other night when you turned to me for comfort. Stop fighting me and enjoy what we have. Bury whoever is in your past and start living now."

The serious tone of his words startled Catherine. Perhaps she had misjudged him. Maybe the man had some feeling after all.

"Are you asking me to make a commitment?"

Logan jammed his fists into his pockets. "I wouldn't trust you if you did." Turning, he walked to the door. "I had to learn the hard way."

The door slammed behind him and Catherine sank back against the pillow. Logan had almost confided the bitterness in his heart, and his revelation frightened her. Both had been scarred by trust and bitterness, and they were injured creatures trying to heal their wounds. They were like animals circling each other in anticipation of attack, each wary and frightened.

Juanita had breakfast ready, and Catherine stuffed herself. There was no way of knowing when they would stop to eat and she didn't want to do anything on the trip to stir up Logan's anger. If she left her inexperience behind and presented herself as a mature, knowledgeable woman, perhaps Logan would respect her. Her mare was waiting outside, and she mounted and rode to join the men. Logan issued a series of last minute orders and the men rode off, leaving Catherine alone with him.

"You are going to ride next to the chuck wagon. Stay close. We don't want any accidents."

"There won't be any," she said and rode to join Roy at the wagon.

By the time the sun had brightened the sky, they were already heading off the MacLennan ranch. The chuck wagon stayed to the side of the herd and from her position next to it, she had a view of the vast herd. She had never seen so many cattle, and the noise and dust were reminiscent of the cattle pens—only on a larger scale.

The first part of the trip would be the easiest. Water and short grass would be plentiful. It wouldn't be until later when they reached the desert areas that they could expect to have problems.

The wagon went ahead of the herd to get the noon meal ready and obeying Logan's orders, Catherine followed Roy. He set up camp beneath the shade of two large trees and when the first group of men came to eat, the food was ready and waiting. Roy wouldn't let her do any of the cooking, but he did let her portion out the meat and potatoes. Logan was among the last to come through her line almost two hours later.

"Did you help with the cooking?" he asked as she dumped a ladle of stew onto his tin.

"You'll be glad to know, I didn't," she said sternly, but couldn't help smiling at his teasing. "Roy is finding a few jobs for me to do."

"I can find something for you to do."

Catherine immediately brightened. She was willing to do anything she could to help make the trip easier. "What is it?"

"I'll tell you about it later. Right now, I'm going to stretch out under that tree and enjoy my food and drink. I've been eating dust all morning."

Catherine was glad the wagon wasn't stuck in the rear. In the back, the dust was so thick it was almost impossible to see, and she hoped the job he had for her wasn't at the rear.

When everything was packed and the men were gone, Roy tied her horse to the back of the wagon and asked her to join him on the seat. "It gets lonely on the bench."

"How long have you been doing this?" she asked, pulling the brim of her hat down to shade her eyes.

"Almost thirty years. I'd been with your uncle since he came to these parts." He grinned at her. "I've always worked for men, and I ain't never had a lady boss before."

Catherine blushed. "I don't know anything about ranching. Logan is really in charge."

"We were lucky he showed up. For a man so young, he's had a lot of experience and the men trust him.

You'd be wise to keep him in your employment."

"What was the other foreman like?"

"The man was good at the beginning, but he got lazy and worked slacked off. Your uncle fired him." Roy whistled. "I've often wondered if he was the man who shot your uncle. Men will do a lot for revenge."

"I hope we've seen the last of him. I don't want anymore trouble." Catherine would have plenty of problems when she returned and found Cameron at his ranch. She remembered what Logan had said about wanting to meet the man who had taken her innocence. They would practically be working together. Unconsciously, she trembled.

"Something wrong?" Roy asked.

"No—nothing. I was just thinking."

They stopped for the night by a small river. Roy set the wagon on the bank so they'd have a fresh supply of water. The cattle were on the other side of a ridge, but Cat could still hear their bawling. Logan came through the line without mentioning the job he had for her and as hard as she tried, she couldn't think what it could be. Since she didn't do the cooking, Roy had her do the dishes. Gathering the tins, she carried them to the stream. She was almost done washing them when she heard a noise behind her and whirled around.

"Are you being careful?" Logan asked, coming to her side and lifting the clean plates and cups.

"Yes. I did learn a few things from you."

"I'm glad to hear that. I'll help you carry these things back to the wagon."

On the way back, she glanced at him. "Are you ready to tell me about the job you have for me?"

"Not tonight," he said, yawning. "I pulled the early duty and I want to get some rest." Catherine carefully put the dishes in the small space alotted for them. "You better get some rest yourself. It will be an early morning."

She scanned the back of the wagon. Everything was in its place and it was crowded. "It looks like I'm going to have to rearrange a few things."

"What are you talking about?" Logan asked, tossing his hat down on his bedroll and reaching for the buckle on his gunbelt.

"I can't sleep on top of a sack of flour. Would you help me move things?"

"You aren't moving anything." He dropped the belt on the blanket.

"Do you expect me to sleep in the corner?"

His blue eyes challenged her. "You aren't sleeping in the wagon." He pointed to the bedroll near his. "That's your bed."

She took a step back. "You don't expect me to sleep on the ground."

"And why not? All the rest of the men are, and you're not going to get any special favors because you're a woman." She opened her mouth to speak, but he added, "Or because you're the boss."

Thinking of the snakes, spiders, and scorpions, she knew she'd never be able to sleep on the ground. "I'll sleep on the wagon seat." It wasn't a very comfortable thought, but it was certainly better than the alternative.

Logan grabbed her arm. "I don't advise you to make a scene. A few of the men are already looking over here to find out what we're arguing about. You have a raw beauty about you when you're mad that appeals to men—me in particular."

She snatched her arm away. "Keep your hands off of me or I'll slap your face in front of the men."

"I wouldn't try it," he warned, his eyes narrowing dangerously. "Now, go to bed. I'd hate to have to join you in your bedroll to wake you up."

Catherine knew he would do it, so she turned and walked to the flat blanket stretched out on the ground. It was anything but soft, and she winced when her head hit the hard saddle. This was definitely going to take getting used to. Although Logan was less than three feet away, she was surprisingly pleased with his nearness. She might not like him most of the time, but he could protect her if anything happened.

Chapter Twenty-two

When Catherine woke, every muscle in her body screamed in agony. Most of the men were already up and Roy had breakfast cooking. Grabbing a towel, she went to the stream to rinse her face. She would have loved a bath but there wasn't any privacy, and she couldn't risk undressing with so many men around.

Back at camp, she poured herself a cup of coffee and accepted a plate of hash. Sitting against a tree stump, she watched the men get ready to ride out. When she was finished, she washed the tins and put them away.

"You better get your bedroll picked up," Roy warned. "We've got to get moving." Catherine had seen the roll on the back of her saddle, but had no idea how to condense the layers to make them fit. Roy came up behind her. "Having trouble?" he asked and she nodded. Getting down on his knees, he straightened the cloth. "The two blankets go on the inside," he instructed, making the necessary folds. He pointed at the center. "If you have anything special and you can't carry it on you, this is a good place to put it. The tarp goes on the outside to keep everything dry."

It made a neat bundle and fit perfectly behind the saddle. Roy hoisted it on the mare's back and secured the cinch. The leather saddle weighed almost forty pounds and Catherine thanked Roy for his help.

The day was just like the one before it and the one that followed. She was usually in bed when Logan retired, so she didn't know what special job he had planned for her.

The terrain changed. Instead of the plentiful stretches of short grass, they crossed dry land, covered only by short brush. The days were long, warm and dusty. On many occasions, the grime at the front of the pack became so unbearable, she had to draw the bandana around her neck over her nose and mouth.

Logan drove them hard, trying to make each day work to their advantage, and he knew just how hard to push the cattle and still keep them fat enough to market. When they moved into the plentiful grass areas, Logan rested the cattle and Catherine was able to make time for herself. She spent part of the day with Roy, helping to ease his work load.

Occupied with his job, Logan avoided her. He was gone in the morning when she woke and absent at night when she retired, and she wondered if he ever got to sleep. When he came through the grub line, she noticed lines of exhaustion around his mouth.

With the start of the desert, water became scarce and Logan assured the men they would come to a river. Catherine hoped it would be large enough to bathe in and was determined to find the privacy to have a bath. The flatness of the desert gave way to deep canyons, the soil changing to reds and oranges. Catherine was in awe of its beauty and she spent hours studying the deep pits.

One afternoon, the cries of the cattle became

louder and the team regained its spirit. Roy glanced at her and grinned. "We're almost to the river."

Less than an hour later, Catherine saw the shimmering wetness. It was a wonderful sight, and she mounted her horse to get a closer look. The cattle's thirst made them restless, and the men were busy trying to keep the animals from stampeding. Catherine galloped forward, oblivious to the cattle moving in on all sides of her. They reached the river at the same time, and as much as she wanted a drink, she found herself surrounded.

"Having trouble?" A rider asked from her side, and Catherine turned to look at Logan.

Laughing, she glanced at the cows surrounding her. "It looks like we all had the same idea."

Edging forward, he broke a path through the cattle for her to follow him to shore. He unhooked his canteen from the saddle and handed it to her. "You better take your drink from this. The cattle need the water more than you do."

She took a generous swallow of the liquid before handing it back to Logan. "Thanks," she said, looking at the river. "I was hoping to get a bath. Do you have any objections?"

His eyes swept down her body. "Do you want me to scrub your back?"

"Of course not," she said quickly. "I just wanted you to know so you can keep the men away."

"I'll personally make sure you're not disturbed," he promised, the edge of his mouth curving into a smile. "Do you want your bath in broad daylight or after dark?"

"After the evening meal. There should be some light."

"I'll see you then," he said, turning his horse and riding into the herd.

Catherine had her things ready when Logan came for her just before dusk. "I thought we'd ride upstream. There is a private cove you can use."

She rode behind Logan until they found a flat area bordering the river. Dismounting, she secured her horse. She laid her towel down and turned, expecting to see Logan preparing to ride away. Instead, he was unbuttoning his shirt.

"What are you doing?" she gasped.

"I'm going to join you."

"You are not. I refuse to bathe with you."

His shirt slid off his shoulders and he dropped it over a bush. For several seconds she became mesmerized by the muscles flexing across his back, and she experienced a tightening in her stomach. Before her body could betray her, she turned her back on him and took a few steps to the water's edge and stared at the inviting wetness. Dust clung to her clothes and skin making her feel grimy. Bending over, she ran her fingers through the water. If she removed her clothes, Logan would make love to her. They had not been together for weeks, and she realized she missed the familiar feel of his body.

Reaching for the buttons on her shirt, she slowly began to unfasten them. Her actions gave approval for his attentions, but there was no point in denying her need. She wanted Logan. Her blouse dropped to the dirt, followed quickly by her boots and pants. There was a thickness in her throat when she turned.

Logan was standing directly behind her, his body already naked and wanting hers. Keeping a foot between them, he raised one hand and ran a finger along the valley of her breasts. Catherine trembled beneath the gentle caress, her body filling with an aching desire. Her hands rose to his shoulders and her fingers dug into the muscled flesh.

Curving his hands across her abdomen, he followed the line of her hips. Sighing, she parted her lips in invitation. His gaze raked her face and his head tipped forward to taste the softness offered. With a light pressure against his hips, their bodies came together, flesh against flesh, each wanting to satisfy a need in themselves and to give pleasure to the other.

Lifting her, Logan laid her on the small grass-covered landing near the water. They came together quickly, an urgency due to weeks of wanting and remaining unsatisfied. They rose to new heights before wrapped in each other's arms, they achieved the utmost release of their desire.

Catherine was still trembling when Logan lifted her and carried her into the water. There, through the sensuous wandering of his hands, he taught her a world of new pleasures, and she in turn, learned to satisfy him.

Much later, Catherine climbed out of the water, dried herself and dressed. When she reached for her boots, a colorful object caught her eye, and she squatted down to get a better look. Satisfied it was not one of the colorful snakes or insects, she picked it up. Careful examination revealed a leather band beautifully decorated with a multitude of color. She carried her findings to Logan.

"What do you suppose it is?" she asked, admiring the workmanship.

"It's a decorative addition for a ceremonial costume."

"Who does it belong to?"

Logan shrugged. "I don't know. There are many Indian tribes around. It's hard to tell which one."

"Indian tribes?" she repeated. "Do you mean to tell me there are Indians near here?"

Logan tucked his shirt into his pants. "We've been on their land for days. As a matter of fact, they've been following the herd most of the day."

Her eyes darted along the bushes. "I didn't see them."

"Just the same, they were there," he confirmed, strapping his gunbelt around his hips.

Catherine took a step toward the horses. "Maybe we shouldn't be this far from camp."

"When they get ready to talk, we'll see them," he said, chuckling. "I wouldn't have brought you here if it wasn't safe."

"What will the Indians want?" she asked, then rushed on, "did you bring trinkets?"

He shook his head. "They don't want junk. Winter is coming and they need food—cattle to be precise."

She threw her hands on her hips. "Well, they aren't getting mine." She smiled mischievously. "If we have to get rid of any cattle, it will be the ones belonging to the MacLennans."

Frowning, his mouth twisted in confusion. "What do you have against them?"

"Nothing at all," she responded, flipping her long hair over her shoulder. "I want this trip to be profitable."

"If it comes to giving away cattle, it will be done on

an equal basis."

"Whose side are you on?" she argued. "You work for me."

"You might be my boss, but I happen to like Alana, and I'm not going to let you cheat her."

Turning, she walked to her horse. "I thought Lucas was interested in her," she threw over her shoulder. "Isn't she a little old for you?"

She was grabbed from behind and swung around. "Alana is a lady. There is not now, and there never will be, a relationship like you're suggesting."

Shocked by the rage in his eyes, she said, "I like her, too."

Her statement seemed to satisfy him and his hands fell. "Let's get back to camp. I'm on early watch."

"Logan," she said, as he swung into the saddle. "What's the job you have for me to do?"

"Taking care of me when I need a woman." Moving the reins, he turned the horse toward camp and Catherine had little choice but to follow.

They stayed with the river for several days. Logan let the cattle drink and feed on the plentiful food because it would be the last sufficient supply they would have before starting on their final leg across the desert.

The Indians came four days after they left the river and Catherine spotted them when she was in the wagon with Roy. "Look," she said, gripping his arm and pointing to a small ridge. There were at least twenty men on horseback.

Roy nodded. "They have been there for some time.

It looks like they are ready to come down."

"You mean they are going to attack?"

"Depends if we don't agree to give them what they want."

There was no reassurance in Roy's statement and her gaze remained focused on the riders following them. Logan rode up to the wagon, trailing a spare horse behind him.

"Let's go see what they want."

Roy slowed the team and mounted the horse. Catherine jumped to the edge of her seat. "You're not going to leave me here."

Logan's eyes roamed over her excited face. "Would you like to join us?"

She sat back, frightened to be left alone and terrified of approaching the Indians. "I'll stay here."

Nervously, Catherine watched and waited while the men rode toward the Indians. The cattle continued to move past her until she was choking up dust from the end of the pack. Frightened of being left alone, she picked up the reins and urged the team forward. Her hold on the leather strips was tight, and she felt the animals pulling in protest. Rather than cause an accident, she relaxed her grip.

Three of the Indians rode forward to meet Logan and Roy and Catherine moistened her dry lips. She reached behind the seat for one of the spare rifles and rested it on the seat next to her. A few minutes later, Roy turned and rode back toward the herd. He spoke to two of the men, and they began separating cattle. When they had about fifty cows, they drove them toward Logan. The Indians, apparently satisfied with what they were getting, surrounded the herd and rode off.

Logan stopped at the wagon and flicked her a quick, impersonal glance. "Fifty head is not bad in exchange for your life."

Even after Roy had returned to the seat, she couldn't relax. "Do you think they'll be back?"

He shrugged. "It's hard to tell. For now, they are satisfied with what they got."

"What kind of Indians were they?"

"Apache. They are one of the largest bands in this part of the country."

She shuddered. "I hope they leave us alone."

Catherine did not sleep well that night or any night after, and she found herself putting her bedroll closer to Logan's each time they stopped. One night she woke to find her hand stretching the distance between them to rest against his chest. Before he could realize what she had done, she jerked her hand free. Her subconscious response to him frightened her. What did it mean?

When one of their expected watering holes was dry, Roy started rationing their supply of water. From her seat on the wagon, she saw two cattle fall from exhaustion and thirst. This was one way Catherine had never expected to forfeit her herd.

"How many do you think we'll lose?"

Roy shook his head. "Ain't no way of knowin'. Logan thinks he knows where there is water." He pointed north of the direction they were traveling. "There is a watering hole about twenty miles, but Logan thinks he'll find a closer one if we head south."

"He thinks!" Catherine shrieked. "Why isn't he going to the one he's sure of?"

"Logan's the boss. I trust his judgment."

"Well, I won't. Stop the wagon. I want to get my horse."

Refusing to listen to Roy's argument, she mounted her mare and went in search of Logan. It was a large herd and it took her almost thirty minutes to locate him. When she saw him, she waved him over.

"I want to know what you think you're doing?" she flashed angrily.

Logan's brow rose. "What I'm doing," he repeated, "is getting this herd to California."

Her tawny eyes narrowed. "I'm beginning to think you want this trip to be a failure. First you give my cattle to savages and then you refuse to lead them to water."

A muscle tightened in Logan's jaw. "I am leading them to water."

She pointed to the area Roy had indicated. "What is wrong with the watering hole twenty miles away?"

"Nothing, but it is out of the way and you'll lose half the herd trying to make up the extra distance."

"Aren't you gambling on something that doesn't belong to you?"

"I know you need money to run the ranch. I also know if I don't get this herd to California, I don't get paid." His voice hardened. "We keep going in the direction we're headed."

Catherine pushed her hat back on her forehead. "No. I want my herd pulled out and my men will lead them to water."

Logan urged his horse forward until his thigh pressed against hers. The icy blueness in his eyes made her uneasy. "You might be the boss, but you don't know anything about the land. I do, and I'm taking the cattle with me."

"But—" she started to say in protest.

"We are going to do this my way, Cat," he warned in response to the defiant flare in her eyes. "If you contradict my orders, you'll have to settle up with me. I will not hesitate to make a scene in front of the men. Are you prepared to battle with me before spectators?"

Catherine clamped her jaw closed. She wanted to defy him but she didn't dare risk his wrath. His tongue could be as cutting as a razor and she'd only be seen as a fool.

Turning, he pulled his dust mask over his nose and rode into the herd. Catherine silently fumed. She'd given him an order and he had refused. It was unthinkable from a hired hand, but what alternative did she have? Alana had hired him to safeguard the MacLennan cattle, so it wouldn't do any good to fire him. There was nothing she could do but wait and hope he didn't fail.

The next day more cattle fell and she stopped counting the dead carcasses left for the vultures. Her lips were parched, but she wouldn't get a drink until they stopped for the night. Late the next afternoon, they reached water, and it was hard for Catherine to admit to herself she'd made a mistake in doubting Logan. When he came through the grub line that night, each of them kept their emotions hidden. Catherine knew she owed him an apology for doubting his ability. He had proven his capabilities many times, but she could not trust him or any other man. She was too afraid of getting hurt.

The desert remained with them, but the days and

nights were cooler. Winter was coming to the desert and though she knew she'd never see the chilling temperatures she'd known in the East, it was bound to get uncomfortable.

Catherine uttered a sigh of relief when they entered California and reached the first small town. They kept the cattle on the outskirts, but Catherine was allowed to go to town. Roy accompanied her and while she enjoyed the company of the older man, it was Logan she wished was at her side.

Six days later, Logan drove the herd to its final destination. Catherine watched the cattle filling the huge pens with a smile of satisfaction. It had been a long, tiring trip, but they had made it. She looked forward to the days they would spend in town before heading back to the ranch. Without the cows, the return would be faster—but she dreaded it.

That night she took a room in the hotel and enjoyed a long, luxurious bath. She was reaching for her clothes when there was a sharp rap on the door. "Who is it?" she called, wrapping the towel back around her.

"Let me in, Cat," Logan's deep voice demanded. "I have to talk to you."

"Go away." She heard him rattle the lock. "I said go away. We don't have anything to say to each other."

"If you don't open it, I'll break it down."

Catherine knew he wasn't kidding so she quickly turned the key. Stepping inside, Logan closed the door. His eyes swept her towel covered figure. "Very nice," he drawled.

It had been a long time since they had enjoyed each other, and she felt the initial stirring of betrayal from her body. "What do you want?" she asked, noticing the papers in his hand.

"The price you've been offered for the herd wil
more than make up for your losses."

"That's wonderful," she said, smiling. "When do we
get the money?"

"Greedy woman, aren't you?"

"I'm just glad to know I can pay the men and keep
the ranch operating. It was what my uncle
wanted. . . . I wish he could have lived—" Her lower
lip trembled.

"He would have been proud of you, Cat," Logan
said softly, and she looked up in surprise. She had
never expected a compliment from Logan. Usually, he
was hurtling insults at her. "The men who bought the
herd want our ranch hands to take it up state."

Catherine dreaded the thought of more travel. She
wanted to go home. "Can I wait here for you?"

"I won't be going with the men," he said, opening
the paper he held in his hand. "I just got this message
from Lucas. We need to get back to the ranch."

"Has something happened?" she asked in fear.

"Someone named Darrell is at your ranch waiting
for you."

His words came as a complete surprise, and
Catherine was stunned. "Darrell—but I thought he
was dead."

Logan's eyes narrowed suspiciously. "I gather you
know him."

"Of course I know him," she snapped, still unable
to believe Darrell was alive. "So do you. He was the
man you shot the night you met me in the saloon."

Logan rested his hand against his lean hips. "So
that was Darrell. My aim must have been off.

378

hought I had killed him."

Catherine didn't try to hide her relief at knowing he vas alive. "I'm so relieved he's not dead."

"Just how well did you know him?" Logan asked houghtfully. "If I recall, he was rather possessive with ou. He talked about your house with familiarity. Was e your lover?"

"That's none of your business," she snapped. She lidn't want to tell him he'd been a friend when she vas alone and frightened.

There was an ugly twist to Logan's mouth. "Is he he man who stole your innocence?"

Catherine's mouth dropped open. "How dare you!" he screamed, the words flowing from her mouth without thinking. "Darrell was a friend when I needed ne. My life was in shambles. I was alone and carrying child."

Logan's body stilled to tense stiffness. The expression on his face was hard to fathom, but she thought he saw surprise mingled with pain and finally ontempt. "You are even less the innocent I thought ou were." One of his hands tightened into a fist. What did you do with the baby? Did you give it away r leave it in the East?"

His words stung. Even now Catherine ached for the nfant she'd lost. It had been a part of her and ameron, and she had loved and wanted the child. wallowing, she blinked tears from her eyes. "There as an accident on the boat I was traveling on, and I st the baby." Dropping her head in defeat, she ared at the hardwood floor. Her heart ached pain- lly and hated Logan for making her relive the nguish she had felt.

379

"What about the ring around your neck? Were you married to the man?" His eyes fell to the bare flesh above her breasts. "Where is it?"

She wasn't about to admit she'd purposely left it at the ranch. "I forgot it," she lied. "I'm not married," she added, denying any bond between her and the man from her past. She was so confused she couldn't think. "Please Logan, leave me alone." Her shoulder trembled. Why did he have to torment her? She hated him for it.

"Did you love him?" he persisted.

Raising her head, she looked at him through watery haze. "Yes, I loved him." She took a breath. "I loved him as much as I hate you."

Logan's blue eyes filled with contempt, his mouth twisted bitterly. "You've made yourself perfectly clear. Our relationship from now on will be totally innocent." Turning toward the door, he said, "Be ready to leave in the morning."

When he was gone, Catherine threw herself across the bed and wept. Her heart was torn apart from reminders of Cameron and her child. Logan had forced her to admit her past love for Cam, and she knew despite his deceit and desertion there was strong chance her love would rekindle. She needed love in her life, and if it was offered she would grab and hold on to the tender feelings.

Logan understood the commitment she had with the man from her past, but the discovery did not make Catherine happy. For some unknown reason she felt bitter and hurt.

Chapter Twenty-three

In the morning, Catherine got little more than a curt nod from her foreman when they mounted their horses and rode out of town. There was a stiffness and controlled anger in him, but he didn't look her way. Without the cattle slowing them down, they covered almost twice the distance before stopping for the night. Logan built a fire and started the meal. Catherine unrolled her bed, unsaddled her horse and accepted the tin Logan handed her. She offered to clean the plates and Logan snorted approval, turned and went to take care of his horse. From beneath the cover of her eyelashes, she watched him remove his bedroll. He walked toward Catherine but instead of making his bed near hers as she expected, he went to the far side of camp. Without even glancing in her direction, he stretched out and pulled his hat down over his eyes.

Catherine threw a few more sticks on the fire before curling up beneath her blankets and going to sleep. Logan was making the coffee when she woke. Smiling amiably, she said hello, but he merely grunted acknowledgment. She didn't know how much longer she could endure the rigid silence that existed between them, but she learned as the days passed. Logan intended to keep his promise to leave her alone.

Snow appeared on the mountains and the cool days forced Catherine to wear a jacket. They traveled hard and fast, and she wondered why Logan was in such a hurry to get back. To pass the long hours, she thought about Darrell. Her relief at learning he was alive brought a smile to her lips and lifted a heavy burden from her shoulders. His appearance at her ranch puzzled her, and she experienced a prickling edge of fear when she reflected on the inevitable meeting between Logan and Darrell. Logan had shot the gambler because he wanted her, and Darrell liked her enough to defend her. Logan was definitely the stronger of the two, and she hoped it wouldn't come down to a battle of wills. She didn't want to see either of them hurt.

One night after they had stopped, she saw Logan standing at the edge of a clearing some distance from camp. There was something funny about the way he'd been acting, and it frightened her.

"Logan, is something wrong?" she asked approaching him.

He turned, his arm swinging behind his back to hide something in his hand. "Go back to camp," he said tersely.

"What are you doing?" she insisted. She started to step forward, but he moved in front of her path. "I said go back to camp."

This time the earnestness in his voice alarmed her. Jumping quickly to her left, she ran forward and got behind Logan. There would be many days and nights later that she would wish she'd listened to the wiser man. Before her in the bushes were the bodies of a man, woman and child riddled with arrows. Turning Catherine looked at Logan's hand now resting at his side. In it he held a child's doll, the pretty blue dress covered with blood. Wavering, Catherine felt a thickness rise in her throat, then seconds later, she fell in a faint—a faint that mercifully blocked everything out of her mind.

When she regained consciousness, she was stretched out on her bedroll and Logan was nowhere in sight. She lay without moving, trying to force the sight of the massacred family from her mind. Twenty minutes later Logan stepped out of the woods.

He dropped to one knee at her side. "How are you feeling?"

"Sick. It was horrible."

His expression was stern. "I told you to go back to camp, but you wouldn't listen. When are you going to start trusting me?"

Catherine rolled her head to the side to avoid his gaze. How could she trust any man when she'd been taught not to. "Are we in danger?"

"We'll have to be more careful. I've been noticing signs since morning." He ran his hand down his muscled thigh. "We'll go south. There will be more cover."

"Is it the same band we gave the cattle to?"

He shook his head. "We passed their camp weeks ago. This is another group. We are on a slightly different course, faster, but not flat enough for the cattle."

"How much longer before we're home?" She wanted the security of the *hacienda* around her.

"About two weeks," he said, rising. "You better get some sleep. I'll keep watch."

When Logan walked away from her, she held her

breath. How could she sleep knowing they might be attacked by savages? For hours she stared at Logan watching from the shadows. As much as she disliked the man, she would have to put her trust in him. She was giving him her most valuable possession—her life

When Catherine rose, Logan stretched out on his bedroll and slept for two hours. She had coffee and breakfast ready for him. He ate a hearty portion of the food and advised her to do the same. Lunch might have to be skipped.

Logan turned to pick up his bedroll and Catherine watched him fold the blankets. His back was blocking most of what he was doing, but before he made the final roll, she saw him pause to look at something. He studied the object for several minutes before carefully placing it in the center of the blankets and covering it Knowing the center of the bedroll was a hiding place for valuables, Catherine wondered what prized possession he kept hidden.

Catherine was glad to be out of the desert and she enjoyed the shade and changing terrain. They were able to stop for lunch and before mounting up, Logan took a gun from his saddle bag and gave it to Catherine. "I want you to keep this with you."

She accepted the heavy piece of metal. "Do you expect trouble?"

"No, but I'd rather know you had it just in case."

Two days later, they rode through a small valley Logan slowed their pace and led them to a stand of trees and motioned for her to dismount.

"I want to go ahead on foot," he said, securing the reins to a bush. "Stay with the horses."

Catherine shook her head. "I'm going with you."

Whatever he was looking for, she wasn't going to be left alone.

"Do you want to get yourself killed?" She shook her head in response but Logan was already creeping through the bushes.

Catherine watched him weave through the brush and frightened to remain by herself, she crouched and followed. He moved rapidly up a small hill, stopped and stretched out on his stomach. A sharp scream that sent warning chills up Catherine's spine caused her to stop. Logan, intent upon something before him, didn't move. Running forward, she climbed the rise and fell at his side.

"What are you doing here?" he grated angrily.

The tortured scream pierced the air again and Catherine clutched his arm. "What's happening?"

In response, Logan's gaze shifted to the scene two-hundred feet before them. Catherine's gaze followed his and a sickness settled in her stomach. Logan, perhaps anticipating her scream, clamped his hand across her mouth. In an attempt to get control of her emotions, her teeth sank into his finger. When she regained command of herself, she nodded, and he removed his hand.

Before them was an Indian camp with more than fifty wickiups. The houses were dome-shaped and covered with leaves and bark. Two white men and women were surrounded by Apache braves. The men, stripped of most their clothes, were the center of attention. Across from them, the women were tied to stakes and screamed whenever one of the Indians touched their bodies. Occasionally, they were struck with a heavy pole by one of the squaws.

The sight sickened Catherine, and her heart went out to the women. "Do something Logan," she whispered to the man at her side. He kept his eyes on the scene before him and she gripped his wrist. "Logan, do something to help those women," she said louder, and this time he turned his head. Putting his hand over her mouth, he dragged her down the small hill. They were almost to their horses when he released her.

"What do you think you're doing? Those women need help."

He untied the horses. "So do the men, but there is nothing I can do for them."

Catherine was appalled by his heartless declaration. "What are you saying? You've got to help them."

Logan's gaze hardened. "There is nothing I can do. If either of us are seen, we'll become their next victims." He hesitated when he saw the color wash from her cheeks. "Is that what you want?"

"Of course not—but it was horrible. The women must be terrified."

Logan agreed. "The men will be dead by nightfall and the women will become slaves, prized by the men and beaten by the women."

"I feel so helpless," she said, shaking her head.

For the first time in weeks, Logan spread his fingers across her cheek. "I know—so do I." He paused to stare into her eyes. "If I get you far enough away, I might be able to sneak back and kill them. Do you think the women would rather be dead?"

It was not a decision Catherine could make. As long as they were alive, they could hope for freedom. His thumb brushed the soft skin. "Trust me, Cat."

Catherine had heard that plea from Cameron. Now

386

she was wiser and she realized as she looked into Logan's eyes, they had shared too much for her not to believe in him. "I do."

A strange light flickered in his eyes when she made the concession, and Catherine knew as she mounted her horse and followed him that she had made the right decision. They rode most of the night, stopping only for a few hours rest before continuing. Logan was constantly on his guard, and Catherine responded immediately to his demands without arguing or questioning his reasons. In his eyes she recognized a new respect, and his gentle treatment lacked the bitter contempt usually present.

They traveled nearly three full days before Logan felt it was safe to make camp. They found a small stream in a secluded wooded area and he built a fire. An amiable companionship surrounded them while they prepared the meal. Some of Logan's hard exterior shell relaxed, and she saw a quick picture of a totally different man — one who was gentle, caring and understanding, and she was surprised to find herself responding to him once again as a man.

When they finished the meal, Catherine did the dishes and packed everything away. She sat on her bedroll next to the fire and watched Logan gather wood. It was a cool night and he wore a jacket, but her eyes became rivited on the fabric tightening across his back. Unwillingly, she remembered the feel of his flesh beneath her fingertips, and her desire for him flared and threatened to consume her.

Trembling, she ran her fingers through her hair and rose. Logan looked up and when their eyes met, she knew her past animosity and uncertainty had been washed clean by the flood of her need for him—a need she realized was more than physical. She had not only given the man her trust, but she had started to lose her heart to him as well. It was frightening, but at the same time exciting. Cameron was still a part of her life, and the love and passion they had shared would always be a memory. Her future with the Scotchman remained too uncertain to put him out of her life, but she knew it was time to set him aside because of her attraction for another man.

Her needs beckoned strongly, and she took one step and then another, each one becoming easier as she walked toward Logan. Stopping within inches of him, she stared at his dark profile. Her memory of Cameron was all in darkness, but both held a similar attraction for her. Her breath was unsteady as she raised her hand and touched the solid wall of his chest. Beneath her palm, his heart pounded, its beat steadily increasing. Her other hand crept up his neck to touch the thick hair at his collar.

"Are you sure, Cat?" he asked softly.

She nodded, for the first time offering him what he'd always taken. "It's what I want."

Logan still did not touch her. "What about the man from your past? You said you still love him."

"He will always be a part of my life. He was the first and only other man besides you I've ever known. I will never be able to fully erase him from my life. I love him, but he deceived that love. It made me bitter and destroyed some of my ability to love. Instead, I learned to hate." She moistened her lips. "Some of that hate has changed. I have feelings for you that frighten me." Logan's eyes flashed at her announcement.

"Was the man from your past Darrell—the man waiting at your ranch?"

Catherine had often wondered the same thing, and now that Darrell was at her ranch at the same time Cameron was supposed to return, her suspicions grew. "I don't know. I never saw the man who gave me his child. We always met at night, and I never knew his face—only his name . . . Cameron MacLennan."

"Cameron," Logan said in astonishment. "Alana's son?" Catherine nodded. "Things are a little clearer now. Did your uncle want you to marry MacLennan?"

"I think he hoped we'd marry, but he was shot before he could tell me everything he wanted to say."

Logan whistled. "When you get back to the ranch, you are going to have three men after your body—or maybe only two if Cameron and Darrell are the same person."

"Darrell could be Cameron, but I never felt the same toward the two men."

"Why aren't you and Cameron together? You said he deceived you."

Catherine nodded. "I can't talk about it." Her fingers eased between two buttons to touch his chest. "I'm glad you know the truth. I told my uncle everything before he died, but I've carried the burden ever since. I never thought I could trust another man or feel the way I do, but you—" She stole a glance at his eyes and found them smoldering lights of blue passion.

He reached for her and she arched her body along the length of his. His hands cupped either side of her head and his mouth very lightly touched hers. Drawing back, he looked into her eyes. "Are you absolutely sure? If I bed you, there is a chance you'll find yourself in trouble again."

Catherine knew he meant he might give her a child, but she was no longer afraid. Her feelings for Logan were too strong, and her need was too great.

"I'm very sure."

He parted her lips quickly, devouring their softness. He gripped and held her tightly, her breasts pressed against his chest, aching to be freed to the feel of his hands. She felt the flare of his desire and it ignited a searching need in her body. Flattening his palms against her hips, he drew her closer to his length.

Her fingers parted the buttons on his shirt to tease the curly hair on his chest and in return, Logan's hands slid beneath her shirt to cup her full breast. Catherine's head fell back and his mouth nuzzled her neck. With a muffled exclamation, he removed her shirt and ran his lips along her breast. Bending her body over his arm, he playfully aroused every inch of her skin before drawing her back against his chest. The rest of their clothes were shed, and Logan carried her to the waiting bedroll. Stretched out at her side, he continued to explore the secrets of her flesh, bringing her to a level of uncontrollable need.

Catherine drew him against her, her fingers running over his naked torso to elevate him to the same pitch of passion. She welcomed his weight as he rolled on top of her. She found his lips with hers, one kiss melting into another until it became a continuous blending of their bodies. His hand slid along her thigh and across the swell of her breast. They came together, their bodies in perfect unison to the calling need of their desire.

Sated, Logan slid to her side and cradled her in his arms. It had been a wonderful, satisfying experience, and they felt fulfilled. She kissed the line of his jaw. How could she have felt hate for him when he fulfilled so many of her needs? Had she despised him because she hated the emotions he created in her? Catherine no longer hated Logan, but what were his feelings? He had shown his contempt for her many times before and after making love. She ran her hand over his chest and across the firmness of his flat stomach. His flesh was warm from their love-making, the skin moist.

"Logan," she began tentatively.

"Hmm," he muttered, turning his head so his lips brushed her forehead.

"Do you hate me?" She held her breath for his answer.

"Hate you?" he chuckled softly. "After the way you made me feel I could never hate you."

Catherine rose on one elbow to look into his face. "You told me many times that you hated me—once after you bedded me—and I've seen the contempt in your eyes." She grew hopeful. "Did tonight make any difference?"

The angry glint and twist of his mouth was gone, and his eyes were like the clear blue sky. "I don't hate you."

She sighed with relief but his answer wasn't enough. "Why did you say it, Logan? I want to know."

Turning his head, he stared into the campfire. There was a nervous twitching in his jaw and Catherine felt the tension creep through his body. Logan had asked for her trust, but he didn't trust her. More than anything she wanted to understand the man who had broken the defenses she'd erected around her heart and made her feel like a woman. Raising her hand, she caught his chin and turned his head.

"Logan, we have shared something wonderful together. Don't shut me out. You asked me to trust you, now I want your trust."

Logan put his hand on her cheek. "You are so beautiful, but I have learned never to trust a woman."

She kissed the finger caressing her lips. "But why Logan? What happened to make you so bitter?"

A hooded mask slid over his eyes. "I loved a woman once, and she ran out on me. You ask me to trust you, yet we both know you're going to come face to face with your past as soon as we get back to the ranch. Am I supposed to believe you won't fall into Cameron's arms? If I made a commitment to you, and you chose another man, it would be the same thing happening all over again. I won't go through that kind of misery again."

"You still feel the pain?"

"Yes," he said, sliding his fingers into her hair. "But being here with you right now makes the hurt lessen." Pulling her head down, he ran his tongue along her lips. She playfully nipped at the tip in a teasing attempt to avoid the sensitive touch. His hands slid down her back and across her buttocks, drawing her slender length against his hips. Catherine's fingers freely ran across his chest and thighs until he twisted and pinned her beneath his body. Once again Logan carried her toward the sky and together they glided back to earth. When the night cooled, Logan drew a blanket across their nakedness, and they slept together, their arms and legs entwined, breast against breast, hip against hip.

Catherine had never slept so soundly, and she felt

completely rested when she woke. Opening her tawny eyes, she studied Logan's face inches from hers. His dark hair and sun bronzed skin made him one of the most attractive men she'd ever seen, and even the tiny scar from a fight at the side of his face did nothing to detract from his looks. His lips parted as he took a breath, the line of them sensual even as he slept. His eyes were so changeable in reflecting his moods that they could be as cutting as a razor or as gentle and sensual as a lover. She preferred the latter, though she had been on the other end of his emotions often enough.

Their love-making had changed their relationship, but without a spoken commitment between them, Catherine could never be sure about the future. Logan was afraid she would return to Cameron.

Until his deception, Cameron had been a gentle, caring man considerate of her needs. Her love for him had been the love of a young, immature girl who knew nothing of the world. She could never recapture the innocence of the woman he had known. She was gone and he had partly been responsible for killing her.

In contrast, Logan was a hard man. Only lately had she recognized another side to the tough exterior he presented; he was also skilled in knowing her needs. As she reflected on the days since their meeting, there had been many hard fought battles between them but he had always been there when she needed help. Many times she had been humiliated and acted foolishly, but he had never abandoned his guard over her despite the hate she flung at him.

With Logan she had become a woman knowledgeable in the ways of life. He had taken the young confused girl and showed her how to meet the challenges of life. He had never tried to destroy her free searching spirit in its quest for growth and freedom.

She had leaned on Cam for support because she was young and inexperienced. Although she hadn't been afraid to try something on her own, she had relied on him. Logan wouldn't accept that dependency. While he watched over her, he had also been a teacher, helping her to learn to survive by herself.

Cam had been outfitted in expensive clothes, but at the ranch he would cast aside his fancy dress and wear a gun and western garb. It would be a Cameron she didn't know.

"What are you thinking?" Logan whispered, and Catherine was reminded of all the times Cameron had whispered his words of love.

"Nothing," she lied.

"Were you thinking about Cameron?" he asked and she nodded. "Are you afraid to see him again?"

"He is not going to be the same man I knew, and I'm not the same woman."

Logan's eyes took on a mischievous twinkle. "You are definitely not the same woman I met in the saloon that evening."

Her hand dropped to the scar at his side, then she bent to run her tongue along the marked flesh. "I can't believe I tried to kill you."

"You almost succeeded. When I finally regained consciousness, there was blood everywhere and you were gone."

"I was terrified of what I'd done."

"Lucky for me you hid in Lucas's wagon and I was able to collect for what you did." Catherine blushed, knowing his payment was the love-making they had shared.

"Lucas will be surprised when he learns we don't hate each other. I think he wanted us to get along, but he didn't want to interfere."

Logan chuckled. "We stay out of each other's personal business. Are you going to make our relationship public?"

Once again her thoughts turned to Cameron, and her eyes clouded. "How can I want two men at the same time? You're both so different."

His finger ran along the valley of her breasts. "Are we really different?" he muttered before his lips closed on hers, drowning out all thoughts.

It was late morning before they left camp. There was an inner glow about Catherine as she followed the man before her. Travel was easy and fast and when they finally stopped for the night, they were only two days away from the ranch. They secured the horses to a fallen tree limb and set up camp. It was an unusually dark night and Catherine didn't stray beyond the light of the fire. Logan, however, ventured into the woods and returned with dry wood for the fire. Once when she looked up and saw him silhouetted in the darkness, she drew a sharp breath. There was something unsettling about his appearance, but she couldn't pinpoint what it was. After several minutes of contemplation, she scolded herself for being so jittery and instead focused on the new feelings she'd discovered.

After eating, they went into each other's arms and renewed their passion, their bodies joining in the union that was becoming so common.

Eager to get back to the ranch, they left early the next morning. At midday, they stopped for lunch. Logan was in a teasing mood and Catherine had to continuously fight off his roaming hands. He caressed her body and when she had awakened to her need, he ran up a rocky incline.

"You can't do this to me," she cried, chasing after the man who could satisfy her aching desire.

Logan reached the top of the hill, planted his hands on his hips, and watched her follow. When she had almost caught up to him, he darted away, cautiously skipping over the boulders. Squealing her protest, Catherine chased him. Their game continued on the rocky hillside for almost twenty minutes. Finally, she stopped and threw her hands on her hips.

"Logan," she called, and he stopped climbing to turn. "Don't make me chase you any longer. I need you."

"*You* need me or your *body* needs me?" he threw back in a teasing voice.

"We both do." Her voice changed from a shout to a soft acknowledgment. "I love you, Logan."

His body stilled and from beneath the brim of his hat, she saw his eyes widen first in surprise and then relief. With a shout of joy, he ran toward the woman who had just announced her feelings.

This time Catherine was the leader in their game, her declaration presenting new rules and challenges. I was up to Logan to catch her and demand the prize she was offering, and she ached for the moment he would claim her and smother her mouth with kisses. Her response would be to press her body against his and tell him how much she cared for him. Through her love she would strive to make him forget the past bitterness and she would try to nurture his trust in her. In return, she would try to put her time with Cameron into perspective.

She still had an adequate start on him when she reached the bottom of the hill. After running a few feet farther, she stopped and turned. She was done running; now she would wait for him to come to her.

Logan's boots pounded against the rocks as he made his descent. When she stopped, his motions slowed, and he came toward her with purpose. His eyes locked with hers and he paused. Every thought but Catherine vanished from his mind as he looked at the woman who had just proclaimed her love for him.

Dazed by her announcement and oblivious to his surroundings, he took a careless step and missed a rock. His booted foot slid into a crevice and he grinned at Catherine as he righted his equilibrium. A warning rattle triggered his sense of danger, and he glanced down just in time to see a rattlesnake coiled to strike. His foot had not completely freed the rocks when he twisted to avoid being bitten. His movements were not fast enough and he felt the painful sting against his thigh. Unable to regain his balance, he fell against the rocks at the base of the hill.

Everything happened so fast, Catherine could only watch in surprise, but the sight of Logan sprawled on the ground spurred her into action and she raced forward. She had heard the warning rattle and nervously glanced over the ground before dropping to his side.

"Logan, Logan," she called, gently nudging his shoulders.

When he didn't respond, her panic increased. His

head rested against a rock, his bronze cheek in the dirt. Certain he'd been bitten, she searched his lower clothing for puncture wounds. Finding nothing, she rolled him over and gasped at the mat of dark red in the corner of his hair. She wanted to wipe the trickle of blood running down his cheek, but his head wasn't her present worry. If he'd been bitten, it had to be taken care of before the poison spread through his body.

She found the tiny holes in his left thigh. Quickly grabbing the knife from the sheath at his waist, she cut a hole in his pants to display the wound. The puncture marks were clearly visible in the swollen, discolored flesh. Sinking her teeth into her lip, she cut two slashes across the skin. With her lips against the wound, she sucked out the poison and spit it on the ground. When the injury was bleeding freely, she turned her attention to the cut on his head. It had stopped oozing blood, and she realized it was more of a bruise than a gash.

"Logan, Logan," she called again, but his eyes remained closed, his lips unresponsive. It was necessary to get him away from the rocks or by night they'd be in danger from other snakes. The campfire was about fifty feet away, and he would need the warmth. Logan was a tall man, his frame solid despite his leanness. Locking her arms under his shoulders, she dragged him a few feet before exhausted and panting, she sank to the ground. She had to rest almost ten times before she decided he was close enough to benefit from the fire. Running to the horses, she grabbed a spare shirt from one of the saddle bags and tore it up. She opened the canteen and poured water on the cloth, then lightly touched it to his head. His unconsciousness frightened her. He needed to be awake to tell her what to do.

Using some of the remaining fabric, she bandaged his thigh. She called his name repeatedly, but he remained oblivious to her pleas. Out of desperation, she placed her lips against his, hoping it would create a response, but they remained cold and unmoving.

It wasn't long before she noticed a moist clamminess to his skin. Running to his horse, she grabbed his bedroll. At his side, she dampened the cloth and rubbed it across his forehead and lips. She nearly cried in relief when his lips moved. Leaning over, she put her ear against his mouth, but he didn't speak.

"Logan, wake up. You've got to talk to me. I don't know what to do. I need your help."

He trembled, and Catherine reached for the bedroll. Her fingers were shaking so hard she had trouble untying the band around the blankets.

"Cat." She heard the faint whisper and glanced up. His lips moved again. "Catr—"

Unable to understand what he was saying, she shook her head in confusion. "Logan, open your eyes. I'm here with you."

His head rolled to the side and his blue eyes slowly opened. "Cat—so cold."

Catherine had his blankets half unrolled when Logan reached for her. His fingers fastened so tightly around her skin, she winced. "Dona leave me."

With her free hand, she finished unrolling the blanket. In the center, she found a small cloth bag and remembered seeing Logan studying the contents. Whatever it was it had to be important or he wouldn't keep it in the special place. His grip eased and she spread the blanket over his body.

"The cloak," he murmured. His eyes were open and fixed on her face, but the blueness was glazed with confusion.

"Logan, I don't understand you. What are you trying to tell me?"

His head rolled to the side and his speech became a series of mutterings. " 'Tis cold. Ye need ye cloak."

Catherine's gaze fell to the object in her hand. Did she have the right to pry into Logan's private business? Intrigued, her fingers tugged at the opening of the small bag and she reached inside to touch a hard, metal object. It fell out in her hand, but she didn't have time to look at it. Logan's body twisted, his blue eyes opening wide to capture hers. His lips curved in an attempt to smile.

"Catriona, ye came back. Dona leave me. . . . Ye love me."

There was a heaviness in Catherine's throat as she stared at Logan's face. Her eyes shifted to her palm and she slowly opened it to display the odd shaped metal coin that had belonged to her father. Catherine was too shocked to move. Why did Logan have her coin? Unless—

"Catriona, ye canna have a bairn when ye have no husband. I will marry ye."

Tears streamed down Catherine's cheeks and her heart pounded heavily against her breast. Cameron and Logan were the same man. She'd fallen in love with the man she'd met in her aunts' garden. In all the past months, she had never guessed his identity. His appearance had changed drastically. The scar at the side of his face was new, and for weeks he had been rough-shaven. Several times she had been disturbed by the sight of him in the dark, and now she realized it was because her subconscious mind remembered the way Cameron had looked in the shadows. Cameron had been a gentle man while Logan had been the opposite—hard and unrelenting. It was only the last few days that she had seen some of Cameron's gentleness in Logan, but until now she had never put everything together.

He moaned softly, and she wondered why he hadn't told her the truth. "Catriona, ye be my wife. Ye canna leave me."

Did he believe she had deserted him? Cameron had been the one to deceive her through faking a wedding. In the far reaches of her mind, she wondered if he believed they had truly become husband and wife. Her thoughts flashed back to the time when he had found the ring around her neck, and she had denounced the presence of a husband. Agony tore at her heart when she remembered how the color had washed from his face when she told him of the child she'd lost. There had to be explanations for what had happened. They had hurt each other so much that their pain had become bitterness with neither of them being able to trust. Logan had been happy when she'd told him of her love, and she wondered which was the real man.

When darkness descended, Catherine threw more wood on the fire. Logan was restless, his head rolling from side to side. He muttered part sentences, reflecting on the time when she'd known him as Cameron. Over and over again he asked her not to leave him and Catherine tried to reassure him she would stay at his side. If he looked at her, his blue eyes were crazed with the fever that held his body in trembling chills and burning sweat. She frequently checked the snake bite, the skin around the area broken and bruised. The poison was racing through his body and she didn't know what to do to help him.

Catherine slept sitting at his side. Toward dawn, he woke and grabbed her arm. "Catriona, help me." The desperate plea in his voice made her want to scream her helplessness. The man she loved was dying and there was nothing she could do.

"Logan, tell me how to help you."

He lapsed into unconsciousness and her cry went unanswered. Catherine wet one of the cloths and dabbed his forehead, but the coolness did nothing to relieve the fever. She had to find help. If she waited much longer, he'd be dead. Their exact location was unknown, but she knew the ranch was less than two days ride to the northeast. If she took Logan, she might reach help in time. With her decision made, she stored everything in the saddlebags and put out the fire. She led Logan's horse to where he lay and knelt at his side.

"Logan—Logan, can you hear me?" She turned his head. "Logan, I need your help."

His eyes slowly opened. "Catriona, I canna wait to love ye."

Under other circumstances, she would have been thrilled with his statement, but she knew it was only the fever talking.

"Logan, I have to get you on the horse." She pulled the blanket off him. "Try to sit up."

With her arm behind his neck, she tried to pull him

up. "Logan help me," she pleaded. Sweat covered her brow when she finally got him to a sitting position and slipped her thigh behind his back to support him.

Logan's hand slid up her arm to touch her cheek. "Will ye wed me?" Catherine met the blue eyes glazed with fever and thought for a minute that he was aware of what was happening around him. "Please Catriona. Say ye will be my wife. Promise ye will ne'er leave me."

With tears in her eyes, she smiled. Logan would forget what had happened, but right now it was something that would make him happy. "I promise. . . . I will marry you." The color of his face was a sickly white. "First you need help. We have to get you on that horse."

After minutes of exhausting work, Logan got to his feet. Catherine thought her body would break in two under his weight, but she managed to get him to the horse. He clutched the saddle horn and after several attempts, put a booted foot into the stirrup. He was weak, and she had to use all her remaining strength to push him into the saddle where he promptly fell against the stallion's neck. She quickly pulled the lariat off the saddle horn, cut it into three sections, secured his ankles to the stirrups and his hands around the animal's neck. He would not be comfortable, but speed was absolutely necessary and he didn't have the strength to stay on without help.

After mounting her horse, she grabbed the reins of the second horse. She checked the position of the rising sun and rode north. She didn't know if her endeavor would be successful, but at least she was trying.

Catherine stopped every two hours to give Logan

water. His breathing was slow and irregular and she worried about the pallor of his skin. Toward dusk, she stopped for an hour to rest the animals but didn't dare take Logan off his horse. Standing at his side, she brushed the dark hair from his forehead. She felt so helpless in giving him aid and now with the darkness descending, she was frightened. The sun had been their guide in keeping them on a path toward the ranch, but it was gone now and with it her sense of direction. Raising her eyes to the sky, she frowned. Heavy cloud cover shielded the North Star and she didn't know if she should risk getting them lost.

Logan moaned, "Catriona, help me."

Brushing the back of her finger against his cheek, she made the decision to continue. Mounting, she guided the mare forward, then let the animal choose its own path. After midnight, the clouds cleared and Catherine searched the sky for the North Star. After locating its shining brightness, she altered their direction and proceeded at a faster clip.

Several times she caught herself dozing in the saddle. Her back ached and the line from her elbow to shoulder was stiff from holding the reins of the horse behind her. With the beginning of the new day, they left the densely covered land for the short grass where cattle could graze. Though she knew they were not on the ranch, travel would be faster.

During one of their stops, she used the last of their water and realized they would have to find help soon. In the afternoon Logan started shivering, and she threw a blanket over his shoulders, but it didn't seem to help—nothing did.

Toward dusk, she tried to calculate how close the

ranch might be, but she knew they could miss it by miles. Logan had said it was a two day ride, and they had already traveled the equivalent of three long days without finding help. Exhausted, her head fell against her chest and her eyelids drooped. A jerking against her arm straightened her in the saddle. Glancing over her shoulder, she stared first at Logan and then at the animal. The stallion's breath was short and heavy. Wearily, Catherine climbed down from the saddle and nuzzled the animal's nose.

"What's the matter fella?" she asked. "I know you're tired and thirsty, but it's just a little longer." She ran her hand along the mane, trembling when she realized the stallion was covered in a thin sheen of lather. The animal had been carrying a heavy load for too long without adequate rest, water and food. Catherine knew he wouldn't travel any farther. In her inexperience, she had not considered that the horses might betray her search for help, but then she didn't know how hard an animal could be pushed before it collapsed.

Transferring Logan to her horse would not be easy. Her mare was not sweaty, nor was it breathing hard, but it wasn't carrying near the weight and she didn't know how long it would be before it collapsed beneath the added burden. After untying Logan's feet and hands, she pulled her mare alongside of his. He was floating in and out of consciousness, but she finally thought he understood her request for help. She freed the leg caught between the horses and eased it over the back of hers. Logan wrapped his hands around the saddle horn and between him pulling and her pushing against his other leg, she managed to get him on the mare. She secured his hands and feet and turned to the stallion. Perhaps the animal could live if it was turned free. She unfastened the leather straps and let it fall to the dirt. Saddles were costly, but there was no way she could take it with her and she remembered seeing another one in Cameron's room at the MacLennan's house. The bridle followed, then she rubbed her hand down the animal's neck.

"Good luck fella." Snorting, the stallion slowly walked away and Catherine realized she was faced with a serious dilemma. If she walked they could travel more distance, but it would take them longer. On the other hand, if she mounted behind Logan, it would increase the animal's burden, and she doubted it would hold up for more than a few hours. Without the horse, she would be totally helpless.

She pulled the rifle from its case on Logan's saddle, picked up the reins and started to walk. Logan's stallion trotted ahead of them, but at a different angle. Before long, she had lost sight of it completely.

Twice Catherine tripped over rocks and more than once wanted to give up in exhaustion. She had rubbed a blister on her left heel and it ached with each step. Time became unimportant and after a while, the rifle became a crutch to support her weary figure. More than once, she wanted to give up, but her determination and love wouldn't let her quit.

It was just after midnight when she realized her body would not carry her much farther. It was too dark to look for familiar landmarks so she picked up the rifle and fired a shot into the air. Perhaps if they were lucky someone would come to help her. Logan was shivering, and she adjusted his blanket and kissed him on the cheek.

A second shot disturbed the night's silence, then she picked up the reins and forced herself to continue. She stumbled repeatedly until she had to drag herself to her feet. She fired shot after shot until there were no shells left. She retrieved the handgun Logan usually wore and pulled the spare one from her saddlebag. She fired again and again until the cylinders clicked empty.

It was not hot, but she was thirsty and very tired. The mare snorted in protest when she pulled against the reins to move them a little farther.

Out of desperation, she began to shout for help, each cry becoming weaker and weaker until her raspy voice couldn't be heard. Her knees buckled and she fell to the dirt. The mare's nose struck her in the back of the head, nudging her onward. When she didn't respond, the mare pulled against the reins. Catherine was too tired to even consider the reasons for the horse's actions, but she climbed to her feet. The mare's pace quickened and Catherine stumbled along beside the animal. The reins slid from her fingers and she cried out in panic when the horse trotted away. She couldn't let the mare escape with Logan tied to the saddle; he was totally helpless.

"Whoa girl," she called, but the animal ignored her call. Tears stung her eyes as she stumbled forward, tripped, righted herself, then fell again. Finally she was too tired to move. She had failed Logan. Unknowingly, he had put his trust in her and she had failed him.

It was a bitter admission to make and it tore at her mind as she lay sobbing in the dirt. She wanted to rise but the pain of her weary body made it impossible. In her agony, she was heedless of the hands that touched her shoulders and lifted a canteen to her lips.

"It's over now, Catherine. Everything will be fine."

In the belief she was dreaming, she ran her hand over her eyes, then looked at the man holding her. "Lucas," she whispered. "Lucas—the horse carrying Logan ran away. We've got to find him."

"He's safe," he reassured her. "What happened?"

"Logan got bitten by a rattlesnake. I drew out the poison and bandaged his thigh, but he's sick. I didn't know what to do." She swallowed a knot of fear. "He is delirious. . . . He hit his head. . . . I don't know how the wound is."

"Don't worry. We'll take care of him."

Relieved to have someone else assume the burden, Catherine sighed and let the blackness block out all memory.

Chapter Twenty-four

When Catherine woke, the darkness around her was alarming and she experienced minutes of panic before remembering she had found help. She was still exhausted, her limbs weak, but she had to know how Logan was. Pushing aside the covers, she slid her legs over the side of the bed. She was wearing a thin cotton nightgown that didn't belong to her so she knew she wasn't in her room. It took her several seconds to reach the door and step into the hall. She was at the MacLennan ranch.

The door to Cam's room was closed but she turned the knob and stepped inside. Recognizing the dark head on the pillow, her heart burst with the love she felt for him. Her steps were unsteady as she crossed to the bed and sat on the edge. A lamp burned on an adjacent table and cast a yellow glow over his features. His breathing was steady and she thought there was more color in his skin. Lifting one of his hands, she brushed her fingers over the knuckles. The fever was down and she was sure it was a favorable sign.

Raising her hand, she smoothed the dark hair from his forehead, then let her palm linger on his cheek and jaw. It was still hard to believe Logan and Cameron were the same man. There were so many questions she wanted to ask him, and she was still haunted by his deceit at the church. What had he hoped to gain by pretending to marry her? Was the thought of marriage totally abhorrent to him?

"Catriona," he muttered in his sleep, and she rested her hand against his chest.

"Yes Cameron, I'm here." Cameron would always be the Scottish man and Logan the tough cowboy.

"Catriona, Catriona."

She knew he was talking in his sleep, but his plea for her made her heart soar. Content, she rested her head against his chest and listened to the pounding of his heart. She ached to crawl into the bed with him and let him wake to the feel of her body against his, but there were still too many questions in her mind. Catherine had openly admitted her love, but Cameron's feelings—if he had any—were locked away.

Catherine was still resting against his chest when the door opened and Alana stepped into the room and stilled at the sight of Catherine and her son. She was happy to see them together and hoped it meant they had finally worked out their differences. Ever since their return she had hated to deceive Catherine about Cameron's identity, but he had made it clear that she was not to learn the truth. For weeks Logan had been carrying a bitterness in his heart, and though she suspected Catherine was involved, he refused to discuss it. Perhaps if the truth was known, the two of them could find happiness.

Stepping forward, she lightly touched Catherine's shoulder. "Catriona," she said softly. "Ye shouldna be here. Ye need to rest."

Catherine raised her head and turned to look at Alana. "I had to see him. . . . How is he?"

410

"He's been very sick, but I think there be improvement. It will be several days before we ken for sure," she said, sliding her arm around Catherine's shoulders to steady her. "Both of ye need rest." Alana helped her back to bed, then covered her with a blanket. "I will see ye in the mornin'," she said and turned to leave.

Catherine caught her wrist. "Wait. . . . Please. I have to talk to you." Alana wanted her to rest but there was determination in her voice so she lit the lamp.

"Wha' be troublin' ye lass?"

She ran a trembling hand across her forehead. "I felt so helpless. Logan and I were laughing and running over some rocks. . . . I said something that distracted his attention and he wasn't as careful as he usually is. The snake struck and he fell and hit his head." Tears filled her eyes. "I tried to help him, but he got so sick."

"I tried to reassure ye that he would be fine, but I canna do more. Ye be both exhausted and have slept for almost twenty-four hours."

Catherine gasped. "You mean I didn't just arrive here this evening?" Alana shook her head. "We were lucky Lucas found us."

"Aye, a few hours earlier Logan's horse came into the yard. We couldna ken where ye be. Lucas gathered up the few men at the ranch and rode out to find ye. They heard shots and finally yer calls. Ye be lucky."

Sinking her teeth into her lip, Catherine regarded the older woman. "Why didn't you tell me about Logan?"

"I dona ken," she said with a shake of her head.

"I know Logan and Cameron are the same man."

There was a look of relief on the older woman face. "Aye, they be the same. I didna want to deceiv ye, but Logan asked me nae to tell ye his rea identity."

"But why Alana? I don't understand. . . . Do yo know we became acquainted at my aunts' home?"

"Cameron tol' me," she said, smiling. "He wro that he'd fallen in love wi' the wee lass Catriona an had made her his wife."

Catherine wanted to weep with relief that Camero had loved her the nights they made love, but couldn understand why he would tell his mother they ha been married. The events surrounding the false cere mony puzzled her.

She wrinkled her nose in confusion. "Alana, w aren't married." In dealing with the past, Catherin could only think of Logan as Cameron. "Cameron me me at the church and we went through a ceremony but later I learned the wedding was not valid."

Alana shook her head. "I dona think ye ken. Whe Cameron returned he saed ye were wed. . . . He to the same thin' to ye uncle. Why would my son trick y like that?"

"My uncle knew?" she asked and wondered if h would have told her the truth had he not been shot.

"Ye must be mistaken. Ye be my daughter-in-law

Catherine shook her head. "The man who calle himself Reverend Peters and wed us was not the sam man who talked to me later. In fact, he was attacke the night of our wedding so someone else could per form the ceremony."

Alana frowned. " 'Tis somethin' wrong here lass. My son believes ye be wedded."

Catherine wanted to settle the misunderstanding by marrying the man she loved, but it would be up to Logan to suggest it. "If he thinks I'm his wife, then why didn't he tell me who he was? Why did he make me believe he was Logan?"

"Ye must ken my son. He be a proud man and his feelings are nae given easily. When he returned to the ranch, he be a bitter man. He saed ye be wedded, but he didna acknowledge yer husband." She hesitated. "He saed ye hated him. Cameron was angry."

The bitterness Alana spoke of had traveled with them all the way across the Midwest. Logan had taunted her and made her hate herself because she had responded to another man when she'd given her heart to Cam; Logan despised her for not being loyal to Cam and after they made love, he hated himself for still wanting her. If he believed they were married, then his bitterness had centered on her because she had denounced their vows and refused to admit any commitment to the man who had given her a ring. He hated her for responding to him as Logan, and he probably believed she was committing adultery.

"Why did ye run out on Cameron?"

Catherine paled. "I didn't. My aunts wanted me to marry a stranger and I had to escape. When I realized he had tricked me, I was filled with intense bitterness and hurt." Tears moistened her cheeks. "I was carrying his child. I didn't have anyone to turn to so I came here."

"What happened to the bairn?"

"I had an accident and lost the baby."

Alana understood Catherine's turmoil and lightl
patted her hands. "I be sorry for ye and my son. 'Twa
nae an easy time for ye. . . . Get some rest. We ca
talk in the mornin'," she said, extinguishing the lamp
and walking to the door.

Rolling to her side, Catherine stared into the dark
ness. There were so many things she wanted to under
stand. Logan could supply the answers, but would sh
like what he said? If he believed they were married
she could understand his resentment toward her whe
she responded to him as another man. She had pro
fessed a deep love for Cameron, yet she bedde
another. Logan was a proud man and if he believe
she had shunned her vows, he would feel deceived an
lose his trust in her.

Logan had been acting out of jealousy and hur
when he shot Darrell. Seeing her in the saloon dres
had triggered an already smoldering resentment an
when Darrell defended her, Logan believed thei
familiarity was because they were lovers. Darrell wa
still at her ranch, and she would have to explai
everything to him before he met Logan.

At last she fell into a soundless sleep, too exhauste
from the complexities of her life. Tomorrow would b
plenty of time to sort out her problems.

It was late when Catherine woke. She sat up an
stretched, and aside from a few sore muscles, she fel
relaxed and almost back to her usual self. Tossin
aside the blankets, she found clean clothes on a nea
by chair and changed.

She paused outside Cameron's door and listened

She wanted to step inside, but something held her back. She had openly declared her love for him, but never once since she had known him as Logan or Cameron had he expressed his feelings. It was his turn to come to her. He would have to sort through the bitterness in his mind and decide if she was to be part of his life.

Catherine found Alana and Lucas in the kitchen enjoying a cup of coffee, and she joined them at the table.

"Ye be lookin' wonderful this mornin'," Alana said, getting Catherine coffee and biscuits.

"I feel good." Her gaze switched to Lucas. "Thank you for finding me. I had gone as far as I could go."

"It was your shots and yellin' that led me to you." There was a look of admiration in his dull blue eyes. "It took a lot of courage to do what you did. You really proved yourself to be one of the women who can endure the hard life in the West."

Catherine laughed. "I won't survive long if I have many more challenges like I had with Logan." Her eyes shifted to Alana. "How is he this morning?"

"He be restin' comfortably."

"Is he going to be all right?" There was an unexpected dryness in her throat.

"Logan is tough," Lucas reassured her. "I've seen men die from rattlesnake bites but most survive. I think he'll be fine."

Catherine hid her relief by taking a sip of the hot liquid. "Lucas, did you know Logan's real identity?"

His eyes darted quickly to Alana, and Catherine saw an approving look pass between them. "I've known that Logan used the name Cameron MacLennan from

time to time, but I didn't know it was part of you
cause for grief. I was with Logan in the East." Lear
ing forward, he rested his arms on the edge of th
table. "He had gone there to take care of some bus
iness and to see you. I knew he was involved with you
but one day he said we were leaving. I asked him
you were coming and he just sneered. He wouldn't dis
cuss you other than to say you had tricked him an
left."

"But I didn't," she protested.

"I know, Alana explained what happened. Whe
you showed up in the wagon, I wasn't sure if you wer
the Catherine that Logan despised. I asked him, bu
he warned me not to interfere. We had traveled to
gether a long time and I wasn't going to let it ruin ou
friendship, so I kept my mouth shut."

"I don't want Logan to know anything I've tol
you."

"But why?" Alana protested. "Ye shouldna hide th
truth from him. He has a right to know."

"I'll tell him." Her gaze shifted to Lucas. "I'd like t
get back to my ranch. Would you take me?"

"Catherine, there is something we haven't tol
you," Lucas said cautiously. "There is a man, Darre
Coleman, in your house waiting to see you."

Catherine smiled. Darrell had been a friend an
there was no reason not to want to see him. "I kno
him. He helped me when I was in trouble."

"Aye, Darrell be a good lad," Alana agreed.

"Do you know him?" Catherine asked, knowing the
were both of Scottish descent.

"Aye. I've known him since he was a wee lad."

She remembered the times she'd mistaken Darrel

for Cameron, and it had proved embarrassing in more than one instance. "When I first met him I thought he was Cameron."

Alana expelled a sharp breath. "Ye thought he was my son."

Catherine nodded. "Cam and I always met in the darkness, and I never got a look at his face. I knew the Scottish accent and when a Scotchman appeared on the same flatboat with me, I thought it was more than just coincidence."

"Aye, when my son becomes Cameron MacLennan, he adds the brogue."

"He had me fooled. His accent is as real as yours."

"Aye. Cameron learned to speak the Scotch tongue when he was a wee lad in Scotland. When he came to America, he dropped the accent."

There was a lot Catherine didn't know about the man she loved. For now, she was anxious to return home. "I want to get back to the ranch and see Darrell," she said, frowning. "I thought he was dead. Logan shot him in a saloon in Saint Louis."

Alana sobered. "Darrell tol' me. I dona want trouble between the lads. I have talked to Darrell, and I will talk to Logan. I will try to make him ken."

Finishing her biscuits, Catherine rose. "I'm anxious to get home. Let me know if Logan improves."

Lucas finished the coffee in his cup and rose. "I'll get the horses ready." Out of the corner of her eye, Catherine saw Lucas wink at Alana, and she wondered what had transpired between them during their absence.

On their return to the ranch, Catherine told Lucas about the success of the cattle sale and when he could expect to see the other men. She had never imagined she would experience such strong feelings of relief when her home came into view. They rode to the front of the house.

"I'll be in the bunk house or barn if you need me," he said and rode off.

Catherine smiled at Lucas's protectiveness. He was worried about her meeting with Darrell and wanted her to know she could call on him if necessary. She had just dismounted when the front door swung open and Darrell strode out.

"Catriona, ye be back." He smiled, the planes of his face as striking as she remembered.

"Darrell, it's been a long time."

His green-eyed gaze slid over her figure. "Ye have changed," he said, but she saw nothing in his glance that was negative.

"I've been through a lot since our last meeting."

Darrell's eyes dulled and his hand absently went to his chest where Logan's bullet had pierced his flesh. "For many weeks, I didna think I would e'er see ye again."

Catherine's eyes softened. "I feel responsible for what happened. I thought you were dead."

"Ye shouldna feel any guilt. Wha' happened was between Logan and me."

She searched his face for some remaining bitterness, but didn't see any. Alana said she had talked to Darrell, and if she also talked to Logan, perhaps trouble could be prevented.

Sliding her arm through his, she said, "I want to have something to drink, then I have promised myself a nice long bath. We can talk after dinner."

Darrell's long fingers briefly closed over hers. "Aye, we will talk later, and ye can tell me wha' ye have been doin' these past months."

Juanita was delighted to see Catherine and gave her an affectionate hug before going to the kitchen to heat water for the bath. Catherine spent nearly an hour in the refreshing hot water before scrubbing her skin to a healthy pink color. After dressing and combing her long tawny hair, she went to find Darrell. He was on the patio, so she grabbed a jacket and joined him.

"Ye have a beautiful home. I was sorry to hear about ye uncle. Ye must have been saddened by his death."

"He offered me a kindness and permanence I had not known for years. I will always be grateful to him for it."

Darrell studied her thoughtfully. "Ye be so different; I canna believe the change. On the flatboat, you were shy and cautious about everything. . . . Now I sense a recklessness about you — almost as though I was ne'er seein' the real Catriona."

"You did see a very different woman," she agreed. There had been a time after Cameron's deceit when she'd felt beaten, but deep down inside, she knew her free spirit would eventually resurface. She had found that freedom in Logan's arms, and their continuous battles had revived the smoldering spirit. "I had been through a difficult time in my life. When I lost the baby, I experienced a deep loss."

Darrell nodded, his eyes sadly remembering her anguish the day he had told her about the accident which claimed the unborn child. "Catriona, is Cameron MacLennan the man — was he the child's father and the cause of ye past unhappiness? Ye called his name when ye were sick and more than once ye mistook me for him. . . ." A teasing gleam crept into his eyes. "Nae that I minded."

Color crept into Catherine's cheeks. "Yes, he is the man." Her announcement didn't seem to surprise Darrell, nor did she see disappointment on his face. "I'm sorry if you thought there could be anything between us."

"Nae lass, I've thought a lot about our time together. Ye needed help and I wanted to give it. . . . I know I tried to kiss ye once, but dona blame me. Deep down I knew t'would ne'er work. After I was shot, I couldna get ye off my mind. Ye had become like a sister to me, and I knew when I recovered I would find ye."

Catherine was touched by Darrell's concern. In her time of need she had regarded his kindness as a blessing. "You are going to make me cry," she said, wiping her eye.

"Nae lass. I just want to see ye happy."

Catherine knew her happiness would never be complete until Logan held her in his arms and professed his love. If Logan had any deep feelings for her, he would be jealous to learn Darrell was in her house — no matter how innocent it was. She shuddered at the thought of the men meeting.

"Are ye cold? Let's go inside. 'Tis gettin' chilly at night."

Juanita had already started a fire and Catherine held her hands against the warming blaze. Then Juanita brought them sandwiches and they sat on cushions to eat. When they finished and their plates were set aside,

Catherine leaned forward and rested her elbows on her knees.

"Darrell, Cameron is at the MacLennan ranch."

His brows shot up. "When did he get back?"

"He returned with me a couple of days ago."

Darrell smiled. "Then we'll be meeting soon."

She couldn't understand why seeing Cameron would make him happy but she thought Darrell didn't know Cameron and Logan, the man who shot him, were the same person.

She moistened her lips. "There is something you should know. . . . Cameron and Logan are the same person."

"Aye," he said with a shake of his head. "Alana tol' me."

"She did?"

"Aye. Alana and I have seen each other many times."

"She said she has known you since you were a young boy." He confirmed her statement and Catherine rose to her feet. "I'm frightened about your meeting with Logan. I don't think you would want to harm him, but he has an explosive temper. . . . I'm afraid one of you might end up killing the other."

Rising, Darrell placed his hands on her shoulders. "Catriona, I willna hurt the man ye love."

"But he might provoke you into a fight."

"Nae. He will lose his bitterness once he talks to Alana." He grinned. "Besides, I be the one who would seek revenge. He shot me, yet I dona want to hurt him."

"But you don't know him like I do."

" 'Tis a lot I dona ken about my brother, but I want to get to know him."

"Your brother!" Catherine gasped and felt Darrell's fingers tighten around her arms. "Cameron—Logan—is your brother?"

"He be my kin," he said, his green eyes raking her pale face. "I didna mean to surprise ye."

"On the boat when I mentioned Cam's name, why didn't you tell me you had a brother with the same name? It is not a common name."

"I didna know," he said, guiding her to a two-seated settee and sitting her down. "Let me tell you what I do know," he said, joining her. "I be five years younger than Cameron, but when I was born, Cameron had already left Scotland."

"He left when he was five. But what about Alana?" She couldn't understand a child of five leaving home.

"Alana wanted to come to America, but she couldna earn enough money. She met a wealthy American couple who wanted a boy to learn their business techniques from a very young age. They couldna use Alana, but 'twas a chance for her son. Times were bad in Scotland and she believed she could someday earn the money to join him. As it turned out, she didna get to America till I was fifteen years old."

"Where is your father?"

"Logan's father died and Alana remarried. I dona know where my kin is. I saw him two years ago when I was in a poker game, but he didna acknowledge me as his son."

Seeing the distant pain in his eyes, she covered his hands with hers. She knew the agony suffered when family failed to return affection. "I'm sorry, Darrell."

He shrugged. "He was nae a man to like. He was fine to Alana in the beginning when we had money, but when times got hard, he became bitter and greedy. I dona miss him."

"Then Alana is still married," she said, reflecting on the interest Lucas and Alana had in each other.

"Aye, they be still wedded."

"But I still don't understand why Alana never told you and Logan about each other."

"I canna sae. Perhaps she wanted to keep her lives separate."

"When did Alana and Cameron get back together?"

"She came to the ranch when he be gone to the East."

"Why did she wait so long?" Catherine asked.

"My mother didna come to America wi' me till I be fifteen. Things with her husband were nae good, so she indentured herself for seven years and we came here to start a new life. I didna like her puttin' herself in bond, but 'twas nae I could do. After two years, she tol' me to make a life for myself, and I turned to poker." He ran his fingers through his dark hair. "We kept in touch 'til she finished her years of servitude, then she saed she be goin' west to work on a ranch. I be on my way to visit her when Cam shot me."

"Perhaps she had decided to bring her sons together."

"Aye, she wanted us to know about each other."

"Is Alana going to tell Logan the truth?"

"Aye, and I expect to see him this afternoon."

"Darrell, Logan was bit by a snake. He's very sick."

His brows came together in concern. "Will he be all right?"

"Yes, but I don't expect to see him for several days."

Darrell flashed her a reassuring grin. "I dona want

ye worryin' about Cameron."

That night in bed, Catherine took the time to sort through all she had discovered. Learning that Darrell was Cameron's brother had been a shock, but it explained why she often mistook him for the man she loved. They had a similarly shaped head and build and in the darkness one had looked like the other. What would Logan think when he learned the truth? She experienced several minutes of horror when she realized that Logan had shot his brother in the saloon. Had he killed him and learned the truth about his identity, it would have been a hard reality to face.

Catherine and Darrell went for a ride after breakfast. Darrell had given up his fancy gambling clothes in favor of the more practical pants and boots. It was an enjoyable morning and they were relaxed in each other's company. When they got back to the ranch, there was a horse tied near the door. A bubble of apprehension lodged in her throat as she dismounted and started toward the house. The door opened and Alana stepped outside.

"Is Logan with you?" Catherine asked immediately.

"Nae, but he be sittin' up in bed."

" 'Tis a good sign," Darrell said from her side. "Hello *Mathar*," he said, leaning forward to kiss her cheek.

Alana's gaze darted uneasily in Catherine's direction. "So ye know the truth."

She nodded. "Darrell told me everything last night. Did you talk to Logan?"

"Nae. I want to wait a few more days till he be stronger."

Catherine had many questions, but as hostess she had to make her guests comfortable. "Come inside. I'll have Juanita fix something to drink."

Darrell touched Catherine's arm. "I'll take our horses to the barn. 'T'would be good for ye to talk alone."

When the women were settled before the fire, Catherine looked at Alana. "Has Logan asked for me?"

There was a sadness in Alana's eyes. "Nae lass. He hasna mentioned ye name."

"But doesn't he care about me?" She had visions of the cold Logan returning. "I love him Alana. Doesn't he know. . . . doesn't he know how I tried to save his life?" She bordered on hysteria.

"I dona know. He doesna talk to me. He either sleeps or stares into space."

"Are you certain he is all right? He took a nasty blow to the head. . . . Perhaps he has forgotten part of the past."

"I canna say wha' the lad be thinkin'. I want Lucas to come back and talk to him. Perhaps he can draw him out."

"I'm so frightened Alana," Catherine sobbed. "Logan has to remember. He has to know I love him."

"Would ye come to see him?" she asked, her blue-green eyes regarding Catherine hopefully.

"I can't. If he has forgotten what happened between us the last few days then he will hate me as before. I couldn't bear to see the contempt in his eyes." Rising, she covered her face with her hands.

"I ken lass," she said sympathetically.

Darrell came into the room, his senses immediately picking up on the tension. "Has something happened?" he asked, noting her anxiety.

Catherine's eyes were brimming with tears as she threw herself into Darrell's arms. "Logan is not acting like himself. Alana said he won't talk to her—and he hasn't mentioned me."

He looked over Catherine's shoulder at his mother to confirm what Catherine said. With the bobbing agreement of her head, a muscle tightened in his jaw. "Wha' can we do?" he asked.

Alana shook her head. "I hope Lucas will make a difference."

"I tol' him ye be here, and he be comin' to the house."

Alana rose. "Try nae to worry."

Darrell put his arm around Catherine's shoulders and they followed his mother outside. Lucas was coming up the walk, his thoughtful expression breaking into a smile at the sight of Alana.

"Darrell told me you were here."

"Aye," she said, returning the warm grin. "I came to see ye and Catriona about Logan. He be awake, but he willna talk to me. And he hasna asked for Catriona."

Lucas's expression was grave. "His behavior is not a result of the snake bite," he said, scratching his head. "But I don't know about the bruise on his head." He turned. "I'll get my horse and ride back with you."

Catherine and Darrell stayed outside until Alana and Lucas had ridden out of sight. "Try nae to worry. Maybe his pride be wounded and he willna talk because ye havena seen him."

Catherine considered Darrell's comment but knew she could never again risk seeing the contempt in Logan's eyes. It would be too painful.

At dinner Catherine picked at the food on her plate and nothing Darrell said to her made any difference. She listened for Lucas's return, finally putting on her jacket and standing outside on the patio to scan the darkness. It was near midnight when he rode up to the house. Catherine rushed forward to meet him and Darrell stepped out of the shadows where he had been waiting to help Catherine if she needed it.

"How is he?" she asked, before he had dismounted.

"Let's go inside. You'll catch a chill out here."

Catherine led the men into the warm house, then turned on Lucas. "How is he?" she demanded this time.

"He is a bitter man," he answered.

Lucas's news was a blow to her. "Did he tell you why?"

"No. He wouldn't talk to me. I've ridden with Logan for years, but I've never seen him filled with such hate."

The older man's words frightened Catherine. What had happened in Logan's mind to make him so angry? She had done nothing but offer her love. "Is it me he hates?" she managed to ask.

"I was afraid to question him. I know he is angry about something, but he keeps things to himself. He's my friend but if I get into a fight with him, he might shut me out completely."

Despite their past conflict, the news about his brother troubled Darrell. "Wha' does Alana think?" he asked.

Lucas shrugged. "She doesn't know. We decided to give him two more days, then we'll try again."

Logan's bitterness and pain were almost too much for her to bear. The man she loved was filled with

427

hate, and it was probably all directed toward her. He
eyes were misty when she raised her head. "Excus
me," she mumbled and ran to her room.

With her door closed, she cried to vent her fear
and anguish. How could she help Logan overcome hi
bitterness? She had done everything she knew to gai
his trust. Her torment was more than she could bea
and she sobbed late into the night.

Catherine woke before daybreak, dressed in warr
clothes and saddled her horse. She hoped an earl
morning ride would help sort out her thoughts. Wit
the wind whipping through her hair and the cold stin
of the morning air against her cheeks, some of he
tension eased. When she returned to the ranch, Luca
and the men were getting ready to ride out on th
range.

Lucas drew her away from the men. "How are yo
this morning?"

"I was upset last night, but I realize I have to b
strong enough to face whatever happens. Logan wi
be in bed a few more days and maybe he'll come t
grips with whatever is troubling him."

"I think you've made the only possible decision. Th
men and I will be back later this morning. Don't ex
pect to see Darrell until lunch. We had a card gam
last night and it didn't finish until almost dawn."

Catherine chuckled. "Are you richer or poore
today?"

"I'm not as bad off as two of the men, but I felt th
pinch. He really knows his way around a deck o
cards."

When the men were gone, Catherine rode her mar
to the barn, unsaddled her and turned her loose in th
corral. Juanita had coffee ready when she got to th

house and Catherine took her cup out on the patio. It was really too cool to sit outside but she hated to be closed inside the house. She wanted the freedom of the outdoors.

Fifteen minutes later, her attention was drawn to a rider approaching the ranch. It was early for company but she drained her cup and went to greet the rider. The horse had entered the main yard before she recognized who it was, and a building knot of tension began in her chest and tightened through her limbs. Logan had come for the confrontation.

Darrell's room was on the other side of the house, but she still walked away from the building so their exchange could be conducted in private. She tried to brace herself for what was to come, but she could not prepare herself for the way Logan looked. His illness had definitely taken its toll on his body, and there were lines of exhaustion on his face. He was leaner and unsteady and it was clear he had no business being out of bed. His hat hid his upper face but she knew he was watching her. She noticed the gun low on his hip when he swung out of the saddle.

"Logan, you shouldn't be up," she scolded.

His head snapped up and she got a look at his eyes—a blue so chilling and remote that there was no doubt about his hate. "No, I don't imagine you are glad to see me," he drawled, and the bitterness in his voice surprised her.

"I am glad, Logan," she protested. "You don't understand."

Grabbing her arm, he pulled her against his chest. "I understand everything. . . . You're a liar."

His hold on her arm was painful. "I've never lied to you. Stop. . . . You're hurting me."

429

When she tried to wrench herself free, his arms closed around her back, fitting her against his length. "You said you loved me."

"I do, Logan. I love you." She couldn't bear the painful embrace.

"Do you also love Cameron?"

"I loved him first, but I also learned to love Logan." She raised her hands to his shoulders. It was time to show him how she felt. Pushing his hat to the ground, she ran her fingers through his dark hair. "I want both of you," she said, rising on her toes to kiss his mouth. "I want to marry you and have your children."

"You are already my wife even though you refuse to wear my ring and use my name."

Catherine's caresses stilled. She'd forgotten that Logan believed they were married and knew her next words would hurt him more, but he had to know the truth.

"We're not married Logan. The ceremony was fake."

His hand closed along her jaw and he forced her head up until she met his eyes. "On my orders, my legal counsel made the arrangements."

Despite the pain he was causing her, she ran her hand against his cheek. "You were tricked. Someone beat up the real Reverend Peters and we were married by an impostor."

There was a dawning light in Logan's eyes and she knew he must be remembering something from the past. "It's possible," he conceded, his grip loosening slightly. "It would fit with something else that happened."

"What was it, Logan? Please tell me." She didn't want to be closed out of his thoughts.

"I was afraid to go to the church myself so I sent a legal man in my place. He asked the reverend to meet me to discuss the details. The man I met was the same one who married us."

"Then you were tricked. Someone wanted to make us believe we were married and only that person would still know we had our freedom," she said, watching him closely. "Do you know who is responsible?"

Frowning, he ran his hand through his ruffled hair. "Aye, it was—" Logan stiffened, his gaze swinging from a point in the distance to focus on her face. "So you want me to believe you love me. After I got hurt, you promised to stay by my side. . . . I needed you, and you let me down. You pushed me aside for—"

"That's not true," she cried frantically. She had to make him see reason. "Logan, you want me at your side, but you have never told me how you feel. Do you love me?"

There was no softening in his hard features. "Cameron loved you, but Logan hates you."

His words were a hard blow, and Catherine staggered backward. "You don't mean that. . . . You can't."

His gaze left her face to stare at the house. "Your innocence and beauty drew me to you but something changed all that. When I met you as Logan, you were a hard, bitter woman."

"You made me bitter, Logan. You ran out on me and left me alone and carrying a child."

"I didn't run out on you," he sneered. "I was away on business, and when I got back you were gone. The next time I saw you, you were working in a saloon and keeping company with a certain gentleman." There was a hardness in his blue eyes. "I tried to kill him once, the second time I won't miss."

Logan's fingers dropped to his holster and his thumb released the safety strap holding his gun. Catherine was first confused then horrified when she followed his gaze toward the house and saw Darrell standing on the patio watching them.

Catherine threw herself at Logan. "There was never anything between Darrell and me. . . . Logan, you've got to believe me."

His gaze dropped briefly to her face. "Is that why you came here—to be with him instead of waiting at my side?"

"This is my home."

"But I am the man you professed to love," he said, throwing her aside.

Darrell, oblivious to the potential danger he was putting himself in, saw Logan's ill treatment of Catherine and started toward them. The murderous intent in Logan's eyes warned Catherine that he didn't know the truth about Darrell.

"There will be no poker game this time, Coleman," Logan said, his hand inches from the gun.

Darrell stilled. He had moved close enough to see Logan's eyes and recognize the danger he was in. "Ye must listen to me Cameron. Ye dona ken."

"I understand what I see." His hand hit the handle of the gun and it was eased from the holster.

"You can't shoot him," Catherine screamed. "He's your brother!"

There was a stiffening in the hand movement and a flicker of doubt on the harsh features. It was long enough for Catherine to get control. Lunging forward, she hit him at the knees with all her strength and they fell to the ground.

Racing forward, Darrell kicked the gun out of the way and pulled Catherine off Logan. He glared at his brother. "Wha' she says be the truth. Will ye listen to her?"

Logan's stonelike expression didn't give anything away. Slowly, he rose, his balance unsteady and cautious.

A horse galloped into the yard and Alana dismounted. "I didna know he be gone."

"Alana, tell him the truth," Catherine demanded. "He almost killed Darrell."

The uncertain glance Logan gave his mother tore at Catherine's heart. What a way for him to find out about his family!

Alana slipped her hand around Logan's waist. "Come into the house, Cameron. I must talk to ye."

"Put him in my room," Catherine shouted before they disappeared inside. She turned to Darrell. "I didn't know he intended to get so hostile. I'm sorry."

"Alana better straighten him out. 'Tis the last time I want to be lookin' down the barrel of his gun."

Her shoulders slumped in rejection. "He hates me, Darrell. You should have seen his eyes."

He slid a comforting arm around her shoulders. "Nae lass, he loves ye. Havena ye e'er seen a jealous man?"

Hope brightened her tawny eyes. "Do you really think so?"

"Aye lass, he loves ye, but he might be too proud to admit it. 'Tis up to ye."

Alana came out of the back room an hour later and joined Catherine and Darrell. "What happened?" Catherine asked quickly.

"I tol' Cameron everythin' and he would like to see his brother."

"What about me?" she asked hopefully. "Does he want to see me?"

Alana shook her head. "He didna mention ye lass."

Darrell gave Catherine's shoulder a reassuring pat before he went to the back of the house. Defeated, Catherine threw herself in a chair. "What a mess!" she sighed. "How did Logan take the news about Darrell? He came very close to killing him."

"Aye, I ken Logan's temper. 'Tis nae to be fooled wi'." She smoothed the dark hair from her cheek. "Logan be a proud man, but he will apologize to his brother."

"But Logan thinks Darrell is my lover."

Alana laughed softly. "My son be stubborn and refuses to admit his real feelings. Darrell will tell him the truth."

Catherine curled her legs on the chair. "Why didn't you tell Logan and Darrell about each other?"

Alana sighed softly. " 'Twas because of Darrell's father."

"Darrell said your husband made your life miserable."

"I was a rebellious young woman who refused to conform to my wealthy parent's wishes. I ran awa' and met Logan's father. We be married and Logan be born. Several months later, my husband took a job on the sea. After a year, I received word he was dead. Logan was almost two." She sighed, her mind back on her earlier years. "We didna have much money, but I wouldna go to my family for help. I didna want my son to be raised near my domineering parents. When I realized our only future could be in America, I found a

ouple who agreed to take Cam to the States and train
im in business. 'Twas hard to let him go, but I had an
heritance I could collect if I pretended to be single.
Vhen Cameron sailed I went home to get the money."
ne sighed. " 'Twas a disaster. My family wouldna give
e the funds and instead used my wealth to find me a
usband. The marriage be against my will. To protect
ameron, I ne'er mentioned him or my first
arriage."

Catherine recognized the lines of strain on the older
oman's face. "If this is too painful for you, we can
lk about it later," she offered.

"Nae. Ye need to know the truth. Darrell was born
the first year. I ne'er loved my husband and he
ade our lives miserable. When things became impos-
ble, I took Darrell and indentured myself to get to
merica. My husband learned my plans and we had
flee without our personal belongings. Among my
othes there be letters from Cam, and they were filled
' disapproval for the man who was makin' my life
iserable." Alana trembled. "My husband, Duncan,
uldna find Darrell and me, but he did go to Cam-
on. They hated each other on sight. . . . I ne'er
entioned my sons to each other because I feared my
usband would use them against me. I knew when I
id served my period of indenture, I would bring
em together and hope they would forgive me."

"I'm sure they understand. Do you know where
arrell's father is?"

"Nae lass, I dona know wha' happened to him."
here was a forlorn look in her eyes. "Cameron prom-
d to search for him in the East, but I canna believe
had any luck."

"You must not give up hope."

"I willna give up hopin'. Lucas would like to we
me and we be makin' plans to be together."

Catherine's heart ached for the two lovers wh
reached for happiness but found it just beyond reach

"Alana, do you think Logan cares for me?"

"Only my son can answer ye." Her blue-green ey
softened. "Ye canna let what has happened ruin ye
lives."

Chapter Twenty-five

Darrell found Catherine outside by one of the barns. "Lass, I be finished wi' Cameron. Are ye goin' to visit him?"

Catherine pulled herself up on the fence rail. "How is he?" More than anything she wanted the two men to come to terms with their relationship. She didn't want rivalry between the brothers.

"We had a long talk," he said, smiling. "Cameron was surprised to learn he had a brother. He is a cautious man and very suspicious of my actions."

"Did you convince him there is nothing between us?"

"I dona know, but he is skeptical of your feelings toward me. Go to the man and make him believe we have nae been romantically involved."

Darrell was asking her to do something she didn't know if she had the strength to do. She loved Logan, but despised his mistrust.

"Catriona, do ye still love him?"

"Yes."

"Swallow ye pride and go to him, ye have suffered enough anguish because of my brother. I've nae wish to see ye hurt." Darrell grinned, and she was amazed by the likeness to Logan. "I dona want a brother who believes I'd try to take his woman."

"I'll think about it," she promised and watched Darrell walk toward the bunkhouse for an evening game of cards.

Pushing herself off the fence, Catherine walked toward the short grasslands. She needed time to think and decide what to do. She knew she would go to Logan, but she was frightened of his response. She would have to be totally convincing in her affections for him, and it was essential that he believe she had only loved one man.

She pulled the collar of her coat around her neck. Back home it would probably be snowing, but in her new home north of Santa Fe, the fluffy whiteness had only touched the mountains. Strolling across the grass reminded her of the days she had walked to the pond and let her real self emerge. Then there had only been the constant pressure from her aunts and she had not let it weigh her down and keep her from being happy. Each day she had held a false mask in place, refusing to let her aunts crush the spirit that lived within her.

Catherine stopped. Her problems with Logan had not only crushed her liveliness, but she had let it keep her from being happy. She wanted to once again feel the freedom she had known in the woods by the pond.

Pulling her hat from her head, she tossed it into the air and watched it float back to the earth. Despite the cold, her jacket followed the hat, then she was off and running across the fields. Her long tawny hair flew wildly behind in defiance of her early reservations. She tripped and fell, her body rolling over and over until giggling, she stopped to stare at the cloudy sky. Cradling her head in her hands, she watched the fluffy formations and refused to dwell on anything but the peace and contentment she felt. The semidarkness and cold air reminded her of how long she'd been gone, and she rose and retrieved her hat and coat.

With her hands in the back pockets of her pants, he stared at the house. From her position, she had a lear shot of her room and she wondered if Cameron as inside. In the past few hours, she had made peace ith herself and now it was time to make peace with he man she loved. She felt ready to face a confronta- ion with him.

By the time she reached the house, dusk had settled o darkness. She wanted her meeting with Logan to be rivate, so she went around back. Her door was closed ut she detected a very dim light through one of the indows. Sliding her palms down her thighs, her teeth it into her lip. This meeting could change her life nd she had to make him believe her feelings were enuine. Her love for him was total and she needed im in her life.

The door was unlocked and Catherine slowly ushed it open. The light next to the bed reflected the hape of someone beneath a pile of blankets. Before he lost her nerve, she stepped inside and closed the oor behind her. She silently removed her boots and ft them at the door. The wood floor was cold against er feet as she tiptoed to the bed.

Logan's dark head rested against the pillow, his lips ightly parted in sleep. Moving around the bed, she cked the door to the room and extinguished the mp. In the darkness, she undressed, her hands trem- ling as she unfastened the buttons of her shirt. There as already an aching need in her body as her pants ll unnoticed to the floor. The chill in her limbs was ot from the cold room, but from the urgent sense of eed she felt. She wanted to be loved by this man and old a special place in his life.

Naked, she drew back the covers and slid in besid
him. She'd been holding her breath and she silentl
released it as she found a place against his side. Loga
did not move, and she could tell by his deep breathin
that he was in an exhausted sleep.

She took a few minutes to study the shadows of hi
face. It was the face of Cameron, but why hadn't sh
recognized him before? His lips closed, then parted, a
his head rolled to the side. His face was so close sh
could feel his warm breath on her cheeks. This wa
the man of her dreams, the man who had introduce
her to new feelings and who made her seek the com
panionship and love of another. He had made it im
possible for her to remain aloof from people and hid
in her own private world. Logan had fulfilled a
empty spot in her life and made her whole.

She wanted to show him her love and let him kno
how deep her emotions went. A lock of dark hair ha
fallen across his forehead and she gently brushed i
aside. She wanted to press her body against his an
run her hands through the silky threads, but it was no
yet time. First she had to awaken his passion an
make him feel the same urgent need.

Sliding her finger across his forehead and down th
bridge of his nose, she brushed the soft flesh on hi
lips. His mouth twitched, his tongue sliding out t
push away the irritating tickle. When he touched th
tip of her finger, trembling waves of awarenes
flooded her body. Her fingers became more insister
and they ran down his neck to gently slide beneath th
blankets. Without making contact with the flesh, sh
ran her palm over the curly hair covering his ches
Her hand slid down his abdomen and over his hip, de
lighting in the realization that he was naked. Inchin

closer, her young eager body pressed against his. He lay on his back, and she twisted on her side to throw one leg over his lower torso. She caressed his chest, her tongue sliding out to tickle the soft hair. Upward she went, her mouth pressing against the skin at the neck and onward to his cheeks. Here she stopped, her tongue sliding out to moisten her lips.

Logan was awake. She could sense the change in his breathing and now, even though she couldn't see his eyes, she knew he was watching her. She wanted to voice her love, but it seemed more important to show him.

Pulling herself up, she nuzzled the skin on his cheek, her lips sliding sideways until she found the corner of his mouth. She teased the flesh long enough to stir his blood, but not long enough to satisfy him. Opening her hands, she threaded her fingers through the thick dark hair. Leaning forward, she kissed his eyelids before returning to his mouth where she became more demanding in her search for a response.

"Logan . . . Cameron," she muttered. "You are the only man in my life. The only person I have ever loved in a passionate way. Darrell never meant anything to me," she said, her teeth nibbling his lip.

Logan was not totally impassive. If his mind refused to respond to her, his body was beginning to betray him. Feeling his response, she pressed her body closer to his, refusing to let an inch separate them. She ran her palm down his arm until she found the hand resting limp against the mattress. She wanted to feel it against her body, creating in her new sensations and desires. After kissing each finger, she laid his hand against the curve of her hip. Even without his caress, the contact burned through her limbs. She moaned

441

her need, frightened that he would not respond, yet refusing to admit defeat.

Her hands became bolder in her study of his body — a body she had known as two different men. Her fingertips grazed the scar at his side before running along the muscular thigh.

Suddenly, she was no longer the pursuer. Logan came to life, his arms closing around her to drag her across his chest. His hands seized her head and forced her lips to his. Contrary to Catherine's fears, there was no punishment in the pressure of his mouth and she allowed herself to be swept into the churning emotions he created and from which she didn't want to escape. His lips plundered hers, robbing her of every control she had left.

Logan did not just take — he gave back, renewing her faith in his need and bringing them closer to the bond she had been seeking for months. Tickling the skin across her back and buttocks, he drew her closer.

"Oh, Cat," he muttered in her ear, and she trembled at the emotion she heard in his voice. Rolling her to her back, he nestled against her side. His leg pinned her thighs to the bed while his hands created a havoc that heightened her senses. His fingers raced across her abdomen promising, yet not fulfilling, what her body begged for. After playfully nuzzling her shoulder, he dropped his attention to the curve of her breast where his tongue teased and caressed the already aroused flesh. She arched and he relented by covering her body with his. Brushing the hair from her cheeks, his mouth swept down to build a rising need. Finally, he shifted and brought them together toward the land they'd been seeking and toward the fulfillment of their dreams — at last in each other's arms.

"I love you, Catherine. . . . I love ye, Catriona," he muttered, and her heart soared with a hope that wanted to burst something inside of her.

Trembling, she curled against Logan. He had brought her to the point of her desire and promised that love with his body and voice. For hours they lay satisfied with each other's nearness.

"Cat," Logan whispered, his fingers playing with a strand of her tawny hair. "Can you forgive me for deceiving you about my identity?"

"Why didn't you tell me who you were?"

Logan smiled. "But I did tell you. . . . Cameron MacLennan."

She tugged at the hairs on his chest. "You know what I mean. Why didn't you tell me you knew my uncle?"

"I was in the East looking for Alana's husband. He is a dangerous man and I felt you'd be safer with your aunts. I had a room in a boarding house but I was gone most of the time, and I didn't want you alone." He kissed her forehead. "When I got back from my last trip, you were gone."

She didn't detect any bitterness in his voice and hoped it meant he had forgiven and understood her abrupt departure. "Duncan wanted to change the wedding. I had to flee. . . . When I went to the church and learned about our marriage, I thought you had tricked me."

Logan growled in his throat. "Alana's husband learned I was in the city and he led me on a false trail. When I got back you were gone. . . . I thought you'd deserted me. . . . I hated you for it." He hugged her closer. "I tried to find you but you had vanished without a trace."

"Then our meeting in Saint Louis was accidental?"

"Partly. I suspected you would try to reach you uncle's ranch and I knew Independence and Sain Louis were the last stopping points for the West When you showed up in the saloon wearing tha revealing dress, I was hurt and furious. Darrell's atten tion to you made things worse."

She had to clear the air once and for all. "Darrel supported me when I needed help. You should b grateful to him."

Raising his hand, Logan covered his eyes. "I almos killed my brother."

Feeling the trembling in his limbs, she leaned forward and kissed his jaw. "When I learned you were brothers i explained why I mistook him for you."

Logan playfully nipped her earlobe. "You better watcl it. I'm a very jealous man where you're concerned."

Rolling to her side, she propped herself up on one arm "When you took me to the hotel room, why didn't you te me who you were?"

"I was in a rage at finding you dressed like a chea whore. I never bargained that I had such a wildcat on m hands." He took her hand and rested it against hi scarred side. "I didn't believe you would try to kill me t protect your virtue when I'd already taken it from you a Cameron."

"I believed I was married to Cam, and I gave my in nocence freely because of my love. Logan was a hard embittered man who wanted to take what I wasn't of fering. My feelings for Cam were still too fresh."

"I hope they are still fresh and can be stirred an renewed by the love we share." He was displaying th kind gentleness she had loved in Cameron. "I didn tell you at the wagons because I hated you for tryin

444

to kill me, then leaving me to die. Despite everything I still wanted you, and I hated myself for that. When I took you I was satisfying my own lust. Your response made me wonder if your vows and professed love for Cameron were real."

"I never shut Cameron out of my life. I love him too much."

"Catriona—my wild, beautiful Cat. *Am pos thu mi?*"

"What?" she asked, wrinkling her nose.

Laughing, Logan said, "Will you be my wife?"

"Oh Cameron—Logan," she cried before kissing him hard on the mouth. Smiling, she drew back. "Which man am I marrying this time?"

"I am one and the same. In Scotland, the clan name is MacLennan, but the family is Logan. Would ye like to call me Cameron Logan," he asked, curving his arm around her shoulders. "I will respond to either name."

"Mmm," she muttered against his mouth. "When Logan gets tired of me, I'll just go see Cameron."

"You wildcat," he accused and covered her body with his.

Much later, when the birds had started their early morning calls, Logan reached over Catherine to the night table. "I found this in the drawer." He opened his palm to display the ring he'd put on her finger at the church. "When we went through the ceremony, I believed I was making you my wife. The words will not change when we stand before a preacher the second time. The ring is yours to wear now, and I believe you are my wife." He slid the band back on her left hand.

Tears misted Catherine's eyes. "Oh Cameron, you've made me so happy. It's not everyone who gets to marry the same man twice. Let's be more selective in our witnesses and preacher next time," she said, kissing his jaw. "And let's get a paper proving our vows."

"I have a paper, but it's probably not legal. I promise we'll do it right the second time."

A pounding against the door woke both of them. "Cameron," Darrell called. "Are ye all right? We canna find Catriona."

Catherine and Logan exchanged smiles. "Everything is fine, she's with me."

They heard his muffled chuckle as he walked away. "What is he going to think?" she scolded playfully.

"Probably that you spent the night in my bed."

"It's my bed," she reminded him quickly. Kissing him lightly on the mouth, she rolled to the side and rose. "I believe you are trying to embarrass me."

"Where are you going?" he asked, reaching for her, but she avoided his grasp.

"I missed dinner last night, and I'm starving."

Frowning, Logan threw himself back against the mattress. "I'm hungry too, but not for food."

Catherine pulled her pants up over her hips. "I'm going to hold you to your promise to make an honest woman out of me."

"Did you think I would try to get out of it."

Catherine gave him a teasing smile and felt the weight of his ring on her finger. It was a promise of his love. "Maybe," she joked.

"Just to let you know my intentions are honorable, we will leave for Santa Fe this afternoon."

She finished buttoning her shirt. "You're not strong enough, and a few days won't make any difference."

Logan tossed aside the blankets. "Would you like a

446

demonstration of my strength?"

Laughing, Catherine grabbed her boots and scampered to the door, unlocked it and glanced over her shoulder. "I believe you, let's make it tomorrow."

Catherine was still grinning when she entered the kitchen and sat down. Alana and Darrell exchanged smiles in response to the glow surrounding her.

"Good morning," she said, taking one of the empty chairs.

"I hope ye didna mind my takin' ye extra room, but I couldna find ye last night to ask ye permission." A sly glance passed between mother and son.

"You're welcome anytime. . . . As a matter of fact, I expect we'll frequently be in each other's company." Catherine didn't know which house would be their home, but she was certain they would be a close family unit.

"Why?" Alana asked with a posed expression of puzzlement.

"Logan—Cameron and I are getting married."

Catherine accepted their congratulations and through breakfast, they discussed the future ceremony. If they were lucky, they could make the trip in two days. Both Darrell and Alana agreed to come, and Catherine was certain Lucas would also want to be included.

When she had finished eating, she fixed a tray and carried it to Logan. He was sitting at the side of the bed pulling on his boots.

"What do you think you're doing?" she demanded, setting the tray on the table next to the bed.

"I'm sick of resting," he complained. "There is nothing wrong with me."

Catherine frowned. "I'm not sure you should—"

447

Grabbing her wrist, Logan pulled her across his lap. She wound her hands around his neck. "Didn't I prove to you most of last night that I'm strong and healthy?"

Catherine blushed, her lips eagerly returning Logan's passionate kiss. "Are you going to prove it to me again this morning?"

He nudged her off his lap. "No. I'm hungry," he said, reaching for the tray. Groaning, Catherine had to be content sitting near him. Their light, playful teasing was a pleasant change from the heated arguments they usually shared, and she knew her life with Cameron would be filled with both.

Alana stopped in their room to offer her congratulations and announce her intention to return home. Catherine offered to ride with her and Logan said he intended to join Lucas on the range.

"Would you like to meet me at the lake for a swimming lesson?" she asked Logan when Alana had gone ahead of them.

"In this freezing weather?" he argued, but he was already warming to the idea.

"I can think of another time when we almost made love in the garden."

Logan winked at her. "And I remember a time in the early fall when a beautiful, innocent young maiden left her aunts' home and traveled a worn path to an isolated pond." Catherine listened with interest. How did Logan know about her private haven? "There she removed her clothes and raised her arms to the sky."

"Logan," she said in shock. "You saw me?" She had never imagined that anyone had observed her moment of privacy, let alone had seen her naked. "Why were you spying on me?"

"I was sleeping in the bushes. You woke me."

This man was baffling. "Why were you sleeping in the woods?"

"I had played poker the night before and lost," he said, grinning. "I got involved in the games hoping to find my mother's husband, Duncan. I knew he liked to take risks."

"Are you going to meet me at the lake?"

"I'll be there."

Still showing signs of exhaustion, Logan strapped his gun to his hips and followed her outside. After a quick kiss, he walked toward the barn, and the women rode to the MacLennan ranch. After a three hour visit, Catherine left to keep her appointment with Logan.

The air was cool, and she turned up her collar to ward off the chill. Stopping at the lake, she skimmed the surrounding shore for Logan. She was early but wanted to be there when he arrived. Dismounting, she tied her horse to the brush and walked to the water's edge. The lake had not frozen but it was icy to the touch. The crisp air prohibited her from undressing and wading into the blueness. Removing her hat, she laid it on a bush and pushed her hands into her pockets. In a few days she would be Mrs. Cameron MacLennan or Mrs. Cameron Logan, whichever she wanted to be. She looked forward to a life with him and hoped in time they could have a baby. It would never replace the one they'd lost, but it would be a baby conceived in the honesty of their love.

The crunch of stones and a soft whinny announced the arrival of a rider and Catherine swung around with a smile on her lips expecting to see Cameron. The smile froze to a look of horror, and her hands fell to her sides. There was a sudden dryness in her mouth and she was certain her tawny eyes reflected her surprise.

"What are you doing here?" she demanded of Duncan Alexander.

"I came to get my fiance," he said, walking the horse to within a few feet of her.

"I'm not your fiance," she spat, no longer the shy girl he'd known at her aunt's home. Duncan was not to be trusted, and she cautiously judged the distance to her horse. If Logan didn't arrive, she'd have to escape on her own.

"Your aunts agreed to the marriage and accepted the money I gave them. I intend to make you my wife."

"The agreement is no longer binding." She stepped to her left.

"You will marry me. I've waited too long for you to mess up my plans."

"Why do you want to marry me? You could have many other women. Why me?"

"Because you are the owner of a very large ranch."

If she could keep him talking Logan might arrive. "Why do you want the ranch?"

Duncan leaned forward. "Because my dear, it is the only large source of water on the entire range. If I control it, I can become a very rich man."

Without water, the MacLennan ranch would not survive. "Well, you're not going to get it?" she flung at him. "My uncle owns it," she said, hoping the lie would discourage him, but she didn't know the depth of his determination.

He assumed a casual, uncaring position on the horse's back. "I know he is dead. . . . I killed him," he said bluntly.

Drawing a sharp uncertain breath, Catherine staggered backward. Duncan had murdered her uncle in cold blood, and knew she had inherited the ranch. When

450

uncan married her, he would take possession, and
rough depriving the MacLennans of water, he could
entually obtain their ranch. Terrified of the man
fore her, she scanned the trees for Logan. He had to be
arned before he rode into a trap.

"He's not coming, Catherine."

She pretended ignorance. "Who's not coming?"

"Logan—Cameron—whatever you call him. I created
little diversion that should keep him busy for hours."

His words frightened Catherine. "What did you do to
m?"

"I didn't do anything, but I scattered his herd all over
e countryside. It will take him days to round them up."

"You're lying," she accused. "Most of the herd went to
alifornia."

Duncan's eyes narrowed. "Would you rather have me
ll you he is dead?" he asked, chuckling at her pale
pression. "Well, he's not . . . not yet."

Logan's life was not worth the ranch. "I'll give you
erything. Just leave Logan alone."

There was a brightening light in Duncan's eyes. "You'd
ve up your wealth for Cameron MacLennan?" His gaze
ked her face. "That's very interesting."

"What did you do to Logan?" she snapped, certain
mething was detaining him. Duncan Alexander was
t a man to be trusted.

"I blew up one of the range shacks. When I left, there
as a fire. If they don't control it, half the prairie will be
st."

Forgetting the violence Duncan was capable of, she
relessly shot off her mouth. "That wasn't very smart,
uncan. If you want a successful ranch, you need grass
r the cattle."

451

His nostrils flared angrily. "Logan is too capable to l[e]
it happen."

"No?" she asked haughtily and threw her hands o[n]
her hips. "Then you better looked behind you."

Duncan's head swiveled to the brush and Catherin[e]
raced toward her horse. Logan had not arrived, but [it]
was a means of distracting his attention long enough t[o]
attempt an escape. She was still some distance from he[r]
mare when she heard thundering hoofs. Throwing [a]
glance over her shoulder, she stumbled, and the sta[l]
lion struck her shoulder. It was a powerful hit and sh[e]
was knocked to the dirt. Without considering possib[le]
injury, she sprang to her feet. Reaching her horse w[as]
out of the question, but if she escaped into the brus[h]
she'd have cover. She had almost reached the woo[d]
when Duncan caught her long hair and jerked her to [a]
stop. Her eyes watered from the pain and the more sh[e]
struggled, the tighter he pulled. Finally, she su[r]
rendered, and he held her against the side of his hor[se]
while he dismounted.

"Don't try to cross me," he warned, pulling th[e]
tawny strands. "I've waited and planned too long fo[r]
you to spoil things for me."

"They'll catch you," she threatened, but knew he[r]
words were just idle threats. This man was devious an[d]
nothing would stand in his way. He had initiated his pla[n]
months ago when he wanted her for his wife.

Pulling a length of rope from his saddlebag, Dunca[n]
jerked her arms behind her back. The rawhide strips cu[t]
painfully into her wrists, but she didn't cry out. Grabbin[g]
her arm, he dragged her to the mare and lifted her to th[e]
saddle.

"You're not going to get away with this," she screame[d]

"Shut up or I'll gag you," he said, mounting.

With her hands behind her back, she had difficulty maintaining her balance when the horse settled into an easy gait. She looked behind her at the lake where she was to meet Logan. Because of Duncan she wouldn't keep her promise and she wondered how Logan would feel when he got there. Would he doubt her expressed sincerity at being with him. Tears had started to moisten her eyes when she saw her hat on a bush. In the West, the hat was never forgotten, and hers lay on the dormant brush in proof of her adduction.

Duncan was careful to remain in the cover of the trees as long as possible. When it became too overgrown, they rode over rocky terrain to avoid leaving a trail. Catherine tried to knock off her boot as evidence of their location, but almost landed in the dirt. After nearly two hours of travel, she suspected most of their movement had been in circles to discourage anyone who might come looking for her.

When they finally stopped, Catherine was so confused that even if she could escape, she wouldn't know where to go. Duncan led her into a densely covered area and branches tore at her hair. When they reached a dead end, he parted some branches and guided them into a tree sheltered area. He dismounted and dragged her off the mare.

"This is where you'll stay," he said, pushing her toward a small, unlit campfire.

Catherine didn't know if he intended to leave her alone, but decided the prospect would certainly be better than having his company. At least alone, she would have hope for escape. She hated the man for murdering her uncle and trying to destroy her happiness.

Looking up, Duncan saw the loathing in her eyes. "You look as though you hate me, my dear," he said, obviously amused by her glare.

"I do. Thank goodness I never married you."

"You will be my wife, but we have to wait until I take care of some other matters."

"Do you think I would stand quietly at your side without telling everyone what you'd done?"

"If you don't keep your mouth shut, I'll kill the priest. Would you want to be responsible for another death?" She gave a negative shake of her head. "I didn't think you would. Later when you have served my purpose, you'll meet with an accident." Catherine was not surprised to learn her fate, but hearing the verbal acknowledgment frightened her. "I'm quite good at organizing weddings, you know." Her confusion showed in her eyes. "Ah, I can see you don't understand me," he said, enjoying her torment. "I am talking about your wedding to Cameron. I knew he was in town, and I was afraid he would try to marry you to get control of your uncle's ranch. I had to remain in command of your life, so I bribed his legal counsel to inform me if he made a move to arrange a ceremony. When he decided to take you for his wife, I was able to substitute my own man." He pointed to the saddlebags. "I have your marriage certificate, and once he is dead I intend to use it to prove you're his widow."

"Was your man a preacher?" she asked, curious to know if the ceremony had been valid.

His mouth curled into a sneer. "I don't think I'll tell you."

"I suppose you were responsible for injuring the vicar."

"That's right. I couldn't marry you until I got Cameron out of town. Reverend Peters was going to preside over our wedding, so he couldn't conduct the service with Cameron."

"Did you follow me the night I went to the ceremony?

And later did you ask my aunts to see if I was in my room?"

He pulled the saddle off her horse. "Yes. I was waiting for you when you left the house. You got suspicious and I lost you near a tavern. When the service was over, Cameron started looking for me and I had to go into hiding."

Tugging at her bonds, she tried to plan an escape. She would not be the bait for Logan's entrapment. She realized the more she knew about the situation, the better position she would be in to do something to help. There was a nagging suspicion in the back of her mind and she needed confirmation.

"Duncan, why are you obsessed with getting the ranch and controlling the land? There must be a simpler, more direct way of obtaining wealth and power."

Beneath the brim of his hat, Catherine thought she saw his eyes narrow. Had she hit on an important discovery? "Humph," he said.

"I think you had an ulterior motive. I believe you are out for revenge."

There was a noticeable stiffening in Duncan's body, but he continued working with the horses. Perhaps if she continued to pester him, she'd learn by the truth. "If you hated my uncle, then you had your revenge by killing him. I think you had another reason for wanting the ranch." She rose to her knees and came back down on her hands. There was a densely covered area to her left; she had to make a try for it.

"You think you're pretty smart," he called to her.

"I'm more intelligent than you'll admit! I think you're after revenge on the MacLennans. I believe you are the man Logan went east to find. I think you are Alana's husband and Darrell's father."

Duncan swung around, his face puffed up in anger. "Did Cameron tell you, or did you figure it out for yourself?"

Catherine met his gaze without fear. Combining the things Logan and Darrell had told her had given her clues to his identity. Everything was too closely tied together to be coincidence.

"I'm Alana's husband, and that young whelp Darrell is my son. . . . But it is Cameron that I hate the most." He turned his back on her and she knew he was reliving the bitterness he had held in his heart for so long. "Alana never told me about him, but she was proud of the son who had made a life for himself in America. All I had was a gangly kid who would never be much of a man."

Catherine sprang to Darrell's defense. "You have a son you can be proud of. It is just a shame you had to be his father."

Duncan sprang toward her, grabbing the front of her jacket and hauling her against his chest. "Shut your mouth."

She knew better than to provoke his anger and she could not risk being gagged or tied to a tree. Freedom meant escape. Duncan threw her to the ground, knocking the breath from her body.

"This is just a sample of what you'll get if you fool with me."

With her cheek pressed against the dirt, Catherine tried to recover her breath. Now that she knew the truth, sparring with Duncan could be dangerous, and she put escape as top priority. Darkness was settling early in the densely wooded area and it offered the best cover for her flight.

It became evident they were staying the night when Duncan unfolded the bedrolls. She would have to plan her escape soon or risk spending the night with him. If he decided to make advances, she'd be totally helpless and the thought of him touching her body made her stomach churn. Her struggles would be useless and she would be degraded by his lust.

Duncan worked on the fire, adding branches until he had a healthy flame. He glanced her way several times and she pretended to sleep. After prying the lids off two tins, he dumped the contents into a small pan. Twisting, he retrieved his saddlebags and rummaged through the contents.

When Duncan was intent upon his work, she dragged herself to a sitting position. Getting to her feet proved to be difficult and she had to be careful not to kick any stones. Standing, she held her breath and waited for him to turn. After a few seconds she relaxed and carefully tiptoed toward the trees. Pausing at the edge of the dense growth, she made sure she was undetected before disappearing from sight. Moving noiselessly made progress slow and several times a branch cracked beneath her boot. The darkness, which she thought would hide her escape, hindered her movement.

Duncan's bellow of rage warned Catherine that he knew she was gone. The necessity to flee for her life was brought to reality when the brush behind her crashed beneath his weight. He made no attempt to be quiet in his pursuit and she heard his mumbling shouts. Repeatedly, Catherine tripped and fell and with her hands behind her back, it was a painful struggle to get back on her feet. Nevertheless, she defied the difficult and plunged onward, intent upon getting away.

Twice she heard animals scamper out of her path, but she pushed aside her fears and centered her attention on escape. As the minutes passed, she staggered more often, and it became apparent she wouldn't be able to continue much longer. Her movements were exhausting and her shoulders ached with stiffness.

Pausing, she scanned the dark surroundings. To her right was a combination of rocks and brush and she ran toward the possible hiding place. If she couldn't leap over the rocks, she climbed them backward using her hands and feet. On the far side, she crawled beneath some brush and lost herself in the cover. The possibility of entering a wild creature's habaitat entered her mind and she waited for the deadly rattle or piercing sting. After a few seconds, she relaxed and listened for Duncan.

Her hiding place was not large, and she was forced to bend forward at a funny angle. It wasn't long before lines of pain raced up her arms and across her back. Resting on her side helped ease some of the discomfort, but she still lay in agony and fear. Once she heard the brush crackle, and she held her breath in fear of discovery. Whatever it was passed, and she sighed her relief.

It wasn't long before Catherine recognized a new danger. Duncan had brought her into the hills and she knew it would be a chilling night. The coldness crept into her feet, numbing them until they no longer seemed a part of her body. Freezing to death was a real possibility and her only chance of survival was by gaining her freedom.

Her small hiding place did not offer security and if she didn't move, it would become her grave. To save her life she would have to risk detection. Crawling out of her hiding place, she sat up. There were rocks all around her nd if she was lucky she'd find one with a sharp point. Leaning back, she opened her fingers to the rock-covered round and began her search. It was a long slow process nd her hands were beginning to tingle when she found a agged edged stone. Wedging the rock against another, he lay on her side against it. Moving her hands back and orth, the rope rubbed the rock. Several times she craped her wrist, but after an hour of hard, tiring work, er bonds snapped and her hands were free. Blood ushed through the deep indentations in her wrists caused y the ropes and she clenched her teeth against the gony. Wiggling her fingers, she waited for feeling to eturn to the numb flesh. When her body began to unction again, she realized how exhausted she was. The rge to rest was strong but she had to keep moving for a ew more hours.

Her legs felt weak from the cold and her toes tingled, ut Catherine stepped forward. Without the bonds, er movement was faster, and she covered distance apidly. She tried to move away from his camp and oped she didn't get confused. It was a few hours efore sunrise when she stopped to rest. Ducking beeath some brush, she leaned against a tree trunk; she as asleep within minutes.

The chirping birds woke her at dawn but Catherine losed her eyes and dozed for another hour. Her head ad fallen toward the side and when she opened her yes, she was staring at an ugly bug. Squealing, she prang to her feet and ran out of the bushes. She ouldn't stop the shudders that shook her small frame s she brushed off her clothes to make sure nothing was rawling on her.

In the daylight her cover didn't seem as dense. Sun-

459

light peeked through the trees and gave her fresh hope of finding her way back to Logan. There was a bounce in her step as she walked through the woods. She had to reach the flatlands, but first she needed a high point to scan the area. A short time later, she stretched out on a flat rock overhanging a valley and looked things over. Fortunately, there was no sign of Duncan, but unfortunately, nothing was familiar.

Suddenly Catherine grinned. If she didn't find help, Logan would find her hat at the lake and organize a search party. Rising, she began to climb down the mountain. It was just a matter of time before help came. All she had to do was avoid Duncan.

Chapter Twenty-six

Logan rode into the clearing by the lake and scanned the area for Catherine. Thinking she might be hiding from him, he galloped toward a strand of trees and called her name. When she didn't answer, he scowled. He was hours later than he should have been and he had looked forward to a romp with her beneath the blankets.

The fire in the shack had been started to distract his attention, and he was certain he knew the man responsible. Duncan Alexander had caused him grief for years and it wouldn't end until the man was dead. He thought of Alana tied to him by the bond of marriage—an obstacle to her happiness. In her case it had been a sentence to a life in prison. Logan had pretended not to notice the affectionate glances exchanged between Alana and Lucas, but he doubted he'd ever seen a more perfectly matched couple.

In America, Logan had stayed past the years required to fulfill his indenture agreement because he liked Paul and Linda Morrison, the couple who had given him a chance in the country of opportunity. Over the years he had kept in touch with Alana and knew of her marriage to a man who was cruel and greedy. He had asked her to join him on numerous occasions, but she kept refusing. Soon after one of her refusals, he received a letter that she was coming to

America to work for a wealthy family. Several months later, Duncan showed up and introduced himself as Logan's stepfather. The dislike was instant, and Cameron threw him off the property.

A business venture took Cameron to California and when he returned, he found the Morrisons' business floundering. Too late to prevent its total destruction, he watched it crumble. The final draw was the accidental death of the couple who had been family to him. Hurt and confused by what had happened, Cam searched for answers and found evidence pointing toward Duncan.

Set on revenge, Cameron picked up his trail and followed his stepfather. His chance to get even came three weeks later when he sat down at the poker table opposite Duncan. He'd been winning for the last two hours and a huge pile of money rested on the table before him. The cards were dealt and Cameron picked up his hand. He had learned the game from a gambler, and although he couldn't be a professional, he had a face that concealed all emotion.

Having Cam on the opposite side of the table made Duncan careless. It was a high stake game and after nearly four hours of playing, Duncan was penniless. Several of the men ribbed him about his failure to beat the younger man and Duncan was furious. Rising, Cameron calmly stacked the money and looked at his stepfather.

"Thanks. You just bought me a ranch."

He turned, his booted feet hitting the wooden floor, as he started across the room. A sudden click froze his motion and he felt a prickling of fear along his spine.

"You're a dead man, MacLennan," Duncan said.

Cameron did not slump under the threat of death. All

his senses remained sharp and focused on his problem. The gun on his hip was a familiar weapon but it was useless when he was under someone else's trigger.

"I've waited a long time to kill you," Duncan said, hating Alana's son by another man. Cameron MacLennan was too proud and successful.

"If you pull that trigger, you're a dead man," a voice from the bar said, and Cameron's eyes shifted to the man leveling his gun at Duncan. He was an older man, large and broad shouldered, and the hat pulled low over his forehead hid most of his face. "Drop the gun!"

Duncan glared his hate for the man who dared to interfere in his fight with Cameron, but when the stranger pulled the hammer back, his gun fell to the floor with a thump. Several of the men on the sidelines snickered, and Duncan's fury and humiliation increased.

"We better get out of here," the stranger said to Cameron, and they left together. Outside Cam shook the stranger's hand.

"Thanks for what you did. That man hates my guts and I know he would have killed me."

The stranger pushed his hat back and Cam got a glimpse of the pale blue eyes. "Glad to do it."

Cam gave the man a hard look. "Do I know you?"

The stranger grinned. "You're Cameron MacLennan?" he asked, and Cam nodded. "Several years back I bought two prime bulls from you." He chuckled. "You drove a hard bargain."

Remembering the incident almost ten years before, Cam smiled. "They were two of the best."

"I bought some of the Morrison wagons a few years ago. They were some of the best made." He frowned. "I was sorry to hear about the death of the Morrisons and I couldn't believe their financial destruction."

463

Cam's jaw hardened, and he jerked his thumb toward the gambling hall. "He was responsible, but I can't prove it."

The stranger loosened the reins of his horse. "I don't think this town is a healthy place for either of us."

"I couldn't agree more." He tapped his pocket. "I'm headed west to buy a ranch. Care to ride along?"

"Sure," he said, swinging into the saddle. "Are you buying this ranch for yourself? Or do you have family?"

"Myself," he said, unwilling to mention his mother's existence so close to Duncan—a man she hated. Once he got settled on a ranch, he would send for her. He never imagined it would take more than seven years to achieve that dream.

"By the way," the older man said as they were riding out of town, "the name is Lucas."

Logan bought the ranch north of Santa Fe. For years, he and Lucas worked hard to make it a prosperous spread. When Alana finally agreed to join him, she asked him to find out if Duncan was still alive. Leaving the ranch in his neighbor's hands until Alana could arrive, Lucas and Logan began the long trip east. In exchange for Ben's help, Logan promised to look for Catherine.

From the first, he'd been drawn to her incredible beauty, and he responded to her innocence like an inexperienced youth. Never in his wildest dreams had he imagined her response to his lovemaking would be with a wild carefree spirit. From the beginning when she'd reached out for help, he had been there to support and comfort her. He was ashamed of the way he had concealed his identity and refused to be sympathetic to her needs. He had been a brute, and the gentle Cameron she had known was covered by the overpowering hardness of Logan. While despising her response to him, he found himself unable to keep his desire under control. He had taunted and teased her about her inability to cope with the hard trail west, but realized his anger had been at himself for not being more sympathetic and understanding.

Dismounting, he stared across the blue lake. It was a beautiful place, and he hoped she could forget the tragedy that had occured on its shore. In time, he wanted it to be a special place where they could laugh and love. He'd teach her to swim, and they'd frolic happily in the water before admitting their love beneath the open blue sky.

A movement on the ridge caught his attention and his gaze swung to the tawny cat standing in magestic attention above the water. Its beauty and grace matched Catherine, and Logan stood in awe of the animal and woman. One he could only stand and admire; but the other, he would hold, love and cherish. Catherine was his life, and he would make up for the past hurt.

Perhaps in time they could share the love of a child. She hadn't known his true identity the day she told him about the baby she'd lost, and it had been a staggering blow. After the initial shock, he'd covered his emotions with a hard shell, but inside he ached the loss.

Logan ran his fingers over the brownish bush at his side. They had been given a second chance to find happiness and he was determined to make it work. Had he not been detained, she would be in his arms right now.

He felt a familiar tightening in his loins and knew it was time to return to the ranch and Catherine. Turning to his horse, he froze, his eyes glued to the hat tossed carelessly on the brush. In seconds it was in his hand and his lips had thinned. It was Catherine's hat, and he scanned the surrounding land.

"Catherine—Catriona," he called over and over, but the answer to his call was silence. She'd been here, but why had she forgotten her hat? Since leaving Independence she'd learned the importance of keeping it with her and he could only contribute it to her old carelessness. He grinned. She was certainly one for surprises.

Returning to his horse, he mounted and rode toward the ranch. He was almost halfway home when he saw Lucas approaching him from the MacLennan ranch. Logan reined in his stallion and waited.

"How are things at the house?" he asked Lucas when they were once again headed for the ranch.

Lucas grinned. "Things couldn't be better."

"I'm glad to know about you and Alana," Logan told the older man. His mother's loneliness often troubled him and he was glad she had found a good man.

"After all these years, why didn't you tell me about her?" Lucas scolded. "The day I met you at he saloon you led me to believe there wasn't any family."

"If you recall I'd just had a run in with Duncan, and I wanted to protect her." He didn't know how much Alana had told him, but eventually there would be a showdown and he wanted Lucas on his side.

"I know there is something troubling Alana, but she won't discuss it."

"Do you know about Darrell?"

Lucas nodded. "I know he is her son, and I also know

e man you were chasing is Darrell's father."

"He is also Alana's husband," Logan regretfully
ninded him.

"The man has no hold over Alana. . . . I've been
>king for a woman like Alana since I was a young man
d we intend to build a life together."

"Nothing could make me happier," Logan said,
iling. "You both have my blessings."

Lucas grinned. "That makes things easier." He
sted his hand on his thigh. "I'll never let Duncan
in Alana's life," he said, his voice edged with deter-
nation to protect the woman he loved.

"I'm glad you know the truth. Duncan has been
er me for years. I ruined him in that saloon and
's out for revenge. I think he's responsible for the
>uble at the shack."

Frowning, Lucas said, "I think I better spend the
xt few nights with Alana."

Logan chuckled deep in his throat. "Weren't you
ing to do that anyway?"

"Probably," he admitted honestly. Looking at
gan, his expression softened. "I'd be proud to call
u my son."

"All right—Dad," Logan teased.

Leaning over, Lucas playfully smacked Logan's
gh and for the first time noticed the hat hooked to
saddle. "Isn't that Catherine's hat?" Logan
dded. "Weren't you suppose to meet at the lake? I
re hope the two of you aren't fighting again."

"Not this time," Logan said, grinning. "I was late
d I guess she got tired of waiting."

"I'm surprised she forgot her hat," Lucas said
>ughtfully. "She never went anyplace without it."

'She probably had other things on her mind." He

certainly had pleasant thoughts occupying his mind and it was a shame Duncan had to cloud his happiness. "I better keep a close watch on Catherine," told Lucas. "I don't know where she fit into his plan but he wanted to marry her. With her uncle dead she's a rich woman."

"I'll alert the men," Lucas said, stopping in yard at the younger man's side.

Eager to see Catherine, Logan shouted her name. He had just dismounted when Darrell came outside.

"Wha' be ye shoutin' about?"

"I'm looking for Catherine. Where is she?"

A puzzled light entered Darrell's green eyes. "She at the lake waitin' for ye."

"I just came from there," he said, holding up hat. "She'd been there and gone."

"Maybe she went to visit Alana," he offered to e the concern on his brother's face.

"I was at the MacLennan ranch," Lucas supplie "She's not there."

Logan and Lucas exchanged concerned glances. think we better start a search."

"I'll get my gun," Darrell said and disappea inside.

Most of the men were not back from the cattle dr to California so there were only a handful to join the search. Logan shouted orders and horses w saddled. Each man was given a specific area to sear and everyone rode out of the yard. Darrell came ba outside and picked up the reins for his horse.

"Where do ye want me to go? I dona know countryside, but I dona think I'll get lost."

Logan put his hand on his brother's shoulder a took a deep breath. "There is something you sho know," he said, his blue eyes staring into his brother's green ones. He had already caused him enough pain, but he had to know the truth. "I think Duncan is nearby. Lucas and I believe he's responsible for the fire on the range."

Beneath his hand, Logan felt the tightening of his brother's muscles and Darrell voiced what the other man hated to consider. "Do ye think he has Catriona?"

"It is a possibility," Logan said, letting his hand fall. "I'll understand if you'd rather not take part in the search. Duncan is out for revenge and things could get nasty."

"Nae, I've nae love for my father. He be a bitter man, and if he has Catriona, we must help her."

They mounted the horses. "I'll go get Alana. She'll be safer if she's riding with me," Lucas said and left.

The brothers rode together for several minutes before splitting up. At dusk everyone congregated back at the ranch, each hoping someone else would have Catherine with them.

"I went back to the lake and found two fresh sets of tracks," Logan said. "I followed them into the rocks and lost them. Maybe tomorrow, when it's light, I can pick up their trail."

"Then ye think Duncan has her?"

"I'm convinced of it. I'm going to get a fresh mount and go back out."

"Logan, Lucas said, grabbing his arm. "It won't do any good. You won't find anything in the dark."

Shaking himself free, Logan looked at his friend. "I know and I feel so helpless."

Logan was up early and had the horses saddled and

waiting when the men gathered outside. He decided to try and pick up Catherine's trail in the rocks. Alana and Lucas would scout the land around the lake, and Darrell would go to the north. The ranch hands were assigned to the grasslands and shacks covering both properties.

There was a rigid determination in the men when they rode out of the yard and separated to begin their search.

Chapter Twenty-seven

Catherine's stomach grumbled its protest. If it had
been spring or summer, she would have found a sufficient supply of food, but as it was almost winter, the
berry bushes were barren. She had frightened several
rabbits, but without a weapon, she didn't eat. Thirst
was not a problem because of the cool temperature,
and springs were plentiful in the rocks. To avoid total
exhaustion, she frequently stopped to rest. She fought
the urge to shout for help because it might alert
Duncan to her location. She never forgot the threat he
posed and moved cautiously, watching and waiting for
attack.

Reaching the flatland, she stayed in the cover of the
brush. Nothing was familiar to her, yet she refused to
give up the hope of finding a familiar landmark. She
was staring at the dirt before her when she heard the
whinny of a horse. Stiffening, her eyes darted over her
surroundings for a place to hide. A cluster of bushes
ahead of her offered the best protection and she dove
behind them. Holding her breath, she parted the
branches and saw the horse come into view. Her gasp
of relief was loud enough for the rider to hear, and he
pulled the horse to a stop.

Catherine stumbled from her hiding place. "Darrell
Darrell, over here."

"Catriona," he said, swinging off his horse. "Are ye

all right?" he asked, folding her in a hug. "We ha[ve]
been worried about ye."

"Is Logan okay?" Darrell nodded. "And what abo[ut]
Alana?" Again he nodded.

Drawing back, she looked into his eyes. "Darre[ll,]
I'm afraid I have bad news for you. Duncan is he[re]
and he's determined to get revenge."

He shook his dark head. "Aye, lass. I know
about it. Ye dona have to worry."

She lightly touched his sleeve. "I'm sorry, Darre[ll.]
Trouble is coming and I wish I could spare you t[he]
pain. I know your father is filled with hate."

"Dona worry. I know the man be evil, and I have
loved him for years."

Catherine knew if there was trouble with Dunca[n]
Logan would try and shield his brother. "Do you ha[ve]
anything to eat?" she asked, grinning. "I'm starved[."]

Reaching into his saddle bag, Darrell pulled o[ut]
some jerky. " 'Tis nae much, but ye can have it,"
said, handing it over. "I think my horse can car[ry]
both of us, and I want to get ye back to Logan. He
worried about ye."

She was thrilled to learn of Logan's concern a[nd]
agreed they better leave immediately. "Duncan
searching for me, so we'll have to be careful," s[he]
cautioned.

"Duncan is right behind you," a voice said, a[nd]
both of them wheeled around. Darrell's hand aut[o]
matically rose to his gun. "I would't try it," Dunc[an]
warned, his gun already drawn and leveled at th[eir]
stomachs. Darrell dropped his hand.

Duncan was on foot and Catherine decided it w[as]
why they hadn't heard his approach. He looked at [his]
son with a bitter twist to his mouth. "You would[

want to kill your own father, would you?"

"Ye nae be kin to me," he said, looking his father in the eye. "Ye be a snake."

Tightening his hold on the gun, Duncan brought it down against the side of Darrell's head. His son staggered backward and hit the side of his horse. A trickle of blood ran down his face from a cut near his brow. Using the cuff of her shirt, Catherine wiped the blood from his eye.

"I won't stand for any insolence," Duncan cautioned.

Catherine was furious with Duncan for the needless attack. Keeping her hands on Darrell, she turned her head and glared at her captor. The flecks of gold in her tawny eyes sparked daggers of hate.

"Shut up," she warned. "Can't you see he's hurt?"

She was so intent upon watching his face, she failed to see him shift the gun to his left hand, freeing his right. She was totally unprepared for the blow he dealt across her cheek with his palm. The stinging contact snapped her head back and she fell against Darrell.

"I don't want any of your lip. Put out your hands, Darrell," he ordered, giving Catherine a rope. "Tie him and make sure it's tight."

Reluctantly, Catherine put the rope around Darrell's wrists, but didn't pull it as snug as she could. When he was immobile, Duncan told him to get on the horse. Catching the loose reins, Duncan pulled the animal forward and grabbed Catherine's arm. Her mare was a short distance away at the edge of the clearing.

They mounted and Duncan led them across the grasslands. Catherine was surprised he would risk being seen, but he was intent upon reaching a destination. Darrell was behind Catherine, and she lifted to see if he was all right. The wound on his head had stopped bleeding but there was a sense of failure reflected in his green eyes. Flashing him a reassuring smile, she knew they would find a way to stop Duncan.

They rode onto the MacLennan ranch from the north. Pausing briefly, he waited to see if anyone appeared in the yard, then with his gun drawn, they rode directly to the barn. After dismounting, Duncan put the horses in the stalls to keep them out of sight. Catherine was hoping he would secure the barn doors. If they were closed it would alert riders of possible danger, but Duncan was no fool and the doors remained open.

"Get to the house," he said, shaking the gun in their direction.

Catherine kept hoping someone would arrive, but they reached the house unnoticed and she knew everyone was still out looking for her. In the kitchen Duncan pushed his son into a chair and turned his attention on Catherine.

"I had to miss breakfast and lunch on your account, so I want you to fix me something to eat."

"But," she protested, knowing she was an absolute disaster in the kitchen.

"I don't want to hear any excuses. Now get to work."

After lighting the stove, she filled the coffee pot. There was a sufficient supply of food, but she didn't know how to fix most of it. In the pantry, she found bread and meat and decided the best thing to make was sandwiches.

"Can I fix something for Darrell and myself?" she asked.

Duncan was standing by the back door watching the barn. "Fine, just hurry up," he said, letting the curtain fall over the glass.

She made six sandwiches and put them on the table. Duncan sat at the far end, keeping one chair between him and his son. Darrell's head was bent in defeat, but when Catherine put the plates down, she caught the glow in his eyes. He was planning something and she wanted to help him when he made his move.

She put three coffee cups on the table and reached for the pot. Trembling, she poured the hot liquid and gave Darrell a cup. He looked at her with such intent she knew he was trying to tell her something, but she didn't understand. Confused, she pushed Duncan's cup toward his hand, but the cup hit a rough spot on the wood and upset. The scalding liquid poured over his flesh.

Screaming, he jumped back, his hand pressing against his shirt to remove the sting. Darrell sprang to his feet and lunged at his father. He caught him full in the chest and they crashed to the floor. Turning, Catherine reached for the heavy skillet to smash against Duncan's head, but Darrell blocked her clear path. Darrell's bound fists beat at Duncan't face and chest. He didn't try to protest himself and a few seconds later, Catherine knew why. Darrell's motions stopped and Duncan chuckled.

"Get off of me," he ordered, and his son fell to the side. Duncan had managed to free his gun and stick it in Darrell's stomach. His eyes narrowed when they focused on Catherine. "Don't try any more stunts like that or I'll shoot him."

Catherine always met with disaster in the kitchen. "It was an accident," she explained, frightened for her friend's life. She might do something careless and Darrell would be killed. "I didn't plan it."

"Get into that chair," he ordered Darrell. "If you try anything again, I'll kill you." Returning his gun to the holster, he crossed the room to Catherine. "As for you," he said, grabbing her hair and twisting it around his fingers. "I'll take care of you later—and in my own way." His gaze roamed over her frightened face. His hand crept to her breast and she shrank back when he kneaded the tender flesh. "You never did like me to touch you," he snarled. "I wonder if your innocence has been saved or if you threw it away on Cameron's false promises?" Pulling her against his bulky frame, he ground his mouth against hers. Catherine kept her teeth clenched and the assault was only a few seconds. "Am I going to expect an experienced wife in my bed?"

"I'm not going to be your wife," she spat at him and turned her head to wipe her mouth against her shirt.

"You will be, but first I have to get rid of my obliga-tions to Alana."

"Alana doesn't want to see you. She has made a new life for herself."

Releasing Catherine, Duncan looked at his son. "Where is your mother?"

"I dona know." His voice was tight and noncommittal.

Duncan seized Catherine's arm and jerked it behind her back. Her body arched in painful protest. "Where's your mother?" he repeated, bending her elbow toward her shoulders.

Catherine tried to fight the pain, but her arm felt like it was being stripped from its socket and she

476

shrieked. "She's out with Lucas," Darrell said quickly, no longer able to protect his mother at Catherine's expense."

"Who's Lucas?" Duncan demanded without relaxing his hold on Catherine. She dug her teeth into her lip to fight the streaks of pain running along her arm.

Darrell's face was a mixture of pain and helplessness. He didn't want to see Catherine hurt, but he didn't want to give out any information. "Logan's friend."

"A friend," he muttered thoughtfully. "Is he part of Alana's new life?" This time he directed the question at Catherine. When she remained unresponsive, he jerked her arm back. "Answer me, woman. Is Alana involved with Lucas?"

"Stop — you're hurting me." A scream of agony ripped from her throat.

"Aye," Darrell answered for her. "Now let her go."

Duncan's large chest puffed with his deep breath, and he slowly relaxed Catherine's arm. Staggering against the counter, she rubbed her shoulder.

"So the tramp has found herself a new lover," he sneered.

"Dona speak about my mother. She isna cheap," Darrell defended.

Duncan glared at his son. "She's a tramp. When I married her, she was supposed to be pure. She had been with another man and given him a son." He slammed a fist against the table. "Both of them are rotten. . . . I'll make them pay." He stared at Darrell. "You are one of the biggest disappointments in my life." Darrell flinched, then straightened in his chair. "You make a living with a deck of cards in a saloon.

You never know if you'll be rich or poor."

"Ranchin' be a gamble. Ye dona know if the weather or sickness will kill ye cattle. I be good wi' a deck of cards, and there are nae many to beat me. Ye be wrong about my money. I have investments but I dona touch them. Gamblin' be in my blood, but I dona let it run my life. Ye be welcome to wha' I have if ye will let Catriona go."

It was a noble gesture on Darrell's part, but Duncan only laughed. "You are a fool, Darrell Alexander."

"Dona call me an Alexander. Ye have made me ashamed of ye name. I havena used it since I came to America."

Duncan despised his son, but he stiffened at the shun of his name. "You may not use the name, but you are still my son."

"Nae father would tie his son. I dona respect ye, and if ye think I be a weak son, then 'tis because ye are a weak man."

It was the wrong thing to say. Reaching across the table, Duncan slapped his son repeatedly. Catherine lunged for his hand and managed to stop the attack. Darrell's green eyes glazed in pain. Blood gushed from the wound on his head and his lips were torn and bleeding.

"Ye can beat me to death, but 'twill nae change a thin'." He never saw the anger on his father's face. His head dropped forward and he fell across the table.

"Now look what you've done," she cried and rushed to his side. "He needs attention."

"Then give it to him. I want him awake."

Grabbing a towel, she poured water into a bowl. It was several minutes before she'd cleared the blood from his face. Bruises stood out vividly on his cheekbones and one eye was badly swollen. She kept the cloth against his forehead until he regained consciousness.

"Sit him up," Duncan ordered. "Stand away."

Darrell was weak and groggy when he hit the back of the chair, but he steadied himself with his hands, and Catherine stepped back. Walking around the table, Duncan stopped next to his son.

"When and where are you suppose to meet Logan?"

Catherine doubted Darrell's pain-filled mind ever heard the question. Duncan grabbed his hair and jerked his head back. His fist caught Darrell in the ribs. "Where are you meeting Logan?" There was no answer, and he hit him three more times.

Darrell's moans of pain frightened Catherine. "Stop," she screamed.

Duncan threw her an ugly look. "You're just lucky I don't kill him," he said, slamming his fist into his stomach.

Catherine rushed forward. "Let me ask him." Releasing his grip, Duncan stepped back. Gently placing her hands on either side of his face, she looked into Darrell's eyes. "Can you hear me?"

"Aye, lass."

"Where are you meeting Logan?"

Darrell moistened his torn lips. "Here."

"When?" she asked.

His mouth moved but nothing came forth. His eyes rolled upward and he slumped against Catherine. He was heavy, but she managed to lower him to the floor. He'd never stay in a chair unless he was tied. With a towel cushioning his head, she carefully wiped his face. His breath was short and she wondered if Duncan had injured his ribs.

"Get away from him," Duncan ordered, leaning against the counter with one of her sandwiches.

Catherine wanted to defy him, but after seeing what he'd done to his son, she backed away and sat at the table. Her shoulder still throbbed, but her pain was less than Darrell's. He didn't move and she didn't know if he was unconscious or sleeping.

Toward dusk, Duncan moved to the door to watch outside. It was another hour before they heard the sound of hoofs. The animals stopped at the front out of sight.

"Keep your mouth shut or I'll blow off his head."

The door from the kitchen to the living room was open and the outer room was in darkness. The front door opened and slammed shut. After a few seconds a lamp was lit and Duncan stepped behind the door and drew his gun.

Catherine edged forward on her seat as if to cry out and he leveled his gun at Darrell's head. There was no love between father and son, and she knew he wouldn't hesitate to pull the trigger.

Catherine didn't know who was in the outer room but she was terrified Duncan intended to murder them when they stepped into the kitchen. Voices came closer, then Alana walked into the kitchen.

"Catriona, ye are back." Her welcoming smile vanished when she saw Darrell stretched out on the floor. "What happened?" she asked, dropping to her knees at her son's side. "Lucas, come quickly."

Lucas rushed into the room and into Duncan's trap. The door banged shut behind him and he whirled around. Stepping out of their way, Duncan centered his gun on Lucas.

"Would you like to try for the gun?" he asked. "I can kill you now and get it over with."

Alana scrambled to her feet and stepped in front of Lucas.

"Nae Duncan, 'twill be nae killin'."

Her statement amused Duncan and he chuckled. "Well, Alana. It's been a long time."

"Nae long enough," she retorted sharply, and Duncan's eyes narrowed. "Ye were ne'er anythin' but trouble to me. I canna sae I be glad to see ye."

"We have some unfinished business. Where is your son?"

"Right there," she said, pointing to Darrell. "What have ye done to ye kin?"

"He made a very valiant effort to protect Catherine, and he was reluctant to part with certain information." He sneered at the man on the floor. "Don't call him my son. I never wanted him."

"Nae, but ye forced yeself into my bed enough. Ye've only yeself to blame."

"You had the looks, Alana—still do, so it wasn't any chore to bed you. Even if you had been ugly, your parents offered such a large dowry I wouldn't have refused." He sniffed. "They were generous for many years but finally the money stopped."

" 'Tis when ye started wi' ye bitterness."

Lucas's hands moved and Duncan twitched his gun. "Move away from him, Alana."

"I dona want ye killin'," she said without moving. She wanted to protect the man she loved. Realizing her intent, Lucas put his hands on her shoulders and set her aside.

"Slowly unbuckle your gun and drop it on the

floor," Duncan ordered. The man who had caused Alana years of unhappiness stood before him, and Lucas ached to kill him. With the gun aimed at his middle, he didn't have any choice. Dead, he wouldn't be any good to Alana. "Now sit at the table and put your hands on the top."

The belt dropped with a thud and Alana was left standing to face Duncan. "Why are ye doin' this?"

"Don't you know?" he snorted. "Your parents told me you were pure. You weren't a maiden when I took you, but I never guessed you'd been married and had a son." His nostrils flared. "You tricked me. I don't like being made a fool of."

"Ye hated me before that, and ye have nae reason to hate Cameron. He didna do anythin' to ye."

"I went to him as his stepfather, but he didn't want anything to do with me. I hated his pride and success." He grinned. "When I got done with the Morrisons, they were destroyed, and Cameron was left with nothing. I intend to do it again. I've had Ben's old foreman rustling cattle and poisoning water holes. Unfortunately, he had served his purpose and had to be killed." He looked at Alana. "I want what your rich son has. He wasn't a failure like my own," he said, pointing to Darrell. "He's a sniveling whelp."

"Ye be wrong about ye son."

"Would you care to expound on his qualities?" he asked in an amused voice.

"Ye son owns two hotels and interest in a shipping fleet."

Duncan eyed her uncertainly. "He's a gambler. He might own them today and lose them tomorrow."

"Nae, he canna lose his business to gamblin'. He ha legally protected it from e'er happenin'. Both my sons be h men. . . . Ye be the failure."

Grunting, Duncan's lips thinned. "I won't be once I
t control of the ranch. Logan cheated me at cards to
t even with what I did to the Morrisons and the money
used to buy the ranch was mine."

"He won the money in a fair game of poker," Lucas
id. "You tried to kill him."

Duncan's eyes narrowed and he regarded Lucas
oughtfully. "You're the man who interfered." Lucas
dded. "You won't interfere again. I'll have this ranch,
d when Catherine becomes my wife, I'll have
erything that belonged to Logan."

Alana and Lucas shot Catherine puzzled looks. "I've
eady told him I won't marry him," she defied. She
ld up her hand and displayed the wedding band. "I'm
eady married."

Duncan chuckled. "I know. Are you forgetting I
ve your wedding certificate? Once Logan is dead
u'll be his widow and owner of the MacLennan
nch. For me to become your husband I have to get
l of my wife."

Lucas threw up his hand. "Alana has no hold over
u. She is with me now and doesn't want you in her
."

"How very touching," he sneered. "She's nothing
t a tramp." Lucas started to rise, but the sound of
unding hoofs forced him back to his seat. Logan
d come to their meeting.

Every nerve in Catherine's body tingled with fear for
e man she loved. Duncan backed to the window, his
e heightened to a reddish hue, his body stiffening
the forthcoming battle. He shoved the curtain aside
the horse thundered into the yard and stopped.

There was no rider and Duncan experienced moment of panic. Unable to bear the suspens Catherine screamed, "Logan run."

Duncan swung around. "Don't waste your breat There isn't a rider." Grabbing Catherine's arm, I jerked her to his side. He motioned to Lucas. "C outside and tell Logan to come in." He shoved the gt into Catherine's side. "If you try anything I'll kill her

Slowly, Lucas rose, exchanged a quick smile wi Alana and walked outside. With Catherine blockii most of his body, Duncan stood in the doorway ai watched. Lucas approached the horse, whisperii softly when the stallion's head jerked. Holding t' reins, he called Logan's name twice, but there was i answer. He walked to the side of the horse just out Duncan's view.

"Get back here now—or she's dead."

Lucas came back to the house, his head bent to t ground. He stopped just outside the door. There w an unusual stiffness about his large frame and instantly put Catherine on the alert.

"Logan, you better come out," Duncan shouted. have Catherine."

Raising his fist, Lucas slowly opened his finge "He can't, he's not here." Catherine stared at I blood-covered palm. "There is blood all over I saddle. He must have had an accident."

"No," Catherine screamed and slumped agai Duncan. It was like a bad dream. Logan couldn't hurt.

"Stand up, Catherine," he ordered, and she st fened.

Tears misted her eyes. "Lucas, what do you thi happened?"

There was a stern expression on his face but it didn't resemble the sense of loss she'd seen when he thought Logan had drowned. "I don't know Catherine, but there's a lot of blood. If we don't find him tonight, he'll be dead by morning."

Forgetting Duncan's hate for Logan, she turned. "We have to find him. He needs help. He'll die if we don't."

Duncan sneered. "That's exactly what I hope happens. He's a dead man either way."

"No," she sobbed.

"With him out of the way, all I have to do is take care of my wife. Get over here, Alana," he called, and she left her son's side. Duncan stepped out of the doorway. "Get outside with Lucas. It will make less of a mess."

Lucas's arm closed around Alana's shoulders. "Are ye goin' to kill me in cold blood?" she queried.

He raised his gun. "I have to be free of my marriage to you."

"Alana is not your wife, Duncan," Lucas said. "There is no reason to kill her." His fingers tightened on her shoulder. "Tell him the truth."

With the man she loved at her back, Alana met Duncan's questioning gaze. "We arena married. I was ne'er ye wife."

A tremor shook Duncan's body. "What are you saying? We were married in Scotland."

"Aye, we went through a ceremony, but I was ne'er free to marry ye."

"Woman, you're talking foolishness. You weren't married. Your first husband was dead."

"Nae, Duncan. I thought he was 'til a few weeks

ago," she said, reaching for the man behind her. "Lucas be my husband."

"You're lying," Duncan accused, and Catherine felt his tension.

"Nae, 'tis the truth. I thought he was lost at sea. When he came back home, I'd moved to escape the memories."

The admission was so surprising, Catherine felt Duncan's uncertainty. "Get inside, both of you." He motioned toward the house. Alana passed him and Lucas followed. Lucas had just cleared the door when he twisted and brought his fist into Duncan's side. Catherine was still blocking most of his body and the punch was ineffective. Lucas went for his head, but a sharp explosion threw him to the floor and blood coated his shirt.

"No," Alana screamed and dropped to his side.

"We're leaving," he told Alana. "Get up."

She turned wild accusing eyes at Duncan. "I canna leave him to bleed to death and my son needs attention."

Duncan shrugged. "Neither of them mean anything to me. Catherine and I are going for the horses. While we're gone, I want you to get some food together. Don't try anything. I'll have Catherine under my gun the whole time. Be ready when we get back." Shoving Catherine down the semidarkened path, he holstered his gun. "Mount up," he said, catching the reins of Logan's horse. He nudged her toward the stallion and her hand hit the saddle. Thick blood covered her fine skin and she screamed.

"I can't go on this horse," she shouted hysterically. "Get mine from the barn and I'll go with you."

Grumbling, Duncan dragged her toward the barn. Two lamps helped brighten the dark interior, but she still stumbled over a rock when they stepped inside.

"Don't try anything," Duncan warned, but Catherine had lost the will to fight. Logan was dead, Darrell beaten and Lucas shot. This man had caused enough trouble in her life wouldonly be another addition in a long line. He would achieve what he had set out to do and all the people who had stood in his way would be dead.

Her depression snapped, and she realized a halt had to be put to his madness. He would never stop hurting and causing misery. She stopped suddenly and Duncan tumbled into her. She twisted to get a look at his face. "I'm not going with you," she said in a clear voice, her strength and strong will returning.

"If you don't come, you're a dead woman."

Twisting out of his grasp, she turned to face him. "Then kill me now because I'm not going."

"Get on your horse," he commanded, reaching for her arm. His fingers bit painfully into her skin. "I said get on your horse."

"She's not going with you," a clear deep voice said from a dark corner, and both of them turned in time to see Logan step out of the shadows.

"Logan," Catherine cried in relief and tried to run toward him, but Duncan had no intention of letting her go.

"So we meet again," the older man said, eyeing his enemy with caution. From past experience, he knew not to take Logan lightly. He could be a dangerous man.

Catherine couldn't take her eyes off the man she loved. She knew him well enough to recognize his dangerous intent. He faced Duncan unafraid, his body tall and proud. Both arms hung loose at his sides, ready to reach for the gun low on his hips. The long, hard jaw was set with determination, and his blue eyes had a warning glint that was not to be overlooked. He had discarded his hat, and his dark hair hung loosely over his forehead to give him the final picture of a man in command.

"Let her go," Logan warned, his gaze never leaving Duncan's face, though Catherine wished he would look into her eyes and see her love.

"No, she's mine. I won't let her go."

"Cat is free. She belongs to no man."

Duncan smiled. "Are you saying she doesn't care for you? He twisted Catherine's arm. "Do you love him? Are you trapped by him?"

She looked straight at Logan. If she was going to die, she wanted him to know the truth. "I belong in bondage to no man. If I did it would kill my spirit. Logan has given me the freedom to love and find my happiness. He is everything to me, and when I fall short, he is there to support and encourage." Her eyes softened. "I have given him my life."

"Very touching," Duncan sneered. "We know she cares for you Cam, but how much do you care for her? Do you value her life?" he asked, pulling her in front of his body like a shield. Drawing his weapon from its holster, he pointed it at her side. "Let's see how much you do care." He shoved the gun against her shirt. "Get rid of your gun or I'll shoot her."

Logan's gaze flicked briefly to Catherine, but in those seconds, she saw all the tender moments they had shared. His love was without question and she would always treasure the memory of their past.

Bending, Logan reached for the string strapping his gun to his thigh. He straightened, his lean brown fingers loosening the buckle.

"No," Catherine screamed as it hit the dirt, leaving Logan defenseless against Duncan. Tears flooded her eyes. He had offered his life for her, and she could do no less for him.

The gun sticking in her ribs turned to the front. "Don't kill him," she pleaded. "I'll go with you. I'll give you the ranch."

Logan glanced at the open door as though he was expecting someone to appear. "No one is coming. There is no one left to help you."

A muscle tightened in Logan's jaw. "What happened to Alana?"

"Nothing, she's fine for the moment. She's gathering food for our trip and probably taking care of Darrell. I had to beat him up."

"You're a poor excuse of a man," Logan flung at him.

"Alana was also taking care of your father."

There was no change in Logan's expression and Catherine couldn't tell if he knew the truth about Lucas. Until now, she hadn't made the connection.

"My father is dead," he said flatly.

"Lucas is your father," Duncan countered, enjoying his revelation. "Alana is married to Lucas," he snarled. "I'm the one she never married."

Catherine held her breath for Logan's reaction but his expression never wavered. She realized if he did know the truth, he had carefully hidden his emotions behind the hard exterior.

Logan's eyes flicked to Catherine, then Duncan. "Let's get it over with," he said in a bored tone.

"The man is eager to die," he said, locking his arm firmly around Catherine. "Say goodbye to the man you love."

His request was something she could never do. Logan meant too much to her to just stand by while he was gunned down. Dropping her head, she snapped it back, catching Duncan full in the face. Blood erupted from his nose and his balance wavered. She brought her heel down on his toe and succeeded in freeing his grip. Dropping, she rolled to the side.

Lunging forward, Logan knocked the gun aside and tackled him. His fist smashed into Duncan's side and in return he dealt a blow to Logan's jaw. They rolled sideways toward one of the stalls, and the horses pranced nervously. The sound of fists striking flesh came with sickening frequency, and Catherine could only stand in awe of the fight, her full faith in Logan.

The men came to their feet, circling each other. Logan was a tall man, but Duncan was twice his size and when he hit his jaw, Logan spun back against the horse. Catherine screamed a warning when Duncan jumped forward and the men went to the ground. The horses were restless and the nervous movement of their hoofs around the men terrified Catherine. Logan caught Duncan in the stomach, doubling him over. Staggering to his feet, the older man caught his opponent's jaw and sent him to the dirt. A horse reared and Duncan lunged for Logan. The horse rose again, and Catherine heard the hoofs strike flesh.

Horrified, Catherine raised her fist to her mouth. There was a stiffness in her body when the horse topped moving. There was no way she could prepare herself for the sight of Logan's trampled body, but she took a deep breath and stepped forward.

There was movement, then someone fell out of the tall on their hands and knees. Running forward Catherine fell to her knees. His head came up and Logan folded Catherine into his arms. She sobbed her relief against his shirt until she was able to draw back and take his face in her hands.

"Logan—I was so scared. Are you hurt?" Her thumb caressed the purple mark on his cheek.

"Nothing serious. I was lucky."

Leaning forward, she lightly kissed his lips. "How could you take such chances with your life? You could have been killed."

His fingers threaded through her tawny hair. Because I love you, and I'd give my life for you." He grinned. "Besides, I was banking on that wild, troubled nature of yours and hoping you'd do something unpredictable."

"Oh, Logan," she sighed and snuggled against him.

He drew back, his features etched in pain. "As much as I'd like to hold you close, my ribs hurt. Maybe after I've had a hot bath you could help me feel better."

"I'll even wash your back."

"Mmm," he muttered and slowly climbed to his feet.

"What about Duncan?" she asked without looking toward the stall.

"He's dead." There was no emotion in his voice.

Sliding her arm around his waist, she said, "Let me help you to the house."

Catching her chin, Logan raised her face to his. There was a seriousness about his blue eyes that puzzled her. "Is it true about Lucas? Is he my father?"

Catherine thought she detected a glimmer of hope. "Yes."

Logan smiled. "I've always been fond of him. I guess now I know why." The frown returned. "Was he really shot?"

She nodded. "Let's go to the house."

Alana glanced up when they walked through the door. Darrell was still on the floor, but resting against the wall. His relief at seeing Catherine and Logan brought a smile to his lips and a wince of pain.

Alana was kneeling next to Lucas, who had wedged himself in the corner. She was trying to stop the flow of blood from a wound on his shoulder. "Lucas tol' me ye be outside. I knew ye'd take care of everythin'."

"But how did he know?" she asked puzzled, then realized he hadn't been truly upset over finding blood on the saddle.

"I tracked Duncan here. I wanted him to believe I wasn't a threat, so I killed a calf. Lucas and I had done the same thing a few years back." Logan dropped to the older man's side and looked into the dull blue eyes. The color of his own had come from his father, but the piercing color had been from his mother. "Are you really my father?" he asked for second confirmation. He remembered the time he had jokingly called him "Dad" in response to Lucas' mention of him as his son.

There was no denying Lucas's pleasure. "I've wanted to tell you for years, but I never did." He reached for Alana's hand. "Your mother was very special to me, and I thought she was dead; she thought the same of me." He took a painful breath. "My full name is Lucas MacLennan. I was born in America to Scotch parents. I was visiting relatives when I met Alana." He coughed. "When I gave up the sea, I traveled. It wasn't long before I heard your name mentioned in connection with the Morrisons. I've watched over you ever since."

"That's why you were in the saloon when Duncan tried to kill me," he said, and Lucas nodded. There were no words that could convey his feelings. Leaning forward, he embraced his father.

"Ach," Alana said, her eyes cloudy with tears. "Lucas be a sick man, and ye dona look very good yeself."

Rising, Logan looked at his brother and grimaced. "You look as sore as I feel," he said, crossing to his side.

Darrell tried to smile. "Ye dona know how my bones ache."

A seriousness settled over Logan's features, and Catherine dropped to the floor and took his brother's hand. "Duncan is dead. . . . I'm sorry things had to turn out the way they did."

Darrell took a deep breath. "He was ne'er a father to me. I willna morn his death." He looked at his brother. "I be glad to hear about ye father. Ye can be proud of ye heritage."

There was a sadness in Logan's eyes. "You shouldn't be ashamed of your background."

"Nae, Cameron. Our mother gave both of us her love. We couldna ask for more."

"Let me help you to a bed," Logan said, taking his

arm. Catherine got on his other side and together they lifted him to his feet. Before leaving the room, Logan flicked a glance at Alana. "I'll be back to help you with Lucas."

She shook her head. "Get yeself to bed. Lucas be fine."

In one of the spare rooms, Darrell stretched out on the mattress. "Feels good. . . . Are the two of ye really married? Duncan saed he had ye weddin' papers."

"I'll look for them tomorrow, but I think we'll go ahead with a second ceremony regardless. I want to see the face of my bride."

"I hope the two of ye will wait 'till I be on my feet."

Logan put his arm around Catherine. "We can wait. You're going to be one of the witnesses. We don't want any doubt about the ceremony," he said, smiling fondly at Catherine. "I hope you'll think about staying in this part of the country. It's nice to have a brother."

Darrell managed a half smile. "I still need to win back the money ye won from me in Saint Louis. Ye be a good player."

Chuckling, Logan's arms tightened around Catherine. "I was just lucky that day."

Logan led her down the hall to his room. "I'm going to take care of you and go help Alana," Catherine said.

"It might take you all night," he teased when the door closed. She lit a lamp and remembered the day she had first seen Cam's room and dreamed of sleeping with him in his bed.

"I still don't know which name to call you. Sometimes you are like the Cameron I knew in the garden at my aunts' home, and other times you're the hard Logan I knew on the wagon train." She smiled. "Do you do it to confuse me?"

"You'll have to sort it out," he said, drawing her against his body, but not close enough to hurt his tender ribs. "I have enough to do worrying about your wild unpredictable nature. I have a feeling you're going to lead me on a memorable chase."

Tears of happiness stung her eyes. The elements that had threatened her freedom were gone and she was free to love the man of her dreams. Easing out of his arms, she walked toward the bed. When she reached it, she turned and faced him.

"My free spirit is yours, Cameron Logan Mac-Lennan. You have a lifetime to try to catch it."